Shipyard Girls
at War

Nancy Revell is a writer and journalist under another name, and has worked for all the national newspapers, providing them with hard-hitting news stories and in-depth features. She has also worked for just about every woman's magazine in the country, writing amazing and inspirational true life stories. Nancy has recently relocated back to her home town of Sunderland, Tyne and Wear, with her husband, Paul, and their English bull mastiff, Rosie. They live just a short walk away from the beautiful award-winning beaches of Roker and Seaburn, within a mile of where the Shipyard Girls series is set. The subject is close to Nancy's heart as she comes from a long line of shipbuilders, who were well known in the area.

Also available by Nancy Revell

The Shipyard Girls

Shipyard Girls at War

Nancy Revell

arrow books

1 3 5 7 9 10 8 6 4 2

Arrow Books
20 Vauxhall Bridge Road
London SW1V 2SA

Arrow Books is part of the Penguin Random House group of companies
whose addresses can be found at global.penguinrandomhouse.com

Penguin
Random House
UK

First published in Great Britain by Arrow Books in 2017

www.penguin.co.uk

A CIP catalogue record for this book is available from the British Library

ISBN 9781784754648

Typeset in 10.75/13.5 pt
in India by Thomson Digital Pvt Ltd, Noida Delhi

Printed and bound in Great Britain by Clays Ltd, St Ives Plc

To my husband Paul, with love

Acknowledgements

I have endeavoured to be as accurate as possible with the historical and geographical facts I have woven into *Shipyard Girls at War* and it is thanks to an array of organisations, publications, and individuals that I have been able to do this, including Sunderland Antiquarian Society, Sunderland Maritime Heritage, the Sunderland Echo, and Sunderland Museum & Winter Gardens.

A special thanks must go to Elena Notarianni who has been such a great wealth of information in relation to the town and the era in which the series is set, and has also put me in contact with some great women. Bridget Marley told me about her vividly-remembered childhood growing up while bombs rained down on the town, and Meg Hartford spoke to me about her much-loved Aunt Mattie who worked as a riveter in one of the Sunderland shipyards during the war.

I must also say a really big thank you to Jenny Geras for her invaluable editorial guidance, to my wonderful agent Diana Beaumont, of United Talent Agency, and, of course, to my mum and dad, Audrey and Syd Walton, and my husband Paul, who have given me such love, support and encouragement throughout.

Thank you.

'Modo liceat vivere, est spes'
('While there's life, there's hope')

'Terence', a playwright of North African descent
(185–159 BC)

Shipyard Girls at War

Prologue

MRS ISABELLE ELLIOT, 34 TATHAM STREET,
SUNDERLAND, COUNTY DURHAM.

WE DEEPLY REGRET TO INFORM YOU YOUR
HUSBAND PRIVATE EDWARD ELLIOT OF THE
7TH ARMOURED DIVISION OF THE BRITISH
ARMY IS NOW REPORTED TO HAVE LOST HIS
LIFE AS A RESULT OF MILITARY OPERATIONS
ON 11 DECEMBER 1940.
    THE BRITISH ARMY EXPRESS THEIR
PROFOUND SYMPATHY.
    LETTER CONFIRMING THIS TELEGRAM
GIVING ALL AVAILABLE DETAILS FOLLOWS.

WAR SECRETARY OF STATE, WAR MINISTRY.

Chapter One

Friday 27 December 1940

Polly found Bel huddled up on the floor in the far corner of her bedroom.

Her arms were wrapped around her legs, which were pulled up tight to her chest. Her head was bowed down, with her forehead pressed against her knees. Her body, tucked up in a ball, was rhythmically rocking back and forth.

She wasn't making a sound. Polly couldn't even hear the resonance of her sister-in-law's breathing. Instead the room was filled with the most mournful silence.

It was daylight outside, yet the blackout curtains had been pulled shut, as was the tradition when a close family member passed away, although in this case 'passed away' was too gentle a description for the life that had been so brutally taken. 'Passing' suggested the natural end of a life well lived; a life that had reached the stage where it was time to move on.

The life being mourned in the Elliot household, however, had not by any means been ready to move on. It had been snatched away. Robbed. Stolen. Like so many others during this past year. It was a wrongful death. An injustice that could never be righted.

In normal circumstances the closed curtains served the dual purpose of letting neighbours know a death had occurred, as well as keeping the inside of the home dark and cool, as the deceased's body was usually kept there until the funeral took place.

In the Elliot household, though, the curtains had been drawn merely as a sign that the family was in mourning. There was no body to bury, as Teddy's shrapnel-filled corpse had already been laid to rest in a foreign cemetery in a place none of the family had ever heard of: Sidi Barrani in Egypt – a town just a few miles away from where Teddy had been blasted to death by an enemy landmine less than three weeks previously.

He had been one of the first casualties to die at the start of Operation Compass, the first large-scale military action in the Desert War following the Italian invasion of Egypt, which, despite being hailed a success, had resulted in the loss of 624 British soldiers.

Teddy Elliot, aged twenty-six, formerly a shipyard worker from Sunderland, County Durham, had been one of those 624 fatalities.

As Polly edged her way into Bel's bedroom, a few rays of sunlight splintered through the gaps in the blackened cloth, illuminating the outline of her sister-in-law. As Polly's eyes adjusted to the darkness, she recoiled at the sight of her friend. Her brother's wife. Now her brother's widow. Bel looked almost feral, and for the briefest of moments Polly felt fearful of this young woman she had known and loved for almost her entire life. She hesitated before making her way across the room, almost tiptoeing out of respect for the quietness.

She then slowly crouched down.

'Bel,' she said in an almost whisper. 'Bel . . .'

She stretched out her hand, still dirty from a hard day's work, and touched Bel's crown of thick blonde hair.

The rocking continued.

'Bel . . . look at me,' Polly gently coaxed.

The rocking went on, but the head moved, and Bel slowly showed her face.

Her skin was a ghostly shade of milky white, and the dried outline of mascara-laced tears had painted grey, salty streaks down her cheeks.

Bel had been like this all day, and probably all night too.

The previous day, after receiving the telegram telling them of Teddy's death, Bel had taken to her bed, or so Polly and her mum Agnes had presumed when they had watched her shocked figure disappear into her room on the ground floor of the mid-terrace house they all shared in the town's east end.

Shortly afterwards, Polly had also sought solace in her own room, and Agnes, who had managed to hold herself in check in front of her daughter and daughter-in-law had, once on her own, wept bitter tears, until the early morning light showed her another day had begun; still shrouded in a veil of disbelief that her worst fears had become reality and that one of her sons had gone for ever, she had gone to wake Polly and told her to get ready and go to work. Agnes knew that by trying to keep some semblance of normality and routine, it would help her daughter deal with the loss of her beloved brother the best way she could. She knew that Polly needed to be active and, moreover, feel that she was somehow fighting back; by going to work and repairing and building ships for war, she was helping to defeat the enemy that had taken her brother from her.

Her daughter-in-law, on the other hand, needed to stay at home. Agnes knew Bel as though she was her own flesh and blood, and realised she would not be in any fit state to even leave the house, never mind go to work. Bel needed to rest, to take time to grieve for the only man she had ever loved – who she had adored ever since she'd been a small child. Entering Bel's bedroom that morning, she was glad she had had the foresight to send Bel's daughter, Lucille, to stay the night with their neighbour Beryl, for she was greeted with the heart-wrenching sight of her daughter-in-law rocking silently to and fro in the corner of her room. Agnes guessed Bel had been like that all night, as her bed was untouched, but she knew everyone needed to mourn in their own way, and so she had left her there. Agnes had also lost her husband Harry, at around the same age as Bel, at the end of the First World War; she knew only too well the searing pain her son's wife was going through – and would continue to go through for a long time to come.

When Polly had returned from work later that day, though, and Bel still had not surfaced, Agnes had told her daughter 'enough was enough' – it was time for Bel to emerge from her self-imposed cocoon. So Polly was carrying out her mother's wishes.

Now, as she stood looking at Bel, she felt a chill run down her spine, for the woman she loved dearly was staring back at her with what could only be described as dead eyes. There seemed to be no light or life behind the enlarged black pupils now gazing up at her.

This, Polly realised, was what grief looked like in its purest form. It was as though the death Bel was grieving had somehow pervaded her very being, and in doing so had also taken a part of her own life from her.

Polly braced herself.

'Bel, come with me . . . Give me your hand,' she said gently, taking both of Bel's cold, clenched hands in her own and pulling her up.

Polly was thankful this person she had known since they were small children playing on these very streets on the other side of the blacked-out windows did not fight her guidance.

As Bel stood unsteadily on her feet, Polly put her arm around her slim frame, and as she did so she was struck by how aged and fragile Bel felt. She was only twenty-four but seemed decades older.

Polly helped her newly widowed sister-in-law out of the bedroom and down the hallway, before guiding her into the kitchen. A fire crackled and spat as it blazed angrily in the lead range, and a pot of hot tea stood steaming on top of the big wooden table.

'Come. Sit down, Bel,' Agnes told her daughter-in-law. 'Drink some tea. You have to be brave. You have to be strong. Your daughter needs you.'

And with that Bel sat, and with shaking hands picked up a cup of tea and forced herself to take a sip. Forced herself to live. If not for her own sake, then for the sake of her daughter. Her beautiful child who was like her daddy in so many ways. A daddy she would never see again. Never get to know. Never be loved by. Nor love herself.

As if realising she had become the focus of the women's attention, little Lucille, who was lying curled up in her blanket-strewn cot, stirred from an afternoon slumber that had been aided by the sombre quietness of the house. Polly went and picked up her two-and-a-half-year-old niece and sat her on her knee.

There was no chatter amongst the three women as they sat in quietness and moved cups to their mouths. Instead they simply thought their own thoughts and felt their own terrible sadness.

Agnes for the loss of a son.

Polly for her big brother.

And Bel for the love of her life.

A love she felt she could not live without but knew she had to, if only for the sleepy child snuggled up opposite her in her aunty's lap.

Chapter Two

One month later, January 1941

'What's that young lad doing?' Dorothy asked the ship-yard's head welder, Rosie Thornton, as she watched a boy who looked barely a day over fourteen clamber between a line of huge wooden blocks. They had been laid down in a long line and resembled the vertebrae of a steel spine running along the bottom of one of the yard's dry docks.

'It's part of the shipbuilding tradition,' Rosie started to explain as she shielded her eyes from the sun's glare. In this light you could clearly see the small splashes of scars scattered across her otherwise very attractive face. Dorothy thought she would have personally tried to cover them up with a thin layer of foundation or powder, but her boss did not seem to care.

As Rosie talked she wiped a tear away, her overly sensitive eyes struggling to cope with the early morning show of sun. Today, like most days that had greeted the New Year, it was bitterly cold, and there were patches of ice on the yard's greasy, concrete surface, but, as if in celebration of the day's events, the sun had come out for a short spell. It seemed appropriate that the ceremonial laying of the ship's keel should have a blast of sunshine. It was a good omen.

'Haven't you learnt anything since you've been working here?' Gloria ribbed her workmate. By way of reply, Dorothy stuck her tongue out at the woman she loved to hate and who seemed to love to hate her back in equal measure.

Gloria rolled her eyes at Dorothy's juvenile gesture and continued. 'The yard's youngest apprentice has to put a coin down on one of the wooden blocks that go under the keel to bring the ship luck . . . and for those of you who *still* don't know,' she added sarcastically, 'the keel is the long wooden thing that runs from the bow to the stern – that's the front to the—'

'All right,' Dorothy interrupted, 'I may be stupid, but I'm not *that* stupid!'

Rosie sighed. Ever since they'd started at the yard, Gloria and Dorothy had been incapable of saying anything nice to each other, even though, strangely enough, she knew they didn't actually dislike each other. Far from it.

'The day that woman utters a civil word to me is the day I start to worry,' Dorothy muttered to her friend, Angie, who was standing close by, scrutinising the events of the ceremonial laying of the keel being played out in the depths of the dry dock just yards away from the edge of the River Wear.

As usual, whenever there was a break, Angie would climb out of the square metal cabin of the massive crane she spent her day operating, and go and find Dorothy. The pair of them had become inseparable these past few months after they had bonded over a two-timing philandering riveter called Eddie who had been dating them both behind their backs.

'The laying of the keel,' Rosie continued, eager to stop any more squabbling, 'is a tradition that dates way back to when ships were built out of wood. It's one of the four specially celebrated events in the life of a ship, the others being launching, commissioning, and decommissioning. And, like Gloria said, the coin is meant to bring luck to the ship while it's being constructed, and then later on to the captain and crew.'

'Rosie make a good teacher, no?' Hannah said with only the slightest hint of a foreign accent as she nudged her fellow welder Martha, who had been renamed 'Big Martha' by the yard's mainly male workforce. It was a nickname that was also a play on words, as the town's massive anti-aircraft gun had been christened Big Bertha due to its formidable size.

Martha did not seem to mind the fact that her name had been given a prefix. She had told Hannah and the other women as much when they had asked her if her new moniker bothered her and she had simply told them, 'but it's true'. And, to be fair, it was a pretty appropriate description of Martha, as there was no denying she was certainly big; in fact, it wouldn't have been too much of a push to call her a giant. She certainly fitted the description of a 'gentle giant', as she had an incredibly quiet and unthreatening nature in contrast to her huge bulk.

When Martha had first started at the shipyard as a novice welder, it had taken the women a while to get to know her as she had hardly spoken a word. What they hadn't realised then was that Martha had hardly spoken many words at all in her entire life, never mind at her new place of work. Since she had settled in at the yard she had become far more verbose, although she was still a million miles away from being a chatterbox.

'. . . And as you are all more than aware – being almost shipyard veterans,' Rosie gently teased the women, knowing full well that, although they were no longer trainees, six months in the yard had also not made them old-timers, '. . . the keel is the backbone of the vessel, and the laying of the keel is the first piece of the jigsaw puzzle to be put down . . .'

'So, all this hoo-ha is to celebrate the start of the ship's life.' As usual Dorothy had to stick her oar in, and true to form her words were followed by Gloria's dry cynicism.

'Well, let's hope this ship's life is a long one and that it doesn't get bombed to smithereens by some Jerry U-boat as soon as it's out the harbour.'

Gloria's words were met by a communal grunt of agreement from the women as Hitler's stealth-like submarines had already succeeded in blowing up a few ships just three miles up the coast.

As they watched a couple of the town's suited dignitaries make their way down to the dock where the boy apprentice was standing awkwardly, coin in hand, Gloria ran her hand over her small bump that was still well hidden under her bulky overalls. Only the women who now stood around her knew about her pregnancy, and, more importantly, were the only ones to know why there was a need to keep her condition a secret for as long as possible.

'. . . and when the ship is finished, the owners will be presented with the wooden block – complete with coin.' Rosie finished off the women's lesson of the day.

'Blooming typical,' Dorothy exclaimed, having now lost interest in learning anything more about keels or shipyard ceremonies as she spotted Helen Crawford and her mother Miriam hobnobbing with the other VIPs.

'Might have guessed Helen would get her ugly mug in on the action,' she said to the women as a photographer lined everyone up for an official picture.

Dorothy was being even more bitchy than normal, but she was only voicing what the others were thinking. None of them reprimanded their workmate for her catty remarks, because none of them had an iota of sympathy for the woman presently flaunting her hourglass figure to all and sundry just a few hundred yards from where they were now standing – for Helen Crawford had committed the cardinal sin of trying to steal Polly's beau, Tommy Watts; and, worse still, she had tried to do so with deviousness and outright lies.

As Helen clapped her hands in delight when the keel was carefully lowered down on to the wooden blocks lining the floor of the basin, Polly scrutinised her former love rival. She still felt angry when she saw Helen, despite the fact she had not succeeded in coming between Polly and Tommy.

'All right. The show's over,' Rosie said, picking up her welding mask. 'Back to work.'

Her words were met by a general groan, but as the town's luminaries were now making their way over to the administration offices for their sandwiches and sherry, there was nothing more to see. The women were also under pressure to get a number of metal panels welded on to the hull of a cargo vessel; it had had a hole blown in its side after hitting a floating mine that Jerry had dropped along a popular shipping route.

'Hannah,' Rosie said, nodding her head over to the group's 'little bird'. The name had initially been coined by Dorothy, but it had stuck, as Hannah, who had come over from Czechoslovakia shortly before Hitler rampaged through her homeland, really was like a tiny, fragile sparrow. She'd struggled with the gruelling workload since starting at the yard, but had kept going, much to everyone's surprise.

'There's some touching-up work that needs to be done over with the riveters,' Rosie told Hannah, who immediately looked relieved that she would not be spending the rest of the day with her arms held high doing overhead and vertical welds.

As they walked over to join the other shipwrights, Rosie glanced down at Hannah and looked at her slight frame and naturally pale skin and wondered just how much longer she could cover for her and keep finding her less labour-intensive welding jobs.

When the yard manager Jack Crawford had been there, he had been more than happy to make exceptions for Hannah, but since his daughter Helen had taken over the reins for the few months he was away in America helping with the production of a new ship, it had become much more difficult. Helen had already started to query Hannah's work output and question her viability as a ship-yard worker.

Today Rosie was thankful Helen's attention had been taken up with the keel-laying ceremony and rubbing shoulders with the bigwigs, as it meant she had been able to get Hannah in with the riveters without too much fuss. But she knew it would only be a brief respite from Helen's scrutiny and that the boss's daughter had her claws out for all the women welders. Helen was clearly going to make not only Polly, but all of Polly's friends, pay for getting Tommy.

And Hannah was an obvious and very easy target.

At least she's in safe hands here, Rosie thought as she approached the half-dozen men Hannah would be working with over the next few days. Most of them were well into their forties and early fifties, too old for military service but, even if they hadn't been, would have been exempt from conscription due to their shipbuilding skills being desperately needed if this war was to be won.

'We got the bairn with us today?' the head riveter said on seeing Hannah. Rosie smiled. Hannah was nearly nineteen but she still looked like a child, with her coarsely cut mop of thick black hair and short fringe.

'Yes, Jimmy,' Rosie said, 'the bairn's yours today.'

'Well, dinnit worry about her, she'll be fine with this lot,' he said, as he showed Hannah to her first weld of the day.

As Rosie returned to the rest of the women, she thought about Jimmy and the men like him who could come across as hard, no-nonsense northerners, but who hid the softness of their hearts well. The men in the yards always seemed to champion the underdog, and Hannah was most certainly that, here in this metal jungle, where workers had to be strong and tough to survive the backbreaking and dangerous work it demanded.

As Rosie turned on her welding machine, she quickly checked on the remaining four women. She'd hoped Dorothy's mate, Angie, might consider leaving her job as a crane operator and learn to weld, as she needed another pair of hands to make up her team, especially as Gloria was now in the family way and Hannah was being regularly lent out to the other fitters. When she had suggested the idea to Angie, though, she had not seemed keen. And why would she? Her wages weren't quite as good as those of a welder, but the work was a damn sight easier and she wasn't collapsing exhausted into her bed at night like the rest of the women.

When the klaxon sounded the end of the day shift, the women pushed their masks up and turned off their machines. They would all have a tea break and some sandwiches before doing another few hours' overtime.

Rosie, however, had to go. She had told the yard's timekeeper that the damage to her eyes caused by her 'accident' meant they could not deal with more than a day's work; not with the constant flashes of light and the bright smouldering metal that welding entailed.

In reality, though, it was because her second job she went to on an evening had become more demanding. She was needed there now every night from seven until well after midnight, but it was worth it as it was paying dividends. She was now easily earning enough to cover her monthly outgoings – even managing to put some savings aside for the future.

As Rosie waved goodbye to her team of welders, she thought of the group of pretty young women she would be in charge of this evening and how very different they all were from the overall-clad, dirt-smeared women waving back at her now.

Chapter Three

By the time Polly finished work it was dark, and she hurried to catch the last ferry that would take her from the north dock back across to the south side of the river. As the tired old steamer chugged across the choppy waters, Polly looked up at the huge, whale-like barrage balloons floating above her in the darkened skies, and her mind wandered back over the past six months and all it had brought into her life – and taken from it.

As the ferry's rough passage caused Polly to grab hold of the railings to steady herself, she spotted the battered old ship moored by the river's edge, ready to be towed between the north and south piers to block an invading fleet of enemy ships, and for the first time she wondered if the Allies would really be able to win this war. Since she had found out about Teddy, it had felt as if his death had somehow lessened the country's chances of victory. She knew her logic was foolish – one man's death did not hasten a defeat – but she thought it all the same.

'How's that Tommy of yours?'

Polly jumped when she heard the loud, croaky voice of the ferryman bellowing over to her.

Polly turned to look at Stan and, on hearing her lover's name, she smiled. Any kind of talk about Tommy never failed to lift her spirits, even if those spirits were tinged with anxiety about his welfare.

'He's well, I hope,' Polly shouted back, 'fingers crossed.'

Stan had known Tommy since he was just a nipper, and had always given him a free pass on the ferry.

'I got a letter last week and he seemed fine, although it's hard to tell what's really happening over there.'

As Polly spoke, she unconsciously felt inside the top pocket of her overalls and touched the engagement ring Tommy had given her before he had left to join the Royal Navy. She kept the ring with her at all times, and sometimes even put it on when she went to bed, as it made her feel close to the man she had promised to marry once the war was over.

'Aye, I know. But if anyone's ganna sort Jerry and those Italians out it'll be wor Tommy,' Stan said with complete conviction.

Polly smiled at the old man, who must have guided this boat back and forth across the breadth of the Wear innumerable times over the course of his life.

As the ferry bumped the edge of the south dock, and Polly prepared to hop off on to the stone steps that led up to the concrete landing, she squeezed Stan's arm affectionately.

'I'll tell him you were asking after him in my next letter,' she promised, making the old man's face light up.

'Thanks, pet, that'd be grand,' Stan said, giving Polly a toothless smile.

When Polly arrived home, Agnes was still up, and, for the first time in a long while, she looked happy and excited.

'Joe's due to come in on the three o'clock train tomorrow,' she said in hushed tones as Bel and Lucille were already in bed.

'Oh, Ma, that's great news,' Polly said, giving her mum a big hug. Agnes enjoyed her daughter's open display of affection for a moment before pushing her away.

17

'Not with them grubby overalls on, thank you very much. Get them off and I'll give them a wash.'

Polly ignored her mother's command and instead sat down at the kitchen table and poured herself a cuppa.

'Mind you, it's about time. It's taken him long enough to get back here.'

Agnes headed back into the scullery to fetch Polly a large slice of sausage and tomato pie left over from supper.

'I know, but we just have to thank our lucky stars that he's back at all.'

After being blasted by a landmine back in October while he and Teddy were fighting in North Africa, surgeons working in a makeshift field hospital had not only managed to save Joe's life but, after removing a load of deeply embedded steel shards, his leg too.

His injuries, however, prevented him from returning to the front line, and he had been put on a hospital ship, which, despite clearly displaying the markings of the Red Cross, had been forced to dodge attacks by the Luftwaffe and the German Navy.

Polly felt they had all been holding their breath for these past few months, praying that Joe made it back in one piece. They had been able to heave a sigh of relief last week, though, when news come through that his ship had successfully navigated its way back to British shores unscathed, and had berthed in Glasgow.

'How's Bel today?' Polly asked, taking her supper off her mum. 'Was she pleased to hear about Joe?'

Both Agnes and Polly were still worried about Bel, as she had not once spoken about how she was feeling about losing the man she had loved so fiercely all her life. Since that first long day, she had not shown anything of her grief to anyone – even to Polly and Agnes, the two women who were, for all intents and purposes, her family. It was as if she had become encased in a hard, impenetrable shell that was stopping anyone from getting anywhere near her.

Agnes was glad Bel had not gone back to work on the buses, but was helping out with the laundry she took in from local businesses to earn some extra cash, as well as with Aggie's Nursery, the unofficial child-minding service she was running to help out the women round the doors who needed to go to work.

There was plenty for Bel to do, but more than anything it enabled Agnes to keep a much-needed eye on her daughter-in-law.

'Mm,' Agnes mused, sitting down next to Polly and pouring herself a cup of tea. 'She didn't really say much, but then again, that's nothing new at the moment. She still seems a million miles away.'

'I know,' Polly agreed, 'and it's starting to affect Lucille. She's been so much more clingy with you and me. I know she's feeling rejected.'

Agnes sadly nodded her head and drank her tea.

After Polly finished her supper, she went to clean up in the little washhouse in their back yard.

It had been over a year and a half since they had waved Joe and Teddy off to war. The twins had both been determined to fight Jerry despite being on the official list of reserved occupations that stipulated shipyard riveters were exempt from conscription.

Since then they had only had the very briefest of communications with the brothers through the odd letter, as it often took three months for any kind of correspondence to get back to Britain.

As Polly took off her dirty overalls and poured a jug of water into the basin, bracing herself for a cold wash-down, a wave of apprehension hit her.

Her brother had been through so much in such a short time. Within the space of just a year and a half he had gone from being a shipyard worker in a town he had never left, to a soldier in a country halfway round the world. He had been blasted by an anti-personnel landmine and nearly died – and had then been told of his brother's death.

How would Joe be when they all saw him?

How should they treat him?

And how on earth was he going to cope without his twin, who had always been by his side, even before they had been born?

Chapter Four

The next day Agnes, Bel and Lucille hurried to the main entrance of the town's busy railway station.

It was a dismal, overcast day. The sky was a mixture of oddly shaped clouds of varying shades of grey – not that Bel would have noticed any kind of colour in her surroundings, for since her husband's death her world had become black and white. It was as if she had suddenly become colour-blind.

Bel's widowhood had catapulted her into a dark, miserable life of endurance, the only reason for continuing with her existence being the child now staring up at her with a confused look on her face.

'Daddy?' Lucille asked shyly, as she tugged at her mother's coat arm, pointing her small pudgy finger in the direction of the man walking towards them through a throng of fellow travellers.

Bel shook her head tersely in response to her daughter's question. She had told her enough times that the man they were meeting today was her uncle Joe – her daddy's brother.

'Daddy?' Lucille's voice had now become more animated as Joe became momentarily lost from vision by those dodging past him, trying to fight their way into the station, against the tide of people – like himself – hurrying out to reach loved ones.

As Joe reappeared, hauling his tall, lanky body along the cobblestone paving with the aid of a single wooden crutch tucked securely under his arm, it took him a few moments before he again spotted his mother, sister-in-law and niece; when he did so, a big smile spread across his face.

In his smart khaki-green uniform and beret, Bel could not help but think that her brother-in-law did look exactly like the photograph of Teddy, which she had put next to her bed, and which Lucille had looked at every day since her father had gone off to war.

'Daddy!' Lucille's declaration was no longer a question, but a statement. Encouraged by Joe's welcoming smile, she had clearly made up her mind that this man was her father.

Bel stopped walking and bent down to explain to her daughter that this was *not* her daddy – that this was her father's brother, but as she did so Lucille suddenly pulled her small hand free from her clasp and started running towards Joe shouting, 'Daddy! Daddy!'

Bel opened her mouth to stop her daughter, to tell her to *come back here now . . . this is not your father . . . your father is dead. Gone. For ever*.

But it was too late. Lucille had bolted with surprising speed for such a little girl and was now running as fast as her legs would go.

Joe knew instantly that this was Lucille, his brother's daughter. His niece. The one who had been just a year old when he and his brother had left for war.

And she was truly divine.

Joe could not fail to be captivated by Lucille's joyous face and be struck by the pure innocence of her smile. He had not witnessed such unadulterated happiness in a long time.

Without thinking he dropped his crutch and opened his arms to this bundle of life as she barrelled towards him. As she threw herself at him, Joe automatically bent down to catch her with his big, strong hands and, balancing on his good leg, he lifted her up to the heavens above.

Looking up at the rosy, cherub-like child in his arms, for the first time in many, many months, Joe seemed content.

His delight at the vision of this miniature angel he was now holding aloft lasted only for a moment, however, before it was broken by the sound of a harsh woman's voice, shouting out to the little girl: 'He is *not* your daddy!'

The voice was familiar but sounded angry and full of panic. As Joe put the child down and looked up, he saw his brother's wife, Bel, and for the second time in as many minutes he was struck by another vision of outstanding beauty. The slightly wavy, thick blonde hair was almost identical to that of the toddler, who was now standing hugging his good leg and looking up at him in awe.

'Lucille! Come here!' Bel demanded. 'This man is not your father.' Bel continued to reprimand her daughter. 'Your daddy's not here any more. I've told you. He's in heaven now . . . This is your uncle. Your uncle Joe.'

The little girl's face looked crestfallen by her mother's harsh words, but when she looked back up at Joe she beamed again, as if she didn't care what her ma said. In her child's eyes this man *was* her father. He certainly looked like her daddy. Same sea-blue eyes, same cropped, thick, dark brown hair. He looked as tall as the man in the photo whom she had been told was her da. And he was wearing the exact same uniform as the man in the photo.

But that man was just a picture on a piece of glossy paper, encased behind glass, and surrounded by a wooden frame.

This man here was real.

This man *was* her father.

'I'm sorry, Joe,' Bel said, bending down to pick up her brother-in-law's crutch from the ground. 'She doesn't seem to understand yet . . .' Her voice trailed off.

Joe seemed at a loss for words and simply stood staring at Bel and then at Lucille.

'Come here, Joe.' Agnes stepped forward, desperately trying to keep the tears at bay, and the overwhelming emotion she was feeling out of her voice. 'Give yer old ma a hug,' she said, leaning up and wrapping her arms around her son's broad chest.

Joe hugged his mother back, kissing the top of her head.

'I think you've shrunk since I've been gone,' he joked, finding his voice again. 'And is that grey hair I see?'

Agnes put a hand to her hair, which was scraped back into a bun, and laughed, but her laughter nearly turned into tears as the relief that at least one of her boys had safely returned finally hit home.

After Bel gave Joe a stiff, obligatory embrace, the four of them walked through the busy town centre, then down the side streets that led to the east end, before they all reached the top of Tatham Street.

Agnes walked next to her son, firing a string of questions at him about his journey, how he was feeling, and if he had eaten anything – while all the time Lucille danced around Joe, chirping the word 'Daddy, Daddy' every few moments, in spite of Bel's increasing annoyance and commands to 'calm down' and 'hold my hand or you'll get run over'.

When they finally got through the front door, Bel practically stomped into her bedroom, emerging seconds later with a framed photograph of Teddy.

'This,' she said sternly to her little girl, 'is your daddy. This man here.' Bel jabbed the photograph with her finger, determined to make her point before marching into the kitchen and placing the frame in the middle of the mantel-piece for all to see.

Agnes looked up at her son's puzzled, slightly confused face, and at her daughter-in-law, who seemed to be the embodiment of fury, then down at her ecstatic grand-daughter, still bobbing around her uncle's legs, and she sighed inwardly.

She had known the waters that lay ahead for them all were going to be difficult to navigate; had known it was not going to be a smooth ride, but she realised as she stood there that their future under this roof was going to be challenging – much more so than she had anticipated.

'Joe! Joe! You're back!' Agnes's ominous thoughts were broken by Polly's jubilant cries erupting from behind as her daughter hurried through the open doorway. Joe turned to look at his sister, her face smeared with the familiar soot and grime of the shipyard, and at her grease-stained over-alls, and he let free a loud hoot of genuine laughter.

'Well look at you. Is that my baby sister I see behind all that dirt and denim?' he japed before hobbling forward and giving Polly a big bear hug.

Polly had to choke back tears of both joy and sadness. It seemed so strange to see Joe without Teddy by his side.

'And look at you' – Polly brushed away a tear that had sneaked out and trickled down her cheek – 'my big brother looking every inch the handsome soldier. You're going to have all the girls after you.'

In reality Polly had been taken aback by how much her brother had aged. His skin was tanned from the months he had spent out in the hot Egyptian climate, but his face looked sallow and worn. And when she'd hugged him, she had felt his bones and the outline of his spine. He must have lost a good few stone, not that he had had a lot of meat on him before he had left for war.

As if reading her daughter's thoughts, Agnes announced, 'Dinner time. I want everyone cleaned up and sat at the table by the time the kettle's boiled.'

Ten minutes later Agnes, Polly, Joe and Bel were seated around the kitchen table, tucking into a steak-and-kidney stew and dumplings that had been keeping warm in the oven and had cost Agnes most of her food rations for that week. Lucille insisted on sitting next to Joe; a big cushion had been placed on the chair so that she could reach the table and eat with the adults. The little girl seemed entranced by Joe, dribbling gravy down her chin as she watched every mouthful he consumed and listened to every word he spoke.

As the five of them ate, Joe asked Polly about her welding job. He'd been intrigued when he had learnt that his little sister had become a part of the family's long line of shipbuilders, and he listened intently as Polly told him all the latest news.

No one, however, mentioned Teddy. The subject of his death was still too raw, although his handsome smiling face looked down at them all from the framed photograph now taking pride of place on the mantelpiece.

After they had all eaten and the dishes had been cleared away, there was a knock on the door. It was Beryl, carrying a home-made cake and accompanied by her teenage daughters, Iris and Audrey; a few minutes later, Tommy's grandad, Arthur, arrived, armed with a bottle of whisky he had been keeping for a special occasion.

For the first time in many weeks the house felt jolly and genuinely celebratory. Joe looked tired but contented and seemed more than happy to give Lucille the attention she was demanding.

Polly had prepared herself for a change in Joe, and it was clear the war had taken away the remnants of boyishness he had carried with him into adulthood, and that what he had seen had painted a sadness in his eyes. But, despite this, Polly could see that Joe was still 'their Joe'. He still had his spark about him – that had not been extinguished.

As the clock chimed nine, Bel told her overtired daughter – amid howls of protest – that it was way past her bedtime. When she came back into the kitchen after putting Lucille to bed, Joe looked at Teddy's photograph and then back at Bel; he seemed to be about to say something to her, when there was a loud knock on the front door.

The room fell quiet as everyone looked at each other, wondering who on earth would be calling at this time of the evening.

Agnes got up, but before she had even reached the entrance to the long, tiled hallway, the front door was flung open by their late-night visitor.

'Don't worry . . . it's only me!' The voice was shrill and sounded a little tipsy.

Agnes's mouth fell open as she looked at the scrawny, sallow-faced woman, who had dumped her green and brown battered suitcase on the floor and was now jauntily walking down the hallway, her skinny arms stretched out in anticipation of a hug, acting as if she owned the place.

'Eee, you've not changed a bit, Agnes. How long's it been, hinny?' she asked.

Agnes immediately folded her arms, shielding herself from any kind of embrace. Words seemed to escape her as the heavily made-up blonde, wearing an outfit that was more suited to a twenty-year-old than a forty-year-old, sidled past her and into the hub of the kitchen.

The woman stood looking at the faces staring slightly agog at this late-night apparition. As she quickly scanned the room, her eyes fell on Bel and her face lit up in panto-mime delight.

'Isabelle,' she said, flinging her arms wide once more, 'come and say hello to yer ma.'

Bel did not move a muscle but stood rooted to the spot; she visibly winced at hearing herself being called by her full name.

'It's Bel, Ma,' she said, still making no effort to move even an inch towards her mother. *No one* calls me Isabelle.'

Chapter Five

Tatham Street 1920

'I won't be long, Isabelle.' Pearl touched her five-year-old daughter's dirty cheek with uncanny tenderness before turning on the worn-down heels of her shabby leather shoes and walking out of the room.

Bel jumped at the sound of the thick wooden door slamming shut and didn't move as her ma turned the key to lock the door that led out into the hallway.

Bel and her mother lived in 'rooms', or rather they lived in *a* room in a large Victorian house on Tatham Street. There were six others in the three-storey building and there lived a family in each.

Pearl had told Bel how lucky they were that there were only the two of them in their bedsit, and not a crowd like the McCanns upstairs, who, in her mother's words, seemed to 'spill out a child in the blink of an eye'.

Bel, however, thought she would have much preferred to have been squashed up with the McCanns rather than be with her own ma in their sparsely furnished lodgings, for there were always nice smells coming from the McCanns' and she often heard Mrs McCann singing lullabies to her youngest.

As Bel now listened to her mother's forced laughter from behind the locked door as she joked with the wiry, weasel-looking man who had been waiting for her out the front, she didn't move a muscle. She strained to hear what was being said, but the sound of her mother's voice gradually faded away as she clomped down the cobbled main road.

A little while later – Bel had no idea how long it had been, although it felt like hours – she heard children's voices as they played out on the street. When she caught one of the boys' voices she leapt to her feet and ran to the window. She pushed the grey rags that acted as curtains aside and pressed her face against the dirty pane. The glass was so filthy on both the inside and the outside that the two boys and the little girl playing looked as if they were running around in a pea-soup fog.

Bel desperately banged on the window, shouting out the names of the children who were playing tag on the street outside – names she knew, even though she had never had the nerve to talk to them.

'Teddy . . . ' she shouted out, 'Joe . . . Polly . . . '

But it was no good. The passing trams and general hubbub of the street drowned out her little voice.

Bel only stopped shouting when her throat became hoarse and her knuckles started to split and bleed due to her constant banging on the thick glass.

Bel's mother did not come home that day.

Nor that night.

In fact, she forgot to come back home for two more days, by which time Bel had taken to eating small, scrunched-up pieces of newspaper she had found under the threadbare rug. Her stomach felt as if it was gnawing into her very insides, and there was a fire burning in her belly that would only be extinguished if she was just able to eat one tiny morsel of food . . .

The next time Pearl tried to leave Bel in the room while a man waited on the front step, she went hysterical and scratched and clawed at her ma, who tried to push her daughter back so she could shut and lock the door.

But a desperate Bel managed to dodge past her mother's bare legs and escape into the hallway, before running like the wind, through the front door, past her mother's low-life suitor, and out on to the street.

Pearl had swung at her daughter with an open palm as she had skirted past her, but had only succeeded in catching a wisp of her daughter's dirty, nit-infested blonde hair.

Bel scurried round the corner and hid behind a mound of coal that had been left piled up in a heap in the back lane. She barely allowed herself to breathe as she listened to her mother's calls that started off nasty, demanding, 'Isabelle, get back here *now . . . or else*,' before turning sickly sweet, spewing out bare-faced lies that she would get Bel some sweeties if she came back – before, once again, she started growling threats of a 'good hiding' if Isabelle didn't get her backside *'here this very minute'*.

After a short while Bel heard the deep intonation of the man's tetchy voice, and then her mother's cloying utterances, trying to please and appease.

Bel's body sagged when she carefully peeked out from behind the stack of blackened stones and watched her mother walk away with the impatient-sounding man.

Bel stayed there for a short while before convincing herself the coast was clear, that her mum had gone and would not be coming back to lock her in the room again. She cheered up then, pleased just to be on her own, with her own thoughts, devising games she could play by herself. The tramlines always gave her endless hours of fun – her favourite imaginary game being to pretend she was an expert tightrope walker – the kind she had seen pictured on posters plastered around town before the arrival of the travelling circus.

When she got hungry she managed to scavenge a few scraps of food from the lad down the street called Dennis, whose mum ran the local grocery shop, but when it started to come in dark she returned to her own front doorstep, simply because she didn't know where else to go – and if the woman from the welfare turned up, like she often did, she could make out that her mam was round the corner, or had just nipped to the shops. There was no way she was going to end up in one of the workhouses just because her ma was no good.

It got cold and Bel started to cry, but just quietly so that no one would hear her. She felt so miserable and so cold and hungry that the tears just started to fall down her face, and she felt her chest heave as if she was short of breath.

And it was then that the girl she knew called Polly, who lived on the same street with her twin brothers, had seen her and approached her.

Bel and Polly were around the same age, although Bel believed the pretty girl with the long brown hair was older as she was so much taller than her.

'What you doing sitting there?' Polly asked.

'Me ma's gone out.' Bel immediately felt ashamed that someone had caught her weeping. Her ma had always given her a backhander if she had ever caught her crying, or, as she put it, 'turned on the waterworks'.

'Well, you'll just have to come to ours,' Polly told her, as if she had known Bel for ages and it was the most natural thing in the world to suggest. She stretched out a warm hand and took Bel's smaller and much colder hand in her own and the pair walked back down the street and into Polly's home, where Bel was immediately hit by the most scrumptious smells and enveloped in a blanket of warmth.

'And who have we got here?' Polly's mum asked.

'My name's Isabelle, but I like to be called Bel,' she told the older woman, who had bent down to introduce herself to the little stray her daughter had brought home.

'Well, Bel. I'm Agnes and these are my sons, Teddy and Joe,' Agnes said, turning to look at her boys. Bel forced a nervous smile that was followed by a genuine little laugh when Teddy and Joe both grinned in unison.

'And, as I'm sure you've guessed, they're twins,' she said, taking off her pinny, and standing back up straight.

'Don't be fooled, though – they may look the same, but they're like chalk and cheese really.'

Bel looked at Agnes and the two boys, who must have been at least a couple of years older than her – and then at her new friend Polly.

And at that very moment, it was as if a light had been switched on in her life – and, much to her joy, it stayed on thereafter.

Chapter Six

Friday 31 January 1941

Rosie had decided to get the ferry over to the south docks rather than get the bus from Thompson's to see if it made her journey home any quicker. She had recently moved out of her bedsit near the bus depot in the centre of town to a slightly better class of accommodation on the town's Borough Road which, geographically, was situated more or less exactly midway between her two places of work.

She still popped in to see her old neighbour, Mrs Townsend, who would probably never move from her room in the three-storey Georgian house on the corner of Grange Terrace. During the year Rosie had lived directly above her, she'd grown attached to the old woman, whom she called Mrs T for short, and every week Rosie would pop by with a couple of slices of cake or some iced buns she had bought from the town's bakery, and the two of them would drink tea and eat their treat and talk about all the latest goings-on.

Rosie had a suspicion Mrs T knew about her second job and that her 'welding accident' had not been some careless mishap at work but something far more sinister, but she never mentioned it, and Rosie was glad of the old woman's discretion and, more so, that Mrs T did not judge her for it.

Rosie had promised to take her little sister to see Mrs T when she visited during the summer holidays. It would be the first time Charlotte had actually come to stay with her. After their parents' death five years ago, when Charlotte had started boarding school, it had been arranged that during the holidays she would go to stay with their mum and dad's elderly friends, Mr and Mrs Rainer, as they lived just a bus journey away from her school in Harrogate. It was because Rosie had wanted her younger sister to come and occasionally stay with her that she had decided to get a proper flat and not just a room. And now that she had increased her income quite substantially from her investment in Lily's, she could afford it.

As Rosie started walking along Low Street up to the main road that led into town, she saw a familiar face coming towards her, wearing the same smart but well-worn black woollen three-piece suit, with a narrow, perfectly knotted dark blue tie. His overcoat was flapping open, failing to keep out the winter cold. It took just a few seconds for Rosie to place the man, and a few more to recall his name – or rather his surname and rank.

'Ah, Detective Sergeant Miller,' she said with a smile. 'What a surprise to see you here.'

By the look on DS Miller's face, he was not only genuinely surprised at having bumped into Rosie, but also very pleased.

'Good evening, Miss Thornton' – he stopped, took off his trilby hat and put out his hand to greet her – 'but please call me Peter. DS Miller is far too official.'

'As is Miss Thornton,' Rosie replied.

Rosie would more than likely have let the detective keep to the more formal 'Miss', had she not been feeling in such a good mood. Happy even.

'Rosie,' she said, releasing her hand from Peter's firm grip, 'is just fine by me.'

'All right, Miss Thornton, sorry . . . I mean Rosie . . . how are you? And how is work going at Thompson's? I know you've all got a heck of a workload over there.'

Rosie looked into the detective's grey-blue eyes and saw he was genuinely interested, and it surprised her that she wanted to talk to him. She would normally have just gone through the usual 'how do you dos' before carrying on her way, but something made her want to chat to the man she had only met twice in her life, but with whom she shared a strange kind of alliance.

For the next few minutes she told the detective about recent developments at work, including the yard's very particular pride in having their owner Cyril Thompson chosen by the British Admiralty to go over to America with a new design for a cargo vessel called the Liberty Ship, which might potentially help the Allies win the war. It was a Sunderland ship, and the Yanks needed help in going through the design and being shown how they could build it more quickly by welding rather than riveting.

'Our yard manager's still over there helping out with the production . . . But, anyway, enough shop talk, what are you doing in these parts? Aren't you usually based at the police headquarters in town?'

DS Miller sighed. 'A lot has changed since I last saw you – and again, my condolences for the loss of your uncle.'

'Please, no need,' Rosie interrupted, 'I barely knew the man. And by all accounts, from what you told me, that was a blessing.'

It had always been a source of amazement to DS Miller that Raymond Gallagher, the convicted rapist, whose body they had pulled out of the River Wear, had actually been related to this woman now standing before him. And, just like when he'd gone to inform Rosie, as the next of kin, about her uncle's death, he was again struck by how attractive she was, and by how the smattering of small scars on her face did not detract from her natural beauty in any way.

DS Miller forced himself to concentrate on their conversation as he explained to Rosie that he was now working for the Dock Police, who, as he was sure she was well aware, had a cabin by the sea lock on the south dock, near to the *Fire King*, the town's floating fire engine.

'That's where I'm going now,' DS Miller explained. 'The graveyard shift, as they say.'

'Well, I'd better not keep you from catching any villains,' Rosie said, aware that they'd been chatting for longer than was just good manners.

'Of course, I've kept you long enough,' DS Miller said, although he made no effort to move.

Rosie said her farewells and continued her walk up to the main road, while DS Miller remained where they'd both been chatting, watching as she became lost in the throng of fellow shipyard workers all hurrying home or off to the pub after the end of a long, hard day's work.

Rosie's basement flat was still very much a novelty, as she had just moved in over a month ago; she still revelled in the luxury of having a lounge, a little kitchenette, a large bedroom and, best of all, a bathroom, complete with a washbasin, roll-top bath and toilet.

Rosie changed out of her overalls and had a quick washdown. As she carefully pulled her figure-hugging navy blue satin dress over her head, and adjusted the pussy-bow neckline, thoughts of her surprise meeting with the smartly dressed detective – with his thick salt-and-pepper hair, and eyes that crinkled when he smiled – pervaded her mind.

Rosie wondered where he lived, and if he was married and had a family. There was something about him that suggested he was on his own, although Rosie didn't know why exactly she presumed that. An intuitive guess, perhaps, or the way he seemed to want to chat – as if he missed female company.

After quickly covering her facial scars with a pale-tinted foundation she had acquired off the black market, and which was so much easier to apply than the thick theatrical make-up she had been used to putting on her skin, Rosie dabbed a little rouge on her cheeks and brushed her long eyelashes with a smear of mascara, before grabbing her long, light grey herringbone trench coat and checking she had locked her front door. Rosie's living accommodation was completely separate from the rest of the house, affording her the privacy she required for the hours she kept.

A short tram journey later, and Rosie was walking up the long path of the beautiful Victorian terrace house on West Lawn, an exclusive, wide, tree-lined residential street in the affluent area of town known as Ashbrooke. Now that Rosie had bought into the business and was managing the girls, rather than simply being one of the women who worked there, she could enter the premises through the main, very grand, wooden front door, and not by the small back entrance that the working girls and the clients had to use in order to keep the comings and goings of those who frequented the property as discreet as possible.

Luckily, the people living on either side of what amounted to a three-storey mansion were both elderly, and paid no heed to the life around them. As long as there were no disturbances or noise, the neighbours on both sides seemed happy for them all to keep themselves to themselves.

They had, of course, all met Lily, who owned the house, on a number of occasions over the years she'd been there, and they all seemed to have accepted their slightly eccentric-looking neighbour, even if she was not quite of the social standing normally expected in such an upmarket area of town. It had aided neighbourly relations that Lily had told them, in the most beguiling French accent she could muster, that she was a designer, specialising in fashion and textiles, which they had not for one moment doubted, having been overcome by the cloud of Chanel No. 5 perfume in which Lily doused herself on a daily basis, as well as her very obviously dyed mass of auburn hair, worn up in an outlandishly large and rather chaotic bun.

Just the other week, shortly before leaving for her trip to London to find premises for her new venture, Lily had paid her neighbours a visit, taking with her two little pots of pâté de foie gras as a present to both households, not only to keep up the charade that she had French origins and still had connections with her homeland, but also to reassure them they had a kind and respectful resident next door.

They would, of course, have been horrified had they known the truth: that Lily was not really a madame but a madam, and that they were, in fact, living right next to an establishment they would most definitely have viewed as a wickedly sinful den of iniquity.

As Rosie turned the key and stepped over the threshold of the place known by those who went there as Lily's Bordello, she could hear the gentle murmur of people talking and the soft tinkling of the piano coming from the back reception room.

When Rosie looked up the wide, gently curving staircase, she saw one of the girls, a very attractive platinum blonde called Vivian, hurrying down the thick-carpeted stairs with a pleading smile on her face.

'Rosie,' she said in a husky voice, which was partly put on, as Vivian wanted to sound like a sultry Mae West, and partly genuine, due to the number of cigarettes she smoked, 'can I ask a favour?'

Rosie smiled. She knew exactly what Vivian was going to ask her. It was always the same with her. Money seemed to slip through the girl's fingers like water; she was always asking for 'just a little advance'.

'Ask me later on this evening, Vivian,' she told her firmly but good-naturedly. It had taken a little while for Rosie to make the transition from being one of the girls to being their manager. All the young women who worked there had tried their luck with her in some shape or form, and it had been difficult for her to strike a good balance between friend and employer – but she had managed and they all seemed to have accepted her graduation from fellow worker to boss without too much trouble.

As Vivian sashayed past her to greet one of her regulars who had just walked through the back door and was handing his hat and coat to the cloakroom attendant, Rosie heard the sound of a key in the front door. She turned just as it opened.

'*Je suis rentrée*,' Lily announced as she stepped through the doorway, shaking out her umbrella – although Rosie was sure it hadn't been raining – and somehow filling the whole of the wide, grandiose hallway despite her small stature.

'Lily, I didn't expect you back until tomorrow evening,' she said, going up to the woman who was now her business partner and giving her the obligatory kiss on both cheeks, something Lily had told all her girls to do as it was '*très chic*'.

'*Oui, ma chérie*, I was, but you know me . . . full of surprises,' Lily declared, grabbing Rosie's arm and steering her into the back parlour.

Rosie smiled as she detected a hint of Lily's true cockney accent break through the faux French. Every time Lily returned from the country's capital she caught traces of her true accent sneaking to the fore.

For the next couple of hours, the two women chatted, in between greeting clients, speaking to the girls, and making sure there were enough drinks and canapés for their guests; and, of course, taking care of the steady stream of cash payments for services rendered.

As the evening started to draw to a close, Lily poured them both a glass of Rémy Martin. Rosie allowed herself a very small tipple, but was wary of drinking too much; she had started to rely on it heavily during the hellish few months she'd been caught in the vice-like grip of her uncle Raymond. She had vowed nothing would ever control her again. Not anyone. Nor any kind of addiction.

'So, now, I want to hear about you, my dear,' Lily implored. 'What news is there in *ta vie* . . . your life?'

Rosie would have normally skimmed over Lily's question with a simple, 'Nothing. It's been nice and quiet. Just the way I like it,' but for some reason she found herself telling Lily about bumping into Peter on her way home after her day at the yard.

'Oh, *mon dieu*,' Lily said, trying unsuccessfully to hold back her excitement. 'Do I detect a little *je ne sais quoi* . . . a little frisson of attraction, *peut-être*? Could I even go as far as saying there might well be a little chemistry between you and this Peter?'

Rosie gave a short laugh and waved her hand at Lily, as if physically batting away her accusations.

'I do recall the way you talked about him back then . . .' Lily started to say, but then she stopped herself. Lily hated to recall that awful time last year when Rosie had been reduced to a wreck by that heinous man who had nearly killed her and had scarred her beautiful face for life. But at least when the whole horrendous debacle had come to an end, DS Miller had ensured she got her so-called 'inheritance', money believed to have been Raymond's, but that had in fact been Rosie's; her hard-earned money that had not only bought her uncle's silence, but also protected her sister Charlotte from his perverted threats.

And it was thanks to getting this money back that Rosie had been able to buy into Lily's business – and Lily herself had then been able to invest in a new enterprise in London.

'There was no frisson, as you put it, or chemistry,' Rosie rebuked Lily. 'He just seems a nice man. I thought it was a coincidence we bumped into each other and that he's now working with the Dock Police.'

Lily looked over her new half-moon spectacles. She claimed she needed them as her sight was deteriorating, although Rosie suspected Lily's eyes were perfectly fine and that the ornate horn-rimmed glasses were to make her look more sophisticated and intelligent, which, to be fair, they did.

'Oh well, let's hope DS Miller doesn't do his job too well, otherwise we won't be getting our usual supply of much-needed black-market goods through,' Lily clucked. 'And I'll be forced to stash our little essential luxuries in my suitcase and haul them back up from London.'

Both women were still chuckling at the thought of Lily trailing her booty up from the nation's capital when Vivian knocked on the parlour door. 'About that favour?' she asked. Vivian had chosen her moment well, having heard the women relaxing and in good spirits.

Lily rolled her eyes to the ceiling in dramatic fashion, before telling Rosie.

'Ten shillings. Not a penny more.'

Lily then swung her gaze back to Vivian, who, she noticed, had done a really good job of looking like a young Mae West, with her curled bob and wonderfully arched thick eyebrows and over-the-top false eyelashes.

'Young lady,' she said sternly, 'I really believe you're going to have to find yourself a very rich husband. You spend your money before you've earned it, and that is never going to put you in good stead for the future.'

Vivian threw her head back, causing her imitation diamond drop earrings to jangle back and forth as she laughed loudly. 'I know, Madame Lily. Do you not think I am looking for one?' she said, her normally disguised Liverpudlian accent peeking through.

Still chuckling, Vivian took the ten-bob note off Rosie, who then marked the debt up in her ledger, before shutting it and placing the thick, leather-bound book back inside one of the large kitchen drawers.

Just as Vivian was leaving, George arrived at the doorway to the parlour.

'Ah, George.' Lily turned to welcome her friend. 'I've missed you so. Come here and join us for a nightcap.'

George practically lived at Lily's, so much so that Rosie had wondered whether it would be a good idea for him to move in and pay a small amount for board and lodgings. Lily had chuckled and told Rosie she was born to be an entrepreneur and that she would chat to him about it.

As George walked into the room, Rosie noticed that his limp seemed to be more pronounced. She guessed it was down to the wear and tear of age, as George, like Lily, was getting on a bit, and must be approaching the start of his fiftieth decade. George was a veteran of the First

World War, which had left him with a large scar down the side of his face and with a limp he refused to admit had given him a disability; as a result, he did not see the very obvious need for a walking stick.

Lily must also have seen the deterioration in her friend's mobility for, as George limped into the room, she stood up and declared, 'I have a present for you, George,' before she bustled out of the parlour to fetch her gift.

'Rosie . . . always a pleasure,' George said, taking her hand and planting a chivalrous kiss on it before sitting down and pouring himself a brandy.

When Lily returned she was holding the most beautiful, clearly very expensive hand-carved cane.

'It's *time*, my dear,' Lily announced, handing the cane over to her friend.

George started to object, but stopped himself. He looked at the walking stick and smiled.

'How can I say no? It's magnificent,' he said, inspecting the ivory head that had a very subtle swirling 'G' engraved into the handle.

For the briefest of moments, Rosie recalled a very different cane – the one owned by her uncle; and how the ghoulish-looking ram's head carved into the handle had, in fact, been a dagger that he'd used to force her head over a spitting weld.

Rosie pushed all thoughts of that vile man and that horrendous evening in November last year out of her head, and instead looked at what she had now and her hopes for the future.

As Rosie watched Lily and George, she wondered exactly what lay in store for her two friends, who she loved like family. She had often speculated on the exact nature of their friendship, and whether or not it was more than just platonic.

As she listened to Lily tell George about the unique little shop in Kensington High Street where she had bought the cane and had it engraved to her specifications, Rosie thought of her own solitary life and what it would be like to share it with someone else. For the briefest of moments, Rosie's mind wandered to Peter, before she chided herself, pushing thoughts of the detective back to the far recesses of her mind.

Why couldn't she just accept her lot? She could have a good life, but love was not to be a part of it. Rosie had accepted this, even before her face had been scarred for life.

To even think of having any kind of relationship – never mind with a detective – was far, far beyond the realms of possibility.

Chapter Seven

Saturday 8 February 1941

'Anyone for more porridge?' Agnes shouted through from the scullery where she seemed to be banging and crashing a lot of pots and pans about unnecessarily.

'Aye, go on then, hinny. I'll have a dollop more. Set me up for the day ahead,' Pearl shouted back through to her daughter's mother-in-law. Joe had to force himself not to smile as he heard Agnes let out a heavy sigh before plodding back into the kitchen and practically throwing a lump of sticky porridge into Pearl's bowl.

It was a Saturday morning and the Elliot household seemed to be growing by the minute. Just over a week ago there had just been Agnes, Polly, Bel and little Lucille – as there had been for the past year and a half since the twins had gone off to war. Now, not only did they have Joe back home, but they also had an unexpected house guest in the form of Bel's mother Pearl, and within the next hour Tommy's seventy-year-old grandad, Arthur, would also be joining them to live there permanently.

When Agnes knew that Joe would be coming back and that they would need an extra room, she had asked the landlord, Mr Bernie Boyd – whom they all called Mr BB for short – if she could take over the three spare rooms on the second floor left empty by the previous tenants who had done a moonlight flit. She'd managed to persuade Mr BB to give her the extra accommodation at quite a considerable discount – mainly due to the fact he had not found anyone else to rent them out to and it was a case of some money was better than none, but also because he had more than a soft spot for Agnes.

Because of Joe's disability, Agnes had given him her bedroom on the ground floor next to Bel and Lucille, and had moved herself upstairs to the room at the front of the house with a window that looked out on to the main road.

Pearl had taken up residency in the second vacant room on the very night she had shown up. Agnes wasn't quite sure whether Bel's mother had known there was a spare room going beforehand, or if it had just been a coincidence she had turned up when she did, but there was no way she could have chucked Pearl back out on to the street that night, much as a part of her might have wanted to, and even though she sensed she would have had Bel's backing had she done so.

It had, however, been Agnes's idea for Arthur to end his tenancy at the Diver's House on the south dock and to take the third spare room. The old man had more or less become a part of the Elliot family since Polly and his grandson had started courting, and when Tommy had joined up, leaving Arthur on his own in what had been their home for many years, Agnes had argued that it made sense he live with them.

This morning there was just Bel, Lucille, Joe, Pearl and Agnes at the breakfast table, as Polly had already left for work at the yard. She was now working most weekends, often doing a full day on Saturday and half a shift on Sunday.

'Agnes, come and sit down and have your breakfast. You're not our skivvy, you know,' Bel said, glaring across the table at her mother, who she saw was just about to make a grab for the jug of milk.

'And, Ma, we haven't got a cow out back producing an endless supply of milk. There's something called "rationing" going on these days.'

Pearl pursed her lips like a spoilt child, putting the milk down, and eating the rest of her porridge with a sullen face.

'Bel.' Agnes pulled up a chair at the table and poured her tea from her cup into the saucer to cool it down before taking a slurp. 'Would you mind changing Joe's dressing for me this morning, please? It's just that I need to get Arthur's room ready for him before he arrives.'

Bel glanced across at Joe; she realised he was looking at her.

'Yes, of course, Agnes. I've told you before. As long as I'm not working, I want to be doing as much as I can here to help out.'

'Thanks.' Agnes smiled, taking another mouthful of tea, 'I really don't know what I would have done these past few weeks without you.'

Bel had always been a good actress, and she had managed to cover her reticence at having to tend to Joe's injured leg well. In reality, it was the last thing she wanted to do. She would have preferred to clean the lavvy and the washhouse from top to bottom rather than play nurse to Joe.

It wasn't that she had any qualms about cleaning Joe's wound, which was still refusing to heal properly and which meant he had to have clean, fresh bandages first thing in the morning and last thing at night, but that she was finding it increasingly difficult just to be near Joe; or even talk to him.

If she was honest, she could not bear to be in his company at all. Since Joe had returned, it was as though his very presence irritated her. She felt awful for feeling like she did, but she just couldn't help it. She found herself being snappy with him when he didn't deserve it – Joe

48

hadn't done anything wrong since he'd come back. Quite the reverse. He had been incredibly easy-going, even though she knew he was still in a lot of pain with his leg.

But what really annoyed her more than anything was that Lucille seemed to worship the ground he walked on, or rather hobbled on.

She had lain awake at night and thought about why she was feeling so angry towards Joe and so wound up by him. She had practically grown up with Joe, and, of course, Teddy and Polly. She had fallen in love with Teddy, but Joe had been like a brother to her, just as Polly had been like a sister. So why did she feel the way she did?

Bel forced a smile and got up from the table.

'Come on then, Joe, if you sit by the range it'll give me more space and I can get your dirty bandages on the boil . . .'

Bel tried hard to keep any kind of resentment from her tone of voice, but she caught the way Joe looked at her and realised he was aware of what she was thinking and feeling. He knew her too well. She could pull the wool over Agnes's eyes when she really had to, but she'd never had to do so with Joe, Teddy or Polly. All three of them had always been very open with each other.

'Me watch Doey,' Lucille demanded as she slid off her chair, toddled over to Joe and pulled at his hand. Bel was not sure if Lucille genuinely found it difficult to say Joe, or that it was her way of calling him a mix of 'Daddy' and 'Joey'. Bel had given up trying to get her to call him 'uncle', but had come down hard on her when she had kept calling him 'daddy' during Joe's first few days back home.

'No, you're not going to watch your uncle Joe,' Bel said, stressing the words *uncle* and *Joe*. 'Your grandma can take you out for a little while to get some fresh air.'

'Oh, pet, dinnit call me Grandma, makes me feel like a right old woman,' Pearl said, bending down to pick up her granddaughter, who immediately tried to wriggle out of her grip.

'Just you call me Pearl, petal,' she told Lucille, who had sidled up to Joe again.

Bel felt another wave of irritability wash over her.

'What is it with everyone? Why can't we all just call each other what we're supposed to call each other? By our proper names? Joe is "Uncle Joe" and you, Ma, are "Grandma",' Bel said in exasperation.

'Ha,' Pearl blustered, 'that's rich coming from you, Mrs "My-name-is-Bel-no-one-calls-me-Isabelle".' Pearl was triumphant, clearly pleased with herself for getting one up on her daughter. 'I think the proper word is *hypocritical*,' she added, as she got up, and looked around for her cigarettes.

'If you're looking for your fags, I've put them in your coat pocket. You know I don't like to see them cluttering the place up.'

The real reason Bel hated seeing her mum's smokes around was that they reminded her too much of when she was growing up; there had always been empty cigarette packets or tobacco pouches lying around everywhere, as well as an array of overflowing ashtrays. Funny that her ma had always had money for her cigs, but there'd never been a scrap to eat in the house.

Bel pushed thoughts of the past from her mind. Every second thought she had at the moment seemed to be filled with resentment. It was exhausting, and she was exasperated with herself.

'Come on then, petal,' Pearl said to Lucille, 'get your coat and *Pearl* will take you out for some fresh air.'

A few minutes later, when Lucille and her grandmother had headed off into town to look at the large stone lions that guarded the famous Winter Gardens (something she had never done with her own daughter), and Agnes was bustling around upstairs getting Arthur's room as spic and span as possible, Joe and Bel found themselves on their own in the kitchen.

Bel wished she had not been so quick to get rid of her mum and Lucille as she hated being on her own with Joe, more than she hated her mother being around.

There was an awkward silence before Joe asked cautiously, 'It must be hard having your ma around?'

'Just a little . . . But she's my ma whether I like it or not,' she said, not giving Joe any eye contact as she bathed the still raw wound just above his knee.

Joe heard the bitterness in her voice and it sounded unfamiliar. He had never known his sister-in-law to be like this. He was aware that *he* had changed. Of course, he'd changed. War had changed him. The horrors he'd seen had changed him. And, of course, his brother's death had changed him. But he hadn't expected to see such a difference in the people he loved, in those he'd left behind. And yet they'd all changed in their own ways: his mother had become older and wearier, Polly was no longer his baby sister but now a strong, confident woman – and an engaged one at that – and Bel . . . well, Bel had become hard, cold, and bitter. He knew she was grieving, he could only imagine what she was going through, but it still didn't make seeing the change in her any easier.

As Joe gritted his teeth while Bel sponged his leg with warm, soapy water, then dabbed it with salt water before carefully covering the open wound with a piece of gauze, he thought that the only person who didn't seem to have changed was Bel's mum. The years might have taken their toll on her looks, but she was still the same old Pearl.

'She's no different to when we were all kids,' Joe spoke his thoughts aloud.

'I know,' Bel muttered, thinking that Joe was right – her ma had never changed, but she *had* learnt to camouflage her true nature as she had got older, to make herself slightly more socially acceptable.

Bel tried not to touch Joe's bare flesh as she unravelled a clean length of bandage and wrapped the new dressing around Joe's leg. It seemed wrong to have any kind of physical contact with another man. The only man she'd ever touched was her Teddy.

'Has she said why she's come back? Or how long she's staying for?' Joe pursued the subject of Pearl, much to Bel's annoyance.

'Not really,' she said, purposely keeping her answers as brief as possible.

Didn't Joe realise she didn't want to chat?

They were, of course, the same questions she had asked her mother herself, and from whom she had not really got a straight answer.

'I heard about poor Teddy,' Pearl had told her the morning after her impromptu arrival, 'and I just had to come and see my *Isabelle*. My daughter. My *widowed* daughter,' she'd added with her usual lack of sensitivity. Bel's instinct told her that her mother was lying and that there was some other reason she had come back, and that it had nothing to do with Teddy's death, or any kind of care for her daughter, whom she'd never given two jots about.

One thing she did know, though, was that her ma seemed quite at home at the moment, and unfortunately looked set on sticking around for a good while longer.

Chapter Eight

Friday 14 February 1941

'I've got my eyes on you . . .' Dorothy started singing the first few lines of the popular Cole Porter song before Angie joined in for good measure. The pair were more excited than normal for this early in the morning, owing to it being a Friday *and* Valentine's Day – therefore giving them even more of an excuse to go out and paint the town red that evening. They had already announced they would both have found themselves a new beau by the end of the day.

'Good lord, it's like the cat's chorus,' Gloria stressed the point by putting her fingers in her ears. Dorothy and Angie started cackling with laughter.

'Or witches around the cauldron,' Gloria added, but she was clearly fighting hard to suppress a smile. Dorothy and Angie really were a pair. They could be the most annoying women on this earth, or at least in the yard if you weren't feeling full of the joys yourself – or they could be good fun and a welcome distraction from the unrelenting, backbreaking work they were all having to do. Their six – sometimes seven – twelve-hour days a week had meant that often they didn't know one day from the next.

'I don't know where they get energy from,' Hannah said to Gloria, as she finished off a little pencil sketch of one of the half-built ships in the dry basin. Hannah's English was now nigh on perfect, but she still kept forgetting to use the odd pronoun here and there, despite Dorothy taking it upon herself to be their little bird's language teacher by constantly nagging her.

'I know,' Gloria agreed, taking a look at Hannah's very precise drawing and admiring it.

Gloria was going to add that it was the 'joys of being young', as she always felt every one of her forty-one years at the end of a day's hard graft, but she stopped herself – Hannah was around the same age as Dorothy and Angie, but had only a fraction of their vitality and strength.

'Are you working with us today?' Gloria asked. Hannah kept being bounced back to them whenever Rosie couldn't find any light welding work for her to do.

'Yes, I'm afraid so.' Hannah blushed, scrunching up her drawing and chucking it in the metal bin next to their workbench, before adding quickly, 'not that I don't like being with you all. I love being with everyone, it's just—'

'Bloody hard work. I know.' Gloria finished off Hannah's sentence for her.

'That Helen woman,' Hannah continued, 'she say I have to work with you all this week . . . and, how do you say it? For the "see able" future?'

'*Fore*seeable,' Dorothy butted in, adding, 'I *know* – that cow is determined to run us all into the ground. But don't you worry, Hannah, she won't succeed. Just make sure you're working next to me and you'll be okay.'

Gloria looked over Hannah's head and smiled at Dorothy. She might be a total dipstick and man-mad, but the girl was loyal, that much Gloria would give her. Dorothy was their fastest and best welder, and Gloria knew that she would do a good share of Hannah's workload, yet make it seem as though Hannah had done it herself.

'Oh God, speak of the devil,' Angie, who had been standing next to Dorothy, whispered. 'See you all at lunchtime,' she said, hurrying over to one of the huge green cranes she'd just learnt to operate.

'Have you all gone deaf?' Helen spat out the words at the women as she marched across the yard.

She was wearing a full-length leather mackintosh that surprisingly covered her entire body, something she rarely liked to do if she could help it, although she had compensated by pulling the coat's thick belt as tight as she could to accentuate her small waist and womanly hips.

'What did you say, Helen?' Dorothy tried to keep a straight face.

Polly and Martha had now joined the women, and they all managed to supress their giggles at Dorothy's cheek, all apart from Martha, who let out a big guffaw. She might have become more talkative these past few months, but she was still lacking some basic social skills.

'I said . . .' Helen started to repeat herself before realising she had become the silent butt of the woman's joke, which only enraged her even more.

She glared daggers at Dorothy but ignored Martha, whom she never acknowledged; Helen treated Martha as if she was invisible, which was not only demeaning, but actually quite hard to do as Martha was not someone you could easily pretend was not there.

'The horn sounded out at least five minutes ago. Your machines should be on. There's work to be done. Ships to be built, if you hadn't noticed,' Helen scolded.

The only reason Helen had dared to come over and reprimand the women was because she knew Rosie was in another part of the yard chatting to a new intake of apprentices to see if any of them wanted to make welding their trade. It wasn't the most popular choice as it was known to be one of the hardest jobs in the yard. On top of which, many of them had been influenced by the older men, who still believed riveting – and not welding – was the only way to build a ship.

Gloria turned and bobbed down to sort out a pile of assorted welding rods; as she did so she grabbed hold of Polly's arm and forced her to follow suit.

'You've not forgiven her for coming between you and Tommy, have yer?' Gloria said quietly to Polly as they both pretended to be busy.

'I think you have to *want* to be forgiven before you get to be forgiven,' Polly said, while casting a look of pure hatred over her shoulder in the direction of Helen, adding a little too loudly, 'and that stuck-up witch is about as far from wanting to be forgiven as it gets.'

Gloria quickly glanced up to see if Helen had heard and was relieved to see she hadn't.

Gloria looked at Polly and grimaced.

'Aye, yer right there, that's for sure. I don't think the word "sorry" is in her vocabulary.'

Gloria also knew enough about being a young woman in love – could still recall how it felt despite the passing of years – to realise that Polly was also still very jealous of Helen, despite being a lovely-looking girl herself.

Gloria handed Polly a few welding rods, trying to distract her from the harpy in their midst, knowing that if Helen were to just say one out-of-order comment, or cast Polly one of her high-and-mighty sneering looks, that Polly might well react. Gloria was well aware that her workmate had been on a short fuse of late, which was totally understandable. The poor girl was still grieving for her brother, and Gloria knew from others who had lost loved ones in both this war and the last one that bereavement usually came hand in hand with a good dose of anger.

'So, chop chop, off to work you go!' Helen's condescending voice snipped at Dorothy, Hannah and Martha, who were now all glowering back at her.

Gloria shot Polly a warning look.

'Oh dear,' Helen added, looking down her nose at the women, 'if looks could kill . . .' She then let out a sharp, poisonous laugh before turning on her three-inch heels and swaggering off back to the warmth and comfort of the administration offices.

'Please God, bring Jack back,' Dorothy declared to the heavens above as they all turned to their work area and, one by one, switched on their machines.

As Gloria pulled her mask down, she silently seconded Dorothy's celestial plea, not just because Helen really was a complete pain in the backside, and Jack was a far more pleasant and more considerate yard manager to work under, but because she missed Jack – desperately.

It now seemed years – not merely months ago – that they had secretly kissed each other farewell in the shelter of St Peter's Church porch, just a stone's throw away from where they were now. Gloria had known – even then – that it was going to be hard; that she would miss her lover terribly. But she had not expected to feel so bereft. She constantly argued with herself that she was not some love-struck youngster and to pull herself together. But still, she couldn't wait for the day that she would be in his arms once again.

As Gloria broke off from the weld to button up her overcoat, so as to keep out the bitter icy wind that was starting to whip up across the yard, she felt the pull of the thick fabric against her tummy.

'I think your coat's shrunk, Glor,' Dorothy teased, pushing her mask up to speak as soon as she'd spotted her workmate struggling to do it up.

Gloria couldn't help but laugh.

'When I was expecting Gordon and Bobby, I hardly showed until I was about five months pregnant. Slim as a pin I was. This time, though, I've piled on the weight from the second I fell.'

'Yes,' Dorothy mused, 'but you were half your age then.'

'I know, don't say it, I'm old enough to be a "nana" and not a "mammy". I've thought it more than once myself believe you me – but I still can't understand why I'm piling it on. It's not as if I'm exactly stuffing my face – not with all this bloody awful rationing. And to make things worse, I seem to be craving anything and everything even remotely sweet – just typical with sugar being like gold dust these days.'

Just as Gloria was starting to imagine eating a big apple turnover filled with a good dollop of cream and sprinkled with lots of lovely crystals of brown sugar, she felt a tap on her shoulder.

It was Rosie.

'How are you feeling?'

Ever since the day they had all come to Rosie's rescue and saved her from that evil, abhorrent man who they'd come to learn was her uncle, Rosie had made a point of keeping a very close eye on all her women welders. She reminded Gloria of a lioness keeping a vigilant watch on her young – not that Gloria felt even remotely like a small, young cub; all the same, Rosie was determined that no harm would come to either Gloria or the little life growing inside her.

'I'm all right,' Gloria said. 'Everything feels fine,' she added, glancing down at her stomach.

Rosie lowered her voice.

'You thought any more about what you're going to do when Jack gets back?'

Gloria's face fell.

'I just don't know. I can't help but think that it'll feel like history repeating itself for Jack. And,' Gloria added thoughtfully, 'I want Jack to be with me for the *right* reasons. For love. And for love alone. And not just because I'm carrying his baby.'

Rosie nodded. She could understand Gloria's dilemma.

'I know, but it's not as if you've tricked him like his wife did. This baby is very obviously real.' Rosie smiled as she looked at her workmate's expanding waistline.

Gloria nodded her agreement; this child growing inside her was certainly very real – and very unexpected. And they did love each other. Always had. Since they'd been childhood sweethearts.

To this day, Gloria could not understand how Miriam could have done what she'd done all those years ago, stealing Jack off her by seducing him one night and then pretending that his one indiscretion had resulted in her falling pregnant.

They'd all been so young and naïve back then – all apart from Miriam. She'd got exactly what she wanted: Jack, a ring on her finger, and then, after an alleged miscarriage, she'd fallen pregnant for real and given birth to Helen.

'Well, whatever you decide, you know I've got your back, don't you?'

Gloria nodded as Rosie stood up.

'And, just stop if you need a rest or you don't feel good, all right?' Rosie said with a face that showed she meant every word.

When Gloria pushed her mask back down and carried on with her weld, she knew it would not be long before she wasn't all right, and that not only would she not be able to keep up with the workload, more importantly it would not be good for her unborn baby for her to be grafting the way she was now.

Gloria had loved working at Thompson's from the off – had thought the place incredible. She'd never been anywhere that was so full of so many different sights and sounds; she'd gone home after her first day with her ears ringing and her head buzzing. Her love for this huge concrete expanse of metal and steel and half-built ships had grown greater with time, especially after she had started to make sense of the chaos and had begun to understand the whole shipbuilding process.

But, as much as Gloria loved working in the yard, the life of her unborn baby took precedence over everything else, and always would. Ever since the day, not long after she'd found out she was pregnant, and her husband Vinnie had punched her in the stomach so violently she feared she'd most certainly miscarry, she'd resolved that no one, or anything, would harm the life growing inside her.

When the time eventually came and her pregnancy could not be hidden any more, and it was no longer safe for her to work the way she was now, then she'd have to chat to Rosie to see if there was any chance of her staying on at the yard, perhaps in a different capacity. Although she had no idea what she'd do, as she couldn't envisage herself doing office work – and she certainly couldn't see Helen sanctioning a job for her indoors, especially if the truth came out about the real parentage of her unborn baby.

In fact, if Helen were to find that out, Gloria was fairly sure she would not be allowed to put a step over the yard's boundary, never mind still have a job there.

But that was a worry for another time.

By the end of the shift the temperature had dropped even more, and a low-lying sea fret was creeping across the river.

'No overtime tonight,' Rosie said, quickly packing up her belongings.

'Get yourselves off home – or to the pub,' she added, glancing at Dorothy, who had just been joined by Angie.

The women were all pleased they were not required to do any extra hours – all apart from Polly, who would have worked around the clock and quite happily slept at the yard too.

As Hannah and Martha trudged off, followed by an excited Dorothy and Angie, Gloria slung her gas mask over her shoulder and looked at Polly, who was still faffing about.

'Come on, slow coach,' Gloria said. 'If I didn't know better, I'd think you didn't have a home to go to. I thought you'd be racing out of those gates. It's not very often these days we actually get off on time.'

Polly stood up, and sighed.

'If truth be told, Gloria, it's not exactly a barrel of laughs at home at the moment,' Polly admitted.

Gloria crinkled her forehead into a questioning frown.

'The atmosphere is what you might call "emotionally charged". Has been for weeks now. More so since Joe got back, which is madness. You'd have thought his return would have brought a little happiness into the house. But, if anything, it's been the reverse.'

'Go on, tell me more,' Gloria said, linking Polly's arm as they both sauntered towards the yard's main gates, neither in a rush to go home.

Gloria listened as Polly told her that Tommy's grandad, Arthur, was now ensconced upstairs, although that was one change Polly positively welcomed, as she loved the old man to pieces.

'Nice to have just a tiny little bit of the man you love near to you, eh?' Gloria added, feeling her bump and thinking how she felt Jack's presence in the growing life inside her.

Polly smiled and squeezed Gloria's arm.

'Yes, it is,' she agreed, adding, 'but you know I would have thought having Joe at home would have really lifted everyone. It was such a massive relief he was all right and that he got back home safely.' Polly paused. 'His leg's still a worry and Ma's particularly anxious, as she thinks there may be some small bits of shrapnel still in his leg that's stopping the wound from healing properly.'

Gloria nodded her understanding. She knew plenty of war vets who had become amputees a while after being injured due to an infection spreading.

'But,' Polly continued, 'he's being well looked after and he seems happy enough. And it's lovely to see how much Lucille obviously adores him, and how much *he* totally dotes on *her*.'

And it was true; their little niece always made Joe's face light up. In fact, the little girl's buoyancy and natural chirpiness was like a breath of fresh air to them all. Everyone, that was, apart from Bel.

As if reading her thoughts, Gloria asked, 'And Bel. What about Bel? How's she coping?'

'Not well, to put it bluntly. I can't seem to get through to her – at all. It's as though the Bel I've known all these years has simply disappeared in the blink of an eye.

'And what I really cannot fathom out is just why she seems to hate the fact Lucille has taken so well to Joe. You'd think she'd be chuffed. At least her daughter's happy, even if no one else is.'

As they both reached the timekeeper's cabin and handed their cards in, Gloria kept her own counsel on why she thought Bel's behaviour was so out of character. She knew

Polly needed to just talk and she was happy to simply listen to her friend.

As they walked down to the ferry landing, Polly spoke about how awful it was seeing how her brother's death had changed her sister-in-law, and that, although Teddy's death had deeply affected them all, it had wreaked devastation on Bel.

'I suppose that's not surprising,' Gloria said as they waited in the growing queue of workers all eager to get on the ferry and get home.

'She's still young,' Gloria mused. 'If it hadn't been for this damned war, there would have been no reason she couldn't have expected to grow old with your Teddy, and had more children – brothers and sisters for Lucille.'

'You're right,' Polly agreed.

Bel's hopes and dreams of a future had been ripped from her – obliterated with the arrival of a single telegram. It had been nearly two months now since they had found out Teddy had been killed. Polly knew that was not a long time, and that Bel would be grieving for a good while yet, but she seemed to be sinking further down into the dark pit of bereavement, not slowly clawing her way up.

'Perhaps she hasn't hit rock bottom yet – she'll need to do that before she starts to recover,' Gloria volunteered as they followed a group of laughing and joking shipwrights on to the boat.

'And it's not helped that Pearl's back on the scene,' Polly added. 'I can't stand the woman. She just needs to open her mouth to be totally annoying. Heavens knows how Bel must feel; it's her mother after all. But what can we do? We can't just boot her out on to the street, no matter how much I'd like to – and I know for certain Bel would *love* to.'

As the two women looked out to sea, the sound of the waves lapping against the wooden sides of the old ferry and the gentle sway of the boat induced a feeling of calm; even the other workers had quietened down. Polly let her mind flee her present reality and, closing her eyes and lifting her face to the darkening sky, she imagined herself transported across the waters, across Europe, and down to the southernmost tip of Spain – to Gibraltar – and into the arms of her fiancé.

The thought of her and Tommy's first Valentine's Day spent apart made her feel sad, but she knew she was not alone in feeling the way she did. How many other women like herself, who had loved ones away fighting on some foreign battlefield, or holed up on a ship, praying to God they didn't get blasted out of the water or sunk by the Luftwaffe's bombs, were thinking the same. She really had to count her blessings that Tommy, as far as she was aware, was alive and well, and that she didn't have to contemplate a life without ever seeing the man she loved again.

Unlike Bel.

A few minutes later, as the ferry reached the south dock, Polly opened her eyes. To her surprise she spotted Rosie, still in her overalls, her hair tied up in her headscarf, standing halfway up the embankment and happily chatting away to a very smartly attired older man.

Although they were both dressed as polar opposites, and there was a clear age gap between the two, there was no denying they looked good together, and very comfortable in each other's company. If Polly hadn't known it was Rosie, she would have presumed the man and woman chatting away to each other were most definitely a couple.

'Eee, Glor, can you see what I'm seeing?' Polly asked.

Gloria squinted before a surprised looked crossed her face.

'Aye, I most certainly can. Well, that's a turn-up for the books, isn't it?' she said with an amused smile.

*

'We have to stop meeting like this,' DS Miller joked, catching up with Rosie as she made her way up the embankment.

'DS Miller. I mean Peter. Nice to see you. Been catching any black marketeers down that dock?' She smiled.

'Not today,' he laughed. 'Perhaps I might hook one or two tomorrow – along with a nice big crab,' he joked.

There was a moment's pause, before he added, 'I've finished for the day, and I've got a few hours to spare until I go and do my air-raid warden duties. Would it be improper of me to ask if you would like to have a cup of tea with me in the little café at the top the road?'

By the look on Rosie's face, DS Miller was prepared to be turned down, so he was taken aback when she said, 'Yes, why not? I could do with a nice cuppa after the day I've had.'

DS Miller's own face immediately cheered up and he broke into a big smile.

This woman is full of surprises, he could not help thinking, before saying out loud, 'Sounds like an interesting day.'

Rosie laughed. 'If work was just about the welding, it would be a breeze. But add people into the equation and it all gets terribly complicated.'

'Aye, there's nowt as strange as folk.' DS Miller chuckled as they both walked side by side up on to the main road, before making their way to the little tea shop nestled halfway along High Street East.

As they chatted away to each other, Rosie suddenly recalled Dorothy and Angie's dreadful rendition of 'I've Got My Eyes On You', and she realised that today, funnily enough, was Valentine's Day.

Chapter Nine

The next morning in the Elliot household, Bel came bustling out of her room looking spic and span in her smart blue tweed conductress's uniform. It had been languishing in the back of her wardrobe since the arrival of Teddy's death notification almost two months ago and hadn't been touched since.

Unusually for this time of the morning, just about everyone was up: Agnes was in the scullery, Arthur and Joe were sitting at the kitchen table drinking tea, and Polly was stirring a big pan of porridge simmering on the range. Even Pearl was up and was braving the cold, having her first smoke of the day out in the back yard.

'Ah, she's pretty as a picture, isn't she?' Arthur's pale blue eyes shone towards Bel. Joe smiled and nodded his agreement.

Polly stared at Bel for a moment before allowing a wide smile to appear on her face.

'Bel would look gorgeous in a sack,' she said, taking the pan off the hob and serving up four bowls. Neither Agnes nor Pearl were 'breakfast people', as they put it – Agnes just wanted her fix of tea, and Pearl her fags.

'I didn't know you were going back to work, Bel,' Polly said as Bel pulled up a chair next to Arthur and poured herself a cuppa.

'Well, I thought it about time I get out of everyone's hair and start to earn my keep – unlike certain other people in this house,' she said, throwing a derisory look out of the kitchen window at her mother, who was gripping her faded pink cotton dressing gown under her chin with one hand as she smoked with the other. Her slight frame was visibly shivering due to the early morning frost.

Polly's smile dropped. Bel did not seem to be able to speak without either criticising her mother or taking a snipe at someone or something else; but at least she was trying to get herself out and about. Hopefully, this was the turning point that Gloria had talked about.

'I'll make two lots of sandwiches, then?' Agnes shouted through to the kitchen as Polly took her pan into the scullery and plunged it into a sinkful of water.

'Don't worry about me,' Bel replied. 'I'll just get something in the canteen.'

As Polly watched Bel take the first mouthful of her porridge, she sidled up to her mum.

'Well, that's a turn-up for the books,' she whispered. 'Work'll take her mind off everything. Hopefully get her back to her old self.' Polly looked and sounded both relieved and hopeful.

'Mm,' was the only reply Agnes offered, before shouting back through to her daughter-in-law.

'All right, but take some change out of the jar. And don't worry about doing Joe's dressing. You don't want to mark your uniform. And if Lucille's still sleeping, leave her and I'll sort her out when you've gone.'

Bel's face brightened.

'Thanks, Agnes, you're a star.'

Bel pushed her bowl of half-eaten porridge away, and went to stand in front of the mirror in order to pin her hair up so that it would fit under the little peaked cap all the ticket collectors, conductors, bus and tram drivers had to wear.

'You should try and eat a bit more breakfast,' Joe said. He hadn't been the only one to notice just how little Bel was eating at the moment. She'd always been petite, but now she was starting to look undernourished and skinny – not unlike her mother.

Bel shot Joe a sharp look as she stabbed another hairpin into her thick twisted golden hair, which seemed to be fighting to be free.

'You my ma now, Joe?' Her retort was more accusatory than jokey. Both Joe and Arthur looked back to their own bowls of porridge and started eating.

'Not that *she* ever gave two hoots whether I ate or starved.' Bel let out a bitter half-laugh.

Polly came back into the kitchen to see Bel disappearing back into her bedroom.

'You two are as quiet as mice this morning. What? Cat got your tongues?' Polly's cajoling was met by two equally weak and unconvincing smiles.

Polly lowered her voice as she poured a splash of milk on to her porridge.

'It's a start, isn't it? Bel going back to work?' she asked, before tucking into her hot oats.

Joe and Arthur nodded but did not voice an opinion. Neither man looked quite so reassured – or seemed quite as optimistic – as Polly about Bel's return to work.

'Welcome back, Bel!'

The depot manager, Howard, was genuinely pleased to see his former worker back, although he was a little surprised, as it wasn't that long since Bel had learnt of her husband's death and he'd expected her to take a lot more time off to mourn her loss.

Also, she had not told him she was coming back to work, which meant he'd have to redo the day's rota, which was a pain, and always brought a flurry of moans and groans from the other workers. But he couldn't complain, Bel was one of his most reliable and well-liked conductresses – and he needed the staff. Nowadays the Corporation seemed to be constantly short of employees; it seemed like every week one of the young lads working on the buses turned eighteen and was immediately conscripted and drafted off to war.

As Howard walked over to Bel, he put his arms out and, with the utmost sincerity, voiced his condolences.

'I'm so sorry for your loss,' he said, giving Bel a gentle hug, wanting to show just how much he meant what he said.

Howard had known Teddy and his brother Joe from being young lads; he was always chasing them off the trams or the buses for not paying, but they weren't bad lads. And he also knew just how close Teddy and Bel had been, even as bairns. He'd never forget seeing Bel get a right thumping from one of the bully boys on their street when she was playing on the tramlines, and then later hearing the boy's mother sounding off that Teddy had given her little Johnny a shiner. Howard had told the moaning old mare the reason for her son's black eye and she'd stopped her bellyaching.

'I thought it was time I got back to normality,' Bel said, forcing herself to put up with Howard's show of affection. Howard felt Bel go rigid and, sensing her discomfort, he stepped back. It surprised him, as Bel was normally very tactile and had often given him a hug or a kiss on the cheek. He was easily old enough to be her father and he had always felt quite paternal towards her.

'Yes, yes, of course, normality,' Howard agreed.

'Whatever that is these days,' she added with a sad laugh.

Half an hour later, Bel left on the nine o'clock bus service to Fulwell on the north side of the river. Howard had decided not to put her back on her normal Sunderland to Durham route which would have taken most of the morning, but to keep her local, as something told him she still didn't seem quite herself.

As Howard wandered back to his cabin in the middle of the Park Lane depot, he had no idea just how far from herself Bel really was.

'Where to?' Bel practically barked at the first passenger of the day – a grey-haired woman with two young girls, whose age suggested they were most likely her grandchildren rather than her own offspring.

Bert, the driver, looked in his rear-view mirror, surprised at how hard and unfriendly Bel sounded. Also, the woman now groping around in her bag for her purse while trying to control the two little uns had only just sat down and had barely had time to catch her breath. Bert had never heard or seen Bel in a bad mood before, and over the past year or so he had often been paired up with her. The other workers liked to call them 'Beauty and the Beast', as Bert was far from handsome and was knocking on in years, and there was no arguing that Bel was quite a stunner. Bert would laugh it off, saying, 'Ah, she's not that bad, lads!' And Bel always happily joined in the banter.

Today, though, it was Bel who was acting like the beast; he'd never heard her sound so gruff and unfriendly to anyone, let alone any of the passengers, and they'd had a few who had certainly deserved the sharp end of her tongue, but she'd always been the epitome of politeness.

As the journey got going, Bert struggled to keep his attention on the road as Bel's behaviour continued to be totally out of character and a little alarming. Every time she took a fare it was accompanied by a very impatient and audible huffing noise. He also noticed there had not been any 'hinnies', or 'pets', or any other of the kindly endearments that Bel normally used with her fares.

Shortly after the bus, which was now half full, had crossed the Wearmouth Bridge and pulled over at the bus stop in Monkwearmouth, a heavily pregnant young woman struggled to heave herself on board. Bel was standing just a few yards down the aisle, but didn't move a muscle to help; instead she remained resolutely rooted to the spot, glowering at the woman, as if she had no right to be getting on this – or any other – bus.

Bert started to get out of his driver's seat to help, asking, 'You all right there, missus?'

'I'm fine. Honest. You stay where you are.' The woman smiled back at Bert as she successfully pulled herself on board with the aid of the handrail.

A few minutes later, a pair of old grannies clambered on, full of chatter and laughter; their gossiping showed no signs of abating as they got themselves settled in the seats at the front of the bus. They were so busy nattering, they did not see the look of annoyance cross Bel's face, nor her stare as they continued to have a good chinwag.

Bel couldn't stop the anger and irritation rising up in her and, although she knew she should keep her mouth shut, and that it wasn't her place to say anything, she could not stop herself from marching up to the old women and standing, hands on hips, looking down at them, like a headmistress at two naughty schoolchildren.

'Will you two be quiet? Not everyone wants to hear every bit of meaningless tittle-tattle coming out of your mouths, you know.'

The two old women looked up at Bel in shock, but were too taken aback to say anything. Both their mouths had literally fallen open in disbelief at being reprimanded so harshly and so unfairly by the pretty blonde bus conductress.

As Bel turned and walked back to the front of the bus, the women looked at each other incredulously.

'Well I never!' one of them whispered to the other. Her friend shushed her, fearful of another telling-off.

As the bus drove through Fulwell and reached its final stop at the top end of Sea Road, where the main parade of shops was, the pregnant woman started to get to her feet ready to disembark.

As Bert brought the bus to a halt, the woman stood up, but before she had a chance to leave, Bel strode up the aisle and demanded, 'Before you go off to do your shopping, can I just ask why your husband is not off fighting on the front line – but by the look of you would rather stay at home, well out of harm's way, and put you in the family way?'

With each word, Bel seemed to be getting more worked up and more angry.

The woman remained stock-still as Bel continued her rant.

'Don't you think he should be out there fighting Jerry – not knocking you up?'

By now the six remaining passengers, including the two old women and Bert the driver, had all stopped what they were doing and were staring at Bel.

The pregnant woman seemed unable to move, and simply gawped at her inquisitor. Her face had gone as white as a sheet. She struggled to get her words out, and when she did they came out in a stutter. 'He *is* . . . "fighting Jerry" . . .' she said, her voice as quiet as a mouse, but she was clearly determined to defend her husband from Bel's accusations.

'He got a few days leave . . . eight months ago,' she said, self-consciously putting a hand on her enormous belly.

Bel looked at the woman, who now had trickles of tears slowly making their way down her face, and was surprised to find she felt not a flicker of sorrow or empathy for the upset she had caused. Instead she simply turned and walked back down the aisle to the front of the bus.

As she did so, the two old dears shuffled to either side of the expectant mum.

'Come on, dear,' one of them cajoled. 'Let's get you off this bus.'

When Bert closed the doors he looked at Bel, but didn't say a word.

As the bus made its way back into town, he made a silent plea that no more pregnant women or gossipy old ladies got on the bus. In fact, he was secretly hoping there would be no more passengers to pick up before they made it back to the safety of the bus depot.

When the bus finally reached Park Lane, Bert hurried out and made a beeline for the cabin, where he knew he would find Howard.

A few minutes later, a serious-looking Howard appeared and caught Bel just as she was making her way to the canteen.

'Bel, can I have a quick word, please?'

Bel followed Howard into the little makeshift office as Bert left, his head bowed.

'Bel, I've just heard from Bert what happened on the Fulwell run . . . and I'm sure I'm going to hear it from others as the day goes on.' He paused. 'I can't even imagine what you must be going through – losing Teddy and all – but I'm afraid we can't have you upsetting the passengers like that. I really don't think you're ready to come back just yet.'

Howard tried to keep his voice soft and non-confrontational. He hated any kind of argument or conflict – he had seen enough awfulness in the First World

73

War and, despite what he had just said to Bel, he did have some understanding of the complex nature of grief, and knew it was not straightforward. Everyone dealt with it in their own way.

'Have some more time off,' he said. 'We'll have a chat in a few weeks, see how you're feeling,' he added, gently showing Bel out through the door.

Bel didn't object. She knew what she had said was totally unacceptable, but she didn't seem to be able to bring herself to care, or even to feel bad about her behaviour. Instead she forced herself to give Howard a smile of compliance before marching out of the bus depot and making her way back home.

Agnes was getting another load of laundry ready and keeping half an eye on the children she was looking after, who were all playing happily out in the yard, when she heard her daughter-in-law's footsteps stomping down the hallway and into the kitchen.

'Everything all right?' she asked, concerned, as she watched Bel take her cap off and pull the half a dozen or so metal pins out of her hair.

'I'm fine,' Bel said, 'but Howard doesn't think I'm "ready to come back" to work.'

Bel repeated his words in a derisory way, to show that she in no way agreed with him.

Agnes sensed not to push her for more information. When she had heard this morning that Bel was going back to work, she'd thought it was too soon, but knew it was best not to say anything.

'I'm just going to change and I'll be out to help you,' Bel said, disappearing into the bedroom.

As the afternoon wore on, Agnes kept a close eye on Bel. She knew all was not well by the way her daughter-in-law was pummelling a load of sheets on the washboards like she was trying to grind them down to dust, and the vigour with which she was turning the arm of the wringer meant by teatime they'd got through the day's laundry well before they would have normally.

Later on that evening, after everyone had eaten their supper and had either gone out or gone to their rooms, Agnes went round to see Beryl, who always seemed to be the first to hear any kind of local news or scandal, even though she rarely left the confines of her own home.

'You heard anything from your gossip-mongering fishwives?' Agnes tried to make her voice sound light and frivolous but her face told another story.

Likewise, Beryl's face was awash with concern. She didn't say anything.

'Oh dear, that bad?' Agnes said, sitting down on Beryl's settee.

'It's not good, Aggie.' Beryl poured out two cups of tea, adding a splash of brandy to each. 'Get this down yer.'

Agnes accepted the cuppa.

'Come on then, out with it,' Agnes said, taking a big mouthful of her tea and grimacing as the alcohol hit the back of her throat.

Agnes listened in silence as her friend started to tell her what had happened, how Bel had been told to go home – and that it was not because she'd felt unwell, or was still too grief-stricken to face the outside world, but because she had been out-and-out rude to the passengers.

'Did you know she didn't even tell them she was going back to work?' Beryl asked.

Agnes shook her head. 'It was a surprise to us too, but I just presumed she'd arranged it when she'd last been up the town,' Agnes said quietly.

Selfishly, Agnes had not really wanted Bel to go back to her full-time job on the buses; she was becoming increasingly reliant on her daughter-in-law's help with the housework, the laundry and the nursery – and, of course, tending Joe's wound.

Beryl took a deep breath, 'Well, apparently poor old Howard was running around the yard, reorganising runs, only to have old Bert knocking on his office door two hours later with his face tripping him up and looking like he had the woes of the world on his shoulders.'

Agnes let out a weary sigh.

'Go on then, what'd happened?'

'It just sounds so out of character for Bel,' Beryl said, trying to work out the best way round what she was going to have to tell her friend.

'Just spit it out, Beryl. It can't be any worse than what we've gone through,' Agnes said, taking another glug of her tea – glad that it was laced with something which would take the edge off what she was about to hear.

'Well, to cut a long story short,' Beryl sighed, 'it would seem Bel had a right go at two old biddies – just because they were having a good natter and a bit of a laugh. But worst of all she let rip some heavily pregnant woman – demanding to know why her husband wasn't fighting Jerry . . . she actually accused the poor girl's husband of – what was the words she used? – "staying safe and sound at home and knocking her up"!'

Agnes visibly grimaced. This was not the Bel she knew.

'But, worst of all,' Beryl said to a grave-looking Agnes, 'when the young lass started snivelling, Bel apparently just looked at her and walked off. She wasn't at all apologetic . . . I just can't believe Bel would do that. It's just *so* unlike her.'

'I know,' Agnes agreed solemnly.

They both sat quietly for a moment.

'I just don't know what to do,' Agnes said hopelessly.

'I don't think there is anything you can do, hinny,' Beryl said, topping up their cups with more brandy.

As they sat and drank and chatted, the two friends both agreed that all Agnes could do was simply be there for Bel, and hope that she would eventually climb out of the vitriolic pool of grief she was presently floundering around in and return to her old self.

Chapter Ten

Polly's Valentine's card from Tommy arrived a week late, but was savoured just as much, if not more, than if it had arrived on the actual day. Polly kept the little card to herself as she did not want to cause Bel any more anguish or upset, or to remind her of what she no longer had.

The next day, though, she showed it to Arthur, who had held it in his trembling, gnarled hands and told her it was, 'Lovely.' His pale blue eyes looked wet and Polly told him, 'Stop it, Arthur, or you'll set me off.' And the two of them had started to laugh, although their laughter had been mixed with more than a few tears.

Later Polly had gone downstairs to find Bel changing Joe's bandages, but the atmosphere was frosty, so she had taken herself off to bed and lain there until she fell asleep, the little Valentine's card still in her hand.

The following evening she'd been working a late shift, and when she finally arrived home there was just Bel and Joe up. Agnes had gone to bed early, shattered after a day of child-minding and laundry; Arthur too had taken to his bed, along with his newspapers and his little wireless – one of the few possessions he had brought with him when he'd moved in. Pearl, thankfully, was nowhere to be seen.

'Your ma not about tonight?' Polly asked Bel as she went to pour herself a cup of tepid tea from the pot going cold on the kitchen table.

Bel shook her head from side to side, but didn't say any more. She was sewing up Lucille's little dress, which had a rip down the side. Lucille loved her miniature yellow pinafore dress, so it usually ended up being washed most evenings and hung out to dry overnight so that it could be worn again the next day.

Polly looked at her sister-in-law and felt the urge to go and shake her, which she knew was unfair, but these days even Big Martha spoke more than Bel, and that was saying something. It was as if Bel's lack of chatter was a reprimand against them all. As if she was angry with them, which did not make any sense. Polly desperately wanted to take her aside and have a really good talk to her, but so far there just hadn't been the right time. Polly wondered, though, if perhaps she was making excuses and that she simply had to admit that, for the first time in her life, she did not know how to reach out to Bel.

Heavens knew how Joe was managing to exist in this tense atmosphere day in and day out.

Polly had thought they might all get some respite from it when Bel had gone back to work last week, but she had been proved wrong in quite spectacular fashion; Bel's behaviour was still providing the local gossips with plenty to talk about.

Polly took a sip of lukewarm tea, then put the cup back down and went to fill the kettle to make a fresh pot. As she stood by the sink and turned the tap on, it was as though you could hear every splash, it was so deathly silent. The house had never been quiet when Joe was in it. He was always the real live wire, chatting or making people laugh, but now it was as though Bel's refusal to communicate was becoming infectious, as Joe was far from vocal himself these days.

Polly knew what he had been through had obviously affected him and caused him to become more subdued, but so far he had not once spoken about Teddy, or what had happened out in the desert. Polly had understood this to start with, but felt that if Joe didn't talk about it soon it would get pushed so far down he'd never be able to dig it up and give it a good airing, and that instead it would fester, just like his wound seemed to be doing.

When Polly had been chatting to Gloria one afternoon during a tea break, she'd told her that most of the men and husbands she knew, including her own soon-to-be-ex-husband, had come back from the so-called 'war to end all wars' and, in Gloria's words, it was as if they had all taken a vow never to talk about anything related to their time on the front.

'It's not good and it's not healthy for anyone's mind to keep everything trapped in,' she had told Polly as they'd sat in the noisy canteen at work, out of the biting wind, which showed no sign of abating, even though it was almost spring. The weather seemed to have decided it was stuck in winter and was going to stay there for a good while yet. Polly knew that Gloria was speaking from experience as her husband Vinnie had sought solace in drink; every spare penny he got his hands on ended up hitting the coffers of his local boozer as he poured alcohol down his neck, but, worse still, he had taken to using his fists as a way of expressing all his pent-up anger.

As Polly walked back into the noiseless kitchen and put the kettle on the range's hob, Joe looked at his sister. He desperately wanted to break through the awkward atmosphere, even if it was just for her sake. He could see that Polly was working herself to the bone at the yard, and he was sure she was doing even more overtime than she was expected to do, just to stay away from the house.

Besides, he knew if he didn't make an effort to speak, Bel certainly wouldn't.

Joe had not wanted to talk about his need to do something for the war effort, but even though he was still recovering from his injuries, it had been playing on his mind ever since he'd got back; even more so since he'd heard that the other week the German General Erwin Rommel had arrived in North Africa and, two days later, the first units of Jerry 'Afrika Korps' had turned up.

Joe knew that there was never going to be an appropriate time to broach the subject, so now seemed as good a moment as any; and by talking to Polly, it would be a dry run before he told his mother and faced her inevitable wrath.

'I'm thinking of seeing if I can be of any use in the yards.' Joe's voice sounded croaky and a little nervous.

Polly immediately turned to face her brother. Her look of disbelief at what he had just suggested said it all.

She was incensed. Was her brother mad? He had nearly died for his country, and would almost certainly never get back his full mobility – even now he still risked losing his limb if he wasn't careful – and here he was, wanting to go back out there and fight Jerry, even if it was just on the home front.

But just as Polly was about to lambast her brother for his lack of concern for his own recovery, his own wellbeing, as well as for the effect it would have on his mother and the rest of them if he were to fall ill, Bel suddenly chirped up. 'Oh, I think that'd be a great idea.'

Polly's mouth fell open. She stared at her sister-in-law.

She felt so angry at her encouragement when that was quite clearly the last thing her brother needed, she could hardly get her words out.

For the first time ever, Polly looked at Bel and saw her mother in her. Pearl was the most insensitive and least empathetic person Polly had ever encountered. She had never once thought Bel was even remotely like her mother – they both shared the same sky-blue eyes but, other than that, Polly would have struggled to even put them as distant relatives.

Now, however, the pair seemed uncannily similar – and it shocked Polly.

It was as if Bel just wanted Joe out of her sight.

'Really, Bel,' Polly spluttered out. 'I never thought I would ever utter these words, but just then I saw – or rather I *heard* – your mother in you.'

Bel looked at Polly with an expression neither Polly nor Joe could fathom.

Then, as if on cue, Pearl came through the front door, bustled down the hallway and made her entrance. 'I think my ears are burning.'

Her voice was shrill and a little too loud. They all knew Pearl well enough to recognise she'd had a few, although where she got the money for even just a little tipple was a mystery, as she so far had not paid Agnes a penny in board and lodging.

When her words were greeted with silence, Pearl continued regardless, 'Aye well, as long as it's all good, I dinnit mind,' and with that she walked through the kitchen, staggering a little as she passed Joe and using his shoulders to steady herself, before making her way out the back door and into the yard to have a smoke.

Chapter Eleven

Tatham Street, 1920

'. . . and this is Teddy and Joe. They're twins, as I'm sure you've guessed . . .'

Joe and Teddy had just come in from playing outside and were standing next to the warm range. They were both starving and had just been called in for their tea by their ma, who, on seeing them without their little sister in tow, had demanded to know exactly where she was. Before they'd had time to answer, Polly had come trundling in with a little girl Joe knew lived further down the street. Polly was forever turning up with some stray cat she'd found scrounging around the bins, or some flea-infested pigeon with a broken wing, and Agnes would sigh, take whatever Polly had cradled in her little arms, then disappear out into the back yard before coming back in and telling her daughter that either the lost moggie had been reunited with its owner, or the bird had miraculously managed to fly away.

Of course, they all believed her. Why wouldn't they? She was their ma and she knew everything.

This time, though, was the first time Polly had turned up with an actual person. And this time, their mother didn't take the little stray girl Polly had brought home straight back out into their yard – but instead she had bent down and asked her name.

'Isabelle, but I like being called Bel,' the little girl told them.

When Joe looked at the scruffy little girl called Bel, he could see that she'd been crying, as she had tear-stains streaked down her face. Joe continued to stare at this girl standing forlornly in the middle of their kitchen as his mother repeated the same words she always used when introducing her two boys to someone new.

'Don't be fooled, though. They may look the same, but they are like chalk and cheese.'

Joe did not mind his ma's words; if anything he liked the fact that his mother told people he and Teddy were very different, because they were. They had both been born at more or less the same time, but they were complete opposites in personality, if not in looks. Although there'd only been a few minutes between their entries into the world, Joe, who had come out second, had always felt that Teddy was the older brother, and those few precious moments had also seemed to make him just that bit taller and broader than his younger brother.

When Agnes had insisted Bel should stay for some tea, she had not objected.

Joe had sat at the kitchen table, captivated by the girl with her matted, dirty blonde hair, as she had shovelled his mum's rabbit and black pudding stew down as if it was going to be snatched back off her. His mother had seen him staring at their hungry guest across the table and given him a look which had made him concentrate on his own plate.

Later on that evening, Agnes had gone to take Bel home, but the pair of them had returned ten minutes later. Teddy had asked their mother the question that both he and Polly were thinking but did not like to ask – *why had Bel come back?* They rarely had anyone to stay over. There wasn't really the room, and the only children they had ever had stay the night was their next-door neighbour's children, and that had only been on a few occasions when there had been what their mother had called a 'family emergency'.

Agnes had not answered Teddy's question about why Bel had come back that night, but instead simply told them that, 'Bel's going to stay with us.' She'd then told Polly that she would have to 'top and tail' it with their little overnight guest, which had pleased Polly no end.

That night had been etched into all their memories as it had caused great excitement – blankets had had to be retrieved from the cupboard under the stairs, and Agnes had made them all little cups of hot chocolate, something they were only ever treated to on very special occasions; but, best of all, they had all got to stay up way past their normal bedtime.

After that evening they all got used to having Bel around. She quickly morphed from unknown stray into part of the Elliot household. She was an extra playmate for them all and it was clear Polly adored Bel and saw her as the little sister she'd always been on at her mum to have.

Very occasionally, Bel's mum, who they learnt was called Pearl, would turn up at the house. They all remembered her name as she often told them the same story about how she was named after a precious jewel that was found within the shell of a strange kind of sea creature called an oyster. Each time Pearl explained it to them, she did so as if it was the first time. And each time she did, Joe could smell something sickly sweet mixed with the smell of tobacco smoke on her breath; it was a smell he had never noticed on his own mother's breath.

Whenever Pearl turned up at the house, usually late on an evening, she'd bang on the front door, demanding to know where her daughter was, and Joe and Teddy would scramble out of their bed and stand peeking round their bedroom door and down the hallway where they could see their mother, arms akimbo, and the outline of Pearl, surrounded by a fog of cigarette smoke. Agnes rarely said anything to Pearl, but instead would just call out to Bel that her ma was here for her.

Once, though, Pearl turned up really late, banging on the door with her fists and demanding in a loud, slurring voice to know where 'Isabelle' was. Joe and Teddy had sat up in their bed and listened wide-eyed as Pearl had shouted at Agnes, 'What's wrong? You not got enough bairns of yer own without trying to steal *my* daughter.'

Joe rarely saw or heard his mother in a temper, but that night he could tell she was struggling to keep the anger out of her voice as she'd hissed back, 'I'm telling you now, Pearl, you can stand screaming and shouting all night out here, but your daughter is not going anywhere until you've sobered up.'

Pearl had spat a few words that Joe hadn't heard before, but she hadn't stuck around for much longer. A few minutes later they'd heard her singing, or rather caterwauling, and laughing aloud to herself as she made her way back to her own home at the other end of the street.

One time a big burly woman from the welfare turned up at their house with Bel by her side, asking Agnes if she knew where 'this little un's ma is'. Bel had been found sitting on the steps of the General Post Office in town, unsure how to get back home.

It was the first time Joe had ever heard his mum tell an outright lie.

'Oh, Pearl's had to dash off. Her old ma's just taken bad. I said I'd look after Bel until she got back. I wondered where she'd got to . . .' That was the first, but certainly not the last time the welfare turned up on their doorstep;

nor was it the last time he heard his mum tell great big porkies.

None of them ever said anything, but they all knew if she hadn't, Bel would be carted off to the dreaded workhouse, where the orphans and children of delinquents usually ended up.

As long as Bel was under Agnes's wing, she was safe.

Sometimes Bel would have stretches staying at her own home, but it was never long before she was back at their house – and when she was, the first thing Agnes would do would be to give her a good wash and brush her thick, wavy blonde hair. She'd always check for nits, and Joe would often watch fascinated as his mother would sit patiently combing Bel's hair with a strange bit of metal which had lots of teeth in it. Bel's face would always scrunch up as if she was in pain, but she would never cry out or ask Agnes to stop.

If ever he or Teddy got nits, Agnes would rummage around in the bottom drawer in the bathroom and pull out a cut-throat razor and a pot of what looked like hard white soap which frothed up when she added a little water. She would then give them what she called a 'number one', which Joe complained left him feeling as if he'd just been scalped like one of the Red Indians in the Wild West. Bel had chuckled at Joe's comparison and, even though he hadn't meant it to be funny, he loved the fact he'd made her laugh.

After that Joe took great pleasure in making Bel giggle, and would forever be playing the clown, which they all loved, not just Bel. He would have them in what Agnes called 'kinks' with his Charlie Chaplin walk and impressions of their neighbours, or his teachers at school. But even though Joe brought laughter into Bel's life and the pair of them would giggle and chat and have endless fun, it was Teddy whom Bel adored.

When they were younger, Teddy would often complain and tell Bel to go away, because, in his words, she was like his 'shadow', but Joe had always thought that it would be nice to have Bel so close all the time. As they got older, he noticed that Teddy did not complain as much about his unwanted shadow; and by the time they were in their teens and started to take notice of girls, Teddy didn't seem to mind at all.

When Bel and Teddy started to make it known that they had eyes for each other, Joe had forced himself to start taking girls out on dates, but none became serious.

Shortly after Bel became Teddy's wife, though, Joe began stepping out with a young shop assistant called Maria, who used to dress the mannequins for the large glass-fronted window displays at Binns, the town's main department store. Agnes and Polly had joked about hearing the sound of wedding bells for the second time in their home, but Joe had ended it with Maria shortly before he'd joined up. He had said he did not want her waiting for him until he got back from the war – if he got back at all.

This, however, was far from the truth.

The real reason for him breaking up with Maria was very different to the one he gave – but it was one he could never ever admit to.

Chapter Twelve

Friday 21 February 1941

Lily and George were settling into the comfort of their first-class compartment on the ten o'clock train bound for London. Lily had asked George to go with her on the week-long business trip; she was excited about her new bordello that was just about ready to open, and wanted to share it with her trusted friend; and, of course, George had happily agreed to be her companion.

The second-class carriages of the black locomotive preparing to leave the station were all full to the brim with soldiers, hanging out of the pull-down windows, kissing loved ones and waving farewell to family and friends.

'To be young and in love,' Lily mused as she watched a tearful young woman wave her handsome soldier off as the whistle sounded out and the steam train started to judder away from the station platform.

'I do wish our Rosie would find herself a decent bloke,' Lily said, more to herself than to George, who was resting his new cane against the leather interior; although what Lily was really meaning was that she wished Rosie would meet someone who would love and accept her for who she was – and, moreover, *what* she did.

George grunted by way of agreement.

'There's no man I know good enough for our Rosie,' George added as an afterthought.

Anyone listening to their conversation would have thought they were talking about their daughter, and, in many ways, Rosie was not so unlike their own kin as they both cared deeply for her. Loved her. And had been there for her when she needed them most.

'She won't admit it, but I can tell she's taken with that detective of hers. Bleeding typical that Rosie's drawn to someone she really cannot get involved with. If he were to ever find out about the bordello and her part in it, there could be problems. For us all,' Lily said. Her French accent always waned whenever she was on her own with just George for company.

Lily's initial excitement at hearing how Rosie had bumped into DS Miller had ebbed dramatically. She'd chided herself that she'd been so encouraging and enthusiastic, blaming it on the fact she'd been so hyped up after returning from London and wasn't thinking straight.

And then Rosie had mentioned she'd bumped into him again – and this time she had gone for a tea with the damned detective. She'd never known Rosie to go out for a drink with anyone of the opposite sex; it was just so typical that – when she did – the person had to be bloody old bill.

Lily and George were both more than aware that if the bordello was ever raided, it would be the proprietors who would be arrested, and she and Rosie would be looking at a possible prison sentence, or, at the very least, a huge fine that would wipe them out financially. It was a risk they could not take.

'Of course, the other way of viewing it is that Rosie's detective could end up being a beneficial person to have on side,' George chipped in.

'Mm,' Lily mused for a moment, thinking of the VIP clients she knew were already keen to visit her new Marie-Antoinette-themed London bordello. Lily had copied the so-called 'blue-light' brothels she had heard about that had started up in Paris, which were catering for a higher class of clientele. It meant her new venture could be kept well beneath the radar as it would be very small, very expensive, and very exclusive, thereby attracting those of wealth and influence who would be able to pull any strings should the new establishment feel its collar tugged by the long arm of the law.

'No. The impression I get of this copper is that he's straight as a die,' Lily said.

George grunted his agreement again. Lily was usually right about people.

'I could ask around . . . find out about this detective sergeant if you want?' George asked.

Lily nodded her assent.

As the scenery changed, and the view from their carriage window was filled with the most beautiful rolling green landscape, Lily thought about Rosie and how she wanted to tell her what she thought, advise her, help her. They were more alike than Rosie perhaps realised. Lily had also been through the same horrendous abuse when she was just fifteen years old – the same age as Rosie had been when her perverted uncle had taken her innocence, and she knew only too well how that affected a young girl's mind. Lily had come to terms with what had happened to her a long time ago, but she knew it was something that never really left you and was instrumental in forming the kind of woman a person turned out to be.

Luckily Rosie had chosen not to become a victim, but to survive, and although the cards she'd been dealt were not the best by a long shot, she'd played them well.

'She got the sharp end of the stick, but she made the most of what she had – a pretty face and a good head on her shoulders.' Lily spoke her thoughts aloud.

George had started to nod off but shook himself awake when he heard Lily talking.

'Who Rosie? Yes, yes . . . brains and beauty,' he agreed, before sinking back into his daytime slumber.

Lily had seen Rosie's natural flair for business shortly after she'd started working for her. She had just turned seventeen, but was managing to juggle what money she had to pay for her little sister's boarding school fees, as well as keep her own head above water.

For Lily, it had been like looking into a mirror. She had seen the same determination and financial acumen as she herself had possessed when she had started building her own business just after her eighteenth birthday.

But when Lily had suggested Rosie become more involved in the business, she had knocked her back, saying she saw her work at the bordello as just a temporary measure.

Lily, of course, knew the kind of work she and so many other women had done throughout the ages required you to cross a certain, invisible line – one over which you could never return. It was never 'just temporary'.

But Lily knew Rosie had had to learn this for herself.

Now, after last year's nightmare, it seemed Rosie had not only finally realised this, but, moreover, was determined to make it work for her.

It was as if, contemplated Lily as the train pulled into York station, as the scars on her face healed, Rosie had finally been able to accept her life.

Rosie had been heading for self-destruction but, like the phoenix rising out of the ashes, had pulled herself back up and more than dusted herself down. The horror she'd endured at the hands of her sadist uncle might have left her permanently branded and without the advantage of her looks, but it had not pushed her under, but actually made her stronger.

As if echoing Lily's private thoughts, George half opened his eyes and said aloud: 'She's a survivor that girl. Born survivor. They could do with more like her in the army . . .'

And if the past few months were anything to go by, it was working well for the pair of them, as well as the girls they employed.

Which was all the more reason Rosie did not need any man meddling in her life, Lily reflected, gazing out of the window.

'We really don't need any nosy parker copper sticking his oar in.' Lily voiced her thoughts aloud, shuffling uneasily in her seat.

'Life's good for us all at the moment – we don't need anyone upsetting the apple cart.'

George thought for a moment.

'I don't think Rosie wants any more complications in her life at the moment,' he said thoughtfully.

'I hope you're right, George. I really do,' Lily said, settling back into the comfort of the padded seats and closing her eyes for a little cat nap before they hit the hustle and bustle of the capital.

'But,' she philosophised, 'love's so bloomin' unpredictable. It takes you places you just don't expect to go.'

'Here, here. I'll agree with that,' George said, a big smile spreading across his face as he put his hand on Lily's and gave it a gentle squeeze.

Chapter Thirteen

Lunchtime, Saturday 22 February 1941

'Hey, Polly,' Dorothy called over to her workmate. 'Was that your brother I saw here the other day – fraternising with the hoi polloi in the main office?' Dorothy had eagle eyes and never missed a trick; Gloria had often commented that Dorothy really did have eyes in the back of her head as there was no way she could know so much about the yard's comings and goings when her face was covered by a mask all day.

Polly felt her body stiffen and she turned round to look at Dorothy.

'I don't know. He didn't tell me he'd been ... Then again, no one tells me anything any more. Did it look like our Joe?' The strained tone of Polly's voice told Dorothy that she'd said the wrong thing. She silently cursed herself for being so gobby. She had just presumed Polly would know if Joe had come into the yard. After all, they were brother and sister and, as far as Dorothy was aware, they not only lived together, but were also very close; which made it all the more unusual that she didn't know about Joe's visit. Something was amiss.

'I might well have been mistaken.' Dorothy desperately tried to backtrack, did not want to be the cause of any aggro between Polly and her brother, even though she knew the tall, lanky young man who she thought looked a lot like Rudolph Valentino with his short, slicked-back, dark brown hair, and who had struggled to get through the heavy doors to the administration office with his wooden crutch, was indeed Joe. Dorothy had met him a few weeks ago when she'd been heading into town to meet a girlfriend for a coffee and a gossip in the tearooms at Binns, where she'd worked before starting at Thompson's. Joe had been walking back from the museum with Polly's adorable little niece. Before she had recognised the pair, Dorothy had presumed the man and child coming towards her were father and daughter. Apart from their hair colour, the pair of them looked uncannily similar, which, with hindsight, Dorothy realised was not so unusual, given that Joe and Lucille's father were twins, after all. But it wasn't just their looks which had made Dorothy think that, but the way the pair of them had seemed so naturally at ease with each other.

'No, I don't think you were mistaken,' Polly told Dorothy, trying her hardest to keep the anger out of her voice.

It wasn't Dorothy's fault she had seen her brother, Polly reprimanded herself. But still, she couldn't seem to stop the swell of growing fury rising up in her.

'Isn't he still poorly?' Hannah butted in. They all knew about Joe's injuries and Polly's worries that his wound was not healing as quickly as it should.

'Yes, he is – or rather his leg is,' she said, now quietly seething.

Sensing Polly's disquiet, Martha put down the doorstep sandwich she was eating and took a few steps over to Polly. Talking was still a relative novelty for Martha, and she seemed to think that when you did so, you needed to be right in front of the person you were speaking to.

'We find out why?' Martha asked.

Perhaps because of her closeness to Hannah, she appeared to have adopted her pronunciation and slightly off-kilter grammar, and was also in the habit of missing out the odd word. Dorothy constantly had to bite her tongue to stop herself correcting Martha, for fear it might inhibit her foray into speech.

Polly put a hand on to Martha's shoulder, touched by her workmate's concern and offer of help; but before she had a chance to tell her not to worry, and that she was sure she would find out soon enough, Rosie came over to the group.

'Time's up everyone, back to it,' she commanded, before adding, 'Polly, can I have a quick word?'

As the noise of welding machines started up, Rosie took Polly over to the edge of the quayside, a place that always made Polly think of Tommy. She still half expected to see his massive twelve-bolt copper helmet emerge out of the water, and for him to clamber on to the divers' pontoon in his heavy, lead-soled boots, water pouring off his huge metal corselet and canvas body suit.

'I thought you might like to know that Joe was asking about coming back to work in the yard. He'd already been over to Bartram's before he came to us, but they didn't have anything for him either.'

Rosie looked at Polly with concern. 'That was where he worked before the war, am I right?'

Polly nodded her agreement.

'Well, I'm sure he heard the same there, but the office manager here had to tell him straight, though Joe knows it better than anyone, that any kind of shipyard work is physically hard and his leg is just not healed enough, even for operating one of the cranes, never mind riveting.'

Rosie looked at Polly before asking as sensitively as she could, 'Is it money? Does the family need another wage coming in?'

'God, no,' Polly said, 'but even if we were destitute, we'd never agree to let him out to work in the condition he's in. I really don't know what he's playing at. He mentioned this the other night, but I didn't think he was going to go out and look for work straight away . . . He's only been back just over a month.'

Polly put her hands on her hips and tried to stem her frustration before she glanced up at the admin office and saw Helen peering out of the window.

'I'd better get on, otherwise that bossy cow will be out like a shot accusing me of shirking and trying to get me sacked. She'd love that.'

'You're right there,' Rosie agreed as they both turned away from the river's edge and started walking back over to the dry dock where they were presently all working.

And Polly's not the only one Helen's trying to get shot of, Rosie thought as she made a beeline for Hannah, who was struggling with a relatively straightforward vertical weld. She was working shoulder to shoulder with Dorothy, who Rosie knew was covertly doing a good percentage of Hannah's work. Dorothy was as speedy as she was skilled, and, like them all, she would do anything to keep their little bird safe from the yard's circling vulture.

'You just need to angle your rod a bit more like this,' Rosie said, shouting over the noise, which was even more intense than normal today as they were working right next to the riveters. Rosie put her gloved hand over Hannah's and demonstrated to her how it was done. She had shown her many times already, but Hannah just did not seem to be getting any better.

Rosie felt Hannah's arm droop, followed by her shoulders, which then started shuddering.

'Hey.' Rosie turned Hannah around and pushed up her mask. Her pinched, pale face was wet with tears.

'I just can't do it, Rosie,' Hannah said with complete hopelessness. 'Practice does *not* make perfect with me. I've tried and tried . . . and practised and practised, but I just don't get any better.'

'Think of how you were at the start,' Rosie told her sternly. 'And how much you have come on since then. You can do this. Go and have a little breather and start again . . . And pace yourself. Don't worry about going fast, just do what you can and do it well.'

Hannah forced herself to smile, but her eyes looked tired and dejected. Rosie knew she was on limited time here in the yard. Dorothy might be covering for her, but she could not keep on doing it; she'd get caught out before long. Rosie knew she had to think of something, and quickly, otherwise she was going to lose one of her team. She'd been determined from the off, when the shipyards had been forced to give women jobs, that she'd show that shipbuilding need not just be the domain of the men – but that women too could be just as good, if not better than their male counterparts.

So far she was pleased that her little group of women welders were not far from proving her right. Dorothy and Martha were her star players; Dorothy was a natural, whereas Martha had incredible strength and stamina. Polly and Gloria were now just about up to scratch, and certainly worked as hard, if not harder, than the men. But Hannah, unfortunately, was the runt of the litter, and it was looking more and more unlikely that she'd survive the harsh world of yard life.

It took a few minutes for Rosie to make her way over coils of welding leads and snakes of metal chains before she reached the other side of the hull, where Polly, Martha and Gloria were all working.

As she made her way past the flat-capped young apprentices heating up the rivets around their mini-furnace, she spotted Martha's huge frame and realised that she didn't have a welding rod in her hand but a rivet gun.

'You lot aren't trying to pinch my number one worker from me?' Rosie said. Her voice sounded jokey but she meant every word. She couldn't afford to lose any of the women – not with Hannah barely hanging on to her job by her fingernails, and with Gloria having only two months at the most before her pregnancy would force her to stop welding.

And now it looked as if the riveters were trying to poach Martha from her.

Who could blame them, though? Martha was a proper workhorse – had been born to work in the yards; something Rosie had told Martha on a number of occasions.

Looking at the head riveter's slightly guilty face, Rosie might have known they would want her. They had lost too many of their men to the war, and it was not a trade most women had the strength or the will to do. The riveters had been known as 'the kings of the shipyard' for decades; now it looked as if they needed a few queens. Seeing Martha now, standing holding the ton-weight rivet gun as if it were a child's toy, there was no doubt the woman would be a natural and, more importantly, had the strength in her thick, muscular arms to rivet all day long.

'How about we share her for the day?' Jimmy, the head riveter, asked her with a pleading face.

Rosie owed Jimmy because of the way he had helped out with Hannah. It was payback time and they both knew it.

'Just for today,' Rosie told him, but she knew that now she had to find a way not only to keep Hannah, but also Martha.

At the end of the shift, when the women were all on the ferry heading back over to the south side, Polly sidled up to Rosie. Their journey back over the river had reminded her of the evening she had spotted her boss chatting away to the smartly dressed man in the black three-piece suit and trilby hat.

'Did I see you with a rather dashing older bloke the other day on the south dock?' she asked with a cheeky grin.

'Oh.' Rosie laughed a little too loudly. 'That was Detective Sergeant Miller. Remember, the one from last year?' Rosie dropped her voice, so that only Polly could hear. 'The one who came to see me about my *inheritance*?'

'Oh yes,' Polly whispered back conspiratorially, adding, 'You said he was really nice, but not that he was also rather "scrummy", to use Angie's favourite word.'

Rosie laughed again, a little embarrassed.

'Well,' she mused, 'if a middle-aged man with greying hair can be classed as *scrummy* . . .'

The sentence was left open-ended as she looked up the river to the sea lock, where the small Dock Police cabin stood. When Polly stole a glance at her boss, she could have sworn she saw the faintest of blushes appearing on Rosie's pretty but scarred face.

When Polly got home a short while later, she let out a big sigh of relief to find Joe on his own in the kitchen, sitting in front of the range with his bad leg stretched out in front of him, staring into the grated fire that was now just about out, the heap of remaining ashes barely smouldering.

Everyone else – Agnes, Arthur, Bel and Lucille – was in bed; everyone, of course, apart from Pearl, who was, as always, out. Polly had joked with Bel the other day that the term 'night owl' had been invented for her mother, but Bel had not laughed as she would once have done – as the old Bel would have done – but instead had merely huffed her agreement, adding that it was 'better than having her around the house, that's for sure'.

'You must be dropping on your feet,' Joe said as he turned to see his sister entering the room. As he spoke he started to struggle to his feet so that he could sort Polly out with a cup of tea, but his little sister stopped him.

'Don't worry, Joe, just sit down, I can get my own cuppa . . . I want to talk to you,' she said, pouring herself a drink from the big porcelain pot, and pulling out another chair from under the kitchen table so that she could sit next to her brother. As she eased her tired and achy body down on to the chair, she took a slow breath before saying, 'So, what's this about you turning up at the yard asking for work?'

Joe shuffled in his chair and used both his hands to move his injured leg a little to one side. It was done for no particular reason, but it was evidence of his unease. He hadn't been sure whether or not his sister would get to know about his visit to Thompson's. He should have guessed she'd find out. The yard might be immense, but any kind of tittle-tattle or gossip spread like wildfire. He knew because Bartram's had been the same; it gave the workers a reprieve from their exhausting – and also what could be mind-numbing and repetitive – work.

'I know . . . it was stupid. I left there feeling like the biggest fool ever . . . trying to convince them that I was man enough to do a normal day's work . . .' Joe's voice trailed off in thought. It was the lowest Polly had heard him sound since his arrival back home.

'Oh, Joe, you *are* man enough. You don't have to go back to work to prove yourself. You just need to get yourself better. Not just for your sake – but for all of our sakes.'

'I know. I know,' he agreed; what he wanted to add was that he *was* going to get better, and that he *would* get back to work – by hook or by crook. It was just going to take him a bit longer than he had anticipated.

Polly had thought she might have a fight on her hands, but was thankful for small mercies that it looked as if Joe's visit to the yard had brought him to his senses.

'Let's just take one step at a time,' she said, adding, 'and in the meantime, let's try and sort our Bel out – and get her back to the way she was before.'

Joe straightened up in his chair and looked at Polly.

'I don't think we'll ever get her back to the way she was. Some things change you, and you cannot change back again.'

Polly looked at her brother and thought that he was not just talking about his sister-in-law.

'She's just going to need some time. Probably a lot of time. She's got a lot of grieving to do. Bel worshipped the ground Teddy walked on, and always did, even from being a bairn,' Joe said, his mind slipping back to more innocent times; a period when life had seemed so straightforward – not all buckled and bent like it was now.

'And to add to it all,' he added, 'Pearl's suddenly tipped up out of the blue. She couldn't have come at a worse time.'

Polly listened to Joe's words and agreed with him – Pearl's presence in their home was far from helpful, even though she'd claimed to have come back for Bel's sake. They were not fools; they were all well aware that something else had propelled Pearl back into their lives, and that, somewhere along the line, it probably involved some good-for-nothing bloke. What was more concerning, though, was that it looked as if she was set to stay for a good while longer.

But, Polly mused, even though Pearl was a complete nightmare, it still didn't excuse Bel's behaviour. She felt Joe was being too soft on their sister-in-law, too defensive of her, too forgiving, especially as he, out of everyone, was getting it in the neck the most from Bel. That was something Polly could not understand, as the pair of them had always got on so well – from being children; always talking nineteen to the dozen and laughing at some joke, or just being plain silly. Polly had always been surprised that it had been Teddy Bel had fallen for.

Now that Joe was back, though, and they were all living under the same roof once again, it was as if Bel couldn't stand him. And what had really annoyed Polly more than anything was the fact that Bel had actually encouraged Joe to go back out to work, when it was quite obvious he was nowhere near ready, or well enough, to do any kind of work. It really was beyond the pale – and so unlike Bel. She'd always been the most caring and compassionate person Polly had known.

'I don't know how you keep your tongue with her,' Polly spoke her thoughts aloud, adding, 'she's not the only one grieving. We've all been grieving. I know that sounds hard and it's going to be different for Bel because she was married to Teddy, but she needs to realise we're all going through it.'

Polly looked at Joe before adding gently, 'You've not said much, Joe, but I'm sure you've been going through hell as well?'

Polly tentatively tried to open up the conversation, to get Joe to chat to her about how he was feeling, how he was dealing with being back at home, how he was coping with what he had been through over in North Africa and, more than anything, how he was feeling that he no longer had his twin by his side.

'I do miss him, terribly,' Joe said.

But that was all he said before turning back to the fire, which was now totally dead.

Chapter Fourteen

That evening, like just about every night since he had arrived back in his hometown, when Joe went to bed and closed his eyes, he welcomed the images of his adorable little niece that flitted across his mind: her wide-eyed joy at something she'd seen or done, the little frown she had mastered to show she really wasn't very happy at all about something or other, her petulance at not getting her own way. She was definitely going through that determined stage he'd seen in other toddlers, when they were testing those who loved and cared for them – pushing them to see how far they could go and how much they could get away with.

There had been some nights when, lying there enjoying the quietness of the house, Joe had chuckled to himself when he thought of something Lucille had said or done that was particularly funny or mischievous. Today she had been playing with some of the other children in the back yard and it had started to hail. Joe had been getting some coal from the bunker and had seen Lucille throw her head up to the sky and let out such a whoop of unadulterated laughter it was infectious. He'd marvelled at her sheer delight in the sudden, unexpected change of weather, and more so in the fact that she'd kept laughing – as though she was simply enjoying laughter for laughter's sake.

There really was no denying that Lucille was her mother's daughter. She was the mirror image of her mother when she herself was just a child. And not just in looks, but in personality too. Just like Lucille, Bel had always been so happy and so full of fun when she was young. He remembered Agnes saying that Bel was like a 'bouncing ball'. At the time he'd thought his mother had meant her energy; now in hindsight he wondered if she'd also meant that Bel had the capacity to always spring back from whatever life threw at her.

Once, when they were youngsters walking back home, weighed down with bags of the groceries Agnes had sent them out to buy from the market, Joe had asked Bel how it was she was always so happy. So bubbly.

'Why wouldn't I be happy when I'm with all of you?' she had said.

That day Bel's words had stirred in him a hope that she would *always* stay with them. Or rather stay with *him* for ever more. If she was happy, she would not want to leave, would she? And whether Joe had consciously done so or not, he had always tried his utmost to make Bel laugh, to keep her joyful and bolstered up in the hope of keeping her near. And to a certain extend he had succeeded. Bel had often said to Joe how much he made her laugh, often demanding he stop his comic behaviour as it was actually making her stomach hurt. And, moreover, she *had* stayed with them all, hadn't she?

As Joe now lay on his lumpy mattress, looking up at the damp, stained ceiling of his small bedroom, the throbbing in his bad leg started to abate, as it always did when he had it stretched out in front of him and elevated off the ground. He enjoyed these restful moments of peacefulness and solitude before the darkness of sleep took him and he was catapulted back to that other nightmarish world he'd inhabited for the past year: a world of war, of gunfire, of the tormented cries of slow and painful deaths, and of the abhorrent, hellish sight of dismembered bodies – the cruel artwork of the Axis's anti-personnel landmines, hidden in stony, dry terrain, waiting to disfigure, maim and kill.

All of this he managed to keep at bay during the day, but it came back to him with full force at night, when his defences were down and sleep overcame him. He would often wake at exactly three in the morning, covered from head to toe in a sheen of sweat. He'd taken to keeping a towel under his bed, so that when he woke from his night terrors, he could easily wipe down his cold, wet body, while all the time telling himself that he was alive, he was safe, he was here, with people who loved him.

He was home, where he belonged.

Tonight, before sleep forced him back to that godforsaken place and the horror spawned by the bloody battlefields he had fought on, Joe allowed his mind to flood over with calming, happy thoughts of the innocence of life of which Lucille was an embodiment. He didn't feel as if he could ever get tired of that childishness – that absurd and often nonsensical behaviour – because it was evidence of life's refreshing simplicity, of which he could never sicken. It was as if it combated all the horror, all the evil, all the base reality, the worst side of human nature to which he had been a witness.

As Joe heard Pearl return from another late night, trying her hardest to be quiet and tiptoe down the long hallway and up the stairs to her room, his mind wandered to Bel. It was not just the images of Lucille that replaced the horror he carried with him, but also the love he had for her. A love he knew he couldn't have, but which he didn't have the strength to fight like he used to.

Unlike before, he now happily gave in.

As Joe lay there, enjoying the stillness of the late evening, and hoping it would not be broken by the disruptive wailing of the air-raid sirens, he allowed himself to think about his love for Bel. He realised now that he had loved her from the first moment she had come into their house – and had loved her ever since.

As the physical pain in his leg ebbed, the ache in his heart grew stronger as he recalled the anguish he felt as a young boy when he realised that it was his brother Bel wanted – and had always wanted.

In the darkness of his room, Joe allowed himself to indulge his secret thoughts and feelings for Bel, which no one else would ever know – could ever know.

Joe had resigned himself, a long time ago, to the fact that his love for Bel, for the stray his sister had brought home that day, would never be requited. From the moment he had seen Bel's dirty, tear-smeared face, even though he'd only been eight years old, he had felt that he would love this little girl for a very long time.

And now he was older, and felt older still in his head and in his heart, he knew that he would love Bel until his dying day.

He had accepted that now.

Chapter Fifteen

Monday 24 February 1941

'Thank goodness for that!' Gloria's voice boomed across the yard. She was wrapped up in so many extra layers of clothing to keep out the bitter winter cold that she resembled a little barrel.

As she scrunched through the layers of crisp new snow that had just fallen in flurries on the yard's concrete surface, she left the warmth of the roaring five-gallon barrel fire, around which she had been standing with Polly and Rosie as they had tried in vain to combat the freezing early morning temperatures.

The three of them had turned up early to work after last night's air-raid attack on an area of the town where they knew their other workmates all lived. Four bombs had been dropped on houses, along with a clutch of incendiary devices. Word had spread – like the fires that had started up amongst the debris – that three women had been killed in the hour-long attack; another had been seriously injured and taken to hospital.

Gloria's face was a picture of concern as she hurried over to Hannah, Martha and Dorothy.

'You all okay? Anyone you know got hit?' Gloria asked, as she cupped her hands around Hannah's little ashen face and then inspected the other two women, who had stopped in their tracks to be given the once-over by the group's mother hen.

'All fine,' Hannah said.

'All fine too,' Martha repeated.

Hannah and her aunty Rina lived on Villette Road, just a few streets away from Martha and her mum and dad, who rented a little single-storey cottage on Cairo Street. Dorothy lived about a quarter of a mile away in a large detached house, which overlooked the town's expansive Backhouse Park.

'Yes, we all fine too,' Dorothy said cheekily, deliberately speaking in pidgin English and mimicking Hannah and Martha as she sidled over to the women's makeshift mini-furnace to catch some warmth.

'Dor! Dor!' The women looked around to see Angie running as best she could in her oversized overalls and her hobnailed boots across the freshly laid snow, face flushed red and panting heavily, trying to catch her breath in the icy cold.

'Thank goodness you're all right. I was worried sick about you last night. I nearly came over, but my ma was having none of it. And my da said he would thrash seven bells out of me if I stepped out the front door . . .'

'Don't worry, Ange, Jerry isn't going to stop us going to the flicks tonight. I know that's what you were *really* worried about. Who else could you go out with if I wasn't here?' A big smile spread across Dorothy's face as she joked with her friend. She looked as pleased as punch with all the attention she was getting.

Gloria shook her head in mock disapproval at the way Dorothy always made light of the serious, but she was more than relieved to see her workmates were all in one piece. Gloria knew her pregnancy was making her overly sensitive and definitely more emotional and maternal than she would have been normally, but she had decided to give up trying to fight it. Despite all the worries and secrecy that went with this baby growing inside her, she felt happy. So much happier than she had in such a long time. Years. She had been surprised at just how carefree she felt, and had come to the conclusion that it might have been partly down to her pregnancy, but it was also largely due to the fact that she was now on her own, free from the constraints of her husband Vinnie, and no longer having to live under a cloud of threatening violence, unpredictable rages, and alcohol-induced highs and lows.

As Gloria looked at the women all huddled round the fire, all jigging about from one foot to the other and clapping their gloved hands in an effort to keep warm, she thought how she was old enough to be every one of their mothers. And perhaps it was because of her condition but, as she looked at them all now, she realised she would not have minded having any of them as her daughter – even Dorothy.

'I heard Tunstall Vale was the worst hit.' Rosie jaw was chattering as she spoke. She had been at Lily's last night when the hour-long raid had started, and all the girls and their clients had piled down into the cellar, which had been kitted out with plenty of food and drink and comfortable seats; there was even an old chaise longue down there. There had been much chatter and laughter last night with Vivian, as usual, being the centre of attention and giving them a very convincing rendition of Mae West's 'I'm No Angel'.

'No one had time to get to a shelter,' Hannah said, her body shivering from top to bottom – tremors caused not only by the morning's arctic weather, but by memories of the devastation she had seen the previous night.

'The rescue men were digging away, trying to free people who were trapped,' she added.

'It was awful. Chaos. There was dust all around. All you could hear was people shouting, ambulances . . . fire engines . . . It felt like we were all in hell.'

Martha nodded her agreement. She too had seen the decimation caused by Hitler's Luftwaffe, but what she didn't tell the women was that she had spent most of the night helping the wardens and the rescue men shift piles of bricks and wooden beams so they could check to see if anyone had been buried alive. Her mum and dad had also taken in an elderly couple who had lost their home and all their possessions.

When Martha had returned to their modest little terrace in the early hours of the morning, her mother had given her a cuddle and told her, 'Well done, pet,' before sending her off to bed with a large, steaming mug of hot chocolate. Martha's favourite – and a rare treat these days.

'I heard three people were killed,' Polly said sadly, 'with at least a few others seriously injured and taken to hospital.'

When the sirens had sounded out at just before nine o'clock, Polly, Agnes, Bel, Lucille, Arthur and Joe had all made it to a nearby shelter. Pearl was out and had returned about an hour or so after the all clear, with tales of walking wounded and houses that had been reduced to mountains of rubble. It had been Pearl who had told them about the three fatalities as she had puffed on a cigarette standing in the back doorway, turning every now and again to blow smoke out behind her so it wouldn't go into the house. When she had mentioned the women who had died because they had not been able to get to a shelter, Bel had got up and taken herself and Lucille off to bed without so much as a goodnight. Joe's face had also displayed a mixture of sadness and anger. Polly knew what her brother was feeling – he so desperately wanted to be doing more. She had seen the same look on Tommy's face whenever the town had taken a battering from bombs, or there were reports of yet more deaths and atrocities abroad.

As the yard's klaxon blared out the start of the day's shift, the women all let out a collective groan.

'One day I'm going to live somewhere there are no horns, no sirens and no noise . . . in fact, I think I'll just move to the country,' Angie said as she reluctantly dragged herself away from the warm fire and headed off to the other side of the yard, where the crane she was operating was standing idle, its huge metal neck hanging over the river like a docile giraffe about to take a drink from the water below.

'Hah, you'd be bored stupid,' Dorothy said with complete conviction, but also hating the thought her best friend could even think about leaving her. 'You wouldn't last two minutes out in the sticks!'

'All right, let's get to it,' Rosie said, but she didn't need to tell the women twice. They were keen to move and start work, not only to get warm in front of their welds, but because she knew that today of all days they would be even more determined to do something which they felt would help to defeat Jerry – and, more importantly, help to put a stop to any more loss of life.

By the time they all stopped for their lunch break, the women crowded alongside the men to get into the warmth of the canteen. They were all starving, and all eager to get some warm food in their bellies. A few minutes later they were inside and standing in the queue, breathing in the smell of meat stew and warm pies, and feeling their mouths watering in anticipation of having their hunger sated.

'Excuse me . . . sorry . . . can I just get to my friends?' It was Angie, trying not to cause too much upset by pushing her way to the front of the queue so she could be with the women welders.

'Wait till you hear what I've just been told,' she said, grabbing a plate of shepherd's pie and peas which had just been served up by one of the three elderly dinner ladies who worked there.

As the women welders all scraped their chairs back and sat around the table they'd made their own at the side of the cafeteria, Angie took a mouthful of food, and savoured it, before continuing.

'Mildred, who's been taken on as one of the painters, has just heard from her mate who lives up Tunstall way that they found a little baby this morning – alive – in one of the houses which had been bombed.'

All the women stopped eating and were staring at Angie, eager to hear more.

'The poor bairn had been there – *exposed to the elements* – for more than ten hours. The rescue men had been working flat out all night when they heard a faint cry from one of the wrecked houses. They went to investigate and found the baby in one of the bedrooms which didn't even have a roof over it – *or even an outer wall.*'

'Bloody hell,' Dorothy exclaimed, 'the little thing must have been frozen.'

'What about the baby's ma?' Gloria asked, instinctively knowing what Angie was going to tell them all.

Angie's face dropped and the excitement in her voice immediately disappeared.

'The baby's mum was killed . . . They found her bed, which was just next to the cot, buried in a load of bricks and wooden beams . . .'

There was a sad silence as all the women let Angie's words sink in.

Polly's eyes watered as she thought of yet another life gone. Snuffed out. Just like her brother's.

Hannah put her hands together and said a silent prayer, thinking of her own mother and father, from whom she had not heard for some time.

Martha looked at Dorothy, who sadly returned her workmate's stare. No words were needed.

Gloria felt a lump stick in her throat as she imagined the baby swaddled in blankets, crying out for its mother – a mother the tiny little child would never have.

Rosie looked at the women and saw how this news, which was both a tragedy in that a life had been taken, but also a miracle as a life had been saved, had affected them all. She knew the mother's death and the baby's incredible survival would mean something different to them all. But out of all the women, she knew it would affect Gloria the most.

As the afternoon got going, she was proved right; the other women soon busied themselves with work and started up their usual stream of banter again, while Gloria remained in her own world for the rest of the shift. She did the work that had to be done, but it was clear to Rosie that Gloria's mind was elsewhere.

When Gloria got home that evening she was still thinking about the motherless baby. She had bought a copy of the *Sunderland Echo*, which reported the story on its front page.

As she sat down at her kitchen table with her paper and a cup of milky hot chocolate, she took a moment to simply sit and enjoy the peace and quiet.

It was true she loved the noise of the shipyards, the clanging of metal and the whirring of rivet guns, but when she shut her front door at night she liked nothing more than the sound of silence. For too many years her home had been filled with screaming and shouting, anger and drunkenness, followed by the depressing, heavy stillness that fell after a rage or a beating.

As Gloria forced her weary legs to stand up and walk across the kitchen to switch on the little electric fire, before she rallied what little energy she had left to make her supper, she was shocked out of the contemplative quietness by a sudden banging on her door.

Years spent on tenterhooks waiting for Vinnie to kick off verbally or physically had worn down her nerves, and she felt her body jolt with the sound of the loud knocking.

And it was an angry knocking.

A knock that she knew heralded the arrival of only one person.

Just keep calm, Gloria murmured, silently reprimanding herself for feeling the adrenaline rush of fear, and the sudden racing of her heart; her instant, in-built, learnt reactions of old.

Gloria stood up clumsily from the table, knocking the side of it slightly and causing her cup of cocoa, which was sitting on the Formica top, to spill over into the saucer.

You don't have to be afraid now, she tried to reassure herself as she hurried out of the kitchen and into the short, narrow hallway.

He won't hurt you now.

He can't hurt you now.

Gloria reminded herself of the official letter she had handed to Vinnie at the end of last year when she had plucked up the courage and gone to see one of the town's solicitors for advice. She had left a few pounds poorer, but enriched with confidence and armed with a threatening legal document which had spelt out in fancy wording that Vinnie had to leave the marital home or Gloria would report him to the police authorities for the violent abuse he had inflicted upon her. Fortunately the blow to the stomach Gloria had received that day had knocked the stuffing out of her and made her vomit, but she hadn't lost the baby.

The baby that Vinnie still knew nothing about.

Gloria bolstered herself up with thoughts about the letter that had done the job intended and succeeded in getting Vinnie out of the house. In fact, she'd hardly heard a whisper from him since he'd left with his tail between his legs, the lawyer's letter in one hand and the bag that Gloria had hastily packed for him in the other.

Gloria inhaled deeply, and in her most confident and strongest of voices shouted out, 'Yes, coming!'

Gloria's new-found assertiveness, though, was in vain, as her words were drowned out by the loud thudding sound of heavy fists being smashed against her front door, hammering their impatience, demanding to be let in. Gloria knew that Vinnie was, without a doubt, drunk. And with that knowledge her confidence dissolved. She knew that when Vinnie was in drink all reason went out of the window – and all the solicitors' letters in the world wouldn't make any difference.

She had a choice. She could either open the door, or have it kicked in.

As she turned the latch to open the door, she felt her body start to shake with nerves.

When the door swung open, Vinnie nearly fell in as the momentum of his fists which no longer had anything to bash on carried his whole inebriated body forward.

Gloria stepped to the side as the man she had once loved, but who now instilled only fear in her, stumbled into the hallway.

'Right . . .' Vinnie slurred as he steadied himself. Gloria looked at her husband and noticed he was having trouble focusing on her.

'Right,' he repeated, running a hand through his thinning light brown hair, 'you've had enough time now on yer own . . . I'm coming back.'

The words were out of Gloria's mouth before she had time to rein them back in.

'No, you're not.'

The defiance of her words and the strength in her own voice took her aback, but also pushed her confidence to the fore. As she stood there in the hallway, the cold wind whistling through the open door, Gloria looked at her husband, the man she had spent half her life with, and knew what she had known for a long time now: that she no longer even had a flicker of love left for him. But what she had not realised until this moment was that she also did not feel any hatred towards him either.

Other than fear, she felt nothing. Absolutely nothing. Only the need to get him out of the house and away from herself and her unborn baby.

'I'm sorry, Vinnie, but you cannot come back. It's over. You have to accept that.'

In her head she wanted to scream at him that for years she had tried again and again to help him in so many different ways; she had talked to him about his problems, his drinking, his violence; she had loved him, held him, shouted at him, rationalised with him; she had even believed at one stage that she had the power to love him better. What a fool she had been. How little she had known. It had taken her too long, but she had finally realised that she could not help Vinnie – that she had no control over him or his behaviour.

She had realised that he had to help himself. That he had to *want* to stop drinking; had to *want* to stop himself from hurting her.

Her only regret now was that she had not fathomed it out sooner – that it had taken the love of another man to make her understand. She wished she had been stronger and done what she had done long before she had. For her own sake. Her own wellbeing. Her own happiness. But she hadn't.

It had only been the life now growing inside her that had forced her to be strong.

'Go back to Sarah.' Gloria tried to move forward in the hope she could get him back out of the house. But as soon as the name 'Sarah' was out of her mouth and had sunk into Vinnie's alcohol-sodden consciousness, the white-hot flames of violent temper that were always there, lying just below the surface, immediately flared up.

Gloria saw it straight away. Had seen it too many times.

She did not know – had no reason to know – that Vinnie was here because he'd just had an almighty fall-out with Sarah, his girlfriend, the woman he had been seeing for almost two years behind Gloria's back. The pair of them had argued and their words had become more heated, more volatile. Vinnie had kept drinking and the words had kept spewing forth from both their mouths. Then he had felt the devil rise within him and he knew he had to leave, otherwise his fists would take control of him and he would do what he had been doing to Gloria for most of their married life – and he didn't want that.

So, instead he had forced himself to walk away. But the more he'd walked, the more enraged he'd become, and his rising acrimony had brought him back to his old marital home.

As Vinnie now stood towering over Gloria, she saw the familiar madness ignite in his eyes and she felt her bladder instantly weaken; she instinctively stepped back. Her eyes widened in sheer fright as she looked at Vinnie's clenched fist. Her arms automatically wrapped themselves around her stomach.

Her mind screeched, *Not the baby. Anywhere but the baby.*

And then she heard a voice. Her own voice. Although it didn't sound like her voice.

'*Don't!*' Gloria screamed aloud. 'I'm *pregnant*! Don't hurt your baby!'

Vinnie had just been about to let his fist do its worst; he had been unsure whether to punch her in the head or the stomach. If he'd gone for the face his violence would be evident for all to see, and so he'd made the split-second decision to ram his fist into her stomach. She'd always had a bit of fat on her anyway, never really got rid of it after the boys had been born; and she was certainly carrying a little weight on her now – he had thought that as soon as she'd answered the door . . .

Her words pierced his ale-addled brain.

Pregnant?

Baby?

His baby.

Gloria looked at her husband's face and saw the confusion of emotion slosh around inside his beer-drenched mind. She saw his fist drop and knew her baby was going to be all right. She had lied and had done so in the blink of an eye. It had been done without thinking. It had been an untruth born out of fear for the unborn child. A primal instinct to protect.

'You're pregnant?' Vinnie asked, needing affirmation that what he had just heard was right – was true.

Gloria knew the shock of her words had quelled his outrage, but she had to think quickly now. This had come earlier than she'd anticipated. She had purposely put off even thinking about it, as she had thought it would be at least another few months before she would have to come clean to Vinnie that she was with child. And, more importantly, she'd been undecided as to whether or not she was going to tell him the truth – that the baby was *not* his.

Now her decision had been made for her. Vinnie knew she was pregnant, and she had lied. And, of course, he'd believed her. Why wouldn't he?

Gloria had always been the perfect wife. Had been totally faithful and loyal to him. Had loved and cared for him. Had borne his two sons.

'Glor . . .' Vinnie stumbled forward as if he wanted to touch her, hold her, but Gloria automatically flinched and she turned her body away from his outstretched hand – the one he had been going to hit her with just seconds before.

'How come? I mean . . . yer so old now,' he stuttered, still clearly struggling to grasp the concept that Gloria was carrying a child. His child.

'I know,' Gloria said. A part of her wanted to laugh – perhaps a little hysterically – that he was telling her she was *so old*. She certainly didn't feel that old. Her work at the shipyards had actually given her a lot of vitality. Before she had fallen pregnant, her body had felt fitter and leaner than it had ever done before. Yes, she was exhausted most of the time, but it was a natural tiredness which came from hard manual labour.

'It's unusual,' she said, her mind racing, trying frantically to back-pedal and work out the best way to deal with this unplanned scenario, 'but not unheard of . . . it must have happened shortly before you left.'

Gloria was careful to make it sound as if it had been Vinnie's choice to leave. That he was in control.

'But, you know, Vinnie, there's still no guarantee that this pregnancy will go full term,' Gloria added, even though it hurt her to say it as she was determined this baby *would* be born, at the right time, and it would be perfectly formed and totally healthy. But she needed Vinnie to feel as if it might all come to nothing in order to give herself some more breathing space.

'That's why I didn't want to say anything,' she improvised. 'I'll have to give it another few months before the doctors are happy everything is okay . . . you know – me being *so old* and all that.'

Gloria now felt on a roll. She felt like patting herself on the back. He would never know what a doctor would or would not say. He had no idea about womanly things – had never wanted to know either.

'Aye, all right. Yes. That makes sense . . . Bloody hell, that's a turn-up for the books, isn't it?' There was now a half-smile appearing on Vinnie's face.

Gloria was aware his recollection of their conversation would be sketchy when he sobered up, and she would probably still have to prepare herself for more visits after his head had cleared and he'd had time to mull things over – especially as this was really going to put the cat amongst the pigeons with Sarah. She was not going to be at all pleased.

'Let's worry about this baby when we know it's *really* going to happen . . . I mean, there's no need for Sarah to know just yet, is there?' Gloria knew she was pushing it, but if she could steer Vinnie, she had to at least give it a go.

'Why don't you go home to Sarah now? She loves you.' Gloria forced the words out, speaking as calmly and as soothingly as possible.

Vinnie felt reassured by Gloria's words. All he would need to do was to say a few tender words to Sarah, take her out for a drink down their local, and their argument would be forgotten.

As Vinnie stepped back outside and walked up the garden path and on to the main road, he heard the front door shut quietly behind him.

Gloria was right, he ruminated as he turned to walk back home. He wouldn't tell Sarah. Not yet. Sarah did not have to know right now. What would be the point of all that hassle if Gloria lost the baby? And she *was* old, after all. He didn't know of anyone who had had a baby at her age.

As he trundled up the Fordham Road and headed back to Grindon, back to his lover, he thought about Gloria's unborn baby. His unborn baby. His child.

Of course, there was no doubt, it was *his* child.

One thing he had always been one hundred per cent certain about was Gloria's faithfulness. She wouldn't even as much as look at another bloke, never mind anything else.

As Vinnie's mind wandered, he allowed his imagination to stretch its limbs, something it rarely did, and he thought about Gloria and how she had been by his side for over twenty years. After the boys, they had always been careful, as neither of them wanted to have any more children. They had both come from big families and knew the hard work and poverty that went alongside having a load of kids.

He had always 'jumped off before he got to Sunderland', as the saying went.

Obviously he hadn't got off soon enough that time.

If it had been any other woman apart from Gloria, he would have immediately presumed she'd been having it off with someone else. But he would bet everything he had, which admittedly wasn't much, but all the same he would wager every penny he had that Gloria would never play away from home. She would never have seen someone else while they were both married.

Would she?

For the briefest of seconds, Vinnie thought about Gloria having a secret affair – not unlike his own – and he immediately felt the familiar rage that was always waiting in the wings start to kindle and spark up.

As he headed down the road to his local public house, he felt his face flush and his hands clench involuntarily.

'I know one thing for sure,' he said to himself. 'If she's done the dirty on me, she'll wish *she'd* never been born – never mind any baby.'

Chapter Sixteen

Bel was sitting on her bed in her room, which was sandwiched between Joe's bedroom at the front of the house and the kitchen at the back. When the red-brick townhouse had originally been built at the end of the last century, during the reign of Queen Victoria, Bel's bedroom had been the family's dining room, Joe's the living room, and Polly's a small storage room at the very back of the house. The actual sleeping accommodation had been on the first floor, where Agnes, Pearl and Arthur had their bedrooms. The attic on the third floor, which now stood empty, had been the servants' quarters.

But then times had changed: money had become scarce, poverty more prevalent, causing many of the grand houses, like the ones running the length of Tatham Street, to be turned into bedsits and boarding houses.

When Bel had moved back in with Agnes and Polly after Teddy and Joe had gone off to war, she had made her bedroom as cosy as possible, with a colourful patchwork bedspread, a few threadbare but comfy cushions, and an old leather armchair with a floral throw covering it; she had also made a few clippy mats to put on the bare floorboards. Despite a limited budget and scant possessions, Bel had succeeded in making the room homely and snug. She'd put Lucille's second-hand wooden cot next to her own bed, which was where the little girl was now, lying curled up with her chubby little arms cuddling her favourite raggedy toy rabbit. Her gentle rhythmic breathing told Bel her daughter was enjoying a contented, deep sleep.

Making as little noise as possible, Bel got off the bed and crouched down by its side, before carefully lifting up the mattress a fraction, and pulling out a crumpled piece of paper. When she got up, she sat back on the bed and straightened out the handwritten letter.

As Bel started to reread the letter that Teddy had written to her just weeks before he'd been killed, she put her hand across her mouth in an attempt to stifle the tidal wave of grief that broke free from deep within her and powered forward. Through a blur of tears she silently mouthed her husband's final words to her.

Bel's shaking fingers ran over her husband's writing as if she were actually touching him; for once, Bel was not able to stop the torrent of grief, nor push it back down – back to its deep, dark, festering hole in the depths of her soul. This time it was too strong and it rushed, gushing and foaming, to the surface. No noise came from Bel's mouth as she clamped it shut now with the aid of both her hands, but her whole body jerked as her sorrow unleashed itself and she sobbed quietly, tears streaming from her eyes. She was forced to take a huge suck of air as her body cried out for her to breathe. Bel felt she could have wailed with such force it would have woken the whole street, never mind just the Elliot household. Instead she grabbed her pillow, held it tightly against her face and let her muffled angst gush out of her.

When her torment was expended, her body exhausted, and her eyes puffed up and swollen, Bel picked up the letter, now water-marked with her tears and, as she continued to read, her body stiffened as anger stomped over her aching heart.

But I want to stress to you that, should something happen to me out here, it is important that I know you will carry on this life without me, and that you will not waste this life with mourning. Our daughter needs a mother who is happy – not sad. So, I beg of you, if I do not make it back into your arms, you must remain strong and find happiness where you can.

And look after Joe when he gets back. He will not be the same man as you remember who left all that time ago.

I feel compelled to tell you, my love, that I love you and our daughter more than anything in the world.

I must go now, my love, but I always carry you in my heart, and when I close my eyes, it is you I see.

I miss you.

Forever yours,

Teddy x

Bel tossed the letter to the floor.

Her mind screamed: *How can I live without you? How can I be strong without you?*

She wanted to laugh mockingly and bitterly at even the thought of ever being happy again.

How *dare* he ask this of her!

And how dare he ask her to look after Joe!

Bel knew Teddy's words would be forever scratched into her memory, plaguing her, haunting her. There would be no escaping them.

'I won't do it, Teddy!' she hissed under her breath. 'I can't – and I won't! '

And with those words, an impenetrable mask, branded with a coating of bitter, cold resentment, dropped down in place of her spent, raw grief.

And, as it did so, Bel picked up the discarded letter and stood up straight.

She waited for a moment, listening carefully to check there was no one else about, and then she walked quietly out of her room and into the kitchen.

She stepped purposefully across the faded floor rug and over to the stove, where she knelt down in front of the small grated fireplace in the centre of the lead range.

The few remaining coals were barely glowing as she reached to the side of the hearth for the large box of matches.

She struck one.

And then she held out Teddy's letter and slowly moved it over the yellow tip of the burning flame.

And she watched with eyes devoid of any kind of emotion as the paper singed and curled, and the last words of her lifelong love smouldered and burnt before being transformed into mere flecks of feather-light grey ash.

Chapter Seventeen

The next morning, as usual, Polly was the first to rise. She liked to be up and out before Pearl surfaced, as any kind of interaction with the woman seemed to plunge her into an instant bad mood – never the best start to any day, especially one which was going to be a bloody hard slog with, at the very least, a nine-hour shift spent outside in the freezing cold.

Polly had not made any bones about the way she felt towards Bel's mother, and Agnes had told her daughter to pull her horns in a few times – words of admonishment that had just sailed over her head and been blatantly ignored. What Polly didn't like to show, though, was that she also preferred to get out of the front door before Bel got up. She felt sad about that, and sadder still when she started to suspect that Bel was also awake when Polly was having her breakfast but was waiting for her sister-in-law to leave before she ventured out of her bedroom.

'Bloody typical!' Polly cursed Pearl under her breath as she looked at the dirty grate. It was meant to be Pearl's job to prepare the fire and to stack it up with newspaper and kindling and a top layer of coal, so that whoever was first up could simply spark it up straight away and get the house warm and the stove as hot as quickly as possible. It was about the only chore Agnes had asked Pearl to do as she was always the last one in on an evening.

The mornings were freezing. As if it wasn't bad enough being at war, and having to get by on the bare necessities rationing afforded, the north-east was having the worst winter for decades. And it showed no signs of abating. Despite being just weeks from the start of spring, swirls of snow greeted the workers at the yard most mornings – either that or a blanket of freezing fog or a battering of biting winds coming across the North Sea.

Polly braced herself against the blustery cold as she nipped out to the coal bunker at the far end of their back yard, and quickly filled the metal scuttle with a good heap of fuel before hurrying back indoors and into the kitchen.

As she bobbed down on to her haunches to build the fire, she noticed, lying amongst the ashes, the charred remains of a letter. She carefully picked up a small piece of burnt yellow paper and, seeing the words 'miss you', knew instantly it was Teddy's handwriting and that it was the letter he had sent Bel shortly before he'd been killed.

It was the letter she had found Bel sobbing over when Polly had returned home the evening Tommy had proposed to her. It seemed such a long time ago, although in reality it had only been four months.

Polly remembered it as clearly as if it was yesterday. She had initially been puzzled as to why her sister-in-law was so upset, as Teddy was alive, and Joe, despite being injured, was on his way back home. It hadn't been until Bel had gone to bed and Polly had read the letter for herself that she had understood why her sister-in-law had been so despondent – in fact, Polly had felt like crying herself, as there had been something terribly sad about the tone of the letter.

A strange kind of finality.

Now, as Polly held the remaining fragment of her brother's letter between her blackened fingers, she realised his words had been horribly prophetic.

Had he somehow known he was going to die out there in the North African desert?

Or was he just trying to prepare his wife for what could possibly happen?

And, more importantly, *why had Bel burnt her husband's last words to her? What was going on in her sister-in-law's head?*

Polly realised she no longer knew the answer to that question, but she wished she had the letter in her hands now so that she could march into Bel's room and make her reread her husband's plea – so that she could tell her that Teddy would want her to do as he had asked. He would want 'his Bel' to be happy.

Or to at least *try* to be happy.

Polly knew her brother would be devastated if he realised his death had caused such a change in his wife. Bel's mourning had brought out something inside her that none of them had ever seen – would never have thought she had in her.

But it was, and it seemed to have taken over her whole being.

As Polly stacked up the fire and sparked it up, Agnes came into the kitchen, still in her thick winceyette dressing gown.

'Mornin', Pol,' she said, pulling out a chair from underneath the kitchen table and easing herself down into it. Polly looked at her mum and thought how old she was looking. The grey in her hair seemed to have now overtaken the deep chestnut brown, and her skin looked slacker and more wrinkled.

'I'm guessing Pearl forgot to make the fire – again?' she added, looking at her daughter, who was now energetically and rather aggressively working the bellows and succeeding in fanning the fire to life.

Polly did not answer but stood up and said in a whisper, 'She's gone and burnt Teddy's letter.'

It took a few moments for Agnes to work out that her daughter was talking about Bel.

She thought for a moment before getting up to put the kettle on the stove.

'Well, Pol, it's her letter. She can do what she wants with it.'

Polly exhaled air.

'I don't know how she could do that. It's not as if she's got a lot to remember him by – and besides, it might have been nice to keep it for Lucille.' Polly's whisper was getting louder by the second. 'For when she's older . . . A keepsake from the da she never knew.'

Just then Joe hobbled into the room. 'What's the big secret?'

Both women looked up.

Joe thought how sad and weary his mother's face looked, whereas his sister was clearly extremely vexed about something.

'Nothing,' Polly said, grabbing her boxed-up gas mask and canvas holdall from the table.

'I'm going to get to work early. I'll get some tea and a bit of breakfast in the canteen today.' She forced a smile, gave Agnes, then Joe, a quick peck on the cheek, before snatching her coat and scarf from the back of the door and hurrying out of the kitchen.

Joe gave his mum a questioning look as they heard the front door slam shut.

'So, come on, Ma, what's going on?'

'Let me get a cuppa on the go first,' she said, getting up to fetch the big brown teapot from the scullery.

When she returned with the steaming pot, she sighed. 'Before your brother was killed, he sent Bel a letter,' she explained.

'He told her that if anything were to happen to him and he didn't come back from the war that she had to be happy – both for her own sake as well as Lucille's.'

Agnes poured them both a cuppa, before carrying out her ritual of tipping a slosh of tea from her cup into her saucer and blowing on it.

She thought for a moment, wondering just how much to tell Joe about what Teddy had written. Every word of it was imprinted in her memory.

There was no need for her to say that Teddy had warned them that Joe 'would come back a changed man'. She was sure Joe was well aware of that himself, for he *had* returned a different man to the one who had gone marching off to war.

'And typical of Teddy' – Agnes took a sip of tea – 'he told Bel to look after you when you got back – as if she'd do any different . . . As if any of us would do any different.'

Agnes didn't see Joe's body stiffen, his demeanour become more alert.

'That boy always liked to tell people what to do,' Agnes continued, 'was always determined to be the big brother . . .' Her voice trailed off in thought. Teddy had been the more serious of her boys. Joe had been the mischievous one, the joker – her cheeky Charlie who got away with blue murder. Teddy, on the other hand, was more earnest, trying not only to be the big brother, but also the surrogate father.

'There was something troubling about the letter, though,' she added.

'What do you mean?' Joe asked.

'Oh, I don't know. It's probably just me being superstitious and silly . . .'

'But?' Joe prodded.

'Well, it wasn't so much what he said, more what he didn't say . . . like he knew he wasn't coming back.'

Agnes could feel the tears starting and swallowed hard to force them back.

'Perhaps that's why Bel wanted to get shot of the letter,' Joe mused.

Agnes nodded her agreement.

As they sat quietly, Agnes looked at Joe, who seemed to have gone off into his own world.

Joe had become a more pensive, a more private person; Agnes worried that he had not spoken about his brother at all since he'd got back, or about what had happened out in that godforsaken country.

'A penny for your thoughts?' Agnes said quietly. It was one of her favourite expressions, but one she had never had to use on Joe before, as she had always been able to read him like a book. Since his return, though, that hadn't been quite so easy.

'He did the same to me,' Joe said, his mind still not quite back in the here and now.

Agnes was now sitting up straight, eager to encourage her son to open up – to talk.

'In what way?' she asked.

'He made me promise – promise to look after Bel.'

Agnes could see the sadness in her son's eyes – the sorrow at remembering the brother he no longer had by his side. She leant forward and took his hand.

'Tell me what happened.' She gently pushed for Joe to keep going, to keep speaking, to keep unburdening.

'When I was in the field hospital, just before they moved me to the evacuation hospital, Teddy came to see me.

'We both knew it would be the last time we'd see each other before they shipped me back. It was night-time, or at least I thought it was. It was dark at any rate. I was on a lot of morphine . . . sometimes I wasn't sure what was real and what wasn't . . .' Joe's voice dropped.

Agnes took hold of her son's hand and squeezed it.

'But that night I can clearly recall the look on his face. He looked serious – his voice was serious. "Look after my Bel and my Lucille, Joe," he said to me. He kept repeating it, making sure I had understood what he'd said.

'"You have to promise me that . . . Get back safely and get well. If I'm not there, she'll need you. Promise? You must promise me." He kept on and on. I remember wanting to laugh at him and tell him to stop being such a solemn bugger, that the war would be over soon and he'd be back home before he knew it to love and care for his wife and daughter himself – but I couldn't get the words out. I felt so tired, exhausted, every time I tried to speak, my mouth seemed to dry up.

'In the end I just nodded and told him that I would. I promised.

'He seemed happy then and smiled at me. That was the last time I saw him. The last time we ever spoke to each other.'

Tears were now running down both Joe's and his mother's face – Joe in remembrance of the scene, and Agnes in imagining it.

Joe's throat felt constricted, choked with emotion, but he kept speaking. It felt a relief to just get the words out, to let the images out of his head and lay them out for others to see.

'On the long journey back, when I'd been taken on to the hospital ship, I kept thinking about Ted – I couldn't shake the look he had – there was just something in his manner which kept unsettling me.'

Joe paused, thinking about how during that long, chaotic voyage back he would drift in and out of consciousness, and how images of Bel came to the fore, as did those of his mother and sister. Sometimes he even saw the faces of his fellow riveters. On a few occasions he saw the face of his father, who he could not remember seeing as child, but whose photograph was always on the bedside table in his mother's room. But it had been Teddy's words which kept coming back to haunt him the most. Like Bel's letter, they had left him with a sense of foreboding.

'No matter how much I tried to push Ted's words away, they kept coming back to me, and each time they did, I had this awful sense of . . . I don't know what to call it . . . It was like our Ted knew he wasn't going to make it back,' Joe said simply.

Agnes started to weep and nodded her head in understanding.

It was exactly what she too had felt after reading Teddy's letter to Bel back in October last year – the most terrible sense of foreboding.

A foreboding she had felt every day thereafter – until the telegram had arrived and her worst fears had become reality.

Chapter Eighteen

'You had any more word from Tommy?' Gloria asked Polly as the women were having their usual morning catch-up before the start of their shift. Standing huddled round their fire, they were all supping from their flasks, which had just been replenished by the little tea boy now making his way across the yard, carefully balancing his seesawing pole of metal cans across his narrow shoulders.

The women all enjoyed hearing how Tommy was doing – they had all liked him, and had got to know him through his work as a dock diver, as well as through his turbulent relationship with their workmate.

'Oh yes, any more letters from lover boy?' Dorothy asked brazenly. 'I think we're due another instalment.'

Polly didn't mind her workmate's ribbing; she enjoyed nothing more than talking about her fiancé and delighted in keeping her friends up to date on Tommy's life over in Gibraltar; she would often read them excerpts from the letters he regularly sent her. There was always plenty to tell, as Gibraltar was of great strategic importance to the Allies, and controlled virtually all the naval traffic into and out of the Mediterranean Sea and the Atlantic Ocean.

Although Tommy, who was part of a specialised unit of navy divers, was not able to disclose much, he could fill his pages to his fiancée with wonderful tales about the Rock of Gibraltar, and how it housed a kind of underground city, as masses of limestone had been blasted out to build huge man-made caverns, barracks, offices – even a fully equipped hospital.

The women had been mesmerised by Tommy's descriptions of this unique British garrison at the southernmost tip of Spain, and had laughed out loud when he had written about the famous wild monkeys, the tailless Barbary apes, which inhabited the top part of the Rock. They were hoots of incredulity when Tommy told how the British Army had appointed an officer to supervise their welfare, that a food allowance of fruit, vegetables and nuts was included in their budget, and the birth of every monkey was published in the military journal – with each one being named after a governor, a brigadier, or some other high-ranking officer. When he wrote in one letter that one of the monkeys had injured itself and had been taken to the Royal Naval Hospital to have surgery, the women had all refused outright to believe it.

This morning, though, thoughts of Tommy had been pushed aside by the incendiary actions of Polly's sister-in-law the previous evening.

'Oh, please don't mention letters to me,' Polly said with a sad laugh.

Rosie, Gloria, Dorothy, Martha and Hannah all turned to look askance at their workmate; they knew Polly was finding it hard to deal with her brother's death, on top of her worries that the same fate might befall her future husband.

'It's a long story,' she said. 'I'll tell you about it over a drink in the Admiral after work if you all fancy?'

'Definitely,' Dorothy exclaimed, excited by the hint of any kind of drama or gossip.

She immediately tossed the rest of her tea on to the ground, screwed the top back on her thermos, and announced, 'I'll just nip over to tell Angie. She's bound to want to come.'

The women were now familiar faces in the shipyard's prime watering hole, only a stone's throw away from the big metal gates of Thompson's. Over the past six months they had gradually become accepted there, even welcomed – something that would have been unheard of before the war.

The proprietor of the Admiral, an older Irish man called Patrick, whose family had come over to the north-east during the potato famine of the mid-1800s, had a particular soft spot for the women welders, and had told them they brought a 'bit o' fresh air' to the place whenever they graced his 'humble abode'. Patrick's attitude reflected the growing respect amongst the shipyard workers for all the women who worked in the yard; Rosie had even heard some of the foremen and other heads of departments remark that they had been surprised by just how hard the women worked, and, more importantly, how their work output certainly equalled – if not exceeded – the output when there had just been men working there.

'Great! Angie's coming too!' Dorothy came back breathless from the other side of the yard, where her friend had recently been taught how to operate one of the largest cranes; a feat that had greatly impressed the women. Rosie had been secretly disappointed, though, as she was still hoping Angie might consider joining her team.

'I don't suppose we can persuade you to come for a drink too, Rosie?' Dorothy asked, despite knowing the likely answer. The women always invited Rosie out with them whenever they gathered for a drink after work, or went to the flicks as a special treat, but Rosie rarely went. Her presence at the bordello was needed just about every evening, due to the fact Lily was now regularly making trips up and down the country – alternating between the Ashbrooke establishment and her new venture in Soho.

She was getting increasingly excited about her new business, which she had decided to call Lumière Bleue – French for 'blue light' – and which was just about to have its grand opening.

'Sorry, I'm afraid I can't, but when Charlotte visits I'd love it if we could all have a bit of a work jaunt to the cinema.'

'Fabulous,' Dorothy enthused, 'tell me the exact dates when you know and I'll see what's on at the Bromarsh.'

It was accepted that anything related to books or films was firmly Dorothy's domain, just as she was solely responsible for organising any outings to the cinema. She was presently trying to get the women to critique a different picture house each time they went to see a film, in order to find the best one in town.

'Oh, so we get to meet Charlotte – finally!' Hannah chirped up.

Rosie smiled. She was really looking forward to her little sister's visit. Charlotte would get to meet the people who had saved her life; and although Rosie thought Charlotte was still too young to be told about their uncle Raymond, she wanted her to at least get to know the women. They were, after all, like family.

When the klaxon sounded out, the women headed off to the dry dock and Rosie took Hannah over to the plumbers in the fitting-out quay to work on the ship that had just been launched and was now ready to be furnished. At this stage of the shipbuilding process, there was always plenty of 'pick-up work' – touching up spots of welding that had been missed – which was ideal for Hannah. As they walked over, mufflers wrapped tightly around their necks and coats buttoned up against the whistling cold wind, Rosie noticed Helen watching them from the first-floor window of the administration building.

Rosie likened the yard's emerald-eyed sex siren to a kind of Greek goddess of revenge, and, seeing her now, viewing them from above, she did not have a good feeling. The situation with Hannah was nearing crisis point. She was just keeping her fingers crossed that Jack got back from America – and quickly. Hannah would be fine then, but if he got delayed, Rosie doubted very much whether she could keep Helen at bay and away from her intended prey. She knew the group's little bird would be the first in line to feel Helen's wrath, and her almost pathological need to wreak retribution on Polly and all who knew her.

And God help us if she ever finds out about Gloria's baby being Jack's child, Rosie had thought many times these past few months. Gloria too had echoed the same fears, admitting to her boss, 'I don't think Helen will take too kindly to having a half-brother or sister.'

As the day wore on, and the women welders ploughed through another shift of grindingly hard work, they gradually got lost in their own world of welds as they melted metal, and helped create the super-sized steel shell of another desperately needed ship.

By half past five their whole bodies were aching and tired. Over the past six months all of the women, bar Hannah, had developed muscles which would put those of many men to shame. It had taken them a number of weeks after first learning to weld for their arms to feel even remotely normal, after the sheer strain of working such long hours, often in awkward positions. Even their legs had become stronger and tauter as they were on their feet, sometimes up to twelve hours a day; and when there was as rush on, as was more and more the case these days, they could easily end up working over seventy hours a week.

But none of them complained. Men like Polly's brother had sacrificed their lives for their country; Gloria's two sons were presently serving in the Royal Navy on one of the most perilous battlefields of the war – the Atlantic – and Hannah's parents were trapped in a country now governed by a depraved regime.

The rest of the women had all felt the brute force of Hitler's malevolence during the many air raids the town had suffered – bombs whose destination was the very yard they worked in. These merchant ships they were all helping to build were essential if the Axis were to be stopped in their tracks. The women knew it and, although they did not speak about it openly, their exhausted limbs bore testimony to their pure grit and determination to do whatever they could to help win this abominable war.

As soon as the horn sounded out across the yard, signalling the end of the day shift, Dorothy pushed her helmet up and declared, 'The Admiral! And pronto!'

There was no arguing with her, and within a quarter of an hour the women were all settled with their drinks in the corner of the yard's local.

Hannah was still persevering with the 'black stuff', but had been advised by Pat to try 'proper Irish Guinness', as he claimed Hannah would much prefer the taste to that of stout; Hannah being Hannah hadn't liked to admit it, but she didn't like it any more than the stout, but felt obliged to keep drinking it – a part of her still hoping the liquid medicine would have the same effect that spinach had on Popeye and bring about a miraculous transformation enabling her to have the strength and stamina of Martha – or, at the very least, Polly.

Gloria watched their little bird grimace as she took a mouthful of her pint, which left a white tide on her upper lip, and then looked at Martha as she took a big gulp of her beer shandy and asked, 'Letter?'

Gloria savoured her lemonade and smiled at Martha. Martha's intuition was uncanny. Gloria was convinced Martha had known she was pregnant before she had breathed a word to any of the women. When they had watched their first ship launch back in December, Martha had said in her simple, monosyllabic way, 'Baby.' Gloria had nearly toppled over with shock; she'd given Martha a big bear hug and then put her finger to her lips, to tell her that no one else was to know just yet.

When Gloria had told the women her very unexpected news, Martha had again repeated the words 'baby' followed by 'girl'. She was clearly convinced Gloria was going to have a daughter; although Gloria hated to admit it, she was secretly hoping for that. After her two boys, whom she loved dearly and prayed for every night, Gloria thought it would be wonderful to have a girl – not that she was under any illusion that a daughter would be any less worry than a son; she just needed to look at the young women sitting with her now to know that this simply wasn't the case.

'Yes, Polly, *the letter*?' Dorothy and Angie both demanded in unison.

'Well . . .' Polly began, taking a sip of her half-pint of Vaux ale, which was brewed just half a mile away on the outskirts of the town centre.

'Last year, on the night Tommy proposed to me, I came home to find Bel sobbing her heart out. She'd just received a letter from our Teddy . . .'

As the women listened, Polly felt as if a load had been taken off her shoulders. Her anger towards Bel seemed to disperse and suddenly the issue of the letter did not seem to be so horrendous, or painful, or serious. Agnes had always said to her 'better out than in', and after she had unburdened herself on her friends, she realised just how true those words were.

As they all chatted and gave their opinions and thoughts and feelings, Polly felt so grateful she had what she called her 'family of friends'.

She loved Agnes, and Joe, and Bel, but as she sat here, sipping her frothy, hoppy beer, Polly realised just how much she needed these women – how much they *all* needed each other in these very strange times.

Joe was lying in bed when he heard Polly come through the front door. His leg had really been given him gip today and it had exhausted him. He'd been stupid to think he could go back to work immediately, but he was determined it would not be long – even if he had to will himself better.

'I'm home!' Polly announced, as she always did when she walked through the front door.

Joe heard her boots stomp down the tiled hallway and then the muffled sound of his mother's voice, followed by Arthur's, both welcoming the return of their 'Wearside welder' – the nickname Agnes had given Polly after her first day at Thompson's.

Agnes had told Joe it had been a day that had given her a fresh load of grey hairs, and that she had argued until she was blue in the face to try to change her daughter's mind. But time had mellowed his mother, and she had adapted to the daily worry of her daughter working in the shipyards – despite its notoriety for accidents and as the target of just about every bomb dropped thus far on the town.

Listening to the jocular mood in the kitchen, Joe could tell that Pearl wasn't back yet. Heaven knew where she got to of an evening. He didn't really want to know. He had seen the type of men she used to step out with when they were growing up, and the state of her when she returned after what Agnes called her 'benders'. So far there had not been evidence of any men in her life, and if she was half cut when she came back to the house, as Joe suspected, she was now much better at disguising it.

How on earth Bel tolerated her, he did not know. He would have loved to have talked to Bel about her mum. She was keeping so much to herself; he knew she needed to talk, to confide in someone about how she felt, what she was thinking. She was a ticking time bomb at the moment, and he dreaded the day she lost it.

One thing he knew for certain was that if she didn't decompress, then it would not be long before there was an explosion. He knew Agnes thought the same. She hadn't said much, just a few words here and there, but she was a wise, older woman who had been through this herself and knew better than most what Bel was going through.

But Agnes had to be careful with how she dealt with Bel. She might be her unofficial adopted mother, the one who had practically brought her up since she was five, but she was not her biological mum, and now both 'mothers' were under the same roof it made the situation much trickier. Agnes had been forced to take a step back.

Joe knew it was up to him to help his sister-in-law – and not just because she clearly needed it – but because he had a promise to keep.

The promise he had made with the last words he had spoken to his brother.

Chapter Nineteen

Saturday 8 March 1941

'I've always wondered why they call them the Cat and Dog Steps,' Rosie said to DS Miller as they strolled along the narrow pathway winding along the top of the stretch of steep cliffs that began at the seaside resort of Roker, not far from Thompson's, and continued for half a mile until they reached the neighbouring suburb of Seaburn, which had also been a flourishing tourist trap before the war. Both places now resembled military zones, with soldiers patrolling with guns, and an elaborate series of defences and diversions in place along the coastal plain, including pillboxes, tank traps and gun batteries.

The detective stopped and looked down at the thick stone steps that had been carved into the face of rock and curved gently down to the stretch of yellow sandy beach below.

'I've heard two explanations,' he said as they both stared across at the dark green choppy sea, its white frothing waves rhythmically slapping against the walled promenade, creating a fine, salty mist, 'although I'm not sure anyone is completely certain.'

'I'm all ears. Explain away.' Rosie smiled.

She knew she shouldn't have come here after work with the detective, and although her head had told her to reject his kind offer of a walk, her voice had gone off on its own accord and told him, 'That sounds like a lovely idea.'

Her gang of women welders had left on time, eager to make the most of their afternoon, and Rosie had just finished clearing up and was herself looking forward to a few hours off before heading over to Lily's. She had been gazing up at the unusually cloud-free, milky-blue sky, and thinking it seemed a long time since they'd had any even remotely nice weather, when her eye had caught the stocky, slightly lumbering figure of DS Miller in the distance hurrying across the yard, side-stepping thick reels of ropes and stacks of giant chains, his black woollen coat flapping open, waving across to her, his slightly greying hair flopping down in front of his eyes, despite his repeated attempts at pushing it back away from his face.

On seeing him, Rosie had felt an instant jolt of joy. It was as if the day had all of a sudden got much better – and much brighter.

Rosie had sensed that Peter was a little nervous when he explained he had just been to see one of the bosses at Jackie Crown's shipyard, which stood cheek by jowl with Thompson's, concerning 'a bit of trouble they're having over there', and that on the spur of the moment he had decided to see if Rosie was about for a short stroll – it being 'such an unusually pleasant day'. And he was right. The sun was just starting to peek out, hinting that spring might finally be winning its battle with winter.

Rosie had argued with herself that a little excursion along the coast with someone whose company she enjoyed was harmless, and she had pushed back the voice in her head telling her otherwise.

Since their coffee on Valentine's Day three weeks previously, Rosie had 'bumped' into DS Miller on another two occasions, and each time she had found herself happily agreeing to accompany the detective to the little teashop up from the south dock. Each time she had done so, though, the logical part of her brain had told her that this was not a good idea.

Anyone but a copper, it had warned her. But she had argued with herself that it was only a quick cuppa after all.

It wasn't as if they were going out on a date or anything.

Not that she would know what it was like to actually go out on a date, having, unbelievably, never been out on one before. Her work at Lily's had made her a woman of the world in all aspects of physical love, but she had never experienced the innocence of courtship and romance. The night she had been violated by her uncle Raymond had robbed her of that, and afterwards her life had changed beyond all recognition – boys had been the furthest thing from her mind.

But although she might have been a total novice when it came to going out with someone, she knew that women didn't go out on dates dressed in dirty overalls, and wearing big, clumpy, rubber-soled boots, with soot on their face instead of make-up. Rosie had told Lily and George (the only people to know about her meetings with the detective) that he was simply someone she enjoyed talking to. Apart from which, the man was almost twice her age; she guessed he must be at least forty. And more than anything, he was really a kind of work colleague, as he was, for all intents and purposes, a dock worker.

'Some say the Cat and Dog Steps are named after the expression, "it's raining cats and dogs",' DS Miller said, looking down towards the famous Cannonball Rocks, which dated back more than two hundred million years and were known worldwide for their unique, perfectly rounded formations. 'Because when the sea is rough and the tide is in, you can get soaked by the thundering surf smashing against the sea wall. Not unlike it is today.'

'Like being caught in a downpour,' Rosie added thoughtfully.

'Exactly – but the other, less palatable explanation, is that the steps were so named as they give easy access to the beach to drown unwanted pets.'

'Oh, that's awful,' Rosie said, a frown creasing her forehead. 'Sometimes I cannot understand human nature. How can people be so cruel? And why kill the poor things?

'Animals and children,' DS Miller agreed. 'How anyone can take advantage or hurt the most vulnerable in our society has always been beyond me. I've seen too much of it in my job. But the worst part is, there doesn't seem to be any stopping it – and all too often they get away with it.'

An image of Rosie's uncle Raymond flickered momentarily across her mind, but she pushed it away. The day was far too lovely to be poisoned by thoughts of someone whose life's work had been about satisfying his sadistic need to abuse the susceptible and defenceless.

The pair chatted away animatedly about the rights and wrongs of society, both enjoying the freedom of being out by the coast and breathing in the fresh, salty air, even if they couldn't walk along the actual beach, which was now cordoned off with rolls of barbed wire and harboured half-buried landmines to stave off an attempted invasion from the North Sea.

DS Miller explained more about his duties as a law enforcer, and his work with the Dock Police, who had been especially tasked with trying to combat the flourishing black market that seemed to be thriving in most port towns. Rosie pushed back thoughts of Lily and the little entrepreneurial dabbling she was enjoying on the side.

The detective explained that, in current times, his job was particularly varied; it was not just about catching 'the bad guys', as he called them, but also army deserters and 'enemy aliens'. Police forces up and down the country were also being asked to help out the town's civil defence unit, enforce the blackout, and do what they could to assist the rescue services.

As they continued to walk, their chatter turned to the inevitable subject of war and the news that British troops had just landed in Greece, before moving on to the latest goings-on at the yard.

It was a relief for Rosie to be able to discuss work with someone who not only understood the inner workings and politics of the shipyards, but also seemed genuinely keen and interested in listening to her.

Rosie had mentioned the women welders to Peter before, and he had remembered all their names and knew a little about their very different personalities, and so it felt natural to tell him about her concerns for Hannah.

'She's such a lovely girl, but she's just so unsuited to working in the yard. I really don't know what possessed her to even apply for a job there – never mind as a trainee welder. At the moment she's hanging on to her job by a thread.'

Rosie briefly told DS Miller how Hannah had recently fallen under Helen's scrutiny, although she did not go into detail about why Jack's daughter hated the women so much.

'Why do you think Hannah's so desperate to work at Thompson's?' he asked, naturally curious, as he knew a little about Hannah from their previous conversations, knew that her parents had wisely sent her to stay with her aunty in the town's small Jewish quarter shortly before Hitler invaded her homeland.

'You know, that's a good question, Peter,' Rosie said, taking a sidelong glance at her companion and thinking how thoughtful he was.

'I've wondered that myself so many times and never once asked her. Perhaps it's time I did.'

As they reached the small line of shops along the promenade, they agreed a quick cup of tea was called for before they went their separate ways.

As they sat and chatted, Mrs Hoggart, the owner of the café, asked them if they wanted anything to eat. Not surprisingly the little tearoom was empty, as there was next to no passing trade, and the snacks and cakes on offer were scant. Neither of them felt at all hungry, but DS Miller ordered two rolls, which seemed to please the elderly woman.

A short while later, having forced down their rolls, which DS Miller insisted on paying for, the pair walked back out on to the pavement.

'Well, thank you for a lovely afternoon. Perhaps we can do it again sometime?' DS Miller asked Rosie as she started to walk towards the bus stop.

Rosie opened her mouth to answer, but found herself unable to say anything.

Just then her bus came round the corner and she stuck her hand out for it to stop.

'Yes, Peter,' she said, jumping on to the platform, 'it's been lovely.'

And with that the bus pulled away and DS Miller found himself waving to the back of a bus with its 'Shop at Binns' advert and feeling more than a little confused.

Had she meant 'yes' she would like to go out again, or did she mean 'yes' it was a lovely afternoon, thereby successfully avoiding giving him an answer to his request to see her again?

'Bugger,' DS Miller muttered under his breath, as he forced himself to turn and walk away. This woman was a mystery to him. Was that why he felt so drawn to her?

He'd tried to forget her after meeting her for the first time last year when he'd gone to her bedsit to inform her of her uncle's demise. He'd felt the most peculiar pull towards her, and after he'd taken her the cash they'd found in Raymond's room, he'd had to fight with himself not to find another excuse to go back to see her. It would have been the height of unprofessionalism, and that was something he put a lot of value on.

But then he'd met her when she was walking home after work, after which the magnetic draw he felt towards her had become even stronger. Had she guessed that their so-called 'chance' meetings thereafter had been anything but? He hoped to God she had not realised he had deliberately taken to walking by the ferry landing around the time he knew her shift ended, in the hope of catching her walking home. He knew he was being ridiculous. Every time he had waited at the top of Low Street, he had berated himself. He was a grown man, and a widow at that. He had experienced life and death, and through his work just about everything in between, but he just could not help it.

For some reason this woman fascinated him. And she was without doubt very attractive. Of course, most of the men he knew would not look twice at her because of the awful scars she'd been left with after her welding accident, but that didn't bother him in the least. He had watched his own wife die slowly, her English rose looks overtaken by the ravages of the cancer that had relentlessly eaten away at her, but he never once stopped seeing her as beautiful.

DS Miller quickly made his way up Sea Road, where he needed to do a little off-the-clock policing before he started his air-raid warden duties. As he pulled on his black leather gloves, his mind wandered from the immediate task at hand as he realised that it had been almost five years to the day that his beloved Sal had left him. During that time he had never so much as even looked at another woman, never mind wanted to be with one.

That was – until now.

As Rosie sat on the upper deck of the bus which was bringing her back into town, she looked out at the River Wear snaking its way into the North Sea, its journey guided by a canopy of massive overhanging cranes, its waters filled with a vast array of ships, colliers, punts and tugboats. It was a scene she never tired of seeing – of admiring.

And, as always, she felt proud that she was a part of the ebb and flow of this river's life – its vibrancy, its history, and of the wonderful metal miracles it produced.

A few minutes later she made her way down the spiral staircase and jumped off at her stop at the end of Fawcett Street. She had to be at Lily's in an hour, which gave her just enough time to have a quick wash-down, change her clothes and get over to Ashbrooke. As she briskly walked towards the turning on to Borough Road, she slowed down as she approached the entrance to Joplings, one of the town's main stores that had now closed for the day. The feeling of lightness and joy she had been carrying with her since leaving DS Miller instantly evaporated as she stared at the skeletal-looking beggar woman, wrapped in a bundle of dirty, raggedy clothes, sitting huddled up in the wide doorway, her head bowed down and her hand stretched out.

'Kate?' she asked.

On hearing her name, the woman lifted up her head and looked at Rosie.

'Yeh? Who wants ta know?' The woman's voice was defensive. The upturned palm of her begging hand had been immediately withdrawn and was now clenched into a fist.

As her eyes looked up, Rosie saw they were puffy and bloodshot. Trickles of thin red veins ran across her gaunt, hollow face. Her mousy-brown hair was matted; it must have been a long while since it had felt the pull of a brush. Rosie bobbed down so that Kate could see her own face up close, so she could see she meant no harm.

'Kate, it's Rosie. Rosie Thornton. Can you remember me? From school? In Whitburn village? You used to be in my class?'

A slight flicker of recognition crossed Kate's filth-smeared face. Then a cautious smile started to form as Kate's dull, glazed-over eyes scrutinised the scarred but pretty woman wearing overalls and a peacock-green head-scarf who had suddenly appeared right in front of her.

'Rosie . . .' the woman said a little dreamily, casting her mind back, allowing herself to recall a time long ago; a time when her life had been very different to the one she led now. As she remembered her old friend with increasing clarity, a shy smile spread across her face, revealing chipped, yellow teeth.

'Aye, Rosie and little Charlotte,' she said. 'Yer lived in the fishermen's cottages by the beach.'

Forcing back a show of shock and pity, Rosie tried her hardest to mirror Kate's pleasure at their reunion.

'That's right. Although Charlotte's not so little any more. She's nearly fourteen. That must make it – goodness – about ten years since we last saw each other.'

Rosie words were well meaning, but she was lying.

She had seen Kate twice during those intervening years.

The first was when Rosie had been a young girl and she had seen her old schoolmate in town. Kate had been taken into the care of the nuns who ran a home called Nazareth

House after her mother, the village seamstress, had died suddenly. Rosie had hardly recognised her old friend. She had changed beyond recognition and was no longer the bubbly, chatty Kate she had known, who had caused their teachers no end of frustration with her constant questions and talk. The girl she had spotted walking by the side of one of the black-caped nuns was barely a trace of her former self. She looked as if she had had her very spirit beaten out of her – and, by the state of her welt-covered legs, she had suffered more than a few thrashings.

Rosie had been too shocked to approach her old play-mate that day, but later on that evening, when her mum was tucking her into bed, she had told her about Kate and how terrible she looked, and how she didn't understand, as the nuns were meant to be the 'brides of Christ' – kind and caring. It was the first insight Rosie had into a harsher, more unjust world.

She had not seen any more of her childhood friend until last year, when her own life had felt like a living hell and she had spotted Kate begging in town. It had terri-fied Rosie, as it had been a stark reminder of what could happen to her own sister if she did not pay Raymond the money he was demanding from her and he carried out his threats. Her concerns then were for her own flesh and blood, but now her life was on the up, Raymond was gone for ever, and, most important of all, her sister was safe and well.

Seeing Kate now, Rosie knew she could not simply pass her old friend without offering her a helping hand.

'Why don't you come back to my bedsit for a bite to eat?' Rosie asked gently, not wanting to seem too pushy. Kate reminded her of a stray dog that had been beaten too many times and had learnt to back away from any kind of human contact for fear of being hurt again.

'I've no money,' Kate started to say.

'You don't need money. I can offer an old friend a sandwich and a drink, can't I?'

Kate still looked wary, but when Rosie stood up she followed suit.

'Come on then, it's not far from here. I've got a nice can of Spam and a fresh loaf of bread at home – it's not exactly the Ritz, but it's warm and comfortable.'

And with that the two women, one dressed in scruffy overalls, the other in dirty rags, walked together down the main road and back to Rosie's small but cosy basement flat.

When Rosie arrived at Lily's an hour later, she gave the required three knocks before the spyhole was quickly opened and shut and the sturdy back door opened. Lily was chatting to the cloakroom girl when she saw Rosie walk in and was just about to ask why she wasn't using the front entrance when she had her answer.

'Oh, *ma chérie*, I see you have a companion with you this evening.' Lily was dressed from head to toe in the latest fashion to come out of Paris – it was her new 'look' and had replaced her former love of extravagant corseted meringue-shaped evening gowns consisting of layers of red taffeta and plunging necklines. Her style now was chic and sophisticated, and in her words '*très à la mode*'.

As Rosie eyed Lily, she could tell she was working hard at keeping her usually unflappable veneer in place as she took in the sight of Kate cowering behind Rosie.

'Lily, meet Kate. She's our new live-in maid. She can have the spare room on the top floor that's never used.'

Rosie's tone made it clear this was a statement and not a request. It was the first time she had not asked Lily's permission regarding the running of the bordello.

Lily looked over the top of her horn-rimmed glasses, first at Kate and then at Rosie. For once, Lily seemed stuck for words.

Kate, meanwhile, looked up in wonder at the ornate mouldings and cornices on the high ceilings above her and then down at the varnished parquet flooring, before her gaze rested on the vision of this magnificent woman before her. This wonderfully attired queen bee, in a couture black velvet dress, was like nothing she had ever seen before. The woman's voluptuous figure looked as though it had been especially sculptured to resemble one of the shapely Renaissance models she had seen in the oil painting in the town's municipal museum, where she often sought refuge from the cold.

She could not help but be captivated by this incredible woman's ample bosom, ivory pillows of flesh on which rested the most beautiful ruby and diamond necklace. But it was the blaze of orange hair which truly captivated Kate, piled high and artfully crafted so that the end result looked both coiffured and wanton at the same time.

The women's silence was broken by the sudden arrival of George as he walked out of the smoke-filled reception room and into the main hallway. As soon as he saw the tableau in front of him, he too forced back a look of complete disbelief, managing to keep his face deadpan as he asked, 'Ah, do I see a newcomer in our midst?'

The voice he used was soft and unthreatening, as if he was talking to a young child.

Kate didn't seem at all offended by being talked to as if she were a mere youngster and not the grown woman she was. Quite the reverse, she seemed to take to George, allowing herself to venture out of Rosie's shadow.

'Hi, George, yes, this is Kate. She's an old schoolfriend from Whitburn. She's going to be our new live-in cleaner.'

'Oh, splendid! I'm guessing she's going to bunk down in the spare room at the top of the house, which, I hasten to add, has been empty for too long now. Great stuff. Glad to have you on board, my dear.' And with that George swung his new walking stick and continued on into the back parlour, from where he was going to retrieve a bottle of 1935 Bordeaux for one of the evening's guests.

'Ah, so this is *Kate*,' Lily said. Her demeanour had softened and she threw Rosie a look which said she now understood. Rosie had told her many months ago about her poor friend who had been orphaned and sent to the so-called 'care' home in town, run by an order of nuns known as the Poor Sisters of Nazareth.

'Well, we had better get you settled in then, *ma chérie*,' she said. 'Follow me and I'll show you to your room. I think there might be a few garments up there which would fit you perfectly.'

As Lily ushered Kate down the hallway, Rosie watched as she chatted away to her new charge, telling her that one of her girls was very good with a pair of scissors, and had she thought of having one of those new bobs that were so popular at the moment.

Rosie caught a look of complete entrancement on Kate's face as she climbed the stairs, her eyes never once leaving the eccentric older woman who was presently escorting her up the carpeted staircase and towards a new and better life.

Chapter Twenty

A month later, April 1941

'It's getting worse, isn't it?' Arthur said to Polly as they walked home from the fish quay. The old man had met Polly off the ferry and they'd gone to buy Agnes some fish bits so that she could make one of her much-loved and always hastily devoured fish pies. The pair had formed a close bond since Tommy had gone off to war, and even more so since Arthur had moved in. Polly found the old man's gentle manner and thoughtful disposition a welcome relief from the tightly wound, edgy atmosphere that had pervaded the Elliot household these past few months and now seemed to have permanently settled there.

Not surprisingly, Arthur had started to spend more time in his room upstairs, reading his papers and listening to his little wireless, and it had not escaped the rest of the household's attention that Polly would often head straight up to see the old man after work.

'The war out here?' Polly asked, looking at the shell of a bombed-out row of houses they were passing. 'Or the silent one taking place in our home?' Her question was punctuated with a short, sad laugh.

'Both,' Arthur replied as he stopped to take a rest. He was getting more breathless these days when he was out walking, and knew his time was probably running out; a thought that did not worry or scare him. Sometimes he almost welcomed it, as he was pretty sure he was going to be with his beloved Flo again. He wasn't at all religious, but he had always felt a strange certainty that his wife, who had died twenty years ago, had never really left him and would be there when it was time for him to leave this present life.

His only worry about departing this world was for the future of those he would leave behind. What terrified him – much more than the Grim Reaper – was Herr Hitler, and the kind of society in which those he loved would be forced to live, should that evil narcissist achieve his aim and enforce his hate-fuelled and prejudiced way of living on to others.

As Arthur looked at the destruction wreaked during the Luftwaffe's air raid last week, he saw it was now abundantly clear that the war which raged worldwide had now well and truly arrived on their own doorstep, and over this past month had been causing total devastation, obliterating homes and businesses, as well as ruthlessly taking lives, regardless of age or gender.

The most recent air attack had lasted more than five hours and had resulted in the town's beloved Binns department store being gutted. Serious fires had been caused due to an unrelenting shower of hundreds of incendiary bombs; chandelier flares had also been dropped, lighting up the whole town and providing a perfectly illuminated target for the enemy planes droning overhead in a more or less constant procession.

The town's anti-aircraft defence and gunners had fought back and succeeded in keeping the planes at bay, allowing the hundreds of firemen and auxiliaries heroically fighting the flames to do so unhindered and unharmed. Sadly, though, the bombs that were dropped took lives, including that of a seventeen-year-old boy, with dozens more townsfolk seriously injured.

'I *know* what I need to do to help beat Jerry – and that's to keep on building ships – and as fast as humanly possible,' Polly said, 'but I have no idea how to bring about a ceasefire in our own home.'

Arthur nodded in agreement.

'I just don't know what to do, or how to make things better,' she continued as Arthur got his breath back and they started walking again.

'Perhaps there is nothing you can do,' the old man volunteered, 'other than sit it out and weather the storm – and be there to pick up the pieces after the inevitable fall-out.'

Polly looked at her frail, aged friend and thought about the father she'd never got to know. She wondered if she would have got on so well with him, and whether he too would have been as easy to talk to, and would have offered such wise and balanced advice.

Arthur was a much-needed sounding board for Polly, and one she knew she could trust. Her words to him would go no further. She had confided in him and told him how much Bel had changed, and that she wished he had been able to get to know her better before Teddy had died, and to have seen her for the loving and caring person she really was. Or used to be.

Polly could tell Arthur liked Joe, but he too had changed, and she tried to describe what he was like before the war: his youthfulness, the way he would play the fool, his knack of making people laugh. At least Joe's gentle and rather sensitive nature had remained untouched, which was just as well considering the bashing he was getting on a daily basis from Bel's increasingly bad moods and cutting comments.

'It's like she's using him as some kind of mental punchbag,' Polly spoke her thoughts aloud. She knew she didn't have to say who she meant, that Arthur would know.

'Perhaps that's what she needs,' he said after a moment's thought. 'And Joe knows that – is allowing her to do it.'

'Well, there's only so much anyone can take, and if she pummels away much more at him, he's either going to topple over, or have a go back. There's a limit to everyone's patience. Joe's a lovely bloke, but he's no saint, and she'll end up pushing him too far – and then the balloon really will go up.

'And what's more, it's Lucille who'll be the one to suffer. She adores Joe.'

'Aye, the wee thing is definitely determined to make him her da, that's for sure,' Arthur agreed, although he did not say he also believed Lucille's fervour to have Joe as the father she no longer had was also, in part, because Bel had changed so much. Lucille might only be a small child, but she was old enough to sense the change in her mum – a mother who may be there in the flesh, but in every other way was very much absent.

Arthur hated to admit, even to himself, that Bel's reaction to Teddy's death bore a frightening similarity to that of his own daughter, who had never recovered from the loss of her husband, and had ended up taking her own life. It was something Arthur still felt very angry and bitter about, as it had been Tommy who had suffered the most, and had been forced to grow up without either a mother or a father.

'It's a good job Lucille's got you and Agnes.' Arthur tried to give some reassurance.

'And as for Pearl – well . . .' Polly didn't feel the need to say any more. It had been clear from her arrival back in January that both she and Arthur felt the same about Pearl; they could not abide the woman – not that she gave a damn about what anyone thought of her. Polly had commented on more than one occasion to Arthur that her sister-in-law's mother had the skin of a rhinoceros and did not possess a single maternal bone in her body.

'Aye,' Arthur agreed with Polly's unsaid words, wishing he could have talked so easily with Tommy as he was able to with his grandson's fiancée.

'Now there's a disaster just waiting to happen if ever there was one.'

As Polly and Arthur walked slowly down Tatham Street they were both quiet, each immersed in their own thoughts.

When they reached their front door, Polly took a deep breath and gave Arthur a sad smile. 'Here goes. Let's hope all's quiet on the western front.'

Within seconds of walking over the threshold, though, Polly's hopes of a tranquil evening were dashed as she heard Bel's angry voice telling Pearl, 'Ma, when I said to take Lucille out for a treat, that did *not* mean you show her the inside of one of your local drinking dens.'

Bel had become convinced her mother's enthusiasm to take her granddaughter out was so that she could either pocket some of the money Bel gave her to spend on Lucille, or else use it to buy a quick drink and a few smokes in one of the town's many taverns and inns.

'Ah, petal, you make it sound like Sodom and Gomorrah. It was only the Rose and Crown on High Street West – and we were safe and sound in the snug. I know the landlord and he let us slip in there for a while. The little un loved it.'

Bel was momentarily transported back to her own childhood, when Pearl had dragged her around the town centre from one public house to the next, and Bel would have to sit outside and wait until her mother either staggered out voluntarily, or else was chucked out by the barman who had had enough of her lip and drunken antics.

Sometimes some half-cut man would bend down to look at her, breathing beery fumes into her face, and give her a penny in the mistaken belief she was begging. She'd never put them right, though, but instead would quickly squirrel the penny away in her pocket and out of her mother's sight.

There were a few times her mother had come out of the pub with some dodgy-looking man and Bel had been relieved that they were finally going home, only to be told by Pearl to 'hold yer horses – we're not gannin yet'. Bel had then had to continue waiting on the cold stone step while Pearl disappeared down the side alley with the man, only to re-emerge a little while later, straightening her skirt and top and looking dishevelled.

After such occasions they would walk back home and Pearl would wave a coin or a note in front of her daughter's face and tell her they were going to stop off for some fish and chips.

Bel knew it wasn't right, but there were many times she was starving and hoped her ma would go down the back alleys with the men just so they could get a delicious hot fish supper afterwards.

'And I'm guessing those few shillings I gave you were spent on yourself and not your granddaughter?' Bel continued her tirade.

Pearl acted incensed. 'I don't know where you get your devious mind from, *Isabelle*. It's certainly not from yer mother! For your information, the little un got a bottle of pop and a bag of Smith's crisps and then I bought her a pot of cockles from one of the local fishwives who came in. Lucille couldn't have been happier. All the old women drinking their glasses of stout and port were clucking about her like mother hens.'

Polly and Arthur were standing in the hallway, unsure whether to venture into the kitchen in case they got caught in the crossfire. Polly cast a look behind her as Arthur grimaced and pointed his finger up to the ceiling to indicate he was going to opt for the safety of his own bedroom. Polly nodded she understood, before braving the kitchen, a place that had once been the happy epicentre of the family home, but which now, more often than not, resembled a fierce battleground of words and wills.

Polly braced herself and quickly sidled past Pearl, hoping not to be noticed, before arriving safely in the scullery, where she found Agnes peeling potatoes in preparation for their fish pie supper.

'They at it again?' Polly whispered to her mum as she gave her the bag of fish bits. Agnes's eyes rolled to the ceiling in response. Her face looked tired and sad.

Just then Joe hobbled in from the back yard. He had ditched his wooden crutch after becoming frustrated with how cumbersome it was and was now using a walking stick, which wasn't really adequate, but just about did the job. Joe had promised himself that he was going to 'get back to normal', or as near normal as possible, even though he knew he was never going to regain full mobility of his injured leg.

'Hi, Pol. How's everything at the yard?'

Polly knew Joe was still keen to get back to work, if not as a riveter, then in some other capacity, and looking back into the kitchen at Bel and Pearl's angry stand-off, she did not blame him one bit. Over the past month her attitude had changed about Joe going back out to work. His leg was, thankfully, healing, and she knew he needed to get out of the house. She'd even been keeping an ear out for any vacancies in the administration department at the yard. The thought of her brother working anywhere near Helen was a little troubling, but the way things were going at home, it might, unbelievably, be a preferable option to staying here all day.

'Doey! Doey!' Lucille's voice could be heard resounding down the hallway as she returned from her friend's house two doors down where she'd been sent to play for a while after returning home with Pearl. The little girl's appearance immediately stopped the bickering between her mother and grandmother, but her demands to see Joe only made Bel's ire change direction.

'Your uncle Joe is out the back. Now leave him alone for a few minutes,' Bel barked at her daughter.

'I don't mind, Bel,' Joe said, emerging from the scullery.

Lucille charged towards him and Joe lifted her up high while she squealed with excitement.

'She's going to be spoilt rotten!' Bel said. Her face looked thunderous. 'She's got to learn, "I want doesn't always get"!' But Bel's words fell on deaf ears as Joe put the little girl down and then pretended to be a scary tiger, growling and making his niece giggle and scream at the same time.

Bel marched out of the kitchen and into the cool, empty hallway. It was the only action she could take that would prevent her from losing it with Joe. And Lucille. Never mind her ma. At least with her mother she could have a go at her and was justified. Besides which, it was like water off a duck's back for her. Bel could scream blue murder at Pearl and she would probably just shrug it off and go out and have a smoke.

It was harder, though, to keep her temper with Joe. She knew he did not deserve the sharp end of her tongue, especially because he hadn't done any wrong – other than be adored by her daughter; but that didn't make it any easier to hold her temper with him.

Bel took a deep breath, pushed back the anger that was again rising up within her, and stomped back into the kitchen.

'Right, little girl, it's time for you to have a bath,' she said, bending down and picking up her daughter and walking away from Joe, who had just been about to start playing a game of Snap with his excited niece.

'Your hair stinks of fag ash – thanks to your *grandma* constantly puffing away on her cigarettes and dragging you into smoky pubs.'

Joe knew Bel didn't really mind the smell of smoke, unless, of course, it was her mother who was doing the smoking; then the change it triggered in Bel was more than obvious.

As Bel frogmarched her daughter out of the back and down the yard to the washhouse, Joe and the rest of the household, even Pearl, who was normally unaware of anyone else's moods, breathed a collective sigh of relief at the temporary reprieve from hostilities. Eager to remove themselves from the firing line while Bel was busy bathing Lucille, everyone quickly dispersed.

Pearl scuttled out to see her old friend Irene, who had let her kip on her sofa for a few nights when she'd come back up north. She owed her friend a bottle of something strong, as it was Irene who had told her about Teddy's death and that Agnes had a spare room going.

Agnes, Polly and Joe took themselves off to their own rooms.

It wasn't until much later on that evening, after Lucille had been scrubbed clean and put to bed, that Bel realised she had forgotten to dress Joe's wound. She caught herself puffing air through her lips just like her mother did, making her feel awash with fresh anger as she emerged from her bedroom. As she walked into the kitchen, she saw Joe hobbling to his chair, precariously balancing an overflowing bowl of soapy water to clean his leg himself.

'Here. Let me,' she told him sharply, taking the bowl off him and putting it on the table before marching over to the sink in the scullery and quickly scrubbing her hands clean.

Joe looked at his sister-in-law with hurt in his eyes. Not for the first time she had made him feel like a complete imbecile. A failure of a man. She might have chosen his brother to love, but in the past she had never once made Joe feel bad about himself. They had always been friends. And good friends at that. Friends who cared for each other. Made each other laugh. Not cry. It hurt him, and for the first time he felt a wave of anger towards her.

He'd tried to fulfil his brother's last wishes and take care of Bel, but how could you take care of someone who really was making it very plain that she did not want to be cared for?

As Bel wound the clean bandages around Joe's leg, her own mind was also agitating.

She loved Agnes, but she felt resentful that she had been saddled with tending Joe's injuries. She would have done anything for her mother-in-law, who, she felt, had saved her from a life of destitution. She owed her so much that there was no way Bel could refuse to do this for her. Especially as she had so much on her plate at the moment, what with the nursery, the laundry, and a house-load of people – although why Agnes had offered Pearl the spare room, she'd never know. Bel would have quite happily seen her ma leave that night and not come back.

But that was Agnes for you. She had instilled in Bel that it was important to be kind to others, and to care for those less fortunate than yourself. Virtues that Bel had never been exposed to by her own mother.

More than anything, though, Bel's fury was very much aimed at Teddy. She knew it was abhorrent to be angry with the man she loved and who was now dead, but Bel just could not help herself. She felt more than angry – enraged, in fact, that he had written her that damned letter and asked her to look after Joe when he came back.

She had been adamant she would not – had even burnt his letter – but deep down she knew if she didn't do as Teddy asked, she would always feel she had somehow let him down. Her husband had never asked her for anything – had always said she gave him everything by simply being his wife. His asking that she look after his brother was not just his *last* request, but also his *only* one.

She had to do it. Whether she wanted to or not. If she didn't, she would never forgive herself and would always feel she had failed the man she had loved and adored all of her life.

'Thanks, Bel,' Joe said as she finished off doing his dressing, but his words came out harshly. More harshly than he had intended. Bel heard the bite in her brother-in-law's tone of voice and glowered at him in response.

It was a look that was the final straw.

'Bel,' he demanded, 'what have I done wrong? Tell me!' His voice started to climb. 'At least then I can stop doing whatever it is that I'm doing wrong and make your life and everyone else's lives just a little better?'

Bel looked at Joe as if he was the most hated man on earth. She gave him a scowl that was frightening in its silent ferocity.

'There you are again. You're looking at me as if you hate me. Really *hate* me. Tell me, what have I done?' Joe's voice was now starting to reach fever pitch.

From her bedroom upstairs, Agnes heard her son's voice. Teddy had always been the twin who was quick to temper, but when Joe did lose it, he lost it, and if he did the whole neighbourhood would know their business. As she climbed out of her bed and wrapped her winceyette dressing gown around her she sighed wearily, before making her way out on to the landing.

Arthur opened his bedroom door at the same time and looked at Agnes. 'Shall I—' he started to say, but Agnes cut him short.

'No, Arthur, you stay put. There's no need for you to get involved. I'll sort the pair of them out.' And as she made her way down the stairs she added as much to herself as to a worried-looking Arthur, 'This has been a long time coming.'

But by the time she entered the kitchen, it was too late.

The balloon had already gone up.

Just like Joe, Bel had never been one to lose her temper easily, but like her brother-in-law, when she did, she did.

'You really want to know what you're doing wrong?' Bel's voice was practically spitting nails. 'Do I really have to spell it out to you?' Her voice was now loud enough for Beryl to hear next door, and had brought Polly hurrying down the stairs to join her mother.

'Yes, you do!' Joe was not backing down. He was standing, balancing on his good leg, with his freshly bandaged leg bent slightly, but it was strong enough to put weight on and give him his balance. Both Joe's arms were outstretched in front of him, the palms of his hands held up as if he were expecting something to be placed on them.

'Tell me,' he implored angrily.

It was what Bel had been waiting for. Those two words allowed her to unbolt the floodgates and let all her anger and grief come spilling out.

'Isn't it obvious?' she practically screamed.

Joe responded with a genuine blank look.

Bel's exasperation was plain in her look and in her voice.

'You're his *replica*. You look like him. You speak like him. God, you even smell like him! You're a constant

169

reminder of what I have lost. What I will never ever have again in my entire life . . . *You are my daily, never-ending torment.'*

She drew breath.

Joe looked stunned. As did Agnes and Polly, who were now standing by the table, not wanting to come further into the kitchen.

'My God,' Bel continued with renewed gusto, 'even my daughter thinks you're him . . . Is determined you're going to *be* him.'

Bel felt a wave of nausea pass through her as her adrenaline started to kick in. She felt as if she was going to gag, but stopped herself. 'Well, Joe,' her voice had now dropped to a growl, 'you're not him! You'll never be Lucille's father. She doesn't *need* a father! Look at me.' She laughed a little hysterically. 'I managed just fine without one!'

Bel now had tears streaming down her face. It was the first time any of them had seen her crying since they had first been notified of Teddy's death. Both her hands went up to the sides of her head and she grabbed her curly blonde hair as if she wanted to rip it out. Agnes made to go to her, worried about what she would do to herself.

'Don't! Don't, Agnes. Don't anyone touch me. I hate you all,' and with that she turned her gaze to Polly and spat out the words.

'Why the hell did you have to take me home that day? Why did you have to be so bloody nice? Why couldn't you have just left me there, snivelling away to myself? If you had just left me alone like everyone else, I would never have met Teddy, never have fallen in love with him . . . never have lost him . . .

'I wouldn't be going through this hell . . . You could have spared me all of this.' Bel swung her arm around the room, as if the very house were also to blame for her pain. As she did, the sound of the front door opening and shutting could be heard, before Pearl appeared in the kitchen doorway.

She was just opening up her mouth to say something when Bel beat her to it. 'And you, Ma. Well, I'll tell you one thing, if I hate Joe and I hate this family, there aren't words enough to describe just how much I hate you. You just take the biscuit, don't you? What are doing here anyway? What are you really after? I still haven't worked that one out – but I know one thing's for sure, it'll be something you need. Or want. It'll be about *you*. It always is, isn't it, Ma? So don't think I believe for one moment you turned up on our doorstep to come and see your little *Isabelle*. Come to help your little girl get over the loss of the man she loved. The man she adored.

'*The man who made up for all the love you never gave me.*'

Bel's anger was reaching a crescendo. 'You're really trying your hardest at the moment, aren't you, *Pearl*? Well you're not fooling anyone here, that's for sure. You forget we all knew you when I was a child. Oh, but of course, you probably don't remember much of that do you? Because you were either simply not there – or were too drunk to know or care.'

Pearl was struck dumb as her daughter continued her rant. 'Everyone can see right through you, Ma. What's the word? – You're *transparent*. Do you even know what that means? Well, I certainly wouldn't, were it not for Agnes. It was she who taught me to read and write. Not you. Not my own mother. It was *she* who sent me to school. Something you just couldn't be bothered to do. The teachers actually thought I was a new girl when Agnes started taking me. And, you know what, Ma. I let them think I was. I let them think Agnes was my real ma.

171

'What right have you to be here, to just saunter back into my life and wreak havoc like you always do? You've never been a mother to me. Ever. Agnes,' Bel continued bitterly, 'has been more of a mother to me than you've ever been. You do not deserve to be called a mother. A mother is meant to love and care for the children she gives birth to. You don't even know the meaning of love. Unless it's opening your legs for some bloke—'

As the last words found their way out of Bel's mouth, Pearl stepped forward and slapped her daughter hard across her face.

The room fell into a shocked silence. They all seemed rooted to the spot as Bel's hand went to her red, stinging cheek.

She then turned, pushed past her mother, and practically staggered down the hallway, before flinging open the front door and running down the street.

'What's got into her?' Pearl asked.

Agnes was speechless, as she stared at her daughter-in-law's mother in disbelief.

Had the woman really no idea?

Polly looked at Joe. They didn't say a word to each other, but they knew what each other was thinking.

'No, I'm going,' Joe told Polly, and she knew there was no arguing with her brother. She knew intuitively he was the one who could sort this out. Make it all right. Hopefully.

Joe grabbed his stick and hurried from the room and out of the house. Polly followed him to the front door and shouted after him: 'She'll have gone to the Victoria Hall. That's where she always used to go when we were small and she was upset.'

Polly watched Joe hobble off at a surprisingly fast pace, using his stick to push himself forward. She desperately wanted to go after him; to take charge and run and find Bel herself, but she knew she was not the right person to go to her sister-in-law's aid at this moment – to help patch together Bel's fractured self.

Joe was the one at whom her anger and resentment had really been directed. Joe was the only person who stood any chance of remedying the situation that had been going on for too long.

Polly could now see exactly why she had been so angry of late. Of course, she was grieving, but there was so much more to it. Polly felt annoyed with herself for not realising before, but she had been dealing with her own grief at losing her brother, as well as her own worries about Tommy. And on top of all that, she felt constantly exhausted by the number of hours she was doing down the yard. She just had not had the energy to put herself in Bel's shoes and walk around in them for a while.

Of course, now she understood – every time Bel looked at Joe she saw Teddy. The torment and the pain of seeing someone all day, every day, who was the double of the man she had loved and lost must be unbearable.

As Polly watched Joe disappear down the street and into the darkness, she turned back into the house. As she walked into the hallway, she saw Lucille sitting on the top step of the stairs. Next to her was Arthur. Lucille had obviously heard her mother's shouting and hysteria and had sought refuge with the old man. Polly counted their blessings that Arthur had come to live with them. He was the one calming presence in their household. And a very much needed one.

As Polly looked up and saw the upset and confusion on the little girl's face, she beckoned to them both. 'Come on down, you two,' she said, forcing a smile and trying to make light of the situation by adding, 'the coast's clear.'

As the pair slowly made their way downstairs, Polly reached to pick up Lucille and give her a comforting cuddle.

'It always seems worse than it is, you know, when someone shouts and cries.' As she spoke she gave Arthur a sad smile, mouthing the words 'thank you' as they went back into the kitchen, where it was now unnaturally quiet.

Polly could see the back of Pearl in the yard, puffing away on a cigarette, and Agnes was sitting staring into the open fire, lost in thought, but on turning to see Lucille wrapped around her aunty Polly, she snapped herself out of her worrisome thoughts and said, 'All right. Let's put the wireless on and listen to some music, and I think I'll treat this bonny little bairn to some Ovaltine . . . How does that sound?' she said, cupping Lucille's face in both her hands.

Lucille answered with a nod, but she still looked distressed. Agnes and Polly knew she had rarely heard any of them raise their voices, or cry, and certainly not lose it in the way Bel just had.

As Agnes walked into the scullery, she heard her granddaughter's unusually quiet voice ask, 'Where Doey?'

Agnes sighed inwardly. This was not going to be a quick fix. But what did she expect? Her son's death had affected so many lives, and the ripples of his leaving them all would continue for a long time to come – that much Agnes knew.

'He's gone to have a walk with your ma,' Agnes heard Polly say. A reassuring white lie.

Agnes just hoped Joe was able to find Bel and bring her back. She had never seen Bel so angry and so out of control. Not even as a child – and Agnes knew Bel had had every right to be volatile as a youngster after the upbringing she had suffered. Agnes looked out at Pearl, lighting another cigarette from the one she had just smoked, and glared daggers at her back. What had made that woman such a self-obsessed and insensitive person, Agnes had no idea.

As she turned and opened the cupboard door in search of the tin of Ovaltine she knew was in there, her whole body wilted when she heard the whirring sound of the air-raid siren start up.

'Oh God, no . . . not tonight of all nights,' she said, slamming the cupboard doors shut and hurrying back out of the scullery.

Chapter Twenty-One

'Bel! Bel!' Joe had just caught sight of her when the sound of the air-raid sirens sounded out across the town.

It had only been by chance that he had seen Bel, as the blackout meant his search for her really was a stab in the dark. Thankfully Polly had been right, and it looked as if Bel was heading for the Victoria Hall on Toward Road, just next to the museum. Why that place had always been her sanctuary in times of trouble, he had no idea. But at least he had reached her before she had made it to the Gothic, cathedral-like entertainment hall she was so drawn to. He could just about make out the back of her slim figure and the thick mop of her bobbed blonde hair due to the anti-aircraft searchlights that had started to poke huge white tapering fingers of light into the brooding, dark skies.

'Bel ... Bel,' he shouted as loudly as he could, in order to be heard over the whining of the sirens now in full flow.

Bel finally heard her brother-in-law's deep voice hollering from behind and she turned around. Her eyes squinted through the sporadic flashes of harsh light and the tears that were blurring her vision. She looked distraught. Joe had never seen his sister-in-law like this ever before – not in all the time he had known her. But then again that wasn't so unusual; she had been Teddy's girl. If she had ever had any problems, or been upset, it had always been his brother she had gone to – even as children, before the pair of them had started stepping out with each other.

As Joe hurried towards her, it occurred to him that his relationship with Bel had always been one of frivolity, fun and laughter; they had had surprisingly few serious conversations during the years they'd spent growing up together.

As Joe neared Bel, he felt his body sag with relief that she had stopped walking and was now standing stock-still, facing him as he approached. He was desperate to reach her before she ran off again, and was managing to make up the distance between the two of them quickly, considering his bad leg was such a hindrance.

'Just leave me alone, Joe!' she shouted above the deafening sound of the air-raid siren. Her head jerked upwards as her attention was suddenly diverted skyward to a blur of red and white lights as tracers let off their rose-coloured beams in spurts.

Bel had got as far as Laura Street before Joe had caught up with her. It was a residential road on the cusp of the town centre. Men, women and children were starting to spill out of terraced houses that lined the road and were beginning to hurry towards the nearest shelters. Doors could be heard banging shut, as could the piercing screams of babies, upset at the rude interruption of their slumber, and the panicked voices of mothers, wrapping up their babies in blankets and shouting at their other children to 'hurry up' and 'keep close' as they fled their homes.

'Bel,' Joe said as he finally reached her. 'We've got to get to a shelter. It's not safe being out here.' He was out of breath. He hadn't realised just how weak he had become over the past few months. He used to be able to run for ages, barely breaking into a sweat, never mind getting out of puff; he had worked with the dead weight of a rivet gun for just about every hour of every working day since he'd turned fourteen, and would still have the stamina for a game of football most evenings. Now his energy was expunged after just a few minutes' dash.

'Just leave me alone,' she repeated.

Joe looked at her exasperated. 'I can't and I won't.'

He grabbed her by the arm in case she decided to make another run for it.

'Besides.' He tried desperately to inject some humour into the dire situation in which they now found themselves. 'If I let you go now, Ma'll have my guts for garters – she'll hang, draw and quarter me . . . and then she'll make my life even more unbearable than it is already!'

It was typical of Joe to resort to such black humour, and to be so overdramatic, although it was true that Agnes would make his life pretty intolerable if he did not bring Bel safely back home. Luckily, his humour caught Bel unawares and in doing so it broke through a weakness in her defences that, until this evening, had been pretty much rock solid.

As Bel looked at her brother-in-law, it was as if she was seeing him for the first time.

This was the Joe she knew. The one who had always made her laugh. Had always made her feel better. How could she hate him so?

And, at that moment of realisation, as she stood there, surrounded by the chaos, noise, and flashing lights, the barricades that she had put around herself went down and the true wretchedness of her soul became visible.

'Oh, Joe, I'm sorry. Please, leave me. I just want to die. I can't go on like this, please just leave me.'

Joe was shocked to the core by Bel's words, but what disturbed him the most was the conviction with which they were spoken.

'Well, you bloody well can't!' His words came out harshly as he pulled her towards him, and practically dragged her forward, along the pavement, his eyes searching around for some kind of shelter, something that would protect them from the inevitable deluge of bombs that were about to be dropped.

'You've got to live, whether you like it or not. You've got the most amazing little girl. And she needs you . . . so if you don't want to live for yourself, you're going to have to damn well keep on living for your daughter's sake,' he shouted at her as he continued to tow her along by his side.

Joe was thankful Bel offered no resistance. All the fight had clearly gone out of her and she was allowing herself to be propelled along the street as he frantically looked for cover – anywhere that would protect them from the Luftwaffe's imminent attack.

'You might think she's better off with Ma and Polly– but you're wrong,'

Joe's words sent a shock of guilt through Bel. He had read her so well. He had seen right through her. He had read every terrible, awful, sinful thought, for that was exactly what she *had* been thinking, more and more so of late – that her daughter *would* be better off with Agnes and sister-in-law.

Joe pulled Bel behind him. One hand had a vice-like hold on her arm, the other was gripping the top of his walking stick, upon which he was pushing down heavily as his leg was now in agony.

Just then there was a massive explosion. The ground underneath them vibrated and they were both covered in a sheet of dust. Neither of them could see a foot in front of them.

For a split second Joe thought he was back in the desert, his vision blinded by the acrid dust from the harsh, water-deprived landscape.

Then, all of a sudden, a vision of Teddy's face showed itself to him through the grimy mist, and his brother's words resounded in his ears. 'Promise me you'll look after Bel.'

Joe reached out and grabbed Bel's hand. It felt so small in his own. He pulled her away and out of the fog of dirt and debris.

With no air-raid shelter nearby, Joe frantically scanned the immediate area and spotted that the front door of one of the houses had been left swinging open. He yanked Bel to the deserted house and over the threshold. He pulled her behind him down the short stretch of hallway to the cupboard under the stairs. He unlatched its little wooden door. 'It's better than nowhere,' Joe said as he put his hand on Bel's head and forced her into the small storage space, which was empty, bar a large sweeping brush and a few buckets. Joe bent over and followed Bel, pulling the door shut and making Bel sit down with him on the wooden floor.

They both sucked in air, trying to regain their breath; coughing, their throats dry.

'Oh my God! I hope Lucille and everyone else is all right.' Bel felt herself starting to panic.

'They'll be fine,' Joe tried to sound as reassuring as possible. 'They would've had time to get to the shelter. Ma will probably be organising everyone now, and getting them to sing along to some song or hymn that everyone knows the words to.'

Bel's mind jumped back to last summer, when Agnes's little lunchtime birthday celebration for Lucille had been ruined by an air raid, and how her innovative mother-in-law had somehow managed to organise a makeshift party in the cellar of the local church they were sheltering in. She knew Joe was right. Lucille couldn't be in better hands.

Joe put his arm around Bel's shoulders. There was hardly room to breathe, never mind move about. Bel was aware of his closeness, the way he was protecting her, and she let him. She could not fight it any more. She simply didn't have the strength, or the will.

'I'm so sorry, Joe,' she said, trying her hardest to hold back the tears.

Finally Bel's anger started to dissipate, allowing her sorrow to seep through. All her deeply buried thoughts and feelings began to find their way to the surface. To the light.

'Oh God, I'm so sorry, Joe,' she repeated. Her words this time accompanied by tears. 'I feel so terrible. I've been such an awful person. I hate myself . . . I've hurt the people I love the most. The people who have loved me the most. I've just been feeling so angry and it's just got worse and worse.'

Joe looked down at Bel's face, now covered in dirt, and he let her talk, held her as her words came tumbling out with increasing speed. He caught some but not all of what she said, but he knew that didn't matter. Bel had finally let go and that was all that mattered.

Bel cried some more and Joe let her. He didn't say anything, just kept holding her in his arms.

'And, Joe,' she said, lifting her face up to look him in the eyes, 'I'm so sorry for what I said back at the house.'

Joe gently squeezed her shoulders to reassure her. 'Well, a lot of it was true. I do look like my brother. I must be a constant reminder of him. We were twins, after all.'

'In looks but not in your personalities . . .' Bel said.

'*Like chalk and cheese,*' they both said in unison.

'I think my ma used to say that so much because she *wanted* us to be different,' Joe said thoughtfully.

'And you are – were – so different,' Bel corrected herself with sadness.

They both continued to chat; all the while Joe held Bel in his arms, his body wrapped around her, protecting her from any harm.

They remained like that for hours. Sometimes they were quiet; listening to the rumblings outside, the distant sound of gunfire and the drone of aeroplanes. When it seemed to calm down, they awaited the call of the all-clear siren, but it never came; instead the earth shook as more bombs were dropped on the town.

Bel gripped Joe's hand when she heard the sounds of the ack-ack guns, and she prayed for the safety of her daughter and the people she loved.

'Please God, let no harm come to them. Keep them safe. They're good people,' she tried to argue her case, hoping that there was some kind of justice to be had amidst all of this terror – this malevolence that was trying so hard to ravage their land.

Joe listened to Bel's quiet murmurings, but did not offer up any of his own pleas to some unseen, omnipotent God. The war had taught him there was no God looking down on them, caring for them. No God ensuring good overcame evil. No God could have allowed the horror to happen that he had witnessed with his own eyes. No God would have allowed the slow, torturous, undignified deaths he had been forced to watch both on the battlefield and in the hospitals where he had been treated.

After a while, Bel's prayers were spent and she started to talk. Slowly, she voiced all her pent-up frustrations at being denied a happy, long life with her husband. She realised as she let the words tumble out of her mouth that she had been killing herself and those around her with her resentments.

'How could I hate the way Lucille is with you?' she asked, but knew there was no answer. 'I'm so sorry, Joe.

I should have been overjoyed my little girl has taken to you so much. That there is a man in her life who can be a good, father-like figure. I always dreamed of having a dad, used to make up stories about who my dad really was, and that someday he'd come back and save me from the miserable life I was living with my ma.

'But,' she added pensively, 'that faded when Agnes took me in.'

Bel's outpourings were punctuated by tears that had been held back for far too long. Joe knew she just needed to let the words drain away her suffering, and so he just held her, and gave her a gentle cuddle every now and again to show her he was listening, that he cared, and that he understood.

'And when my ma turned up . . .' Bel paused, trying to find a way of describing how her mother's sudden reappearance had made her feel, but failing. 'Well, I don't know what to say. It felt like the heavy weight already crushing down on me had just doubled.

'I don't understand her. I can't understand how she can be the way she is. The way she was. She just doesn't seem to think she's done anything wrong . . . And I'm sure she actually tries to wind me up a lot of the time.'

Joe grunted his agreement. 'She's certainly one of a kind.'

There was a pause and they both said in unison, '*Thank goodness!*'

They both laughed, and Bel's residual anger that was finding its way back up to the surface was dispelled.

'Great minds . . .' she said.

'Think alike,' Joe finished off the sentence.

It was something they'd all said as children whenever any of them had spoken the same thoughts at the same time.

'How can I make everything better? How I take back the words I said?' Bel asked.

As her breathing started to even out, Joe reassured her that it would all be fine. That, of course, they all still loved her.

He wanted to add that *he* would *always* love her, but forced the words back, and allowed her to carry on with her outpouring.

'It was like I just couldn't stop myself. Like I'd been overtaken by some terrible demon. Like I was . . .' Bel was stuck for words.

'Turning into your ma.' The words just came out uncensored from Joe's mouth. He surprised himself that he could joke in such a serious situation. But with his words came laughter. Joint laughter from them both.

And as they chuckled, Joe felt a part of his old self return, and at the same time saw the person he knew as Bel shine through for the first time in a long while.

Over the next few hours, as they sat there, with the sirens and the drone of aeroplanes overhead, and the occasional explosion in the distance, the two of them chatted like they used to before the war. Like the friends they always had been.

When the all-clear siren finally sounded out, Joe felt as if he had to forcibly peel his arms from Bel. He felt he could have held her all night long. Wished he could hold her all night long. They had only spent a few hours together, but during that time it had surprised him that his love for Bel had grown. He would never have thought that possible. But she had opened up to him in such a way that his love and concern for her felt even deeper.

More real.

*

184

'Lucille! Agnes!' Bel shouted out as soon as she stepped through the front door that had been left wide open in hopeful anticipation of her and Joe's return.

'Mummy!' Lucille came shooting down the hallway. 'We've been out all night!' she said, full of excitement. Bel picked her up and held her tight.

'Have you now?' Bel inspected her daughter to check for any signs of injury or harm.

'Mummy, we played games for hours,' she chatted on, happily oblivious to her mother's concern. When Bel was satisfied her daughter was unscathed by the evening's events, she gave her another bear hug, before putting her down, and telling her, 'Mummy loves you to bits – you know that, don't you?'

Lucille nodded up to her mum and a big smile spread across her face before she scampered down the hallway and back into the kitchen, bumping into Agnes coming out.

'Thank goodness you're all right.' Agnes hurried towards her daughter-in-law and wrapped her arms around her. As she looked over her shoulder she panicked.

'Where's Joe? Is he okay?'

'Yes, yes, Agnes, he's fine. He wanted to help the rescuers. It's madness out there. Total bedlam.'

'Thank God you're both all right.' She sighed. 'I don't think I could handle it if anything else happened . . .' Her voice trailed off and they both thought of Teddy.

'I'm so sorry, Agnes,' Bel said. 'I've been awful. Truly awful. I'm just so sorry.'

'Shush. As long as you're here now and in one piece,' Agnes told her softly. 'That's the main thing. We'll get through this. Together. I promise.'

Tears came into Bel's eyes, which she brushed away. 'God, I've cried more tonight than I think I have in my entire life,' she said as she gratefully took the hankie that Agnes had pulled out of her cardigan pocket, and blew her nose.

'Well, that's probably no bad thing.' Agnes spoke her words of reassurance just as Pearl's head appeared around the kitchen door.

'Dinnit worry, Isabelle, your old ma's all right. No need to be asking if I'm safe and sound and not been blown to smithereens by some Jerry bomber.'

'No such luck,' Bel mumbled under her breath, forcing Agnes to push back a smile.

The pair walked back into the kitchen to find Polly shuffling the pack of Snap cards, with Lucille impatiently waiting to be dealt her hand.

'So, what's this about you playing games all night?' Bel asked her daughter.

Bel and Polly looked at each other and smiled. Bel knew she had lots of apologising to do, but she wanted to speak to her sister-in-law alone. Their close relationship had ruptured and they needed to sit down together when they were on their own and mend it. Bel wanted her to know just how badly she felt about the way she'd been of late. Not just for being a miserable old cow with a short fuse and a vicious tongue, but because she had not been there to listen to Polly's worries about Tommy.

'Well,' Polly said, as she started to count out two piles of cards with the pictures of animals on them. 'We ended up in one of the neighbour's cellars. It was huge. It was one of the posh houses round the corner – Mum's all matey with her because her daughter sometimes comes here during the day and she told Mum to go there next time there was a raid.

'Lucille loved it because there was a load of other children there and it was all kitted out with toys and games. Lucille was in her element. Happy as Larry.'

As Bel listened to Polly, and watched her daughter eagerly awaiting the start of her game, she noticed her mother slipping out of the back door for a cigarette.

That's one person I won't be apologising to, she thought to herself. *Every word I said to her was meant.* Bel might have felt as if she'd had a terrible demon exorcised from deep within, but she hadn't quite cleansed herself of all her resentments.

Joe's leg was throbbing and the pain he was in was only just bearable, but as he gritted his teeth as he limped home, he felt good about himself. He was filled with a sense that he had been of some use – had done something worthwhile for the first time since he'd been blown off his feet and carted off on a gurney from the front line.

After the all clear had sounded out, and he had been reassured that Bel really was all right and was going to go home, he had followed the sound of the ambulance sirens and those of the fire brigade and found himself looking at the skeletal remains of Victoria Hall. Masses of masonry from its walls had been flung hundreds of yards around its perimeter, leaving only the shell of the building standing. A row of shops nearby had also been wrecked by an explosion in the middle of the street.

As Joe picked his way over the red bricks and rubble, the dust still lingering in the air, he'd heard an air-raid warden shout out, 'Over here!' And for the next few hours he had helped free three firewatchers trapped in the bombed-out shops. The basic first aid he had learnt during his time in North Africa had enabled him to tend to the men when they'd eventually been released from what could so easily have become their cement-encased coffins. Joe was amazed they had surfaced in one piece, never mind alive, and his mind had flashed back to less fortunate souls he had fought alongside – those, like his brother, whose bodies had been blown into bits, and others who had survived but without limbs.

When all the air-raid casualties had been seen to or taken to the Royal Hospital on the other side of town, local residents had set to work clearing away the debris that had blocked off Toward Road and Borough Road.

The pain in Joe's leg had forbidden him to do any more, and he had hobbled his way back home, passing families standing next to small mountains of wood and plaster, made homeless in a matter of seconds. Some were simply standing in shock, staring at the scene in front of them, others were trying desperately to salvage their possessions from the ruins.

His heart went out to them.

As the early morning sun started to peek through, casting light on the darkness, Joe looked up at the artistry of the pink marbled skies of the breaking dawn, and he wondered at the beauty of nature, and how it was in complete contrast to the ugliness of the man-made hell around him.

As he made his way back through the desolation, a surge of relief suddenly hit him.

Thank God Bel had not made it to the Victoria Hall. If she had, she would not be alive now. The news circulating as he left the bombsite was that ten lives had been claimed during the air raid and a hundred and thirty injured.

Bel could have easily been the eleventh life lost last night, crushed under the building she had ironically always treated as her safe haven. A place which had always been associated with tragedy and death. Not many townsfolk would bemoan its loss, for it had been marred since that terrible day back in June 1883,when 183 children had perished after a stampede for the stage when free gifts were handed out.

Was it this that had drawn Bel to this once magnificent building? Had she somehow identified with the tragedy of the lives of those children? Had she been drawn there by some veiled, unconscious desire to bring about her own death?

Hopefully its destruction would reflect the crumbling walls of Bel's bereavement. Perhaps, she could now try to start rebuilding her life without her husband in it, hard though he knew it would still be for her.

As Joe turned the corner on to Tatham Street, he thought of his brother, and for the first time was grateful that Teddy had made him promise to look after his sister-in-law.

Joe was now sure his twin had predicted his own impending death. But had Teddy also known that his wife's life would be in danger – and that it would be up to Joe to save her?

Chapter Twenty-Two

One week later, April 1941

'So, fingers crossed it stays like this. The only spanner in the works is Pearl, but at least we've got our Bel back. And Joe's leg is on the mend. It's like a great big dark cloud has been lifted from over our house.'

The women welders had decided to forgo their usual trip to the canteen and were sitting around on stacked-up pallets, drinking tea from stainless-steel thermos cups and eating their home-made sandwiches. Polly had just finished telling her workmates all about the night of the air raid when Bel had lost it and run off into the night, pursued by Joe, and how she had returned exhausted, but clearly unburdened and, more importantly, back to a semblance of her former self.

Polly looked up at the midday sun shining through the overhead gantries and towering wooden staithes, and felt it really was a case of nature reflecting life. The weather, like the atmosphere in the Elliot household, had finally turned. There was still a nip in the air, but there was a clear blue sky above and rays of sunlight were shining down on them all.

'That is the best news,' Hannah said, putting the stress on the word best.

'Yes, the best news,' Martha repeated with a big smile, showing off the big gap in her two front teeth and half a mouthful of a cheese and pickle sandwich.

'Now you just need to sort out that nightmare of a mother-in-law,' Gloria said, unbuttoning her jacket as she sat back, revealing her now substantial bump. She knew she couldn't make out it was simply a case of middle-age spread for much longer, and was bracing herself for the repercussions when Rosie went to see the powers that be to tell them about her condition.

'I reckon you should send that old cow Pearl packing,' Dorothy said only half jokingly. 'She's nothing but trouble by the sounds of it. Out all night on the razz and up to God knows what.'

'Sounds like someone I know,' Angie said, appearing from behind their makeshift seats and causing them all to turn round.

'Well, it takes one to know one, Ange,' Dorothy reprimanded her friend in a mock matronly manner.

Angie sidled up to Dorothy and pulled out a big brown paper bag. 'Well, yer all ganna want to know me when I show yer what I've got.' She opened the top of the bag and held it out so that they could all see the contents.

'I'll do yer all a deal,' she said with a cheeky smile on her face. 'A good bit of gossip for these lovely iced buns.'

Angie had bought the buns on Sunday morning from the bakery near to where she lived in Monkwearmouth, which sold leftovers from a hatch in the wall at the rear of the shop. She'd queued up for ages in the cobbled back lane, but it had been worth it as she'd managed to get the slightly battered buns for just a few pennies.

'Ah, Angela,' Gloria said, 'you're a little star.' Her sugar craving had not once abated as her pregnancy had progressed, but rather increased. Even if she had been offered a chunk of prime beef, she would happily have exchanged it for a bag of the white stuff.

'Are you sure you don't want to come and work with us?' Rosie said, leaning over to pick out her sticky bun from the proffered paper bag. Dorothy looked at Rosie and knew that her words had been said in a jocular manner, but that she meant every word. Rosie had tried to persuade Angie numerous times to swap the operating lever of her crane for a welding rod, but with no joy. Angie always laughed off the suggestion, as she did now.

'You must be kidding! Why would anyone swap sitting on their backside all day and twiddling a few knobs with being on yer feet all day welding great big sheets of metal?'

'Because you'd be with us!' Martha's words were spoken just before she demolished her finger-shaped doughy treat in two mouthfuls. Everyone laughed. They all loved it when Martha chipped in to the conversation. And lately she had shown them all that behind that simple-looking façade lay quite a sharp sense of humour.

'Yes, Martha.' Rosie smiled. 'That would most definitely be the case, providing, of course' – she cast a theatrical glare over to their gentle giant – 'no one defects and goes off to join the riveters!'

There was a general murmur of agreement, as they all knew Jimmy the head riveter had his eye on Martha and was trying every which way he could to get her to join his team.

Rosie looked at her mixed assortment of women welders and wanted to add that there might soon be no more 'us' left, after her meeting with Helen later on in the day when she was going to tell her about Gloria's pregnancy. Rosie was going to have to fight tooth and nail just to keep Gloria at the yard, never mind as a welder. She was determined, though, that she was not going to let her little group of women welders go down without a fight. She was getting her guns spiked in anticipation of her meeting, and had organised a get-together with her union rep just before the inevitable locking of horns with Helen. Rosie knew next to nothing about a woman's employment rights once she had fallen pregnant. And why would she? It had never been a concern of hers before. She had no intention of having a baby herself and, apart from that, she had never even known any *women* shipyard workers, never mind ones who ended up in the family way.

Rosie knew Helen would use Gloria's condition as an opportunity to finally get her team of women welders disbanded. With Gloria gone, all she would need to do was prove that Hannah wasn't up to scratch, which would not be hard, and then give in to Jimmy's pleas and move Martha over to the riveters. That would leave her with just Polly and Dorothy, who would then be separated and sent to work at opposite ends of the yard.

Helen would not only have won but, more worryingly, the break-up of her squad would have massive repercussions for the women themselves.

Gloria's employment at the yard had been her lifeline; she needed the support of her friends, and would need it even more after the baby arrived.

As a fairly recent refugee to the country, Hannah did not know anyone else in her new hometown, apart from her aunty Rina, and would not only be out of work, but also incredibly lonely.

Martha, without doubt, would head straight back to her non-verbal world if she had to work day in day out with a load of blokes she did not know, and who would have no idea how to deal with her.

Dorothy, as the youngest of the group, would most definitely be taken advantage of. She tried to act all worldly-wise, but she was very vulnerable underneath all that puffed-up false confidence. Rosie knew the men in the yard wouldn't be able to see beyond her pretty looks, or appreciate what a skilled and valuable welder she actually was.

And Polly, of course, would stay on at the yard come hell or high water, regardless of how difficult her love rival made her life, but she would miss her 'family of friends', as she liked to call them all. Since her brother had died, she had come to rely heavily on the women for their support and advice.

And Rosie had to also admit that she too would be totally devastated if she did not have her band of women welders. She loved these women. Apart from the fact they'd saved her life, they were the only true friends she had ever had. They had all been through so much in such a short period of time. They knew her, and liked her. They accepted her – and moreover they didn't judge her.

As she mentally braced herself for her late afternoon showdown with Helen, Rosie ate her iced bun without tasting it and resolved that she would fight to the bitter end to keep them all together at the yard. She wasn't going to lose them now. And certainly not because some vindictive, spoilt young woman with more money than sense wanted revenge simply because she hadn't got her man.

As the women all silently ate their pastries, Dorothy looked about her and saw the pensive look etched on her boss's scarred face. Dorothy might like acting the fool, but she was far from stupid, and it did not take a genius to work out that their little gang was under threat.

As she turned to look at Angie, now sitting next to her, and then over to Gloria, who was picking the icing off the top of her bun and looking as though she was in some kind of gastronomic heaven, an idea came into her head.

'Hey, Ange,' she said quietly, 'let's have a quick walk over to the canteen to have a neb around – see if there's any new talent about.'

Angie laughed. 'Eee, Dor, yer never give up, do you?'

They both jumped off the pallet they were sitting on and hurried off across the yard.

'Man-mad, the pair of yer,' Gloria shouted after them, licking her lips. 'I just hope you're both careful and don't end up like me,' she added, running a hand over her bump.

Martha also watched the pair hurry off across the yard, gabbing away to each other, but something told her Dorothy's quest, for once, was not about getting a man, but something else entirely.

'You seen any more of Vinnie?' Polly asked Gloria as she finished off her bun with a swig of tea.

'No, thank goodness.' Gloria sighed. 'But I'm going to have to face him soon. He's going to realise that this baby is staying put and he's going to have to tell Sarah. And when he does, I'll have him knocking on my door, there's no doubt about that.'

'Well, as long as he's not hammering it down,' Rosie chipped in. 'Otherwise he'll be getting more than a letter from the solicitors.'

They all knew Rosie meant every word she said as she got up and wandered off to check the welding machines before the start of the afternoon shift.

Helen watched the women welders eating their iced buns from behind the venetian blinds of the accounts office, which had been pulled down due to the bright glare of the afternoon sun coming across the river. The thick wooden slates and the tape crisscrossing the windows in anticipation of an air raid provided Helen with a good vantage point from where she could spy on the women – women she hated with a passion. Women she was determined she was going to get rid of, come hell or high water. She was going to break up their jolly little group if it was the last thing she did. She was going to pick them off. One by one. Starting with the peaky little Jewish girl. She would be the first to go.

Helen reckoned she could get shot of the lot of them, and even if she couldn't banish them all from the yard, she was damn well going to get rid of most of them; any remaining hangers-on would be separated and their working life made hell. She would see to that. She only hoped her father stayed in America for as long as possible, or at least long enough for her to achieve her goal.

She knew that Jack would most certainly scupper her plans if he came back before she had had a chance to do what she wanted to do. She knew he had a soft spot for the women, although heaven only knew why. It was not as if he could possibly find any of them attractive.

Martha was like a man, Dorothy was young enough to be his daughter, and Hannah looked young enough to be his *granddaughter*. Rosie was very womanly and had been attractive once, but was now scarred and, as the saying went, was 'spoilt goods'.

And then there was Gloria, who was around the same age as her dad, and who Helen had heard from her mum had once gone steady with her father another lifetime ago, but lately she had started to resemble a female version of Fatty Arbuckle. She had become a right heffalump these past few months. She was the only woman Helen knew who was putting on weight in these times of food shortages and rationing.

And then, of course, there was Polly.

Why had Tommy thought her so bloody perfect? Helen silently fumed. She stamped her foot on the floor, trying to stop herself thinking about *that woman*. There weren't enough words to describe the pure hatred she had for Polly. She still could not get over Tommy choosing that scruffy little welder over her. Helen had men falling over themselves to take her out on a date, and she had lost count of the number of times she'd been told she was the double of either Vivien Leigh or Hedy Lamarr. So why had he preferred Polly? She really had no idea – but he had, hadn't he? And he'd not just favoured her, *but asked her to marry him.*

Helen was once again filled with the familiar feeling of being totally wronged.

She wanted to scream: *The injustice of it all! Tommy had been hers! She and Tommy had known each other most of their lives!*

Which made it even more infuriating that this overall-clad upstart from the town's east end, who had only met Tommy when she'd started work here, had snatched him from under her nose.

God, it still made her blood boil.

And to add insult to injury, one of her little welder friends had found out that she had spread a rumour that Polly was seeing one of the yard's platers, Ned Pike, and had gone and told his wife. It had been annoying enough that she had not realised the bloke was married, let alone that his wife was heavily pregnant, but it was beyond humiliating when the woman had marched into the yard and actually yelled at Helen, calling her a 'sly, conniving bitch'. The words were still imprinted in her head.

Which was another reason why not just Polly should suffer her wrath, but all the other women as well.

As Helen watched Gloria demolishing the rest of her pastry, she laughed out loud in the empty office; the entire department had gone outside to eat their lunch, craving the sunlight they'd been starved of for so long.

'No wonder you've got fat, dear, eating like that,' she said aloud to herself, smoothing down her figure-hugging tweed skirt and turning away from the window. As she made her way out of the office and down the stairs, she laughed again at her own venomous observations: 'You should give it to Hannah – she could do with some meat on her.'

Helen waggled her way across the yard, enjoying, as she always did, the leering looks and racy comments from the male workers, who had learnt they could get away with it. When she reached her destination, Rosie was just surfacing from behind a load of welding machines.

'I have a very important appointment later on, Rosie.' Helen was lying. She had no such 'appointment', but she wanted to show Rosie who was boss, especially as she had no idea why Rosie had asked to have a meeting with her or what she wanted to talk to her about. 'So I'd like to have our little chat now, if that's all right by you?'

It wasn't really a question – more of a demand.

Rosie responded with a scowl, and Helen had to fight the feeling of intimidation she always got around the yard's head welder. Helen knew she would never get rid of Rosie – that was one battle she had realised she would never be able to win. Rosie was an unknown entity, which was why she had to be on her guard. She was peculiar. What woman in her right mind *wanted* to work in the shipyards, never mind encourage other women to work there too. She was like one of those suffragettes she had learnt about at her girls-only, very expensive, and very boring school on the town's Mowbray Road.

Just as long as she doesn't chain herself to the yard's gates when I put my plan into action, Helen thought.

'Looks like I don't have a say in the matter.' Rosie's voice had a very definite chill to it.

'We'll go to my office,' Helen told her.

'Jack's office?' Rosie made the question sound genuine, although she knew perfectly well that was where Helen meant. It was a veiled reminder that Helen's position was just temporary; she was only boss until her father returned.

And how Rosie wished Jack was back.

Jack was such a nice, decent bloke. How he'd sired such an abomination of a woman she would never know. Helen was the antithesis of her father; by the sounds of it she took after her mother; she had heard from those who knew the family that Helen was a carbon copy of Miriam – in both looks and personality.

Helen forced a tight smile and told Rosie that was exactly where she meant, before the pair walked off for their impromptu meeting, watched with a degree of dread by the women.

They did not have a good feeling.

Rosie and Helen's departure coincided with the end of the lunch break, and as the women were gathering up their equipment to start work again, Jimmy appeared.

'Hey, Martha, you're with us this afternoon.'

There was no Rosie about to say otherwise, so Martha reluctantly put down her welding rod, took off her helmet and followed the riveter's foreman.

A few minutes later the head plater arrived and told Hannah that she was to work with them on the ship's hull this afternoon.

'Boss's orders,' was all he said.

Hannah reluctantly put down her tools and did as she was told. Her face, though, looked woeful, and she was clearly on the verge of tears.

Dorothy, Gloria and Polly all looked at each other.

'Rosie's not going to be at all happy about this,' Polly said.

'I know,' Gloria agreed, 'and there're no prizes for guessing who's behind it all.'

For once Dorothy did not say anything, but she thought all the more. She had been the one to tell Ned's wife about the malicious rumour Helen had spread, the outcome of which had been better than she could have wished for; but she should have known Helen would never forgive or forget. She was baying for blood, and it was not just Polly she was determined to rip to shreds – but them all.

'Am I hearing you correctly?'

Helen put on her best speaking voice, as she knew it had the effect of making most people feel subservient. Helen wanted to rub Rosie's nose in the fact that not only had she benefited from a top-notch education, but that she was a cut above, and certainly a class above her.

Furthermore, she needed every advantage she could muster. She hated to admit it, and she certainly made sure it never showed through, but she always felt a little out of her depth whenever she had any kind of dealings with Rosie. An effect people rarely had on her.

When Rosie had come to work in the office for a short time last year after her accident and wasn't able to weld for a while, Helen had felt uncomfortable in her presence. She couldn't put her finger on why, but the woman made her feel uneasy. When Rosie had opted to go back to work in the yard, Helen had been more than a little relieved, especially as anyone in their right mind would have jumped at the chance of working full time in the administration department. Her father had it all set up for her, soft touch that he was.

But, no, Rosie had chosen to return to the backbreaking shifts required as a shipyard worker, and had done so at a time when they were in the middle of the worst winter they had endured for a long time, certainly in her lifetime.

'Yes, Helen, you are hearing me *correctly*,' Rosie said. 'What is it that you are struggling to understand?'

Over the years, Rosie had managed to curtail her northeast accent, but she had not lost the hard vowel sounds or the singsong inflection in her speech.

Helen let out a breath.

'Well, to be honest, Rosie, I'm having difficulty understanding how a woman of her age is in the condition she's in. Isn't she too old to get pregnant?'

Rosie kept her voice level. 'Obviously not.'

'Well,' Helen said dismissively, 'she'll just have to go. We can't have her heaving her great big belly around the yard. It's just not practical.'

Helen's mind was racing and, as she was speaking, she felt a thrill of excitement. This was better than she had expected. She had thought Rosie wanted to see her about something boring, like buying in new welding rods or helmets, *not to tell Helen that one of her much-loved team was up the duff.* She had thought the woman was just getting fat, not eating for two.

Rosie had to bite her tongue, before adding as coolly and as professionally as possible, 'I'm afraid it doesn't work like that, Helen. There are rules to be adhered to. Employment laws to be abided by.' But her outward confidence belied her uncertainty. Rosie knew she was skating on thin ice: she had no idea what the rules and regulations were, or if, in fact, there were any. It had been for this very reason that she had arranged the chat with her union rep a little later on, in anticipation of her scheduled meeting. She'd been caught on the hop by Helen bringing the meeting forward.

'Well, we'll see about that,' Helen said, moving over to the door and opening it to show Rosie that their meeting was now over. She was determined to end their little tête-à-tête on a high note, and could not wait to be on her own to digest this unexpected and rather excellent news. She could now get rid of Gloria in one fell swoop, followed by Hannah, and then Martha. The dismantling of the women welders' group might be happening sooner than anticipated.

As Rosie walked out through the door, she stopped and looked at Helen. She wanted to say so much. But she did not. Instead she simply said, 'We'll speak again in the next week or so.' She then immediately turned on her heel and walked back out of the office door, allowing it to slam shut behind her.

When Rosie arrived back at the welders' work area, she was fuming.

When she learnt that Martha had been ordered to go and work with Jimmy's squad of riveters, and that Hannah had been hauled off to work with the platers, she struggled to keep a lid on her simmering rage.

Calm down and use your head, Rosie, she told herself.

She had to play this one right. And she needed time to work out her strategy. Helen might have the advantage after this first skirmish, but Rosie was determined to win the war.

Chapter Twenty-Three

Monday 28 April 1941

In the middle of a particularly confused and muddled dream, Bel heard the distant, troubled sound of someone crying out. In pain or anguish. Or both. Her dream was fast becoming a nightmare as the man's voice started shouting out indiscernible words. Then the words changed into a long, mournful howl.

Bel's eyes snapped open.

The dream disappeared into the ether in an instant, but the disturbing audio track continued. She could still hear the terrible cries.

It took her brain a few seconds to comprehend that the disturbing sounds were not a part of the illusions of her night-time slumber.

They were real. And they were coming from the room next door.

It was Joe, and he was clearly in the midst of a horrendous night terror. Without thinking, Bel tossed back her bedclothes and hurried out into the hallway and then straight into Joe's bedroom. She didn't bother to knock, as it was unlikely she would be heard above the alarming din he was now making.

As her eyes adjusted to the dark, Bel could just about make out the thrashing shape of Joe. He was dripping with sweat and tangled up in his sheet. His quilt had been tossed to the floor.

'Joe. Joe,' Bel whispered, but it was no good. He was too deeply immersed in the depth of his nightmare.

All of a sudden he shouted out, 'No! Don't! No!'

Bel automatically raced over to the side of his bed and placed both hands on his arms, which were frantically thrashing about, punching the air and flaying around as if he was fighting off a horde of demons.

Holding them down firmly, in case he caught her with a clenched fist, Bel gently shook him. 'Joe. Wake up!'

This time she wasn't whispering. 'You're having a bad dream. Wake up. Everything's all right.' She stared down at his face, which was contorted with a mixture of agony and anger.

As she stared at Joe she saw he was in pure torment, in some kind of terrible purgatory. She leant nearer to his face. 'Please, Joe, wake up.'

At that moment, Joe's eyes opened, and for the briefest of seconds Bel saw the fear and horror within them. She had never seen eyes saturated with such fright.

'Joe, you are all right. You're here. At home. In your bed.' Bel's instinct told her to immediately reassure him, tell him where he was; that he was safe.

Joe blinked, and the abominations spilling across his mind went – or were at least temporarily pushed back.

'Bel,' Joe slurred. His voice was still slow with sleep. 'God. Where am I?'

His confusion lifted as his mind made the crossover back to reality.

'Bel,' he said, now sounding more awake. 'Blimey. I thought you were an angel hovering over me.'

He smiled up at his sister-in-law's worried face. 'I thought I'd died and gone to heaven.' He forced a laugh.

'Oh, Joe.' Bel could not believe he was making a joke after what she had just seen him going through. Even though she knew the heinousness he had clearly just experienced had only been in his mind, she was pretty sure the nightmare he had just endured had once been his reality. The real-life recollections of a vicious and inhumane war.

Joe became aware of Bel's hands on his arms, still gripping him. He stopped himself telling her that he was fine, in the hope that he might feel her touch for just a few seconds more.

Realising that she was still pinning him down, Bel felt an instant stab of embarrassment. 'I'll let you go now,' she said, giving an awkward little smile.

She looked at Joe and saw that, despite his attempts at joviality, his distress still lay just beneath the surface.

'Do you want to talk about it?' she asked gently.

'No, no, I'm fine, really,' Joe said, but Bel knew he wasn't.

'I'm just sorry for waking you up. I must have been making a right racket?'

Joe had been in hospital with men who had had the dreaded night terrors, and the sounds they made were awful. Not human. More like an animal. An animal that was trapped and in extreme distress. He shuddered to think that he too had been making such sounds. He could see by the look on Bel's face that it had been disturbing. Bad enough to have her dashing out of her own bed and into his room. Something he knew she would never have done unless she had been really perturbed.

He was annoyed with himself. His nightmares had been pretty constant since he had nearly had his limbs blown off. Since he had seen others who had had their limbs blown off. So why was he now crying out in his sleep? The screams had always stayed in his head. Why were they now finding their way out into the open, for all and sundry to hear?

'Joe, you can't help what your head does. Especially when you're asleep,' she tried to reassure him.

'I should know. Look what my mind was making me do, and *that was when I was wide awake.*'

They both laughed.

Despite his own mortification that Bel had seen him in such a state, it was so lovely to see her back to the way she had been. He knew she would never be exactly the Bel of old, but her fundamental essence had been resurrected. That was the main thing.

'Well, you know what your ma says,' Bel said. '"Better out . . ."'

'". . . than in".' Joe finished off Agnes's well-worn mantra.

'I'm just glad you woke me up,' Joe said. And he meant every word; had wanted to add that the awfulness he had just relived had been worth it just to have her wake him up, to have her there now, sitting on the side of his bed.

Before either of them had a chance to say anything else, they both heard another cry, only this one was far less scary – and much more demanding.

'Mummy!' Lucille had woken and realised that her mother was not in her usual place, tucked up in the bed next to her cot.

'Ah, her ladyship awakes,' Bel said with a smile.

Joe put his arm behind his head to prop himself up. 'Thanks, Bel,' he said.

Bel looked down at her brother-in-law as she stood up. She would have liked to have given him a cuddle. He'd been through so much. More than any of them would ever know or understand. And yet he had put up with her sharp tongue and foul moods for months and been nothing but kind and supportive.

'You're welcome, Joe.'

But before she went to see to the needs of her daughter, Bel quickly grabbed hold of Joe's hand and gently squeezed it before bidding him goodnight.

Joe lay there listening to Bel gently coaxing Lucille to sleep. He smiled when he heard her start singing the softest of lullabies. He had listened to her before when his little niece had woken during the night, and Bel's gentle melody had not only comforted and reassured her daughter but also Joe himself.

Joe knew he probably would not sleep now for the rest of the night, but that didn't bother him. He didn't want to go back into that godforsaken world Bel had just woken him from, and more than anything he wanted to enjoy the feeling she had left him with.

Since the night of the air raid two weeks ago, a heavy, dark cloak had been lifted from the house, and it had made everyone living under its roof so much chirpier. The closeness and friendship Joe had shared with Bel before he and Teddy had left for war was gradually returning, and they had even recently shared the odd joke and had the occasional laugh together.

Bel had also made things up with Polly, which had put a smile on his sister's face. Now he would often find them both at the kitchen table, cup of tea in hand, chatting away. Usually it would be Polly telling Bel some gossip from the yard, or showing her a recent letter from Tommy, and he could tell that Bel was all ears and enjoying every morsel her sister-in-law was feeding her.

He knew Bel missed the lively chatter of working on the buses, but since she'd been asked to leave that day, she hadn't shown any real interest in returning; and Agnes was pretty reliant on having her here at home helping out. He doubted his mum could do without her now.

There was, of course, still an unmistakable sadness behind Bel's eyes, but that was to be expected. Teddy had only been taken from them four months previously.

Joe, however, still hadn't been hit by the kind of sorrow he had seen in Bel. He felt that he should be experiencing just a little of the grief he had seen in his brother's widow, but he was not, and it bothered him – greatly. He was not mourning Teddy's death in a way he felt he should be. He missed him massively; sometimes he turned and expected him to be there and was surprised when he wasn't. They had been so emotionally close all of their lives – had even been in close physical proximity to each other most of the time. But Joe had not experienced the kind of deep melancholy he thought was normal – that he should be enduring. He argued with himself that Teddy would not have wanted him to be miserable or sad, but it disturbed him that he had not been subjected to even a modest amount of malaise.

He felt anger at what he had witnessed out in the desert; he felt murderous towards Hitler and the sheer coldbloodedness of his actions, the atrocities being enacted; and he felt a raging fury that this war had taken his brother from him – but he didn't feel bereaved.

When he had been informed of his brother's death, he had been heartbroken. It had felt as if he had lost half of himself. And he had, in many ways. He and Teddy had been so close. Right up until the end. They had been born together, brought up together, worked together, and had even fought in the same regiment as each other, side by side. Joe had felt guilty that he had survived and his brother had not. It made more sense for Teddy to have been spared, as he had a wife and child. Joe had no one. Not even a girlfriend. Yet he had been the one to live.

He did not know why Teddy had been taken, only that there seemed to be no logic to anything any more. What had happened to Teddy had happened. It was war. It was indiscriminate. All reason flew out of the window. The world was now topsy-turvy, as were his emotions, and instead of feeling sorrow for his brother's death, he felt love for his widow. If that wasn't completely upside down and back to front, he didn't know what was.

Since arriving back home, his thoughts hadn't been with his brother, but consumed entirely with his brother's wife, and that had doubled his guilt. But he couldn't stop the way his heart pounded when Bel was around, the way he wanted to care for her, love her – and caress her. He wanted and desired his brother's wife, and he knew it was wrong. So, why did it feel so right?

He wondered whether on some primeval level he saw Bel as a free woman, as she was no longer married, but a widow, and death had released her from her marriage vows. Joe knew how awful that must sound, and he would never express those thoughts to anyone. But was there some truth in it?

It didn't matter whether there was or wasn't, though, he could not stop, or even ignore the way he felt. He had already tried and failed. He had accepted now that he was not able to beat down the longing he had for her, but he knew that he had to do his utmost to hide the way he felt. Out of common decency for Bel and for those he loved. They would hate him if they knew what really lay in his heart and in his loins, and he didn't want to see or hear any more hatred in his life for as long as he lived. He had had his fill. Had seen the physical reality of hatred, and the pain and suffering it caused.

As he lay there, half asleep, half listening to Bel quietly singing Lucille her lullaby, Joe felt a great relief that Bel had finally come out of the ghastly fugue in which she had been locked.

As he started to doze off, his mind held the picture of Bel's tired, worried face leaning down over him, looking at him, and he heard the soft resonance of her voice in his head saying his name, telling him he was home, and that everything was all right.

There was a love there, even though it might only be the love of one friend to another, the love of a sister towards her brother – but the love and care he had felt from her this evening had lifted him up, and left him with the most wonderful feeling, which no amount of night terrors could spoil.

Chapter Twenty-Four

'Morning all!' Pearl declared as soon as she stepped foot in the kitchen. She always liked to make her presence known, unless she was sneaking in late at night.

'You're up early, Ma? What's the occasion?' Bel asked sarcastically. She might have been in a much better mood of late, and she might well have extinguished many of her resentments, but there were still a few lingering about.

'Well, it was that lovely lullaby I heard yer singing last night – made me sleep like a baby.' She took a big slurp of tea, before adding, 'Wasn't quite sure whether it was Lucille or Joe you were singing it to?'

Pearl had crept in late last night and caught a glimpse of her daughter sitting on the side of Joe's bed through his half-opened bedroom door. After tiptocing to the top of the stairs she had stood quietly, trying to listen to them both, but after a few minutes Lucille had woken and cried out.

Pearl's insinuating words made Bel almost choke on her tea. She was just about to tear into her and demand to know what she was implying, when Agnes banged a fresh pot of tea on to the kitchen table. She too had heard Bel comforting Joe. The whole street must have heard him crying out in his sleep.

'Your daughter's got a lovely voice, hasn't she, Pearl? We're always saying she should go on the stage – what with her film-star looks and lean to the theatrical.'

Pearl emitted a short puff of air through her lips, giving off an air of derision. It was one of her habits that Bel found really annoying.

'Bel,' Joe quickly explained, 'came to my rescue last night when I was having a bad nightmare. Thankfully she brought me out of it before I ended up waking the whole house.' As he spoke, though, he had the distinct impression that Pearl knew exactly what he felt towards her daughter.

'And,' he continued, 'the lullaby was for your grand-daughter's ears, although, like you, the sound certainly helped me get back off to sleep. I reckon our Bel should – what's the right phrase – *cut a record*? She'd make a fortune selling her dulcet tones to the nation's insomniacs.'

Polly had caught the barbed interaction as she was getting her sandwiches ready for work and suppressed a laugh. Joe was always quick off the mark. He was no one's fool, although he had his work cut out with Pearl. She could be a piece of work. Always stirring things up.

'See you all tonight!' Polly made quick her escape to a chorus of, 'Bye, Pol,' along with her mother's usual: 'Take care in that yard of yours!'

Agnes's anxieties about her daughter's welfare at work seemed to have been revived since Teddy's death. Polly knew it was understandable, and tried to reassure her mum that she was always really careful and that Rosie was a stickler about health and safety.

'Eee, Isabelle, yer reminded me of that woman, what was her name, Mrs O'Connor?' Pearl persevered.

'O'Cann,' Bel corrected her. She felt her body stiffen at the recollection of the room she'd been brought up in before Agnes had come to her rescue and this house had become more or less her permanent home. 'I'm surprised you can remember, Ma. Wasn't as if you were there much.'

Bel's comment was meant to cut deep, and for once it looked as though her words had hit their mark.

'I remember that tribe of bairns she had and the noise they all used to make,' Pearl bit back, determined not to show her daughter's words had hurt.

'Could never get a wink of sleep with all their carry-on and the constant wailing of babies. God, that woman seemed to drop one every time her fella as much as looked at her.'

Pearl took another swig of tea. 'Ah, well, enough reminiscing about the good ole days, time for my morning smoke.' And with that she was on her feet and out of the back door, not giving her daughter the chance to respond with another stinging comment.

Agnes sat down in the chair Pearl had been occupying and poured her tea into her saucer and blew on it. She gave Bel a sad smile.

'Let it go,' she said to an angry-looking Bel. 'You're going to have to let it go, otherwise it'll eat away at you.'

'I know, Agnes,' Bel said. 'I know. But I just can't.'

Chapter Twenty-Five

Helen had arrived at work just after seven, as she always liked to get in before any of her staff. Her father had told her she had to work harder and longer hours if she was going to be accepted as management. He'd reiterated his words of advice in the weeks leading up to his departure when he'd been prepping her on the ins and outs of his job, adding, 'And that's not just because you're my daughter – but for the very fact you're a woman.'

Helen had been enjoying the relative quiet, before the daily unrelenting clamour of the yard started up, when all of a sudden Rosie appeared at the entrance to her office.

'Oh, Rosie, you gave me a surprise there. I didn't hear you come up the stairs.'

Helen tried to sound nonchalant, but in reality she had got more than a surprise – she'd just about jumped out of her skin.

Rosie too liked to get into work early. Jack had also given the same advice to Rosie when she had started at the yard at the tender age of sixteen, and again after she had been promoted to head welder a couple of years ago – a position a woman had never held in the yard in all its long history.

Rosie had heeded his advice, although today her motiv-ation for getting in before the start of her shift was driven by a very different reason. This time *she* wanted to be the one to catch Helen out unawares, just like Helen had done to her yesterday.

'I thought we'd have a quick chat about *my* squad,' Rosie said. She was pleased to see Helen's startled look on her perfectly made-up face.

'And,' she continued, 'I have to put the stress on the word *my*. Because it is *my squad*. No one else's. So, if any of my welders are going to be moved about to other parts of the yard, to work with other teams, then I'll be the one sanctioning that. Not you.'

Helen's mouth dropped open.

This had been totally unexpected. *She* had been intending to call Rosie into the office later on today to tell her what she had learnt from the solicitor engaged by the shipyard to advise on any kind of legal issues relating to employment or compensation. She had been over the moon with what she'd found out, and had arrived at work this morning champing at the bit, ready to enjoy the look on Rosie's face when she told her.

She was annoyed she'd had the wind taken out of her sails and was now having to deal with the fall-out caused by her own meddling yesterday.

'Well, if you're talking about Hannah and Martha, then I'm afraid you're wrong. In times of what is deemed "extreme need", I can put any of the workers in any part of the yard. And yesterday there was an "extreme need". The riveters were desperately short, as they seem to be all the time at the moment, and needed an extra worker to complete a job that it was imperative to finish by the end of the day. And, let's face it, Rosie, Martha's probably got the strength of two men, so she was the obvious choice . . . And as for Hannah.' Helen took a breath and tried unsuccessfully to keep a spiteful, belligerent smile from spreading across her face. 'Well, the platers needed a welder and I thought she'd be the best choice. I mean, she's such a natural, isn't she?'

Her last words were spoken in an unmistakably catty and sarcastic manner.

Rosie fought to keep her temper. She was on dodgy territory when it came to Hannah; she knew she couldn't say too much as it might well further jeopardise Hannah's position. Rosie wasn't quite sure if Helen had cottoned on to the fact she was constantly trying to find pick-up work for the group's little bird, or any other light welding jobs that weren't too physically or technically demanding.

'Well, next time,' Rosie said firmly, staring daggers at Helen, who had by now managed to position herself behind her big stainless-steel desk, either as a way of asserting her authority over Rosie, or for a form of protection, 'you ask me first, otherwise I'll be forced to seek advice from the union. If you'd done this to any other manager or group head they'd have been straight on to their rep. I may be a woman, but I'm no different and don't expect to be treated any differently.'

Helen was very tempted to make some kind of derogatory remark relating to Rosie's categorisation of herself as a woman, especially as she now had those awful scars everyone pretended not to notice, but she was unsure how Rosie would react, and so she held her tongue. She might have revelled in the moment of being a total bitch to Rosie's face, but she knew there would most likely be repercussions if she did let rip. And what was more, Rosie was well established in the yard, and, annoyingly, generally well liked; Helen had to play her cards right and keep this as professional as possible. If she overstepped personal boundaries she would not do herself any favours. Instead, she decided it was time to play her trump card.

'While you're here, Rosie, we might as well discuss Gloria. And her future in the yard. I've talked to the company's legal adviser and, well, there's no two ways about it, Gloria's going to have to go. As a pregnant woman she's not entitled to any kind of leave, nor do we have to keep her job open for her.'

Rosie's heart sank. She had hoped Helen would have been too busy getting her nails painted, or sipping cocktails in the Grand with some other of the town's '*nouveau riche*' (a term she had learnt from Lily). She'd underestimated her. Helen had clearly done her research. Just like Rosie had done last night when she'd met with her union rep to chat about a woman's maternity rights – or rather, the complete lack of them. The government might have put into force various health benefits for an expectant mum, but there was no legislation whatsoever relating to a pregnant woman's employment rights. It was going to make her battle with Helen much harder. In fact, she was pretty much devoid of any ammunition, but that didn't mean she was going to lie down without a fight. Her women needed her. And she'd made a vow last year when they had rescued her from her uncle's clutches that she would always be there for them, as they had been for her.

'That may well be, Helen,' she said slowly, her mind racing at a rapid rate of knots. Rosie hadn't worked out what she was going to do yet, and had been caught on the hop by Helen's industriousness. She had to think on her feet, and fast. 'But I think you're jumping the gun a bit. Gloria's only a few months pregnant.' Rosie hoped she hadn't gone red. She was a terrible liar, and whenever she told even just a white lie, she would turn a colour which perfectly matched her name.

'She's got a good few months left before she'll have to stop work. As her direct manager, *I'll* decide when I feel that it's time for her to move on.'

Rosie kept her face as stony as possible, knowing she was winging it.

Helen was just about to say something when the start of the shift horn blared out.

'Right, got to get back to the yard,' Rosie declared, backing out of the office just as a chattering group of administration clerks and secretaries came bustling through the main door. 'We've got a busy day today. We're on a tight deadline to get this frigate patched up, which I'm sure you know all about, so I'll be needing *all* of my squad.'

'All right, you lot. Get yourselves home. You've done enough for today.'

Rosie saw the look of relief on the women's faces. Particularly Hannah's. Which was not surprising, as the weather had done its usual masterful trick of squeezing four seasons into just one day. There'd been a brief show of sun, a more or less constant wind, a sudden downfall of rain, and a smattering of hailstones during their twelve-hour shift.

As the women packed up their bags, Rosie went over to see Hannah for a quiet word. 'How are you managing the workload at the moment?'

'Fine. Absolutely fine.' Hannah's words came out convincingly enough, but her face told a different story.

'Can I ask you something, Hannah? But I don't want you to take it the wrong way.'

Rosie's question was interrupted by Gloria, Martha and Polly, who were shouting out their farewells. Rosie put her hand up to wave goodbye, but on looking at Gloria and her increasingly rotund shape, she was hit by another wave of anxiety. She had told Gloria about what Helen had said this morning and seen her disappointment. The woman loved the yards, and on top of everything, she also desperately needed the money, now more than ever before. She was a single woman expecting a baby.

Rosie knew it would not take long for Helen to realise that Gloria was much more than just a few months pregnant, especially when the weather warmed up and she couldn't hide her bump under her bulky oversized winter coat. She needed to find a solution. A way of keeping Gloria at Thompson's. And she had to find it quickly.

Rosie looked back at Hannah, who was patiently waiting for her boss to ask her question.

'Sorry, Hannah. I just wanted to ask you *why* you originally wanted to come and work in the yard. I don't want to get rid of you. Anything but. It was just something that occurred to me the other day – and I realised I had never really asked you your reasons for wanting to do this kind of work.'

Rosie saw water beginning to pool in Hannah's deep, dark brown eyes. It was like looking into the eyes of a baby doe – they were beautiful, but they also emitted a certain vulnerability.

'I know. Everyone must think I'm mad as a hatter. That's the right expression, isn't it?'

Rosie nodded. She had seen Dorothy bring in Lewis Carroll's *Alice's Adventures in Wonderland* for Hannah to read, and had wondered whether that had been the best choice for someone who was still learning the language.

'Well, to be truthful' – Hannah gulped back the tears she felt were starting to threaten to spill out – 'when I first came here from my country, I was so angry because all the learning and all the lessons I'd been taught by my school and my tutors were totally useless. Nothing that could in any way help defeat Hitler.'

Hannah's body sagged. 'So I said to myself, "Hannah, you got to do something practical. Something that will actually help beat this terrible man and his army. Reading a book, or learning calculus, or knowing all about the history of the Romans and Greeks hasn't stopped him from invading your country."'

For the first time, Rosie realised just how Hannah's life had changed since she had been forced to flee her homeland.

'So,' Hannah continued, 'when my aunty Rina took me in and told me this was the world's biggest shipbuilding town, and that it was the ships that would win or lose this war . . .' Hannah paused for breath, lost for a moment in her recall of those first few weeks here in this town '. . . it seemed the only solution. I had to help build ships. And when I saw the advert for the job of trainee welder here at Thompson's, it was like a sign. I knew I had to do it.'

Rosie looked at this young, virtuous girl and thought for a moment.

'I can see the logic to that thinking,' she said, looking at Hannah and then across to the quayside, where one of the cargo vessels had been painted in camouflage colours and was now ready to be sent back out to transport food and fuel across the North Atlantic and prevent them all from being starved into submission.

'Let me have a think about things,' she said finally. 'See what we can do to make your working life a little easier.'

Hannah's face lit up. 'Oh, thank you, Rosie. I'm so glad I've got you as my boss.'

Rosie smiled and watched as Hannah hurried off to get her bike; as she cycled off through the huge gates which dwarfed her small figure, she wondered how easy her promise was going to be to keep – if she could indeed keep it at all.

As Rosie packed up her holdall bag and grabbed her boxed-up gas mask, she noticed one of Hannah's scrunched-up pencil drawings fluttering around on the ground. She picked it up and flattened it out to see a perfect replica of one of the ships that was waiting to be repaired by the quayside.

'If only she could weld as well as she can draw,' Rosie muttered to herself. But as she went to throw the creased-up paper drawing into the bin, she stopped, her mind turning over the beginnings of an idea, and instead she carefully folded up the drawing and put it in her overall pocket. Deep in thought, she made her way out of the yard.

As she began walking down to the ferry, though, she heard someone calling out to her. 'Hey, boss!'

It was Dorothy, who was standing leaning against the outer wall of the yard with Angie next to her.

'What are you two up to?' Rosie asked. 'I thought you'd gone ages ago. Didn't I hear you planning a night out on the tiles?'

'You're right there, miss.' Angie had the endearing habit of calling Rosie 'miss', which always had the dual effect of making Rosie smile, as well as causing her to feel much older than she was.

'Dor's treating me tonight. We're going back to mine to get all togged up and then we're gannin off into town,' Angie said, before adding somewhat mysteriously, 'she owes me one.'

Rosie threw Dorothy a quizzical smile.

'I do,' Dorothy admitted. 'I've struck a deal with Ange here, but, the thing is, it also concerns you. Have you got time for a quick drink while I explain? It won't take long.' Dorothy was aware that Rosie's commitments at Lily's now meant she had to be there just about every night, so her time was precious.

'Well, how can I say no? I'm intrigued.' And with that, the trio of women walked the short stretch to the Admiral Inn where Dorothy got a round of their usual tipples in before explaining in earnest her idea to Rosie.

*

221

Dorothy wasn't the only one to be plotting and planning that day, for Polly's mind was also working overtime as she walked back home along the Hudson Road.

She'd been chatting to Gloria on the ferry, and it was now abundantly clear that Helen was determined to break up their gang of welders. It was revenge for Tommy, as well as for the humiliation she'd suffered when Ned's wife had publicly chastised her.

Polly knew that Helen would realise it was unlikely she would be able to get shot of Polly. She would struggle to find a reason to sack her, and, apart from anything else, the yard needed welders who were speedy and proficient. Rosie had taught Polly well and she fitted both criteria.

No, she knew Helen's ultimate aim would be to make her life a total misery, gloating from her throne on the first floor, and that her revenge would have to be subtle. Polly's guess was that Helen would do what she was doing now, work at gradually dismantling their squad, getting rid of as many of the women as she could, then she would dump Polly with the worst possible team of welders she could find – probably Mickey's lot, who were known to be a particularly lecherous group of old, would-be Lotharios.

Helen was presently in a position of power, but for a limited time only, as she would have her wings clipped when Jack returned. From what Polly had heard today following Rosie and Helen's early morning meeting, it was clear Helen was circling and getting ready for her first kill. But, just before she had left work, Dorothy had told her about her plan to keep Gloria at the yard, at least until the baby was born, which had, in turn, given Polly an idea of how to help out once the baby was born. And it was for this very reason she was now walking into the little confectionery shop at the end of her road, the bell over the door alerting the two elderly spinsters, Maud and Mavis, who lived out at the back of the shop, that they had a customer.

'An ounce of your toffee, please . . . a bag of barley sugar . . . oh, and I'll have this bag of broken biscuits, thank you,' Polly told Maud, as the elder of the two sisters wrapped her black shawl around her shoulders before weighing out the requested amount of sweets, shovelling them into two little white paper bags, then swinging them like a skipping rope and twisting them closed at the ends.

'Oh, and one of your lollies, please.' Polly had nearly forgotten Lucille.

'That'll be fourpence, hinny,' the old woman said, taking Polly's ration book.

Maud and Mavis had known Polly since she was a child, as well as her brothers, and they had watched with sadness from their shop window when the curtains had been drawn in the Elliot home and they had heard it was Teddy whose life was being mourned.

As Polly said her thank yous and goodbyes, she carried her potential bribes the hundred yards or so back to her front door, crossing her fingers that her plan would be met favourably by Agnes and Bel.

Polly was determined to do her bit to keep her 'family of friends' together, and if it took a sack-load of sweets to get what she wanted, then so be it.

Chapter Twenty-Six

When Gloria made it back through her front door she was jiggered, and practically fell into the armchair positioned in front of the little electric fire. Realising she didn't even have the strength to switch the heater on, she decided just to take herself off to bed. This baby was sapping every bit of energy she possessed.

She was beginning to resign herself to the fact that she was not going to be able to keep welding for much longer. And from what Rosie had told her, it was clear Helen intended to boot her out of the yards as soon as she could.

She felt so sad at the prospect of leaving her little clan. They had learnt their craft together, worked together until they dropped, and sweated and frozen together in all weathers. But most of all they had been there for each other these past nine months. Talking and listening to each other's trials and tribulations, and helping each other try to get some perspective on this queer life that they were all being forced to live.

She would miss the women's warmth and their sincerity, but she knew her friendship with the women would not be the same if she was no longer working in the yard. There simply wouldn't be time to see each other, not with the amount of overtime they were doing.

And she had to admit that she would miss the actual work – the cathartic feel of seeing the smooth flow of steel and the iridescent colours a weld produced, the unmistakable smell of hot metal, and the sound of a hissing rod, all coming together to create the perfect pattern of a well-woven weld. Welds she produced day in and day out and which gave her a much-needed feeling of order and control in her life. Neither of which she had had for many a year.

And, strange as it might seem, she would also miss the actual physicality of the work. Although backbreaking, she enjoyed the way it made her body feel at the end of the day – a satisfying exhaustion.

She wanted to push all her worries about the situation at work to one side. She wanted to ignore the sadness in her heart that she might very soon have to leave the one place which had given her so much – shown her a different life, gifted her a group of invaluable mates, and brought back to her the man she had loved all her life.

At least, she thought, as she hauled herself out of her chair and slowly made her way to the bottom of the stairs, *I now have the freedom to do what I want*.

No more worrying about what Vinnie was up to, no more anxiously awaiting his return from the pub, and no more wondering what state he would be in. Her time at the yard had set her free from the restrictive shackles of her sham of a marriage.

She now realised that the love that had bonded her and Vinnie together had never been a true love. When they had parted, she had wondered if Vinnie had ever really loved her; for years she had actually felt that Vinnie didn't even *like* her, but she had told herself she was being paranoid. But when she had found out about Sarah, and that he had been in a relationship with her for years, she realised her intuition had been right.

All along Vinnie had had a second life.

She had felt so incredibly deceived and – more than anything – angry that she had unwittingly been forced to live a lie.

But no more. Not ever again.

As Gloria reached for the bottom of the banister, preparing to expend her last bit of strength to make her ascent up the stairs, there was a knock at the door. Intuitively she knew it was Vinnie, and she wondered if word had already spread around the yard that she was pregnant, that Vinnie was here to talk about what they were going to do now it was out in the open and the baby seemed determined to go full term.

The last thing she wanted to do tonight was talk to Vinnie, though. Every fibre of her being was just screaming at her to go to bed and rest. She didn't even have the stamina to talk. All she wanted to do was lie on her bed and drift off into a restful sleep, thinking about Jack and the few precious weeks they had enjoyed together, and imagining what it would be like when he was finally back in her arms.

That would have to wait, though. Reality had come knocking, literally, and she had to face it head on; there was no running away.

When she opened the door, Gloria immediately relaxed – Vinnie wasn't drunk. Wonders would never cease.

'Hi, Vinnie,' she said, in a world-weary tone. 'Look, I'm not feeling too good – I was just off to bed, so you're going to have to make this quick.'

Vinnie looked totally woebegone. His gaze dropped to her swollen stomach.

'The babe's hanging in then?' He actually sounded normal, although Gloria wasn't fooled. This was Vinnie trying his hardest to be nice, and he could only keep it up so long.

'Yes. Despite me being "so old".' Gloria quoted him from their last confrontation, but doubted he would remember what he had said.

'The baby needs its father.' Vinnie just came straight out with it. 'I think I should come back.'

Over my dead body, Gloria's head screamed, although she managed to hold her tongue. Instead she said, as kindly as she could, 'That's just not going to happen, Vinnie . . . Let's chat about this another time.'

Gloria knew she was now treading on dangerous territory. Vinnie didn't always need to have a drink in him to get violent. A rejection could be just as intoxicating as a barrel of beer.

'I promise to be a better man.' The words tumbled out of his mouth. Words he had uttered countless times over the years. 'To knock the drink on the head . . . Look at me now. As sober as a judge.'

Gloria sighed. How many times had they had this conversation? She had felt every emotion there was to feel about her husband. Pity. Hurt. Anger. Sorrow. He'd wrung her dry, until she had finally realised – or rather Jack and this baby had made her realise – that it was time to walk away.

'Vinnie,' she said, again forcing her voice to sound calm and understanding, 'you're always full of remorse, full of promises that you'll stop drinking, that you will stop being violent towards me.'

Gloria could immediately see his body stiffen. His mouth tighten. She had seen it all before. Vinnie was nothing if not predictable. It had taken her a long time to realise that, but at least now she had – *finally*.

She had trudged down the same path over and over again through the twenty years of their marriage. She'd done everything possible, *tried* everything possible to keep their marriage on an even keel. She had talked to his family and his friends, thought of strategies to help him stop drinking, excused his vile temper and put it down to the mental scars of what he had experienced in the First World War. Deep down, though, she knew it wasn't just the war that had given him his temper – it had always been there, just waiting to rear its ugly head. Which it had done with ever-increasing frequency.

Perhaps there were reasons why he was the way he was; she had learnt snippets of how he had been brought up in Panns Bank, a particularly poor part of town, and how his own father had also not been averse to using his fists on his wife and children. But even if it was a case of 'the sins of the fathers', Gloria had finally had to stop making excuses for her husband.

'I'm sorry, Vinnie. I can't.'

They were both standing just a yard or two apart.

Gloria felt the protective need to put a barrier between the pair of them, and started to slowly ease the door shut. She was tired now. Not just because of this baby inside her, but tired of Vinnie's emotional neediness – and by his violence. She had wasted too much of her life on him. She had no more to give him.

'Vinnie,' she said, 'I really honestly hope that you manage to live a happy life with Sarah. Let's talk about the baby when it arrives.'

When she saw his reaction and the way his face immediately curled up in a snarl, she knew she had made a mistake. She should not have mentioned Sarah. She wondered if he had fallen out with Sarah and that was why he was here now. Had she got to know about the baby and kicked him out?

'You cannot keep fobbing me off, Gloria.' His face twisted up. 'That's my baby too.'

How Gloria desperately wanted to tell him that, no, actually it *wasn't* his child. But she knew that could have fatal consequences. For both herself and her baby.

Gloria's exhaustion was making her slow off the mark; she should have read the signs more quickly – seen that his anger was rapidly rising to the surface.

Too late she looked down to see his fists were clenched.

She went to push the door shut, but in a flash saw it come back at her; felt it rebound against her face.

It shocked her, left her dazed.

Then came another blow. But this one was not from the door – but Vinnie's knuckles.

As his balled fist hit her, Gloria felt a harsh, jarring thud on her face, followed by searing pain. Then it felt as though water was pouring from her nose and down her chin.

Gloria looked down at her chest and saw that the water was in fact blood.

Another punch hit the top of her right eye, and she felt a wet sensation and again another trickle ran down her face.

As Gloria sensed herself falling backwards, she braced herself as best she could, pushing her hands out behind to break her fall, before landing heavily on her back.

The baby!

As long as the baby was all right.

He'd not touched the baby.

As if he was reading her thoughts, Gloria saw Vinnie's vindictive eyes narrowing as he spat out the words into her face.

'Dinnit worry, Glor, I won't hurt the baby.'

Gloria's final thought was, *Thank God*, before the back of her head banged against the wooden floor of the hallway, creating a darkness all around her.

She felt as if she had been immersed in the blackness for hours, but in fact it must have only been a few moments, for when she came round Gloria saw Vinnie's receding figure strutting down the little garden path before turning on to the main road and disappearing from sight.

Gloria slowly sat up, her hand automatically going to her bump.

'You all right in there?' she murmured to her enlarged belly. She already felt that her baby was a real, live person, just not yet fully grown or visible. She also felt intuitively that her baby was well and had escaped uninjured from her husband's sudden and shocking brutality.

Gloria carefully hauled herself to her feet, wearily pushed the front door shut and dropped the catch. She would never make that mistake again, would never again open the door to Vinnie – even if he screamed blue murder and tried to batter it down; even if it meant she had to put a barricade up to stop him from getting in.

For the moment, though, she knew there was nothing she could do, other than clean herself up and go to bed.

Her head thumped as though she had a rivet gun banging away inside her brain as she forced her shaking legs to put one foot in front of the other and climb the stairs. She thought about the letter she had threatened Vinnie with, and how the blow he had just landed on her proved that the expensive piece of legal jargon had served its purpose but was no longer effective. It had succeeded in getting him out of the marital home, but it would never stop his violence towards her. The letter had threatened him with 'criminal proceedings' if he was to hurt her again, but Gloria knew it would be hopeless to go to the local constabulary for help. She could just imagine the look on their faces when she told them that she'd been married to Vinnie for the past twenty years and that they had two sons together. What happened within a marriage was of no one else's concern. Apart from that, there was a war on. Why would they be bothered about some spat between a man and his wife?

Gloria realised that in Vinnie's eyes she would always be his punchbag. She would bet money he wasn't physically abusive to Sarah; would not be surprised if he'd actually come around this evening to take his anger out on her instead of his mistress, knowing he could get away with it. Who knew what went on in his angry, sick head? Whatever it was, Gloria no longer cared. Her baby was her primary concern now. She just had to work out how to keep herself and her unborn child safe from any future outbursts.

Gloria dragged her shattered body on to the top landing and, as she did so, caught her reflection in the little mirror hanging on the wall at the top of the stairs. She could have cried for the face that was staring back at her. Drying blood streaked from the top of her eyebrow down the side of her face, and another, thicker band of fast coagulating blood trailed from her nose, across her swollen lips, and down her chin. Remarkably, it looked as if her nose had escaped being broken.

Gloria knew from too many years of experience that the bruises would blossom overnight and ripen to a deep shade of purple. She realised she had no make-up with which to cover them up – she had not needed any kind of concealer since she had got shot of Vinnie last year.

She would worry about that in the morning, though. She was too tired now; she had a splitting headache and she had not an ounce of energy left in her body. For now she just needed to fix up her face the best she could, scrub out the blood which had dribbled on to her overalls and then go to bed.

Thank goodness Jack can't see me now, Gloria thought as she looked away from her reflection in disgust and traipsed into her bedroom.

Her relief that her lover could not see the state she was in now was not down to any kind of vanity, or a concern that he would be repulsed by her looks, but because she knew that Jack would most surely try to kill Vinnie if he saw what he had just done to her.

Which was another reason Gloria had to find a solution, a way of this never happening again. Jack was due back soon, and if Vinnie beat her again and Jack got to know about it, there would be a tidal wave of repercussions, and it would most likely end with either Jack being hurt himself, or him giving Vinnie such a large dose of the medicine he had been forcing her to take for so many years that Jack would end up in serious trouble with the law.

Gloria was so desperate to see her lover again, but she was also very much in dread of his return. So much had changed in the past five months since his departure. He hadn't a clue what he would be returning to. He still did not know about the baby. How could he? There was no way they could write to each other, as questions would be asked about why she was receiving airmail from America. Even if those questions were not put to her personally, they would be posed behind her back, as the postwoman, a young girl called Jeannie who worked the Ford Estate patch and beyond, was well known to be a terrible gossip; a busybody who thrived on scandalmongering and muckraking, and who paid no heed to a person's right to privacy.

But, more importantly, Gloria still hadn't made up her mind about whether or not she was going to tell Jack that the baby was his. It was all too complicated. Too messy. There was too much at risk for them both. But more than anything she did not want Jack to feel that she had tricked him in the same way that Miriam had all those years ago, and that he was cornered. She knew all about being trapped and would not want to inflict that on anyone.

But that was a decision to be made at another time; for now the throbbing pain in her head was spreading and she just needed to rest.

Gloria let out a deep, heavy sigh as she stepped out of her overalls, pulled on her nightie, and wrapped her dressing gown around herself and her bump.

"'I'll think of it tomorrow . . . After all, tomorrow is another day",' she said out loud to herself, quoting the final words of Scarlett O'Hara in the film *Gone with the Wind* – the film that Dorothy had dragged them all to see last year.

Chapter Twenty-Seven

Tomorrow came all too quickly for Gloria.

Waking from a restless night's sleep, she got ready and left for work earlier than usual as she wanted to avoid any of her neighbours, or anyone else who would be a witness to the aftermath of last night's vicious attack.

When she arrived at Thompson's and was given her time card, she put her hand up against her face, as if to shield her eyes from the glare of the morning light, and felt relieved the young lad looked too tired and bleary-eyed himself to notice her own bloodshot black eye and her asymmetrical mouth, now puffed up and swollen on one side.

Rosie, of course, did notice. Straight away. And the look on her face spoke volumes when she glared at the results of Vinnie's handiwork on her workmate's face.

Her mouth was taut as she spoke.

'I'm guessing you had a visit from Vinnie last night?'

Gloria nodded.

Rosie knew she should have asked if Gloria was in pain, and what had happened, but she did not need to know the answers. She knew them already. And, more than any-thing, she felt too furious to say anything else. Instead, she went to fetch her bag, fished around for a while, before pulling out a little tube of foundation and a compact of powder. Since Rosie had been meeting up with DS Miller, her self-consciousness had got the better of her, and even though she hated herself for doing it (had always been determined that people should accept her and her scars for what they were), her need to feel attractive and feminine had won over, and she had taken to putting a light layer of concealer on her face whenever she knew she was going to meet up for a coffee with the detective.

'Come here, let's sort you out,' she said gently to Gloria. *What she would have given to see Vinnie's face in such a state.*

Rosie swallowed down her fury. It was not what Gloria needed at this moment. For now she just needed camouflage – a mask to protect her from the stares of those who were not quick enough to disguise their own disgust, or, worse still, their unveiled look of pity on seeing her battered and distorted face.

Gloria tried not to wince as Rosie applied the make-up. Just the feel of another person's touch on her face was painful, but she knew it would be worth it, and was grateful that her boss was able to create some kind of façade to hide her shame.

'You'll be working next to me today,' Rosie said, just as Dorothy and Angie came trooping across the yard.

'All right, miss,' Angie shouted from a distance as she headed over to her part of the yard. She sounded full of life, despite her late night out with Dorothy.

Dorothy was just about to regale Rosie and Gloria with tales of her and Angie's high jinks from the previous evening but, as she approached, she clocked her friend: the make-up had done a good job of disguising the bruising, but nothing could hide the way in which Vinnie's fist had temporarily deformed her face.

'Oh my goodness, Gloria, are you all right?' Dorothy's voice always seemed to go up an octave when she was either upset or excited.

'Is the baby all right?' she added, looking down at her workmate's stomach.

Gloria nodded and tried to smile, unsuccessfully, due to half her upper lip being almost twice its normal size.

Just then Polly, Hannah and Martha all arrived together; after registering Dorothy's concerned demeanour, they looked at Gloria and realised why their normally chirpy workmate was looking so unusually stern and serious.

They had all seen Gloria's bruises before, but had believed she had left that part of her life behind when she had kicked Vinnie out – especially so after they had heard Vinnie was living with another woman.

'I thought we'd all go for tea and cake at that little shop on Dundas Street after work.' Rosie spoke into the shocked silence.

'Angie as well,' Rosie added, looking over to Dorothy, who would, ordinarily, have promptly raced off excitedly to tell her best buddy of the after-work meet-up, but who this time simply nodded her compliance.

The blare of the klaxon put a block on any more questions or talk, and the women started work, although they did so under a heavy, sombre, grey cloud, despite the early morning sunshine.

The clink of china sounded incredibly elegant compared to the clattering din of metal and steel they had been serenaded with all day in the yard, as the waitress moved the large pot of tea, followed by cups, saucers, and plates of cake, from the wooden trolley she'd carefully wheeled over. The women were seated round an oval-shaped table, which had a view of the main shopping area that ran along Dundas Street, now teeming with shipyard workers either heading home or bustling into nearby pubs.

'This feels ever so posh,' Angie said, trying to speak in the best King's English she could muster. 'I've lived round the corner from this place since I was a baby,' she continued, slipping back into her natural north-east accent, 'and only ever gawped through the windows.'

'Well,' Rosie said, 'on your new wages, you may be able to come here more often.'

The women all looked at Rosie and then at Angie. And then, tellingly, at Gloria.

'Go on then, Dorothy. Spill the beans,' Rosie said with a smile. After what Gloria had been subjected to last night, this was at least one piece of news that would hopefully lift her a little.

Dorothy looked at Gloria and tried not to show just how truly upset she was at the state of her workmate. Dorothy, though, was nothing if not a good actress; she had watched enough films to know how to put on a good performance to disguise the distress Gloria's battered face caused her, which had also brought back memories of her own child-hood, and her own mother's face the morning after an argument.

Firmly banishing any thoughts of the past from her mind, and replacing them with excitement that Rosie was calling on her to be the one to impart the good news, she said dramatically, 'Well, Gloria . . . How do you fancy doing a job swap with Ange here? Swinging cranes around all day – instead of being hunched over never-ending welds?'

Gloria had already taken a big mouthful of her slice of Battenberg. She might be feeling as if she looked like a freak out of some circus sideshow, with a hellish head-ache to boot, but her need for sugar overrode everything. She could have hugged Rosie this morning when she had made her suggestion of tea and cakes. It had kept her from sinking into a deep depression all day.

Gloria swallowed and looked at Angie, then at Dorothy, and then at Rosie.

'Yer joking me?' she said through a mouthful of pink and white sponge.

Polly, Martha and Hannah chuckled. They had all been in on the secret.

The gobsmacked look on Gloria's face showed her disbelief at what she was hearing. 'You're telling me you want to give up your cushy job on the cranes to be a welder?'

Angie laughed. 'I know. I must be barking mad! But this one here,' she said, nudging Dorothy who was sitting next to her, 'finally ground me down.'

'It will mean, though, Gloria,' Rosie spoke up, 'that you will have to take a little bit of a drop in wages.'

Gloria could hardly get her words out quickly enough. 'Yes, but it's better than no wages at all,' before she added in all earnestness, 'are you sure, Angie? Welding's bloody hard work.'

Angie laughed. 'Tell me about it. I've had Dor' moan in my ear lug about it ever since we got matey. Anyway, if Miss Backhouse Park can hack it, I certainly can.'

Angie lived just up the road from where they were now sitting, in an area called Monkwearmouth, known locally as the Barbary Coast. Its nickname made the area sound quite exotic, but in reality it was a very poor part of the town, although revered for its vibrant and close-knit community.

Dorothy, on the other hand, lived in a far more affluent area of town, on the borders of a magnificent park, surrounded by quiet streets and magnificent Georgian houses, but, like many of the more well-to-do areas of the town, it lacked the same sense of neighbourliness.

'And, if I'm honest,' Angie added, 'I'm getting bored sat in that crane on my lonesome every day.'

Gloria thought that was unlikely, especially as she spent every break with them all. But Angie seemed very definite about her decision.

'So,' Rosie said, 'I've been given the thumbs-up from the head foreman. He was more than happy to do the swap because he's short of crane operators anyway and is just relieved he's got someone to replace Angie.'

'And Helen?' Gloria asked gingerly.

'Leave her to me,' Rosie said, taking a bite of her cream bun.

The women all looked at each other, hoping their boss's confidence about dealing with their nemesis was well founded.

As the women all started chattering away, drowning Angie in the whys and wherefores of learning to weld, and telling her which part of her body would hurt the most, Gloria sat back, her plate resting gently on her bump as she took another delicious mouthful of cake. This was the best and most unexpected news ever.

Rosie was pleased to see how relieved and happy Gloria was about her new job. Now, she mused, as she glanced across at her friend's face, all she had to do was somehow find a way of dealing with Vinnie – once and for all.

Chapter Twenty-Eight

Two days after the women's little tea-and-cake soiree, Rosie was walking with DS Miller up from the docks to the little café that had now become their regular meeting place. After their stroll along the cliff tops to Seaburn, it had taken him almost a week to pluck up the courage to go and see Rosie at the end of her shift and ask if she had enjoyed his company enough that day to want to repeat it. He had driven himself to distraction wondering whether, when he had waved Rosie off on the bus, she had said 'yes' to his request for another date, or simply 'yes', it had been a nice walk.

He could not quite believe a man of his maturity was obsessing so much about this woman. This very-much-younger-than-him woman. It wasn't as if he was mooning about, clicking his heels, with nothing much to do. Far from it. He had not had a minute to spare due to the unrelenting number of air raids the town had been subjected to over this past month alone, and the loss of life and carnage the bombings had brought about. The Luftwaffe was meant to be top notch, but so far they had not once hit their intended targets, but had only managed to kill the innocent and demolish people's homes.

DS Miller had been dogged in his determination to be a part of the war effort; it had frustrated him no end that he had been too young to join up in the last war, having just turned eighteen during the final weeks of the conflict, and now, twenty-three years later, he was very nearly too old at forty-one. His occupation as a police officer ruled him out of military service anyway, but had he had youth on his side, he would have joined up regardless.

All this had propelled him to work just about every spare minute for the town's civil defence unit. Now the few hours' free time he snatched – when he wasn't either working or swapping his trilby for a warden's helmet – was spent with the woman walking next to him; the woman who had brought light into his life – although he was sure she had absolutely no idea just how much she had illuminated his world.

'The usual?' Vera, the old woman who owned the shop called out when she saw her two regulars walk through the glass-panelled door of the café. She kept back a smile, as she enjoyed her notoriety as being a hard, no-nonsense east ender who took no lip from anyone. She had had to be like that as a young woman, serving the rowdy, horny young lads who would pop in for a cuppa or a bacon bap on their way to work – or after they had finished for the day and wanted to take a sandwich or pie to the pub to eat with their pint. The mould she had created for herself had been set early on, and it was now impossible to break, even if she felt like doing so sometimes.

'Yes, please, Vera!' Rosie trilled over to the old woman, who banged the large copper kettle back on to her gas stove to boil up, then jangled cups and saucers and tea-spoons on to an old and battered tin tray.

'I've only got a few flapjacks left today, hinny,' she shouted over as she lifted the glass dome from the cake stand on which her last two remaining oatmeal biscuits were languishing.

'Perfect.' Rosie smiled back, not expecting a smile in return, but knowing the old woman liked them, particularly as DS Miller always left a decent tip – just like he always paid. When they'd first started having tea together, Rosie had insisted on taking her turn to pay, but each time she had been beaten down with a look of incredulity from DS Miller, who seemed unable to believe she had even suggested it. Rosie now no longer offered, but very occasionally brought him a few kippers she got from the docks as a way of returning the favour.

'So, tell me more about Gloria – poor woman. Is she all right?' Rosie had just been telling the detective about what had happened to Gloria. He had been horrified to hear what had occurred the other night, and even more so that it had been happening most of her married life. Not that it surprised him. But it didn't stop him feeling outrage and disgust at what his fellow man could do; what a husband could do to his wife – and, more so, one who was pregnant.

Rosie looked at DS Miller, who she felt was her friend, even though there was no denying there was more to their liaisons than either of them seemed able to admit. Which was just as well. Rosie did not want them to *admit* anything. Did not want this to go any further than tea, cake and conversation. No. That was a lie. She did want it to go further. But she knew that could never happen. She knew she was already playing a dangerous game. Knew she couldn't ever have any kind of serious relationship with the detective. But even though she knew that, she still couldn't bring herself to stop seeing him. She knew the arguments she had had with herself that they were just friends – that there was no harm in it, and that their meetings were innocent – were flimsy at best; but this man's draw was strong. Too great for her to fight at the moment.

And although her feelings for her detective were far from chaste, she really did enjoy their conversations; they got on so well, which was surprising as Rosie was very much a 'woman's woman' and had never really sought out men's company, or particularly enjoyed being with a man for that matter. She was aware that her view on life was off-kilter because of what she had been through early on in her life, coupled with her work at Lily's, but that was just the way it was.

Rosie would never have normally disclosed Gloria's situation to anyone outside her squad – apart from Lily and George, of course, but they inhabited another world and would never use or abuse that information, or utter a word to another soul about anything Rosie told them in confidence – so Rosie didn't quite know why she was confiding in DS Miller. It was just that her instinct told her she could, and that, in some way, it might help her find a solution to the problem.

'Would she not consider reporting the attack to the police?' DS Miller asked but, even as he posed the question, he knew the answer before Rosie spoke. He had seen this happen too many times. And, if he were being totally honest with himself, if he himself was a woman who had been attacked and beaten by her husband, he doubted very much whether he would seek help from the police. Or expect any kind of justice, for that matter. It would have been a different scenario had it been a random attack, and had that attack been committed by a stranger. But this was between a man and his wife, albeit an estranged man and wife, and as such the law seemed to be happy to ignore any kind of wrongdoing that occurred between a married couple – providing, of course, they didn't kill each other.

'I've suggested that to her, Peter,' Rosie said, 'but she won't. She doesn't think there's a lot the police can do, or would do, which I'm inclined to agree with.'

DS Miller nodded, showing he understood, but not quite wanting to go as far as verbally agreeing that both women were probably right. He was passionate about his job. Had been driven by a need for justice for as long as he could remember, had always known from being a youngster that he wanted to be involved in some kind of law enforcement; so it pained him to admit that the police and the British justice system were far from proactive about certain breaches of the law.

And it was these gaps in applying the law in certain cases that had bothered him all his working life, and had become a real concern as he had grown older, and which had particularly contributed to the changes he had decided to make in his life after his wife had died.

After his beloved Sal had gone, something inside him had switched, and he had started to think that sticking to the rules wasn't always the right thing to do – and that sometimes the scales of justice needed a little help to achieve their balance.

As an employee of the Sunderland Borough Police, he had felt compelled not only to make sure the letter of the law was upheld, but that the spirit of the law was also adhered to; as a result, this often meant that society's bad apples, those who hurt or abused others, got their comeuppance – even if that meant he had to occasionally take matters into his own hands.

'Is there anything you think *I* could do?' He looked Rosie straight in the eyes, showing her he meant every word, and would do whatever she wanted him to.

'Oh, no, Peter!' Rosie was taken aback. No one had ever helped her before – apart from her women. Certainly not a man. But, as she voiced her dissent, there was a part of her that wanted to say: *Yes, please!* And she had to ask herself if, deep down, she really did want Peter to help. To sort Vinnie out.

Was that why she had mentioned Gloria's situation to him in the first place?

DS Miller looked at Rosie, as if trying hard to read her thoughts.

'It's just good to get it off my chest, Peter,' she said, before changing the subject.

As their chatter turned to the recent developments in the war – the surrender of Yugoslavia and Greece to the Nazis, and the pro-Axis regime in Iraq – DS Miller's mind kept being tugged back to Gloria and what this poor woman would do next time her vicious ex came knocking on her door, and he knew he would not be able to let it lie. He simply would not be able to ignore what Rosie had told him and do nothing. And, much as he had the greatest respect for Rosie and the kind of strong and determined woman she was, he thought it unlikely that either she or Gloria could remedy the situation themselves.

People like this Vinnie would not take any notice of a woman. Of *any* woman. He knew the type, and they made his blood boil. He just had to think about the best way he could deal with this pathetic excuse of a man, who had been getting away with being a nasty, vindictive, violent bully for too long.

As he watched Rosie finish off her flapjack with relish before getting ready to leave, he resolved to go and see a few of his old mates stationed up at the police headquarters in town and find out a little more about this Vinnie.

'See you soon, Vera,' DS Miller said his goodbyes as he and Rosie left the café.

'Aye, ta-ra,' the old woman said. She would have given anything to have known what the deal was between those two. An odd pair, if ever there was one. She couldn't work out if they were work colleagues, old friends, or a courting couple.

If they were stepping out together, there was a big age gap between the two, but she knew enough to know that the young blonde woman with the scarred face was probably not the type to go with a young, eligible young man from around the doors. She had something about her, that one did. But Vera couldn't quite work it out.

She scolded herself. *She should keep her nebby nose out of other people's business.* Still it was hard not to wonder . . .

As they stood outside the café and Rosie buttoned her coat up, DS Miller cleared his throat a little nervously. 'Would it be rude of me to ask to walk you back to your digs?' he asked, sounding very official.

He was clearly tense about asking the question he had wanted to ask Rosie every time they had met up. 'It's just that it's such a lovely day . . . or, should I say, such a lovely early evening.' He was beginning to waffle now, as was his wont when he was nervous.

Rosie knew she should say 'no', that she was fine making her own way home, that it would be overstepping the friendship mark for him to escort her home and for him to find out where she lived; but even though her brain was telling her to say a firm but polite 'no thank you', she heard her voice telling the detective. 'Why not? You're right. It *is* a lovely evening.'

As they started walking up High Street East, Rosie could feel they were walking very closely to one another, but she didn't move away or do anything to increase the gap between them.

When their arms touched momentarily, she still didn't step aside to give them more space. And then, at the top of the road, just before it turned into Villiers Street, when she felt the soft touch of DS Miller as he tentatively, and ever so gently, took hold of her hand in his, she did not pull away.

And so, they walked like this, hands clasped together, fingers entwined, for the remaining quarter of a mile to Rosie's flat on the Borough Road.

Such a trip would have normally taken minutes, but it took twice as long for DS Miller and Rosie to make their way there, as their pace was slow and their chatter easy. Rosie only let go of the detective's hand when they reached the top of the stone steps leading down to the front door of her basement flat and they said their formal goodbyes.

Walking back to his own living quarters in Holmeside, DS Miller felt as if he was walking on air. The energy he had felt course through his body had been almost unbearable, and he wondered if Rosie had felt the same.

Should he take this as a sign that she might agree to a formal date? Could he hope that she would want to court him properly?

DS Miller's step quickened with excitement. He felt indestructible. Tonight, when he was out patrolling the streets as part of his ARP duties, if a bomb dropped on him he honestly felt it would bounce straight off again.

Nothing could quash his feelings of elation and joy, and – dare he say it – his feeling of love.

Chapter Twenty-Nine

'So, have you been enjoying any more rendezvous with your detective sergeant *amour*?' Lily gently tested Rosie, her French accent now in full flow as she had been wearing her 'Madame Lily' hat and had been chatting with clients in the reception room, making sure they had a drink in their hand, a smile on their face, and one of her girls on their arm.

Rosie was in the front room, which in times past had once been the family living room, but which Lily had converted into a very beautiful, rather lavish office, furnished with either authentic antiques or very convincing reproductions. The walls had been decorated with red and gold patterned wallpaper and then adorned with gilded oil paintings. The centrepiece of the room was a magnificent twelve-branch crystal chandelier, hanging from an elaborate rose coving on the ceiling. The bordello's office had a Louis XIV theme to it, and was where clients went to settle their bill, or pay any other monies owed, as Lily also indulged in a side-line of luxury goods from the black market. It was partly because of this extracurricular moonlighting that she was particularly interested in, and a little concerned about, DS Miller, especially as she knew he was working with the Dock Police.

Lily handed Rosie one of the two bulbous cognac glasses with which she had arrived, and that had been filled with just a splash of French brandy, as both she and Rosie always liked to keep a clear head – at least until the end of the evening.

'We may have enjoyed a few cups of tea together of late,' Rosie said coyly as Lily nestled herself into the large cushioned armchair on the other side of the huge, ornately carved cherry-wood desk behind which Rosie was seated.

Rosie had the thick red leather-bound accounts ledger out, and when Lily had arrived she had been tapping away with the end of her pencil at the keys of the green mechanical comptometer that she had acquired after seeing them being used during her short spell working in the admin department at the yard. She had been finding it hard, though, to concentrate on the lines of figures, as her mind kept pinging back to her tryst earlier on with the detective and, more so, to the feeling she had experienced when he had taken hold of her hand. Every time she thought about it, her entire body seemed to tingle and her temperature felt as if it was shooting up a few degrees.

Lily eyed Rosie over her horn-rimmed glasses as she took a sip of her Rémy Martin and thought that she had never seen her look as happy as she had lately. She knew Rosie had a few troubles to sort out at the yard, but that didn't seem to be making a dent in her jovial, light-hearted, and often dreamy countenance of late.

'So, *ma chérie*, am I sensing the potential for a little *romance* on the horizon with your *nouvel ami* – your new friend?'

'I know what *nouvel ami* means, Lily!' Rosie chuckled. 'You've just about succeeded in making me – what's the right way of saying it – *bilingual*. But you'll rue the day when I get so good that I run off to join the French resistance – or should I say, *La Résistance française*?'

Rosie was enjoying teasing her work partner and creating a distraction, but Lily wasn't anyone's fool, and knew Rosie was avoiding her question.

'Mm? So? *Is* there a fledgling romance on the horizon?' Lily wasn't going to give up easily, and continued to push for an answer.

Rosie laughed out loud. 'As they say in good Old Blighty, Lily, "don't be so bleedin' nosy".'

Lily crossed her legs and sat up straight, pushing her glasses further up the bridge of her nose and giving Rosie a steely glare over the top of the delicate tortoiseshell frames.

'I'm pleased to say your French accent is far superior to your attempts at "Cor blimey cockney". And, I hasten to add, more becoming.'

Lily knew she wasn't going to eke any more information out of her business partner. Rosie had always kept her cards close to her chest – even though she knew she could trust both Lily and George with her life.

'Actually, I think you would make a good undercover operative. If my own personal experiences of your tight-lipped retorts are anything to go by, the Gestapo would certainly struggle to get you to divulge what you had for your supper – never mind any classified top-secret information!'

The women's tongue-in-cheek repartee was brought to a halt by the faint sound of timid knocking on the door of the office, which had been left slightly ajar.

'That has to be Kate,' Lily said, craning her head round and shouting out in the direction of the door, 'Come in!'

Kate slipped through the narrow gap in the doorway, as if she were too afraid to open it wide.

'What have I told you Kate, *ma chérie*? Never be ashamed of your presence. Knock loudly. Speak clearly!'

Rosie stood up on seeing Kate and, making her way around her huge desk, quickly walked over to give her old schoolfriend a welcoming hug. Kate's body automatically stiffened, but her face said she was happy with the show of affection.

'Poor you being stuck with this one day in day out,' she said with a deadpan face, nodding her head over in the direction of Lily. 'She can be a right old nag!'

'Enough of the "old",' Lily interjected.

Kate braved a smile.

'Just say when you've had enough of it here in this mad-house,' Rosie added, but Kate vigorously shook her head from side to side. She had no intention of ever leaving her new home. She had never felt happier, although she kept the feeling of euphoria she had felt, from the moment Rosie had brought her here, well under wraps. She still wasn't sure how long the arrangement would last. And there was a part of her bracing herself for a return to the streets.

Kate's worries were, of course, totally unfounded. Neither Lily nor Rosie would ever allow that to happen, unless it was what Kate herself wanted. Apart from which, Lily was especially pleased to have Kate stay, as she had discovered recently that she had a natural flair for dress-making and any other kind of seamstressing. The girls were fighting over themselves for Kate to make, mend or alter their wardrobes. But they'd had to wait in line behind Lily, who was presently getting Kate to run up some fantastic replicas of French *haute couture* – designs from a few of the Parisian fashion houses before the takeover of the Third Reich.

Rosie hadn't been surprised when Lily had excitedly regaled her with the news that Kate was no longer their cleaner but their own personal dressmaker; how she had given her some old, cast-off clothes to wear, and Kate had found a spare needle and thread in her room and transformed the second-hand garment into a perfectly fitted, boxy A-line dress; and how, on discovering her hidden talent, Lily had immediately replaced Kate's mop with an old Singer sewing machine that had been gathering dust in the cellar.

She had, however, been particularly intrigued to hear that when Lily had asked Kate where she got the idea for the dress from, as it was *'très chic'*, she had learnt that Kate had always chosen to beg near to department stores or boutiques so that she could watch the life-sized mannequins in the shop windows being dressed in a variety of styles and fashions.

Rosie had said to Kate how she remembered her mother had been a dressmaker and used to clothe most people in the village, and as usual her comments had been answered by a shy nod of Kate's head.

Her old schoolfriend still did not talk very much, but the change in her had been quite remarkable since Rosie had brought her here. A good scrub had made a big difference, as well as a few decent meals in her belly, and Lily had given her a very fashionable short, layered bob in the style of Loretta Young, and even persuaded her to dye her newly cut locks a vibrant mahogany red colour, which had suited her surprisingly well – it was a style Lily herself would have loved to have had, and she had admitted as much, but, in her words, she said she had to be careful not to look like 'mutton dressed as lamb', which puzzled Rosie, as Lily's present colour was far from staid, or one she'd seen on many women at all, never mind those of a certain age.

As Kate and Lily chatted about fabrics and ideas for a particular design of skirt she was working on, Rosie sat on the chaise longue at the side of the room, near to the plush scarlet velvet drapes that blocked out sunlight during the day, and also afforded the necessary privacy the bordello required. She was so glad to see that Kate was settling in. Her cuts and bruises, the legacy of her life on the street, had all just about healed, and those that hadn't, she noticed, had been covered with a little make-up; the scars left by the nuns, both those on her body and the ones buried deep inside her, would always be there, a reminder of what Rosie now hoped would be her past life.

It still filled Rosie with an intense fury to think about what they had done to Kate as a small child and throughout her formative years, as well as to all those other children who had been under their so-called 'care'. It did not take a genius to work out that if they had been so abominable with Kate, they would also have meted out the same abhorrent treatment to others. One day she hoped they would get their just deserts – in this lifetime, as well as in the next.

Later on that evening, Rosie took her time walking home, with the aid of her little electric torch, through the darkness of the town's blacked-out streets, enjoying the quietness and the solitude and allowing her mind to mull over her thoughts and feelings: Gloria's joy on hearing the news about her job swap, the tenuous situation with Hannah, how Rosie was going to keep Martha in her squad, and how quickly she could train Angie up . . .

And then her mind came to rest on Peter and their walk home, and the warmth of his firm but gentle touch when he had taken her hand into his own.

How it had made her feel.

Her mind started to wander.

What would it be like to be encircled in his arms and kissed? And caressed?

To lie with him, their bodies enmeshed together?

Before she knew it, she was almost home, and Rosie forced herself to snap out of her fantasy world. She knew she was living in cloud cuckoo land and that it could never go any further.

But she could dream, couldn't she?

Lily was stoking the open fire rather aggressively in the reception room that was now devoid of any of her girls or any of their clients. Those who were left upstairs had already settled their accounts and would let themselves out at the back.

Just like Rosie, Lily also had her mind on DS Miller, but for very different reasons. Rosie's 'friendship' with the detective showed no signs of relenting. From the start Lily had feared that this was not going to be a one-off flirtation. Shortly after Rosie had told her about bumping into DS Miller by the docks, she'd had a feeling that trouble was looming.

'Any news from your friends at the Borough?' Lily asked.

George was sitting at the piano and had been playing quite an impressive rendition of Bing Crosby's 'You Are My Sunshine' that was presently climbing up the music popularity chart in America at a rapid rate of knots.

He rested his hands on the edge of the ivory keyboard. 'I'm afraid, my dear, my contact with the boys in blue tell me that Rosie's detective is as straight as a dye. Old school. Not even a warp in his character, never mind a bend.'

George paused. He hated telling lies. Not that this was really lying. Just being a tad economical with the truth. Rosie's detective sergeant *was* indeed an upright copper. Not at all corrupted. Well, not for self-gain, anyway. The contact he had spoken to in the force had intimated that there might be a question mark over him, but this was more over issues at the other end of the corruptibility spectrum, for it would seem that Rosie's detective had changed after his wife's death, had become almost puritanical in his work. And, in the words of his contact, 'may well be taking work home with him – as it were'. But no one knew anything for certain. There was just a suspicion that DS Miller might be prone to tying up loose ends in his own time and in his own fashion.

But this was not something he wanted to impart to Lily. It was unnecessary, and she had enough worries at the moment, what with all the stresses and strains of starting up her new business and the like.

'He's lily white,' George added with utter conviction, 'if you pardon the play on your name, *my darling*.'

Lily softened when she heard George's term of endearment for her, but only momentarily.

'Bloody typical,' she said, taking out a Gauloise. She very rarely smoked; when she did it was either when she was on her own or with George, and usually only when she was very agitated or in turmoil. 'Trust our Rose to pick a copper, of all people, to fall for. Why couldn't she meet someone – anyone but the Old Bill?

'If DS Romeo had been just a little bit malleable, it could have worked to all our advantages, especially with our little venture in hard-to-come-by commodities, but by the sounds of it he's as straight as a bleedin' rod. It's only going to be a matter of time before he susses out that Rosie's earning a second income, and he's not going to like it when he does.'

'Gawd knows how he's going to react,' Lily agreed. 'I've seen it all before. Seen how angry men get when they find out how the woman they've fallen for earns her money. It's all going to end in tears . . . But what's worse,' she added, 'is that it could threaten the business. If he finds out about us, and we're reported, our whole house of cards will come tumbling down.'

'Perhaps,' George ventured, starting to play the first few notes of 'Moonlight Serenade', 'you need to have a chat with Rosie. Woman to woman. Get a feel of just how serious she is about him.'

There was a few minutes' thoughtful silence before he changed his mind and added, 'Having said that, though, Lily, I really don't think you have cause for concern . . . Like I've said before, Rosie's a survivor, through and through. And she won't do anything to jeopardise her future – or Charlotte's.

'Even for love.'

Chapter Thirty

'"Hush now, had your gobs.
"I'll tell you all an awful story.
"Hush now, quiet please
"I'll tell you about the worm . . .'"

Joe's voice was getting quieter with each line of Lucille's favourite night-time story.

He had already regaled her with the first part of the strange tale about a worm that is thrown down a well and grows and grows to monstrous proportions, and as he moved on to the second verse, he wondered if Lucille's interest in the story had been piqued by the fact the main character was a man who goes off to become a soldier and fight in wars. It would certainly make sense, as that was all the little girl had known.

What an odd perspective on life this must give a child, he thought as he continued.

'". . . the worm got fat and grew and grew
"And grew an awful size.
"It had great big teeth, a great big mouth,
"And great big goggly eyes.'"

Lucille's voice, croaky with sleep, joined in the last line, as it always did, for she seemed to particularly relish saying the world 'goggly'. She'd heard the story so many times her little voice would often chirp up and repeat words or phrases at parts she particularly liked.

It surprised Joe that the story didn't give her nightmares, as the tale was actually quite gory and told of a mammoth worm that fed not just on calves, cows and lambs, but which would also swallow little children – alive. The ending might have been slightly more reassuring, but it was still equally gruesome, with the brave knight slicing the famous Lambton worm into two pieces.

Then again, Joe thought as he looked down at his niece, who was still desperately trying to keep her eyes open, she was not your typical child; Joe didn't think he had come across such a strong-minded little girl in his life. Perhaps it was because she had been brought up by three very forceful women, all headstrong in their own peculiar way.

'Night sweetheart. Love you,' Joe whispered quietly.

'Love you more,' Lucille slurred back sleepily, giving exactly the same reply she did every night that Joe and Bel put her to bed. It had become their saying: Joe told Lucille that he loved her and she told him she loved him back – only more so. Then she would settle down properly and go to sleep.

Bel watched from the doorway as Joe tucked Lucille into her cot, picking her raggedy cloth rabbit from the bottom of her bed and placing it next to her on her pillow.

Bel had now taken second place in her little girl's bedtime routine.

As Lucille snuggled up with her favourite toy, she closed her eyes and instantly fell into a deep, comforting slumber.

'She's gone out like a light.' Joe turned to Bel, who was standing behind him in the doorway.

'Good job I'm not jealous,' Bel whispered to Joe as they both backed out of the bedroom and Joe quietly shut the door behind him. 'I'm now most definitely runner-up in that little girl's world.' Bel smiled as she talked. 'You have definitely knocked me off the top spot.'

Not that Bel minded in the least. She understood her daughter had been deprived of any real male influence from being a baby. She had spent her entire life thus far in the company of women. Most of their neighbours were women, too, as they had either lost their husbands in the First World War or had waved them off at the start of this one.

And Bel couldn't ignore the parallels with her own childhood, and the lack of a father or any kind of paternal influence in her life – she didn't want her own daughter to suffer the same void. Her mother had claimed that Bel's dad had died when she was just a baby, but she had never believed her; even as a small child, when she would occasionally ask her mum about her dad, she would look into her mother's face as she told her that her da had gone to heaven, and she could hear in her voice that she was lying.

In hindsight she had not had any kind of male influence in her life at all, other than the men her mum went off with, with their greased-back hair and sly, darting eyes that always seemed to be scanning their surroundings, checking out everyone and everything.

As she had grown up, Bel had often wondered who her real father was, and sometimes she speculated that perhaps even her mother didn't know the answer to that question.

At least, Bel thought, Lucille couldn't have a better role model than Joe. She knew and trusted him. He was a good man, and he also adored Lucille as if she was his own. Sometimes that still scared Bel but, since the night she'd lost the plot and given up her grief, she had started to accept it. Whenever she felt the old feelings of panic that Lucille was becoming attached to a man who was not her real dad, she had to tell herself that this was no bad thing. Besides, Joe was family – he and Lucille shared the same blood – but most importantly Bel could see that her daughter was happy, and that was all that mattered in the end.

Bel felt guilty for being the way she had these past few months; knew her daughter had picked up on her anger and her desolation. At least now that she was feeling more like her old self, she could see that her daughter also seemed happier, less fractious. In fact, she had never seen Lucille so full of fun and life, since she and Joe had begun getting on so much better and her resentment for her husband's brother had diminished.

Coming back into the kitchen, Bel put the kettle on for a brew, and Joe turned the wooden kitchen chair to face the last throw of heat coming from the dwindling fire of the range. It also enabled him to extend his bad leg, which was getting much better, but still pained him if it was bent for too long. He felt his whole body relax as he enjoyed the feel of stretching it out in front of him.

'How's it feeling?' Bel looked down to Joe's leg as she scooped a few spoonfuls of dried tea leaves into the pot.

'Champion,' Joe said, 'nearly as good as new.'

Bel smiled. She knew Joe's leg would never be as good as new, but at least it looked as if he was going to keep it, and the wound was now almost healed.

'How are *you* feeling?' Joe asked hesitantly, as if he knew he was entering unknown terrain and didn't want to feel he was overstepping the mark. Bel had been so much better of late, but he still didn't want to go too far too quickly and push her back into her shell.

Much to his relief, he saw Bel's face soften and she gave him a smile. 'If I'm honest, Joe, I still feel terrible, but not half as awful as I have done. I think my heart is like your leg – it'll heal, but it will never be quite the same.'

Joe looked into the fire and thought for someone who had been dragged up by her mother and given next to no education, Bel could often be almost poetic in how she talked. Agnes had forced all three of her children to go to school every day until they reached the legal leaving age, but Joe didn't have the way with words that Bel had.

When Joe looked across at Bel as she poured the boiling hot water into the pot of tea, he saw silent tears trickling down her cheeks. His immediate reaction was to go to her, to put his arms around her and give her comfort, but he knew he couldn't. Instead he leant towards her and reached up to touch her arm gently.

'Oh, Joe,' Bel said, trying to keep her voice under control and quiet. 'I wish sometimes I could switch my brain off for a little while. It just keeps going on and on, thinking about so many things.'

'What kind of things?' Joe knew he was taking a risk by asking, but it had to be done if Bel was ever to move forward.

Bel bit her lip, wanting to talk but struggling to let herself confide in Joe. In the end, more tears started to flow down her face.

Bel turned one of the chairs round and put it next to Joe's. As she spoke, she looked into the dwindling fire. 'I just keep thinking of all the words I didn't say and all the things I didn't do,' Bel said, her voice trembling.

'I keep thinking that I didn't love Teddy enough, didn't enjoy our time together like we should have. After Lucille was born, I was so wrapped up with looking after her and trying to do everything right, or rather do the complete opposite of my mum, I neglected Teddy. Perhaps if I had been a better wife, he might have stayed here instead of going off to war?'

The tears were now flowing freely down Bel's face, which Joe thought was still just as beautiful even though she was so upset.

'Bel,' Joe butted in, 'believe you me, there was no way in a million years you could have stopped Teddy from signing up. You could have been the best wife in the world, which, by the way, I think you were . . . and Teddy would still have joined up . . . I know because nothing was going to stop either of us doing what we did. *We had to do it*. Wild horses wouldn't have stopped us.' Joe took a deep breath. 'So cross that off your list of regrets and self-recriminations.

'You,' he continued firmly, 'could not have stopped Teddy from going to war. Is that clear? Do you believe me? It's important you do. I knew my brother better than anyone and I wouldn't lie to you.'

Bel looked at Joe and nodded. She knew he was speaking the truth. He had always been honest, even when they were children. He might have been the naughtier of the two brothers, but he always admitted to his wrongdoing. He would never lie to get out of a good ear-bashing from Agnes.

As Bel's overwrought mind started thinking about the past and their lives as children, she remembered how Teddy had always been there to protect her, and how Joe had always managed to make her laugh.

'Remember when Teddy tried to get us all to become blood brothers . . .' Bel said, laughing at the memory.

'. . . And he got his penknife out,' Joe joined in the recollection, 'and we were just about to start cutting our wrists—'

'But I chickened out!' Bel was now chuckling at the memory of her cowardice. 'Oh, I don't think I was so glad to see your ma in all my life.'

'Aye,' Joe continued, 'she played holy war with us all, didn't she?'

Joe and Bel started to laugh and laugh, both remembering Agnes's outraged face as she snatched the penknife off Teddy and ordered them all inside for a right old telling-off.

The pair were laughing so much and were so immersed in the nostalgic reminiscences of their long-forgotten childhood days that they didn't hear Pearl troop into the kitchen.

They both jumped at the sound of her voice.

'Nice to hear a bit of laughter in the house,' Pearl said, but the intonation of her voice inferred she meant quite the reverse.

Joe's heart sank when he realised the rare time he was enjoying with Bel on her own had been intruded upon. And by Pearl, of all people.

'Well, what's the expression? Laughter is the best medicine,' Joe said, trying to keep the mood of the evening from souring as it inevitably did when Bel and Pearl were within striking distance of each other. He just hoped she would go out for a fag and then slope off to bed.

His hopes were dashed, though, when Pearl pulled out a chair from the kitchen table and poured herself a cup of tea. Both Joe and Bel noticed her hand was shaking a little as she picked up the heavy ceramic pot, which was still half full and piping hot. They also picked up the faint smell of whisky.

'Been on the malt tonight, Ma?' Bel asked, with more than a touch of vitriol in her voice.

'Aye, I have that, Isabelle,' Pearl admitted. 'The landlord of the Dun Cow in town had a nice bottle of Teacher's.'

Joe looked at Pearl and for the first time saw her vulnerability. Her guard was uncharacteristically down. She was half cut, but seemed surprisingly sober, if not a little morose.

'You done anything more about getting a job, Ma?' Bel asked. Pearl had been staying as a non-paying guest at the Elliots' for more than three months now; Bel wasn't the only one in the household to be thinking that it was either time to move on or start paying her way.

'Aye, Isabelle, dinnit you worry your little cotton socks. I've been asking around, but there's not much for someone my age. I'm getting past it.'

'You're not that past it to go out drinking every night,' Bel's retort was sharp.

For a change Pearl didn't come back with a scathing remark, but stood up a little unsteadily and stuffed her hand in her pocket and pulled out her packet of Woodbine's.

'Isabelle,' she said, making her way to the back door, 'I know I wasn't the best ma in the world . . .'

Bel and Joe stared at Pearl. Waiting for her to continue.

Pearl had shown them a chink in her armour – a sliver of vulnerability.

Looking at Pearl, Joe realised she looked beaten down, and he felt a touch of pity for this woman who only ever seemed to leave wreckage in her wake. This rare shot of compassion momentarily transported him back to a time when he was still a boy, but was beginning to become more aware of the judgements of others, and he had seen the mocking looks of neighbours when Pearl walked past, usually when she was inebriated, but even when she was sober. He'd been shocked to see how they literally turned their backs on Pearl, especially if she was done up to the nines and with some spiv on her arm.

She'd been an outsider. And still was.

Joe was just starting to feel something more than simple dislike for Pearl when she turned on her way out through the back door, cigarette firmly between her fingers, ready to spark up.

'I'll let you two *lovebirds* carry on from where you left off, anyway. Don't mind me. I'll be hitting the sack as soon as I've had this.'

The modicum of sympathy Joe had fleetingly felt for Pearl vanished and was replaced by a flame of pure anger. He looked at Bel as she stood up, but he couldn't read her face.

'Night, Joe,' she said, turning towards the kitchen door, all laughter now gone from her. 'Don't pay any attention to what my ma says. She judges everyone like herself.'

Joe watched with sadness as Bel turned her back on him and went to bed.

Chapter Thirty-One

Saturday 3 May 1941

'Bloody hell, Vinnie! What's happened to yer face?!'

Sarah was standing with her red polyester nightgown wrapped tightly around her, one hand holding a burning cigarette, the other reaching out to shadow-touch her live-in lover's face.

Vinnie's eye was puffed up red and bloodshot and was clearly going to develop into a nice shiner overnight. He had blood trickling down his left side from a cut on his brow, and his nose felt like it might well be broken. Blood had streamed from both nostrils for a short time before clotting up. It was now a hard black crust that had totally blocked his nose and was causing him to breathe solely through his mouth.

'Don't touch me!' Vinnie snarled. Just the thought of his girlfriend's touch caused him to flinch.

'All right! Dinnit snap my head off!' Sarah quickly withdrew her hand and stuck her fag in her mouth and took a deep drag.

She watched as Vinnie slumped down on the armchair next to the electric fire, which had one bar glowing orange.

'Some thug jumped me,' Vinnie said. His voice was thick and he sounded as if he had a bad cold.

'Just as I left the pub,' he added, not looking Sarah in the eye, but instead staring straight ahead at the brown tiled fireplace.

'Why, I've never heard the like!' Sarah said incredulously. 'Why would anyone want to mug you? It's not as if you're walking around with a load of dosh on you. Far from it.'

Sarah eyed her man suspiciously. She had known Vinnie for a good few years; had been his mistress for two; and they had been living together for six months now, ever since his missus had chucked him out. She knew when he was telling porkies, but she also knew when not to push it. His fuse was naturally short, and it didn't take much for it to spark up and explode – not that he had ever laid a hand on her, but he'd come close a few times and she knew when to back off.

'I'll get you some hot water and a towel. Get you cleaned up,' she said, stubbing out her cigarette in the overflowing ashtray that she'd pilfered from their local pub.

As she disappeared into the kitchen, Vinnie stood up and looked at his face in the bevel-edged, hexagonal mirror hanging above the mantelpiece of his lover's small flat.

His injuries were almost identical to the ones he had inflicted on Gloria the previous week. The image of her face as she lay on the hallway floor of his former marital home rose to the forefront of his mind as he realised he'd been given exactly the same beating.

His fist automatically clenched as he reran the scene in his head. The shock of being dragged off the main road within seconds of leaving the Grindon Mill public house and being flung down the side alley; the thudding pain as he felt a fist smack him bang in the middle of the face. His attacker had laid him out in one fell swoop, and as Vinnie had gone down and was looking up at the dark heavens above, his vision had been blocked by a balaclava-clad figure. Through his blurred vision he had just about made out two unblinking eyes and a mouth.

A pair of leather-gloved hands, which Vinnie now realised had been worn to protect the man's knuckles so as to leave no incriminating cuts and bruises, had grabbed him by his coat lapels and lifted him up a fraction from the ground, before whispering calmly into his ear: 'If you *ever* raise a fist to any woman again, I'll make sure you'll never be able to lift another pint *ever again*, never mind drink one – unless it's through a straw.'

The man had then pushed him back on to the hard gravelled ground of the narrow alleyway, and walked away.

As he'd turned on to the main road, Vinnie had seen his attacker pull off his woollen balaclava, enabling him to catch a glimpse of a tuft of thick black hair. It could have been anyone. He hadn't recognised the man's voice, or anything about him.

As Vinnie eased his aching limbs back down into the frayed floral-patterned armchair, he wondered if his attacker had been sent by Gloria, or if he was acting on his own volition. His gut told him Gloria wouldn't have had the balls to get someone to do him over, but there was something very professional – something very controlled – about the man's behaviour.

As his hand went to touch his lip, which was throbbing and felt the size of a slice of melon, he knew that he might never find out, but that one thing was for certain – the man had meant every word he'd said. And from the damage he had already done to his face, he would not have any trouble carrying out his threat.

Chapter Thirty-Two

Sunday 4 May 1941

'Ma, what've you got there?' Joe asked, stifling a yawn as he half laughed, half smiled down at the spindly little black and white animal that looked as if it was a jigsaw of breeds. If its genealogy had to be pigeon-holed into one particular pedigree, it would probably be a border collie due to its sleek build and long, silky fur.

'I think it's called a "dog", Joe.' Agnes glared at her son as she bustled into the kitchen.

Joe looked at the dog, which was looking from Agnes to Joe, and then back again to Agnes, with eyes that were both pleading and alert.

'How strange . . .' Joe rubbed his eyes of sleep and looked more closely at the shabby, undernourished canine nervously moving around Agnes's legs as she stood in the middle of the kitchen. Joe, like the rest of the Elliot household, had not slept a wink due to an epic five-hour air raid on the town that had started just after eleven the previous night and continued until four o'clock in the morning.

'One of its eyes is blue – the other brown.'

Agnes looked down at her new-found friend.

'I found him lying next to what used to be the auctioneer's shop on the Hendon Road. He just took one look at me, jumped up and started following me.'

Agnes had gone to see an old friend, who lived a few streets away in an area of the east end known as Hendon, where the shipbuilding industry had first taken root back in the mid-1300s. Thankfully Val, with whom Agnes had worked in the County Laundry and Dye Works before it became the Luxdon Laundry a few years back, had made it to the shelter in time, although she had resurfaced to find that three of her neighbouring streets – Wear Street, Adelaide Place and Hendon Road – had been blitzed by high-explosive bombs that the Luftwaffe had dumped on the area.

'I tried shooing him away, but he wouldn't leave me alone. I asked around but no one seemed to know who the dog belonged to.'

Joe hooted with laughter as his mother dropped her bag and her boxed-up gas mask on to the floor, dragged a chair out from under the kitchen table, and sat herself down with a weary sigh.

'And there was me thinking it was our Pol who was always the one to be bringing back waifs and strays to the house,' Joe said, pouring his mother a cup of tea from the pot stewing on the table.

At that moment Bel came in from the back yard, carrying Lucille, who was sucking her thumb and clutching her raggedy bunny as if her life depended on it. She had been terrified by the earth-trembling explosions she'd heard throughout the night, and had sensed the fear of the adults around her as they'd all huddled together in the cramped public air-raid shelter that had been built underneath a very grand building called Tavistock House, just around the corner from Tatham Street.

'You want to be careful, Agnes,' Bel said. 'If the wee mite's got any sense, it'll know it's on to a good thing and you won't be able to get rid of it . . . Look what happened when I tipped up here – I never really left – and then you ended up with double the trouble when this one came along!' She gently brushed Lucille's blonde curly locks out of her sleepy eyes.

Joe could have eaten his words. He hadn't been thinking about Bel when he'd made his remarks.

'Ah well,' Agnes told her, 'thank goodness you did stay, because I've now got myself a gorgeous little granddaughter. And it doesn't look like anyone else will be giving me any more any time soon.' Agnes threw an accusing look over at Joe. She knew her recent need for more grandchildren had come about since Teddy had been killed. It was as though she yearned for the miracle of a new life to help replace the void left by her son's death.

'Bloody hell, how have we gone from waifs and strays to me giving you grandchildren in the time it's taken you to take one slurp of your tea?' Joe was speaking to his mother, but he could not stop himself giving Bel a quick glance to gauge her reaction.

'Give him a chance, Agnes,' Bel said, sensing Joe's discomfort. 'He's only been back four months – not even that. And he's only just got back on his feet – literally.'

Agnes glanced across at Joe and then up at Bel with a look neither of them could read.

Joe covered his unease by bending forward to stroke the dog, which had now lain down on the floor with its chin on top of Agnes's foot, as if it were a cushion. The oddly coloured eyes were glued to Agnes's every movement. Joe ruffled its head. The dog didn't move an inch, but its long black tail swished across the floor in a wide arc.

Agnes looked down at her little scruffy companion and noticed there were patches of soot and ash on its long silky fur.

'I'll ask around again tomorrow. He's got to belong to someone,' Agnes said firmly.

'Ma, I don't think this ugly mutt is going anywhere,' Joe said. 'It looks like it's got its paws well and truly under the table.'

The dog's head bobbed up, as if sensing it was being talked about.

'And,' he added, 'I think you'll find you've got a *she* and not a *he*. Looks like your eyesight's going as well as everything else.'

Agnes gave Joe a gentle cuff round the head and leant down to stroke the dog. 'You'll be a good girl, won't you, missy. Not like the ones in this house. More hassle than they're worth, they are!'

Just then Polly came into the kitchen, followed by Arthur. They'd both gone for a walk upriver to Robert Thompson's old shipyard, which had been hit by three delayed-action bombs that had not exploded until three hours after they'd fallen from the sky. Luckily, no one had been hurt and none of the working shipyards had suffered a hit.

'Eee, Ma, I don't know how you dare,' Polly exclaimed.

Bel joined in her mock outrage, causing Lucille to stir from her slumber and join in the ruckus; if there was noise to be made, she was going to make sure she was also very much a part of it.

Joe gave a sigh of resignation. 'Looks like we're doomed – destined to be surrounded by women, eh, Arthur?'

The old man chuckled. 'Well, I guess there could be worse things!'

Sensing that her daughter was waking up, Bel turned so that she could show her the new addition to the family. 'Look what Grandma's brought home.'

On spotting the dog, the little girl's eyes opened wide in excitement and her whole body sprang to life. She immediately started trying to squirm out of her mother's arms.

'Doggie!' she cried out, as Bel relented and put her down. 'Don't smother the poor thing, Lu,' she told her daughter.

Ignoring her mother's words of advice, Lucille promptly launched herself at the dog, wrapping both her little arms around its thin neck and giving it an all-embracing hug. 'Doggie!' she exclaimed again. '*Our* doggie!'

As if showing its gratitude at being accepted into the fold, the dog rolled over on its back, its black and white paws flopping about in the air.

'Well, I think I'll get the tea on. At least we've still got a home to cook in,' she said, thinking about the news she'd heard from Val that they'd been at least two dozen houses destroyed in the raid, but, worst still, word was going round that there had been as many as thirteen fatalities, which had, heartbreakingly, included an entire family and a fourteen-month-old baby. It was news Agnes had decided she wasn't going to share. Everyone would find out soon enough. In the meantime, if the dog, which had seemed so determined to follow her back home, brought even a little respite and escapism from all this warmongering and death, then who was she to stop it?

Agnes pushed herself up from her chair, and made her way to the scullery to prepare the Sunday dinner. As soon as the dog realised Agnes was on the move, the scraggy stray scrabbled back to its feet and padded behind her, tripping up her heels, determined not to let its new mistress out of its sight.

Chapter Thirty-Three

The following day, after Polly had gone off to work and the house, as usual, was full to the brim with babies and toddlers (neither Agnes nor Bel had the heart to turn away any harried-looking mum who had just got herself a job), Joe hobbled into town.

The place was like a war zone. A number of the town's oldest and most beautiful buildings, like the Victoria Hall and Binns, were now simply skeleton silhouettes, their guts of bricks and mortar lying in gigantic heaps at their feet. Large parts of the famous and extravagantly landscaped Winter Gardens and Mowbray Park were now just deep craters of mud and stone. The most magnificent houses and shops, built with such style during the opulence of the past century, had been reduced to shells – ripped of their splendour in the time it had taken one of Hitler's harbingers of death to fly over the town's skies. It was as if the town was being stripped to its bare bones, brick by brick.

The devastation Joe had seen since his return, however, had made him even more resolute in his determination to continue to fight the Nazis – in whatever capacity he could.

I may be classed as a cripple, he seethed inwardly, as he was forced to make a detour round one of the many boarded-off bomb sites, hurrying as quickly as he could, and angrily slamming his walking stick on to the paving stones, 'but I'll be damned if I'm going to sit on my backside and do nothing.'

He'd been knocked back when he'd returned to Bartram's, the shipyard where he and Teddy had spent their entire working lives since they'd started there as young apprentices. Despite the warm welcome he had received, he had been told there were no jobs going. He had been told the same when he'd hobbled to Thompson's. He had felt emasculated as he had slowly made his way back to Tatham Street. Everyone knew that both those yards, and others along the Wear, were desperate for workers. They were taking on women, but not wrecks like himself.

Joe had willed himself to get better, and a few weeks later had gone to the labour exchange in town, but again, he had been deemed unfit for any of the jobs going, and had left downhearted, in despair of being any use ever again. He had hidden his feelings well, though; kept up his cheery façade. He didn't want to subject anyone to his woes. Everyone had their own troubles to deal with. But, more than anything, there was no way in a million years he wanted anyone to pity him. It was his worst fear. And, besides, he was alive, wasn't he? But it didn't matter how many times he told himself how lucky he was, he could not escape the inherent need to be a part of the war effort.

When he had helped the ARP wardens and emergency services after the air raid he and Bel had been caught in back in April, he had felt a great sense of purpose, and had returned home believing he was of some value. Unfortunately, his leg had paid the price, and his recovery had taken a step backwards. But after the pounding the town had endured last night, he knew he just could not sit around any more, bad leg or not. Wild horses weren't going to stop him.

Besides which, even if he hadn't been driven by the deep-seated need to be of service to his country, he still needed to get out of the house and find some kind of gainful employment.

The reason, of course, being Bel.

He was around her too much. There had been a part of him which thought, or rather hoped, that his feelings for her might have diminished with time; that the reason he felt so strongly about her was because of what he'd been through, and that, as he recovered, he would also get back his perspective and stop obsessing so much about her.

But, the reverse had happened.

Instead of getting less, his love for Bel seemed to be growing more and more; he just couldn't stop it, no matter how hard he tried.

And now he worried that he could no longer disguise his emotions. He was sure his mother had seen something in his face yesterday when she had made her remarks about him giving her grandchildren; that she'd read the secret yearning, the burning desire he had for Bel – and that, if truth be told, he would love nothing more than to give his mother another granddaughter or a grandson, but that the only woman he wanted to do that with was right there in their house – their very own waif and stray. Their Bel. His sister-in-law. His brother's wife.

You should be mourning – not desiring, he'd screamed at himself again and again.

It was as if his brother's death had opened a door in his mind, allowing thoughts of love, lust and passion to run riot. All those suppressed thoughts and feelings he'd had over the years for Bel had been let loose and were now marauding around, refusing point blank to be reined in.

For God's sake, he'd made a promise to his brother to look after Bel – not steal her away from him, hadn't he?

When he had first returned from war, thoughts of Bel had soothed him. Now they tormented him. If his brother knew what was going through his mind, he would be turning in the foreign grave in which he'd been buried.

Joe seemed to be constantly mentally wrestling with his passionate feelings for Bel, alongside terrible, gut-wrenching bouts of guilt.

His mind was becoming clearer as he adjusted to life back on Civvy Street, and with that came the knowledge that this was not right. His feelings for Bel were all wrong. How could he defile the memory of his brother by taking his wife? Not that Bel would agree to be taken, anyway.

His mind was now no longer just consumed by unrequited love, but also by the most awful remorse.

It had to stop. And the only way to stop it was not to be around Bel.

As Joe passed the partially bombed railway station, his mind was cast back to the shock he had felt after arriving back home in January, and how appalled he had been at seeing the extent to which the town he loved and had lived in all his life had been battered and bombed.

And, listening to the BBC news reports at night, and reading Arthur's newspapers, it wasn't just here, but all the major industrial areas up and down the whole country which were being regularly blasted by Hitler's maleficence. The war wasn't just happening in foreign lands and seas – but on his own doorstep.

Joe realised that he would never again be able to fight the Germans or Axis face to face, but he could bloody well do his best to save his own town: its homes, shops and industries, and most of all try to protect the people in it.

When Joe arrived at his destination, outside what used to be a stationery shop in the centre of town, he stopped to get his breath. He caught his reflection in the large window that was crisscrossed with huge lengths of tape, and saw the slightly gaunt, lanky figure of a worn-out-looking chap leaning on a wooden walking stick and dressed in an old coat that was too big for his slender frame, and wearing a pair of trousers that had seen better days.

He blew out air, straightened his shoulders, then turned towards the front door of what was now the recruitment office for the Home Guard: the country's civilian army, whose job it was to defend the five thousand miles of Britain's coastline, and key targets such as factories, explosive stores, collieries and shipyards.

The tinkling of a bell sounded out as soon as Joe opened the door, and as he walked into the stuffy, smoky room he was immediately greeted by a man's voice, 'Good day, lad!'

The confident and clear voice belonged to a man who looked to be in his fifties, certainly old enough to be Joe's father, who was wearing the khaki green uniform of the Home Guard, along with a dark green tie, starched shirt, and matching black peaked cap. He was also sporting a neatly cut moustache, but was otherwise clean-shaven. The nameplate on the desk said he was the 'Zone Commander'.

'Major Gabriel Black,' the man said, sticking out his hand across the table. Joe automatically stiffened his stance, dropped one hand by his side and, with the other, gave an army salute. As he did so his walking stick clattered to the ground.

Major Black ignored the wooden cane rolling on the floor, and instead kept his eyes on Joe; he nodded an acknowledgement and instructed Joe to, 'Take a seat, young man.'

Joe pulled out the chair, picked up his stick and sat down. His injured leg was splayed out in front of him. His wounds had now healed but had done so at the expense of his mobility and flexibility. He could only bend his right leg a fraction; it was as if he had a slightly crooked lead pipe running down his trouser leg. It was sturdy enough, but also unforgiving in its lack of movement.

'So, I'm guessing you want to join the town's Home Guard, soldier?'

Joe nodded.

'All right,' the major said, pulling out a form from his desk drawer. 'Let's start off with your full name.'

He pulled the cap off his fountain pen.

'Joseph Harry Elliot.'

Major Black carefully inked in the names in the appropriate blank spaces.

'Joseph . . . Harry . . . Elliot – with two ls and one t?'

'Yes, sir,' Joe said.

It took a few minutes to go through the form-filling exercise, which required information on Joe's work before the war and any military service since then. Once done, Major Black put the silver cap back on his torpedo-shaped pen.

'So, Private Elliot, you served in the Desert Rats out in Egypt?'

Joe nodded again.

'And I'm taking it you don't want to sit out the rest of the war at home?' he said, looking at Joe for a reaction.

'Exactly, sir!' Joe was pleased the man seemed to understand him, and felt compelled to elaborate. 'I might have been tossed on to the slag heap and sent home . . .' There was no bitterness in Joe's voice. He knew the army captain in charge of his battalion had not had any other choice but to medically discharge him. 'But I've still got one good leg, the use of both my arms, and I've got something resembling a brain between my ear lugs.'

Joe smiled a little nervously, worried he might have overstepped the mark, as he looked across the desk at the immaculately turned-out, slightly forbidding-looking zone commander sitting opposite him.

'I know I'm not washed up yet,' Joe carried on earnestly. 'And I'm sure I can be of some use to the town.'

'Well, lad,' Major Black said, 'I'm sure you can.' As he spoke he pushed his upper body away from his large wooden desk, and it was only then Joe realised he was in a wheelchair, and that he had no limbs from the knee down.

Seeing the surprised look on Joe's face, Major Black said, 'Lost them at the Battle of the Menin Road Ridge near Zillebeke in Belgium back in 1917. Couldn't find the blasted things for the life of me!'

He let out a loud guffaw. 'But I've managed just fine without them.'

He looked at Joe and his face turned serious. 'Don't you worry, Private Elliot, we'll make good use of you here.'

He spun the wooden wheelchair round the desk and guided it towards a cabinet at the side of the room, where he retrieved a bottle of Scotch whisky and two glasses. He didn't ask Joe if he wanted one, but poured out two good measures, put one of the glasses between what was left of his legs, took the other in one hand, and with his free arm wheeled his chair to Joe.

Joe knew not to go and help the former war veteran, just like Major Black had not made any reference to Joe's disability. Instead he forced himself to remain seated, before taking the proffered glass.

'To King and country!'

'To King and country!' Joe agreed.

Both men downed their shots in one.

'Right!' Major Black said with a big smile on his face. 'Let's get you signed up properly.'

While filling out another form which Joe had to sign, Major Black asked Joe about his year's military service in North Africa; for the first time since his return, Joe opened up about his experiences out there. Encouraged by the major's questions, Joe talked about strategies and the battles his battalion had been involved in, and, of course, the Egyptian desert, and how it was totally unlike what he had expected.

'I thought it'd be blazing sun and sand dunes for as far as the eye could see – you know, like in the films. But it wasn't anything like that – just rocks and dust. Hot during the day, and at night it was like being back here – bloody cold and windy!'

In return Major Black told Joe how the reality of the First World War was also not what he had anticipated; how he had served in the Thirteenth Battalion of the Durham Light Infantry, the same as Joe's father, although Major Black could not recall a Harry Elliot.

'It changes you in ways you could never have foreseen – and in ways those who have not been soldiers cannot possibly understand,' he said.

His kindly eyes, which were the colour of dishwater, became veiled in sadness. It was a mournfulness that Joe knew only too well, and he nodded in agreement. Neither men needed to put into words the abject horrors they had been witness to, the visions of mutilated bodies that would stay with them for ever, and the smell of blood and death that would occasionally come back when they least expected it. It was enough to know that they both shared the same godforsaken memories. They were not alone.

After a while, the conversation turned to the present situation out in Tobruk, a port city in Libya near the border with Egypt, and their hopes that the British Army could keep the Germans at bay.

Major Black then brought the subject back to the Home Guard and, more intriguingly, a separate, unknown section of the country's civil defence called 'Auxiliary Units'.

'These units aren't exactly public knowledge. In fact, they're pretty much top secret,' Major Black said.

Joe's interest was now piqued, and he listened intently to each word the major said.

'They're akin to the French resistance – only British, of course,' he said, pulling out a cigarette and offering Joe one, who declined with a shake of his hand.

'They've been described by those in the know as "Churchill's secret army" – ready to protect our shore should the Hun invade, God forbid.'

Joe was now rapt. His visit had become so much more than he had dared to hope.

'So, what exactly is it they do?' Joe asked, eager to hear more.

'Their aim is to resist occupation by the Nazis at all costs. Each unit is made up of six to eight carefully selected men. Having learnt about your background, you've got a lot of hands-on military expertise from your time on the front line – and you've also worked in the shipyards most of your life. Plus you're born and bred here – you know the area. You've got a lot to offer. I believe you would be perfect for the job.'

Joe felt the beginnings of a self-confidence that he had lost the moment he'd been blasted with shrapnel returning to him.

'The units,' Major Black continued, 'operate all over Britain, but they're especially active in the north-east.'

Major Black took another draw on his cigarette. 'A good part of our units are made up of men in reserved occupations. We've quite a few shipyard workers, as well as miners and farm workers from out near Penshaw and Durham. Some of our patrol leaders are schoolmasters, which is where you come in really. I know you're not going to be running around like some of the younger lads, but, like you say, you've got something between your ears.

'And we *need* to be prepared. We need teams of men with the knowledge and the ability to disable factories, petrol installations, shipyards, and any other kinds of industries should Hitler's evil make it across the Channel.' He sucked hard on his Winston cigarette.

'There is the need for men like yourself . . . But,' he added sternly, 'I cannot stress enough how important it is to keep this under your hat. Not a word. Not even to any of your family or loved ones. All they need to know is that you have joined the Home Guard.'

Joe was sat up rigidly straight in his seat. 'That's one thing I'm very good at, sir. I know how to keep my trap shut!'

'Excellent,' Major Black said, stubbing out his cigarette, which he had smoked to the butt, and leaning across the desk to shake Joe's hand.

'Welcome aboard, Private Joseph Elliot.'

The two men chatted a while longer, with Major Black giving Joe more background on the so-called Auxiliary Units, and how they had been set up in July last year, shortly after France had surrendered to Germany and the invasion of Britain became a very real possibility. The brains behind the specialised teams was a Major General Colin McVean Gubbins, who had set up a training establishment in a large country house down south, where a select band of the Home Guard had learnt how to make Molotov cocktails and other explosive devices before returning to their own areas to recruit potential 'guerrillas' to join up.

'The Home Guard and the Auxiliary Units are the last step between the enemy and our families and homes,' Major Black said solemnly.

As their chat drew to a close, Major Black arranged to meet up the following day so that Joe could sign the Official Secrets Act and formalise his membership of the town's Auxiliary Unit.

After Joe left the recruitment office and made his way home, his mind was abuzz with everything that had been said. He felt as though a part of his old self had returned. He felt proud again. And it was thanks to Major Black. He had filled him with a renewed sense of self-worth, of purpose. Joe was resolute that his crippled leg would not stop him being the best man he could possibly be.

As he hobbled down Tatham Street, ignoring the sharp stabbing pains shooting up into his thigh, which happened when he was on his feet too long, or he'd been walking for more than a few minutes, Joe felt a wave of excitement at getting back to the house.

Although he couldn't tell Bel about the fact he had signed up to form a part of Churchill's 'secret army', he *could* tell her he had joined the Home Guard. This was the happiest he had felt in a long while, and he wanted to share that joy. And, of course, he also wanted Bel to see him as a man, and not just someone whose wounds she had to tend to, and who now walked with a stick.

As Joe hobbled through the front door, he was over the moon that it was Bel who was the first to greet him – the first person he could tell his news to.

'Where have you been?' she asked curiously.

'I've joined up – again!' Joe said.

He was so excited, but stopped dead in his tracks when he saw Bel's face crumple.

'You've what?' Bel said in disbelief. Before Joe had time to answer, to explain, Bel had burst into uncontrollable tears.

Joe took two steps forward, tossed his stick aside, and grabbed hold of her in his arms.

'What's wrong, Bel?' he asked her, feeling her body heaving as she sobbed. She was barely able to get her words out.

'You can't go. You can't go!' she sobbed.

And it was then that the penny dropped. Bel had thought the army were sending him back out to the front line.

'Oh, Bel! No, I was just joshing. The army haven't got use for an old cripple like me. I'd be more a hindrance than a help, yer daftie.'

Bel stopped crying and pulled away from Joe and looked at him with a question on her face.

'I've joined the Home Guard, silly billy. They said I might come in useful, gammy leg or no.'

Bel burst into tears again – only this time they were tears of relief.

'Oh, Joe. I'm so stupid. For one insane moment I thought you were going back out there.' Bel gulped air, before admitting, 'I don't think I could cope if you did.'

Joe wrapped his arms around her once more, breathing in her soft scent, and feeling the brush of her hair against his face.

As she pulled away again and wiped tears from her eyes, Joe caught a glimpse of his mother turning and disappearing back into the kitchen, followed closely by the dog.

Later on that evening, when they were all sitting round the table eating one of Agnes's corned beef, onion and potato pies, the news that Joe had joined the town's Home Guard was the main topic of conversation.

'I won't be running around on exercises like they've been doing down Hendon, you know.' Joe was desperately trying to play it down. 'But they said they'd find something for me to do. Keep me out of mischief,' he said, taking a big bite out of his pie.

Bits of pastry fell to the floor and were quickly snaffled up by Agnes's little stray.

'Eee, Agnes, you're not going to need to bother shaking the mat out – you've got your very own human carpet sweeper here!' Polly looked down at the dog, which was in a state of high alert. 'I reckon she's quick enough to catch any crumbs before they've even hit the ground,' she added playfully.

Everyone chuckled.

'So, Joe,' Pearl said, bringing the conversation back to her son-in-law's enlistment in the Home Guard. 'Do you get to wear one of those khaki green uniforms?'

Without waiting for an answer, she continued, 'The women will be beating a path to your door if you do, that's for sure.' As she talked she swung her gaze across to Bel.

'There's a lot of pretty young women out there – and a very definite shortage of eligible young men. You should make the most of it. There's nothing like a man in uniform – and a war hero at that – to get the girls' pulses racing,' Pearl cackled.

'Oh for God's sake, Ma. Do you have to drag the conversation down to the gutter?' Bel spluttered the words out angrily.

The table fell quiet for a moment, before Polly quickly changed the subject back to the dog, and chirped up. 'Anyway, "mother of waifs and strays", what about this ugly mutt that's getting under everyone's feet? I thought you were taking it back to where it came from?'

'For goodness' sake, Polly, when did you get to be so hard? You were the one that was always begging me to keep every stray you came across when you were little. Poor little thing,' Agnes said, her Irish lilt coming through as she reached down to stroke the dog, which, as usual, was sitting as close to its adored mistress as it could possibly get.

Agnes picked a bit of crust from her pie and slyly dropped it so that it fell next to her furry companion.

'I saw that Ma!' Polly was outraged. 'When did *you* get to be so *soft*?'

Arthur chuckled at the women's verbal sparring. 'Agnes tried to find its owner today. We had a walk back along Hendon Road, but no one seemed to know where it had come from. Bit of a mystery really. But, to be honest, I don't think it would have gone even if we'd found its owner.'

As they started to clear the plates, Bel was glad Polly had changed the conversation. She realised she had come down a bit too hard on her mum; after all, her mother was just trying to join in and have a bit of banter. She didn't know why she had been so sharp. She had just felt annoyed at the thought of Joe being besieged by a lot of amorous young women. Which was stupid. Why would that annoy her? If anything, she should be pleased. It would be lovely to see Joe dating someone. Planning a future with a woman.

Wouldn't it?

'Anyway,' Pearl said, as she helped herself to another slice of pie, 'if the hungry little vagabond is staying put, don't you think it needs a name?'

'The hungry little mite is going to stay hungry with you around. It'll be lucky to get any scraps with Hungry Horace Pearl about.' Bel couldn't help having another stab at her mum, although this one felt justified. She had never known anyone eat so much and still be as skinny as a rake. She was such a scavenger. The dog had competition.

'Good point, Pearl,' Joe said, glad the conversation had swung away from his potential love life to the naming of their new house guest.

'What about Tramp – as in homeless, down and out . . . as in "The Lady is a Tramp"!'

Arthur, Polly, Agnes and Pearl looked at Joe with a puzzled expression on their faces.

'You know, from the musical *Babes in Arms*,' Bel said, before she started singing the lyrics:

'She gets too hungry for dinner at eight
She likes the theatre and never comes late
She never bothers with people she'd hate
That's why the lady is a tramp.'

They all sat and hummed along to the well-known tune; even Arthur swayed a little from side to side.

'Eee,' Polly said when Bel came to the end, 'I've said it a hundred times before. You should be on the stage.'

Chapter Thirty-Four

The next morning before she left for work, Polly went to have a quick word with Agnes, who was in the scullery and had just finished wrapping up her freshly made sandwiches in greaseproof paper, and was now slicing up the loaf of bread she had baked yesterday to make toast for everyone's breakfast.

Polly murmured a few words quietly to her mum, who nodded her agreement before opening up the back door to let Tramp out for her morning ablutions.

As Polly walked back into the kitchen, Agnes shouted over her shoulder, 'Good job your old ma's gone *soft*, isn't it?'

Polly let out a loud laugh and shouted back, '*Touché*, Mother!'

She then sat down next to Bel, who was trying to get Lucille to eat her porridge before she was allowed to go off in search of 'Trampie' – the name she had taken to calling her new, real-life toy. It hadn't escaped Bel's notice that her daughter's raggedy bunny had been somewhat neglected since the arrival of the new four-legged addition to the Elliot household.

'I just wanted to check you're sure about what we chatted about a few weeks ago?' Polly asked, not wanting to elaborate, as Lucille didn't miss a trick, and Polly didn't want her niece getting excited about something that might or might not happen.

Bel looked blankly at her sister-in-law. It took a few moments for the penny to drop and for her to catch on to what Polly was talking about – or rather *not* talking about.

'Ah, what we discussed during the evening of toffee, broken biscuits and sweets?' She laughed. 'Yes, of course I'm still up for it! I've actually had to stop myself getting too excited – you know – just in case . . .'

'I know,' Polly agreed. 'You never know, there may be complications because of her age . . .'

'But, yes,' Bel said, her face looking young and happy. 'Definitely. Tell Gloria we'll all have to meet up – and soon.'

Polly gave her sister-in-law a big hug. 'Thanks, Bel. You're a star,' she said, before grabbing her work bag and gas mask and heading out.

As she walked to the south dock she had to wait for a ferry, as the one she normally got was full; the sunny morning had pulled people out of their beds and on to the streets just that little bit earlier than normal.

'Sorry, Polly. There's not even room for a little un like yourself!' Stan the ferryman shouted over to her as he closed the landing gate. 'Be back as soon as we can!'

'No bother, Stan!' Polly shouted back. She'd still make it to work on time, and it gave her a few moments to daydream about Tommy; she had just received another letter from him, which she had already read to Bel, and which she was going to enjoy rereading to the women later on.

But, before she did so, she needed to grab Gloria for a quick cuppa and see what she thought of her suggestion. The baby wasn't due until the start of August, which meant she still had another twelve weeks to go, but the way the days seemed to be flying by at the moment, her due date would be upon them before they knew it.

*

Five hours later, when the midday horn sounded out, Polly dumped her welding mask on the ground, switched off her machine, and headed across the yard to where she knew she'd find Gloria.

'Eee, that crane suits you, Glor! You won't want to come back to us lot,' Polly shouted out to her friend.

Gloria was sitting in her tank-like metal box, just staring out to the North Sea. She was lost in her own world. On hearing Polly's voice she swung her gaze around and smiled.

'I love it here! Give me a moment and I'll manoeuvre this elephant-like body of mine out of this cage.'

Polly watched as Gloria swung her legs around and heaved herself out of the crane driver's box. She stepped on to the flat concrete expanse of the yard, which was just starting to quieten a little as workers sat down to have their lunch.

'I've got a proposition for you,' Polly said, as they both settled themselves on two metal chairs Gloria had managed to acquire from the draughtsman's office. She was now at the stage in her pregnancy whereby she might well be able to sit down on the ground, but there was no guarantee she would be able to get up.

As they poured out their cups of tea from their flasks and unwrapped their packed lunches, Polly gawped at Gloria's two rounds of sandwiches, which looked as though they had been filled with an entire jar of strawberry jam.

'That baby's going to end up with the biggest sweet tooth ever – either that or it'll hate anything even remotely sugary.' Polly chuckled.

Gloria laughed. 'I know. If it's a girl I think I'll just call her "sweetie" – or "sugar", like the Yanks do.' She took another big mouthful, sighed contentedly and lifted her face to the sun.

'So,' she said, wiping jam from the corner of her mouth, 'you've got me curious. What's this *proposition* all about?'

Polly swallowed her own ham and pease pudding sandwiches, which had been a special treat from Agnes, who Polly was convinced was buttering them all up so that they'd be fine about keeping the dog.

'Well, you know you said you wanted to stay on working in the yards after you've had the baby . . . and that the foreman is keen to have you back as soon as possible . . .'

'Yes,' Gloria said, now looking more serious.

'But, you didn't know if you could because you didn't have anyone to look after the baby during the day when you'd be working here?'

'Yes.' Gloria was looking more and more intrigued.

'Well, you know my ma looks after a load of the neighbours' children while they're out at work . . . and that she's now got Bel there helping her . . .?'

'Yes,' Gloria said, her voice getting louder with hope.

'And that Bel's great with children and, let's face it, she has only ever wanted one thing in life – to be a mum . . .'

Gloria could not contain herself. 'Oh, if I think you're going to say what you are, then, *yes please*! That would be *fantastic*!'

Polly beamed, seeing how overjoyed her workmate was. 'You couldn't want for anyone better to look after your baby,' Polly gushed. 'She really is the best.'

Gloria hadn't met Bel, but she felt as if she knew her, as Polly had talked a lot about her sister-in-law: how understanding and supportive she had been when she was going through her rollercoaster of a love affair with Tommy, how she'd always been there for Polly, whether she needed a shoulder to cry on or just a good old gossip, and, of course, how devastated she had been when she had lost Teddy.

'That's all sorted then. I'll organise a time for you to come round for some tea so you can meet Bel. Ma might even bake a cake!'

Gloria eyes lit up as she polished off her lunch. 'Ah, thanks, Pol. You've all been so brilliant. What with Dorothy getting me this job and everyone being so nice about everything. I don't know what I'd do without you lot,' she said.

They were both quiet for a while.

Polly wanted to tell Gloria that they didn't know what they would do without her either; that she had helped them and been there for them all over the past nine months. She had taken on the mantle of mother hen from when they had first arrived in the yard, and kept a watchful eye on them all ever since, only stepping in if it was necessary. And, she had taken control the night Rosie had been attacked, and dealt with Jack when he had turned up so unexpectedly and seen what had happened.

Which brought Polly back to the present.

'Any idea what you're going to do about Vinnie,' Polly lowered her voice, 'or Jack?'

What Polly was really asking, of course, was whether or not Gloria was going to come clean about who the baby's father was. They had chatted about it before, and Polly could understand why Gloria had not told Jack she was pregnant before he went off to America – he might well not have gone, for Gloria's sake, but they all knew just how important these new Liberty Ships were going to be in the war.

Now, though, that the yard's owner, Cyril Thompson, had returned, and issues regarding the production and construction of the new ship had been more or less dealt with, Jack's work was done. He was due back any time soon. And, boy, Polly thought, was he going to get the shock of his life when he saw Gloria.

'I've no idea,' Gloria answered honestly. 'I feel I'm stuck between the devil and the deep blue sea. I know it's not right to let Vinnie think the baby's his, but at the same time, if I tell Jack it's his, there'll be a holy war on. Can you imagine what'll happen if Miriam finds out. And Helen . . . They'll make it their life's mission to totally destroy Jack – and me. I could cope with it if it was just me, but it's Jack who will lose everything – his job, his family, his good standing. He'll be an outcast. And I know Miriam will make it nigh on impossible for him to get another job anywhere else – especially with the contacts her father has. God, he practically runs this town. Or certainly the business side of it.'

Polly nodded her head in agreement. She certainly didn't envy Gloria, and could not see how she could possible resolve the situation happily. She also knew that the last thing Gloria wanted was for it to even cross Jack's mind that she had done the same as Miriam and had conned him into being with her by getting pregnant unexpectedly.

As Polly got up to go back to the women welders, Gloria asked, 'How's Angie getting on?'

Polly chuckled. 'Let's just say it's been an amusing few days. Poor Rosie, I don't know how she manages to keep her cool. Honestly, Angie and Dorothy are like the female version of Laurel and Hardy. It's like being back at school most days.'

'And how's the little bird coping?' Gloria asked.

Polly's face fell. 'Not good. Poor thing. I really feel for her. Helen's giving her a hard time. She's been pinged across the yard like a yo-yo. And don't get me started on Martha. It's like Helen and Rosie are having a tug of war over who has her. The rope's either going to snap or one of them is going to end up on their backside,' Polly mused.

'Let's hope that it's you-know-who,' Gloria said with a concerned look on her face.

'Anyway, catch up with you later,' Polly said, grabbing her empty lunchbox and brushing off the crumbs from her overalls.

'See ya, Pol. And thank you,' Gloria said, watching as her friend hurried back over to her work place, dodging various groups of fitters, caulkers, and rivet catchers, and fending off the usual litany of cheeky comments from the shipyard's Casanovas.

Chapter Thirty-Five

One month later, June 1941

'I know this sounds awful, but thank goodness Hitler's moved his evil eye on to someone else. I don't know how much more this town could take. If he drops any more bombs on us, there's going to be nothing left other than shattered bricks and mortar,' Bel said to Joe as they walked into town.

Over the past few weeks, just about the whole of the country had been given a reprieve from the constant barrage of air strikes it had been subjected to over the past few months as Hitler had turned his sights on the Soviet Union. There had still been a degree of tit-for-tat warfare – with the Germans bombing London and then the Brits bombing Hamburg, followed by the sinking of the British ship *Hood*, then the *Bismarck* – but, on the whole, it looked as if the intense bombing might finally be over for the time being.

Joe was in his Home Guard uniform and was heading to see Major Black; the two men had become firm friends over the past month, and Joe had become the major's unofficial right-hand man. Bel and Lucille were accompanying Joe into town where they were going to do some shopping and, as always whenever they were all walking together, Lucille was hopping around Joe, as she liked to emulate the way he walked.

As the three Elliots made their way along the wide pavement past the town's museum, Joe suddenly broke off and started walking in front of them, before turning and saying, 'Guess who?' It had been his favourite question as a child, when he would ask the question and then either perform some kind of mime of a famous person or of someone from around the doors, and they would have to guess who it was.

As Bel and Lucille slowed down, Joe started twirling his walking stick, walking as if he had bendy legs, which wasn't hard as his injured leg was naturally crooked, and then he rolled his cap as if it were a bowler hat. His facial expression went still and vacant-looking, staring ahead, unblinking and appearing slightly confused.

It was an act Bel knew well; she had seen Joe perform it numerous times as a child, and it was one that was guaranteed to make her crease up with laughter. She had loved all the silent black and white movies she had managed to sneak into the cinema to watch when she was a child – her favourite, though, had always been slapstick.

Now, just like when they were young, Bel started to giggle, then laugh, as Joe started to ham it up even more, pretending to trip up and looking for the offending invisible obstacle. Before long the tears started to roll down Bel's face. All the while Lucille was giggling away, loving the street theatre and the sound of her mother's carefree, rippling laughter.

Holding her side, and between gasps of air, Bel managed to spit out the words, 'Charlie Chaplin!'

By now Bel's laughter was infectious; passers-by started to smile and chuckle as they walked past, and soon Bel, Lucille and Joe were all revelling in a good old belly laugh.

'Eee. Stop. The both of you. My stomach's killing me,' Bel declared. But she couldn't stop the laughter. Nor did she want to.

'Ah, it's good to see you laugh,' Joe said, putting his cap back on and giving Bel a sidelong glance.

'I know, Joe. It *feels* good.' It was the first time she'd felt the physical pain of laughter in a very long time.

Joe looked at Bel and her daughter with undisguised love, before falling back in line with the two of them, and taking hold of Lucille's little hand.

The happy trio continued their walk into town, when all of a sudden a tinkling voice sounded out from behind them.

'Joe? Is that you, Joe?'

Bel, Joe and Lucille stopped and turned round to see a very pretty young woman, wearing a dark green ambulance driver's uniform, with a thin belt wrapped round her narrow waist. The sleeves of her jacket had been rolled up, showing slender, olive-skinned arms. She was hurrying to catch them up.

'Oh, my goodness, it *is* you, Joe!'

Bel looked at Joe. His face had broken into a huge smile on seeing this woman who was very obviously over the moon to have spotted him.

'Maria!' Joe said. 'Wow! You look incredible!'

Maria blushed and leant in to give Joe a kiss on the cheek.

'Hardly!' she laughed, in a self-depreciating manner. 'I joined the Women's Auxiliary Unit and they've got me driving ambulances. I'm just off to do the afternoon shift . . . Anyway, I'd heard you'd been injured and were back. I've wanted to come round and see you but I didn't know if it was the right thing to do.'

Joe couldn't get his words out quickly enough. 'Of course, you're always welcome at ours. Ma'll be chuffed to pieces to see you. Funnily enough, she just mentioned you the other day. I told her you'd probably got married and had your own family by now.'

Maria's face reddened again. 'No. Not married. Nor engaged,' she said simply.

As she spoke her gaze fell on Bel. 'Oh, Bel, I'm so sorry, how rude of me. I was just so shocked at seeing Joe. How lovely to see you too.' There was no malice in her words. She was simply being honest. She really did only have eyes for Joe.

'And,' she added, bending down on to her haunches, 'this must be Teddy's little girl?' Maria smiled at Lucille, who returned the look with a frown.

'And how old are you?' she asked a disgruntled-looking Lucille, who was very clearly determined to remain tight-lipped.

'She's just about to turn three,' Bel said, before adding apologetically, 'and not normally as rude as this. Lucille, say hello to Maria. She's a friend of Joe's.'

Lucille forced out a 'Hello', but kept the scowl.

Maria smiled and stood back up. She and Joe were now standing close to each other, and all of a sudden Bel felt like a real gooseberry.

'Why don't Lucille and I get on with our shopping, and leave you two to it,' Bel said, moving away and taking Lucille's hand.

'No, don't let me stop you,' Maria said, a kindly smile spreading across her naturally tanned face. 'I tell you what, Joe, why don't you come over for some tea tomorrow? My mam and dad would love to see you. They've always had a soft spot for you.'

And they're not the only ones, Bel thought, before chastising herself.

When had she become so catty? She had always liked Maria and had never really been able to understand why Joe had ended their relationship before he went off to war. He had said it was because he did not want her to wait for him, but something about the way he had said it hadn't rung true.

'Thanks, Maria. That would be really nice. That's a date . . . I mean, not a date, but a date . . .' Joe started to ramble on awkwardly. Maria laughed gently and put her hand on Joe's arm, 'Don't worry, Joe. I know what you mean. I'll see you tomorrow then, about four?'

And with that she quickly said her goodbyes to them all and hurried across the wide breadth of Toward Road before disappearing up Fawcett Street.

Bel was just about to say how lovely it was to see Maria, even though she couldn't quite understand why it felt far from it, when Joe looked up at the clock on the town hall and said, 'God, look at the time, I'll see you both later on this evening.'

He bent down to ruffle Lucille's blonde mop of curls.

'Be good for your ma now!' he told her, before hurrying off as fast as he could, using his well-worn walking stick to push himself forward.

'Bye, Doey!' Lucille waved frantically after him, before looking up to her mother with a less than happy face. Bel looked down into her daughter's deep blue eyes. They were Teddy's eyes, but now that she had been spending so much time with Joe, she realised that her daughter's eyes were also the exact spit of her brother-in-law's.

Strange she had never noticed that before.

As her daughter swung her gaze back to follow Joe's receding figure hobbling up to Holmeside where he was to meet with the major, she had an unnerving feeling that Lucille saw much more than her years should have allowed.

'Come on then. If you do as Joe says and are a good girl, I'll get you a bag of whelks from the market.'

*

Later on that night there was great excitement about Joe's tea date with Maria.

Bel had, of course, told Agnes and Arthur, and made a point of telling Pearl when she had traipsed in, and then Polly when she got back from work.

They had all been as pleased as punch.

'I'll get myself some more grandchildren yet!' Agnes declared.

But when Polly had joked with Lucille that it would be nice for her to have a cousin to play with, her little niece's face had clouded over and she had shaken her head vigorously from side to side.

They had all laughed.

'I think she likes to be the centre of attention,' Arthur commented, although not for one moment did he believe that, for the child's face had laid bare her feelings, and he knew exactly what she was thinking.

Sometimes, he thought, *the older I get, the more I seem to understand the young uns.*

The following evening, when Joe came back from his tea at Maria's, everyone was milling around in the kitchen, awaiting his return. When Joe hobbled through the kitchen door, he took a dramatic step back.

'Whoa! Please don't tell me I'm going to get the third degree,' he said as he made his way over to the stove where Agnes had left a pot of stew keeping warm for his return.

'We thought you might have eloped you've been gone that long!' Pearl said on her way out for a smoke. Much to Del's annoyance, her mother seemed to be around a lot more than normal. It irked her that lately she seemed to be integrating well into the Elliot household. If Bel hadn't known better, she would have said her ma seemed to be enjoying family life.

'How is Maria anyway? And her parents – Fred and Alma, isn't it?' Agnes asked as she put some bacon rind and a few crusts in a little bowl for Tramp, who was partly hidden from view by Agnes's long skirt. The dog was so determined to get as near to her mistress as possible that she often ended up being an extension of Agnes's petticoat hems.

'They're fine. They all seem pretty much the same as before I left,' Joe said.

'And Maria?' Polly ventured. 'Is she the same?'

Joe paused.

'My goodness! Our Joe at a loss for words!' Polly joked. 'It must be love. What do you think, Bel?'

Bel had been sitting listening to the banter while helping Lucille draw a picture of Tramp. She was glad of the artistic distraction, as she was finding it hard to join in the conversation. She was struggling to know what to say, which was so unlike her, especially when it was anything to do with romance.

'Well,' Bel said, taking a breath and looking up from her daughter's sketch, which looked more bunny than dog, 'I think Maria's lovely. Always have done. I think Joe would be mad not to want to court her.'

Bel looked across at Joe, who was staring at her intently and somewhat unnervingly.

All of a sudden he stood up. 'All righ, Lu-Lu. Time for your bedtime story. All this women's chatter is making me tired. "The Lambton Worm", I think.'

'Yeh!' Lucille dropped her crayon, immediately abandoning her pet portrait and sticking both her hands in the air, ready for Joe to pick her up.

Bel got up to follow, but Joe stopped her. 'No worries, Bel. You stay here and organise my love life with everyone else.'

His words were said with a smile, but his eyes didn't follow suit.

As Joe put Lucille into her cot and got out her dog-eared copy of her favourite bedtime story, he wished he felt as excited about his tea with Maria as everyone else seemed to be. Perhaps he just needed to try a little harder.

Besides, Bel was obviously keen for him to see Maria. There had been no hesitation there. Not that he thought there would be. It was just lately he had felt Bel had let her guard down and the pair of them had become close.

But perhaps that was just wishful thinking on his behalf.

After Joe left the kitchen with Lucille, Arthur also said his goodnights, leaving the four women, Agnes, Pearl, Polly and Bel, sipping on their cups of tea, having a good old chinwag about the burgeoning romance between Joe and Maria.

'I don't see why Joe wouldn't want to get back with Maria,' Polly mused. 'He only stopped seeing her because he had signed up to go to war, and now he's back and he's not going anywhere, there's nothing stopping him from picking up where he left off, is there?'

'Mm,' Agnes agreed. 'Especially as Maria's not met anyone else.'

Pearl shuffled in her chair, rotating her cigarette packet on the kitchen table.

Bel looked at her. Her mother was either itching to say something, or craving a fag. Or both.

'I thought he seemed a tad undecided,' Pearl said a little cryptically, standing up and taking a cigarette out and tossing the packet down on the table top.

'Perhaps the war's changed Joe,' she said as she walked out of the kitchen, shoving her cigarette into her mouth, ready to light up, and he wants something different now.'

Bel was the only one to catch her mother's mumbled words, uttered quietly under her breath as she passed her daughter. *Something he can't have.*

Chapter Thirty-Six

Wednesday 11 June 1941

'So, how are your girls doing?' DS Miller asked Rosie, taking a bite of his sandwich and washing it down with a mouthful of tea.

The pair were seated at the same small, square, wooden table they always sat at in the corner of the little teashop on High Street East. Today the café was bursting at the seams with customers: workers, pensioners, women and children – there was even a cat slinking around underneath the tables. Rosie loved this place – the clattering of cups and saucers, the gentle hum of chattering voices, even the hungry cries of a baby. And, in the midst of it all, there was Vera, busily making round after round of sandwiches, pouring countless cups of tea, and slicing up her huge home-made cakes.

Despite the sudden teatime rush, the café's proprietor had made sure no one was sitting at the corner table, as she now did every week for the copper and the woman welder who came to enjoy her patronage every Wednesday – and who had been doing so religiously for the past six weeks.

Vera still had no idea if the odd couple were just friends, colleagues or lovers, but what she did know was that they were both as regular as clockwork with the time and frequency of their meetings, as well as with their very generous tips.

Rosie was surprised but glad that their corner table was always free, and wondered whether it was down to the bountiful gratuities DS Miller left, or whether he was actually paying some kind of retainer so that their favourite place was theirs and theirs alone for their regular weekly rendezvous. It was the only explanation Rosie could think of, as Vera was not the most accommodating of people. There had even been a few times when they had arrived to find customers standing at the counter waiting for a seat, even though their corner table was quite obviously empty, and when Vera had clocked them walking through the door, she had simply nodded in the direction of the table, signalling to them to go and sit down, before making everyone else wait until she had sorted them out with a pot of tea and a round of sandwiches.

For Rosie, these get-togethers with the detective were the highlight of her week. Sitting there opposite DS Miller, their waxed-cloth-covered table so small that their legs occasionally brushed against one another, Rosie felt as if they were in their own little world, their own bubble – chatting, laughing, and philosophising about life, their work, and, of course, the war.

Today, Vera had her little wireless on and, as was the norm, was making no effort at small talk, or any attempt to force her mouth into a friendly smile. Her customers didn't seem to mind, though; judging by how busy it was today, her slightly grumpy, almost unfriendly attitude clearly wasn't affecting business.

'Sorry, Peter, what did you say?' Rosie asked. She felt her stomach plummet to the bottom of her rubber-soled boots.

'How are your girls?' DS Miller repeated the question, this time speaking a little louder to make sure he could be heard over the surrounding chatter.

Rosie could feel her heart hammering. For a split second she had thought he'd meant 'her girls' – at Lily's – and she'd been floored by a sense of sheer panic and shock.

Seeing the slightly confused look on Rosie's face, the detective elaborated. 'You know, *your welders* – your girls?'

Rosie wanted to slap herself. There was no way he could possibly know about her *other* girls.

You are getting paranoid, Rosie reprimanded herself.

'Ah, the girls. Of course, the girls. *My* girls. My welders,' Rosie tried to sound nonchalant and hide any trace of alarm the detective might have picked up on.

'Goodness,' she laughed, letting her body relax, 'where do I start?'

'How's Gloria? Has she been having any more bother with her estranged husband?' Now it was DS Miller's turn to force a certain casualness into his voice.

'No, thank the lord!' Rosie exclaimed a little too animatedly, a delayed sense of relief flooding through her.

'She hasn't seen hide nor hair of him since the last time . . .' Rosie paused. 'He's probably so ashamed about what he did that he doesn't dare show his face – I hope so, anyway. Gloria's got enough on her plate at the moment without worrying about him turning up again and getting nasty,' Rosie added, her anger towards Vinnie resurfacing quickly.

Rosie wanted to tell Peter that Gloria's plate was particularly overflowing at the moment, as she was going to have to make up her mind pretty soon about whether or not to come clean about the baby's paternity. She had heard from the other yard manager, who was presently doing a sort of job share with Helen, that Jack was on his way back from America. No one knew exactly when, as he was travelling back by sea, and that could take weeks in the present climate. But, when Jack was back in town, and moreover when he saw that Gloria had doubled in size and it had nothing to do with her diet, she was going to have to either tell him the truth – that the child was his – or lie and say it was Vinnie's. The woman was in an impossible situation.

Rosie wished she could share Gloria's dilemma, but that was her friend's secret and not hers to tell. She did feel, though, that her detective would have understood; she had got to know Peter over these past few months and could see he was naturally kind and compassionate. She also knew he had been enraged when she'd told him about Vinnie's violence. A lot of men she knew would not have been that concerned – and some would even have blamed it on Gloria.

'But,' Rosie continued, 'Gloria seems as happy as Larry on the cranes, which is a good thing. And, best of all, I think Helen's realised that she can't get rid of Gloria, even if she wants to. According to my union rep she *could* sack her at the drop of a hat just because she's pregnant, but he reckons the big bosses have told her to take heed as Thompson's, like all the shipyards, are crying out for more workers. He said it wouldn't be "prudent" to be seen to be sacking women – especially pregnant women – as just about all of the town's industry is becoming increasingly reliant on what he calls "the gentler sex".'

DS Miller pretended to splutter on his tea. 'Gentler? Mm, I'm not so sure about that!'

Rosie laughed. 'Tell me about it! *My girls*, as you call them, certainly don't fit that description.

'But, anyway, the good news is that Angie's taken to welding really well. Thank goodness. And the rest of the women are all chipping in and helping her learn the ropes. It makes my job so much easier.'

After they'd finished their tea and sandwiches, and Rosie had bought a big piece of cake that Vera put in a box for her and tied with string, the pair left, shouting out their goodbyes and, as usual, being waved off by the old woman as if she was shooing them out of her premises.

As soon as the door had closed behind them, DS Miller took Rosie's hand. It was the part of their date she always looked forward to: the feel of his strong hand wrapped around her own as he walked her back to her flat. Neither of them ever struggled with conversation and they would chat away right up to the moment they parted, but Rosie's mind was always focused on her companion's touch – his warm, large, rough hand as it grasped her own gifting her a feeling of sensuality, of joy, of being cared for, and of love.

Sometimes, like today, their fingers would intertwine and Rosie would feel the deep pull of attraction – something she had rarely experienced in her life and which always caught her off guard.

Rosie was well aware that their weekly ritual of tea, chats and then walking home holding hands was a little odd. Most other couples would be dating properly by now. But she was relieved Peter had not formally asked to court her, or attempted to do anything more than hold her hand. It was as if he intuitively knew she didn't want that. Although, of course, she *did* want that. Very much so.

After they both said their chaste farewells, Rosie let herself into her flat, but as she did so the feelings Peter had infused in her quickly evaporated as she came back down to earth. She reminded herself that their dalliance could never go any further, for she simply couldn't allow herself to become involved with *any* man, but especially one who enforced the law of the land.

She was especially sure of this after her reaction earlier on. There was simply no way Peter could know about her other job.

The only way he could ever find out would be if he went there for any of the services offered by her girls, and Rosie was pretty sure Peter was not the type. Lily had told her that they had the occasional visit from one of the Borough's chief inspectors, but he was always very discreet and only Lily and George knew he was a copper. No one else from the local constabulary had any idea that the beautiful three-storey town house opposite Ashbrooke's Sports and Social Club was anything but the residence of one of the town's more affluent inhabitants.

But her reaction to Peter's innocent question earlier on had given Rosie a shock. It had afforded her an insight into how it would feel should he get to know about her past as a working girl, and her present as Lily's business partner. But worst of all had been the sense of shame that had unexpectedly hit her during that short moment she had thought Peter knew about the bordello.

It's a warning, Rosie told herself as she quickly changed her clothes, *I've got too close to this man for my own good. It has to stop.*

Rosie knew she was playing with fire, and she knew she was going to get badly hurt if she carried on seeing him.

As she dabbed make-up on to her face, covering her scars, her mind kept churning over. She knew if her relationship with Peter went any further, the pain she would inevitably feel would be a very different kind to that which her uncle Raymond had subjected her to – but it was pain all the same. And she had suffered enough hurt and torment to last her a lifetime.

'I've already been burnt the once. I'm damned if it's going to happen again,' she said aloud to the reflection staring back at her in the mirror.

As Rosie finished getting ready, she left her flat and made her way to her old boarding house, just a few hundred yards up from the main bus depot in Park Lane. Rosie hurried up the worn carpeted stairs, taking care as she was wearing her heels and a dress which wasn't exactly figure-hugging but that still didn't allow her much leeway in movement.

Lily had shown her some of the latest 'utility' fashions and how it was becoming increasingly common for women to wear slacks for leisure and not just for work. Rosie had liked the look of them; they appeared comfortable and far more practical than a skirt. She longed for the day overalls became de rigueur but doubted that would ever happen, certainly not in her lifetime.

'Mrs T? You up there?' Rosie shouted out as she reached the second landing.

'Of course I'm here, Rose! Where else is an old blind woman going to be? Out living it up? Painting the town red?' she said with a loud laugh.

'You don't fool me,' Rosie said as she pushed open the old woman's door, which was always ajar. 'You're probably planning a night out on the tiles as soon as you're shot of me!'

Rosie gave Mrs T a big hug and then put her boxed-up cake on the side table. 'This is a fleeting visit, I'm just off out, but I wanted to pop in with this for you to have after your supper.'

Mrs T shuffled over to where Rosie had put the square cardboard box and picked it up and smelt it. 'Ah, you're a little treasure. It's my favourite. Good old-fashioned pound cake. I can smell the vanilla and icing powder. Thanks, pet. You don't have to, you know. You should save your pennies. I know you've not got a lot.'

'If I couldn't afford it, I wouldn't get it. You just look after yourself and enjoy it. I'll do us a quick cuppa and then I'll get off.'

As Rosie made the tea, the two women chatted about their week. Mrs T told Rosie about the new tenants on the third floor, a loud, young woman, with two small but equally vociferous children. And Rosie talked in turn about work, and how she was counting down the weeks and days before her sister Charlotte came to stay over during the school holidays.

'I wasn't sure whether I should let her really,' she told Mrs T a little anxiously, 'especially after all the air raids we've been having of late, but it seems to have quietened down. I think I can risk her being here for a couple of days.'

'I can't wait to meet her,' the old woman said as she lifted her teacup to her lips. Rosie noticed that her hands were shaking more than usual.

'Charlotte cannot wait to meet you too. I've told her all about you – and the girls at work. I think she's quite excited.'

When it was time for Rosie to go, Mrs T didn't ask her where she was going, which pleased Rosie, but at the same time it confirmed what she had suspected for a while now: Mrs T had a good idea where she was going and what she was doing – and had probably known for some time. After Rosie had been attacked by her uncle, and the old woman had felt the scars on her face, she'd stopped asking where Rosie was 'gallivanting' off to, just like she'd never mentioned the sister and family in South Shields Rosie had purported to have; that was a story Rosie had concocted shortly after she had first moved in to explain why she was coming back so late in the evening.

The women had an unspoken understanding. Rosie was pleased the old woman had some idea as to what she did but, at the same time, she was glad she also knew not to talk about it.

Her only slight concern was that if an old doddery woman, who could hardly walk and was blighted with cataracts, had sussed out what she was doing, how long would it take someone like Peter, a detective, and a naturally inquisitive person, to also work it out?

At about the same time that Rosie was leaving Mrs T's to go to Lily's, DS Miller was starting his shift patrolling the north side of the river, where the majority of the bombs had been dropped over the past year. His mind, as it always did when he had time to himself, was replaying his weekly tea date with Rosie.

He really had never met another woman like her. She was totally unique, but he still couldn't quite work her out. Sometimes he felt he knew her well, other times not so well. Like this afternoon, he had picked up on something when he'd asked her about 'her girls', but he couldn't interpret her slightly odd reaction. It was as if she had panicked. Which didn't make sense.

He was usually good at reading people – years on the job had taught him that – and he was also naturally intuitive, but Rosie was different. A part of him was of the opinion that there was more to Rosie than met the eye. That she had a secret of sorts, although he had no idea what that could be. Another part of him was saying that he'd been a copper for too long and had become overly suspicious of people. What he did know, though, without a shadow of a doubt, was that he was falling in love with her. That much was obvious, and he couldn't do anything to stop it. And he didn't want to stop it. And he felt that Rosie was also falling for him, even if she was incredibly guarded about showing it.

The woman was just so contradictory, without being aware of it. She was an odd mixture of worldliness and innocence. He had never come across a woman who gave off such maturity and experience of life, but at the same time seemed extremely young and almost naïve – certainly with regard to any kind of courtship.

Her complexity did not in any way dampen his fervour for her; if anything it fired it up even more. He had never imagined he would ever find another woman whom he loved as he had his wife. But then Rosie had come along and bowled him over.

Every minute they were together, sitting opposite each other in the café, he had to stop himself reaching over and kissing her; just like when he was walking her back home and her hand seemed to burn into his own, he had to physically stop himself pulling her into his arms and caressing her. He did not know how much longer he could keep his amorous feelings for her in check.

Part of him wished he had kissed her the first time he'd taken hold of her hand, but something had made him hold back. Was it something he had picked up from Rosie? He could not be sure. Or perhaps it was his own reticence? A residual feeling of guilt that he was somehow being unfaithful to his wife, even though she had now been gone for several years.

As he walked down Sea Road towards the beach to go and chat with some of the Home Guard manning the pillboxes on the promenade, he made a decision: there would never be a right time, and he might never know the answers to his questions, so he just had to follow his heart and show Rosie how he felt – that he loved being with her, loved her company and her conversation, but that most of all he wanted and desired her as a woman.

And there was only one way of showing her this and it was through actions – and not words.

Chapter Thirty-Seven

The next morning Rosie woke from a disjointed dream about DS Miller that she couldn't really remember, but which had left her with a feeling of light-heartedness, of being happy and loved.

Her night-time slumber had also triggered in her a real need to see the detective; she wished that while she had slept a week had magically passed by so it would be Wednesday once again. Her feelings lifted her and perturbed her at the same time. She was still awash with conflicting feelings. It was as if she was in the throes of an addiction, and one from which she did not want to break free.

She wanted more. More of Peter.

She knew Lily was right. Even though she had not come out and said anything as such – she didn't need to – Rosie knew what she was thinking. No good would come of it.

But Rosie just couldn't put the stoppers on it. Not yet. Not at the moment.

As Rosie got ready for work and headed out of the door and down to the ferry, she decided that she *could* allow herself to keep seeing the detective.

For just a little while longer.

'Rosie. Can you come here, please?'

Rosie's heart sank. She didn't need to turn around to see to whom the voice belonged.

'Ah, Helen. How are you? Lovely day today, isn't it?' Rosie said, squinting up at the sunny, almost faultless clear blue sky, peppered with only a handful of billowy white clouds.

'Any news on Jack's return?' Rosie looked at Helen's perfectly made-up face. Her other girls in Ashbrooke would have given anything to get hold of some of her classy and clearly very expensive poppy-red lipstick, and today she was wearing a very unusual green eye shadow, which made her emerald eyes even more striking than they already were. Not for the first time, Rosie wondered how someone so beautiful on the outside could be so vile on the inside.

'Not yet,' Helen spat out, knowing full well that Rosie's question was really a forewarning that she wouldn't be in this position of power for that much longer, which was all the more reason she should act now.

'I'm afraid Hannah's going to have to go and work with Mickey's lot,' she said, trying to fight back a smile which had nothing to do with joy, and everything to do with spite.

'And, I hate to take your star player off you, but Martha's needed with the riveters again. So sorry, Rosie. I know it's a pain . . .'

Her words were spoken without even a hint of apology, however. Helen was revelling in her meddling and, what was more, she knew Rosie didn't have the standing in the yard to stop her.

Rosie glared at Helen and, without speaking, turned her back on her and went to see the women.

Hannah looked as though she was going to burst into tears when Rosie told her she was being sent to work with Mickey's crew who, the women had all agreed, were like an ageing pack of testosterone-fuelled bulldogs – small, but thickset, and still strong despite their years. They were always given the most strenuous type of welding work, and basked in their notoriety as hard men with whom no one dared mess.

Martha was also clearly far from happy on learning she was being siphoned off to go and work with the riveters. She banged her welding mask down and snatched up her holdall, before declaring in a booming voice to the women, 'I do not like this!'

She then lurched off towards Jimmy and his men over in the dry dock.

Dorothy, Angie and Polly exchanged concerned looks, before pushing their masks back down and cracking on with their day's work.

At lunchtime they all met up, but no one was in a particularly chatty mood. Martha had sunk back into her old non-verbal ways, and when Rosie looked at Hannah, she thought she had never seen her look so white. The poor thing was almost translucent.

When they all headed back to work, they did so without the usual cheery banter – even Dorothy and Angie were unnaturally subdued.

Rosie was fuming. She just couldn't understand how another woman could be like this to others of the same sex. Hadn't her posh education taught her anything? She would have thought going to Sunderland Church High School – the town's only private girls school – would have instilled in her some kind of understanding of the meaning of sisterhood, or what Rosie had heard referred to as 'feminism', rather than a tendency to treat her own gender in such an antagonistic and vindictive manner.

Just before the end of the shift, Rosie went over to see how Hannah was coping. When she got there she could see her childlike body slumped over a weld, and she kept breaking off to rest her arm. When Rosie tapped her on her narrow shoulder and Hannah turned round and pushed up her welding mask, she could have cried. The group's little bird looked well and truly on her last legs. Dark circles encased her eyes and it was obvious she'd been weeping behind her mask, as she had dried tear marks running down her sooty face.

'That's enough for today,' Rosie said, bobbing down on her haunches so that she was facing Hannah. 'I don't have to ask how you're doing,' she said, 'because I can see full well how you're feeling.'

Rosie wanted to add, *and I know exactly who is responsible for this*, but she didn't. There was a part of her that realised, much as she despised Helen, that Hannah would be struggling even if she didn't have the boss's daughter constantly on her back.

Hannah took a big gulp of air. 'I can't go on with this, Rosie. I am defeated.' Her words were followed by heaving gasps, as she dropped her head and sobbed.

Rosie noticed Hannah's overalls were laced with pin burns; she'd been doing overhead welds most of the day, the hardest kind of welding work, and she had obviously been giving herself regular molten showers.

Rosie let her cry for a little while.

She was just about to say something, when all of a sudden Hannah looked up. Her face looked desolate. 'And today my aunty told me she had heard rumours that the Nazis have started to murder thousands of Jews. And here I am – doing nothing!'

She burst into more tears.

Rosie had also read about Hitler's persecution of the Jews, and just about any other minority race in existence; it had been a topic she and Peter had talked about. They had been incredulous that one man was able to inflict such evil. Wield such power. And cause such annihilation and horror.

Rosie put her arm around Hannah and comforted her.

'There are no words to describe how truly awful this is. I know you must be worried sick about your mum and dad, and all your family and friends,' Rosie said, adding as an afterthought, 'Thank goodness your parents sent you over here when they did.'

Hannah voice was muffled as she despaired. 'But what good did that do? I can't even do this' – she threw her pipe-like arms open wide at the weld she was doing – 'to help beat the Nazis . . . I'm useless.'

'No, you're not useless!' Rosie reprimanded her. 'Far from it! Look at me.'

Hannah's distraught face, a picture of pure misery, looked up.

'We need to put our heads together. I've been thinking since our last chat – about why you wanted to work in the yard in the first place . . . that you felt all the learning you'd done had come to nothing and was useless.'

Hannah nodded, and wiped her nose on the back of her overall sleeve.

'Well, perhaps it wasn't. Perhaps you can use it.'

'How?' Hannah asked, the slightest tinge of hope breaking through her voice.

'I'm not sure,' Rosie said, trying to sound reassuring. 'But what I do know is that sometimes you can try too hard and there are times you *have* to give up in order to move on. Sometimes you have to admit defeat and giving up isn't always a bad thing. In fact, it can sometimes clear the way to something good – something better.'

'Mm.' Hannah nodded thoughtfully, before looking back up at Rosie.

'You are – how do you say it – very phil-o-soph-ical, Rosie.'

The horn blared out the end of shift and they both got to their feet.

'I'm not sure I think I really even know what that means,' Rosie said wryly, adding, 'I think I'll round the girls up and we'll treat ourselves to a drink down the Admiral.'

Hannah's face immediately brightened up.

'You know what they say,' Rosie added as they started their trek across the yard, 'a problem shared is a problem halved.'

Hannah smiled for the first time. 'I like that saying. I think you *do* know the meaning of philosophical.'

Twenty minutes later, all the women were standing at the bar in the Admiral, which was just starting to fill up with the end-of-day trade.

Much to all of their relief, Martha had come out of her mute mode and taken the lead on getting the drinks in.

'Gin and tonic?' she said to Dorothy.

'Yes, please!' Dorothy said, adding, 'and the same for Ange here.'

'I *have* got my own tongue, you know!' Angie retorted, but she still nodded to Martha that she was happy with her friend's choice, before heading off to bagsy a table for them all.

Martha looked at Gloria and said, 'Lemonade – with sugar?' Before letting out a loud guffaw at her own joke.

Gloria chuckled. 'Yes please, Martha, shove a double in there!'

'Guinness?' Martha asked Hannah, who was standing so close to Rosie that the pair of them looked attached at the hip.

Before Hannah had time to answer, Dorothy butted in, 'Why don't you give up on the black stuff, Hannah? I really don't think it's working. You've been forcing the stuff down your neck for months now and I don't see you sprouting any muscles. Why don't you try something you actually like?'

Hannah looked up at Rosie and the pair of them let out a splutter of laughter.

'It wasn't meant to be a joke,' Dorothy huffed.

'It was something me and Rosie were chatting about earlier on,' Hannah tried to explain.

'Rosie and I,' corrected Dorothy, before quickly adding, 'So what were you talking about?'

'Let's get our drinks in and sit down and we'll tell you,' Rosie said.

Chapter Thirty-Eight

Tuesday 17 June 1941

'So, you seeing Maria again any time soon?' Polly asked her brother as she helped herself to a plate of her mother's tripe and liver hotpot from the stove. She'd just got in from work and was starving, as she always was at the end of her shift – even more so if she had done a few hours' overtime. There was now a constant pressure at the yard to get work done as quickly as possible, but Rosie had told them that they had to start to pace themselves, as this was going to carry on for a good while yet.

And Polly had to agree. It certainly didn't look as if the war would be ending soon – and so the desperate need for a constant supply of merchant ships would continue. It looked as though they would be in it for the long haul, and that the Americans would be getting involved. There had been a lot of talk amongst the workforce after yesterday's announcement on the BBC home news service that the United States had taken the decision to freeze all German and Italian assets.

Polly sat down at the table, giving her supper a good coating of salt and pepper. Joe was finishing off a game of tiddlywinks he was playing with Lucille before her bedtime. He was then heading straight off for his Home Guard duties, which were now taking up most of his evenings, and sometimes meant he was out all night.

'I tell you what, Pol,' he said, as one of his little cardboard discs fell wide of its mark, much to Lucille's glee, 'if you ever stop working in the yards, you could always set up as the town's official matchmaker.'

'Joe,' Polly said, forking a piece of liver and blowing on it, 'I'm your sister. I have a right to know.'

Joe let loose a caustic laugh just as Bel came in from the back yard. She'd just been sorting out a mound of towels and sheets that were now dry and ready to be folded up.

'I swear that laundry basket is bottomless . . . Anyway, what's this I've just caught about "matchmaking"?'

A mischievous look came across Polly's face. 'I'm trying to wangle it out of Joe, whether or not love is in the air, and if he's going to see Maria again. But he's being very evasive.'

'I'm not being *evasive*,' Joe said, watching as Lucille sneaked in a second attempt at potting her tiddlywink, thinking that he hadn't noticed, 'I just like to have some kind of privacy in my life, which is not easy living in a house full of nosy women.'

Polly tucked into her dinner as Joe told Lucille their game was a draw and it was time for bed. His comments were met with the usual moans, but the little girl was tired, and happily put her arms up for Joe to lift her up and carry her to bed.

'I'll do her bedtime story tonight, Joe,' Bel said. 'You best get yourself off. You don't want to be late for duty.'

Joe was looking smart in his Home Guard uniform, which he always made sure was spotlessly clean and pressed. He was carrying Lucille with one arm and had his walking stick in the other as he made his way out of the kitchen.

'You're right. I'd best get off. I'll just tuck this little girl in.'

Bel followed Joe into her bedroom and watched as he popped her daughter into her cot and wrapped her blanket around her. Just then Tramp came trotting in, making a beeline for the little bed and sticking her wet nose through the wooden railings. Lucille rolled over and stretched her arm out so that she could pat the dog's head. 'Night night, Trampie.' Happy with the show of love, the dog turned and scampered off back to Agnes, who had just come back from Beryl's, where she had been for a cuppa and a catch-up.

Bel stood and looked at Joe and Lucille as they went through their usual goodnight banter. Anyone watching, who didn't know the family, would most certainly presume they were father and daughter. For a short moment Bel wondered if Teddy would mind their closeness. Or whether he would just be pleased that his brother and his daughter had formed such a close bond.

As Joe and Bel said their final goodnights to Lucille, they shut the bedroom door. Bel waited for Joe to fetch his gas mask, haversack and helmet before she saw him off at the front door.

'So, are you going to see Maria again?' The words were out of her mouth before she had a chance to stop them.

Joe looked at her in surprise.

'Well . . . Mm . . . to be honest, Bel, I'm not sure.' He seemed a little flustered. 'I suppose it's finding the time . . .' His voice trailed off as he leant on his stick to step down on to the pavement.

'Eee, I'm worse than Pol,' Bel said, wishing she had never opened her mouth. 'Just tell me to mind my own business. And take care tonight. Fingers crossed it's another quiet one.'

Joe smiled and turned to walk down Tatham Street.

As Bel shut the door, she leant against it for a moment before she went back into the hustle and bustle of the kitchen. She could hear Agnes and Polly chatting and then her mother's very distinctive gravelly voice. She had been out in the back yard chatting away to a widower called Ronald who lived in the house directly behind them. He was a smoker, and her mother was always cadging cigarettes off him.

'You all right there, flower?' It was Arthur, slowly making his way down the stairs. He usually liked to make an appearance at this time and have a bite to eat with everyone. 'You look a million miles away.'

Bel smiled at the old man. She had felt comfortable with Arthur from the start when Polly and his grandson had just begun courting. It had been thanks to Arthur that she had got to know about the love triangle of Gloria, Jack and Miriam, and learnt that he was worried the same might happen with Polly, Tommy and Helen.

'I'm fine, Arthur. Just thinking,' she said.

The old man laughed. 'Never a good thing.'

As they both headed into the kitchen, Bel thought how many a word said in jest was actually very true. She did have a tendency to think too much. It was just that, at the moment, she felt as if her head was all over the place. She was saying things she didn't want to say, and she couldn't understand why she was reacting to certain situations in the way she was. Perhaps it was all still part of the grieving process. Her world had been turned upside down and she was finding her feet again.

But it didn't explain why her immediate reaction to the possibility that Joe might start courting Maria was one of disappointment. It was almost as if she was jealous of Maria – which was absurd, wasn't it?

She should have felt glad for Joe. Pleased for him. He was a handsome man, was great with children – or at least with Lucille – and he was still young.

And besides which, Joe was not cut out to be a bachelor all his life, that much she did know.

Joe had got a tram from Tatham Street into town and then got on a bus at the Park Lane depot which would take him to Hetton-Le-Hole, a small town almost exactly halfway between Sunderland and Durham.

Tonight his mission was to teach the members of this town's particular unit, made up mainly of farmers and miners, how to use the .300 rifles and bayonets that had been provided to them by the Yanks.

Tonight, like on previous occasions, he would be picked up by another 'Home Guard' soldier when he got off the bus, and then taken in a lorry or truck to a patch of local woodland on the outskirts of the town called Rough Dene, where the Auxiliary Unit Operational Base could be found.

The concealed underground structure, built by the 184th Tunnelling Co. Royal Engineers, had a camouflaged entrance and emergency escape tunnel. Joe had been amazed to learn that there were already several secret tunnels and bunkers in place across the county, and around five hundred such bases dotted about Great Britain.

He'd also been heartened by the level of subterfuge already in place should Jerry manage to cross the Channel and invade their shores. Since he had been conscripted to the Auxiliary Units six weeks ago, Joe had learnt a lot about the government's specially trained and highly secret teams of civilians, who had been taught how to use guns, make explosives, carry out ambushes, and commit sabotage in order to fight a larger but less mobile traditional army.

Major Black had told Joe that it might seem like role-playing to men like themselves who had been on the front line and seen it all for real, but that if their beloved country was occupied, then they really did need to be prepared.

Joe had agreed wholeheartedly. If they couldn't fight abroad, then the least they could do was to be prepared for battle if – and when – Hitler decided it was time to try to conquer their country.

'If the worst happens it will be highly dangerous. The projected life expectancy of a member of the unit is just twelve days. If capture by an enemy force seems likely, then members are expected to shoot themselves rather than be caught.'

Joe had taken the major's words on board, but had decided that if Jerry did invade, he would not be killing himself. There were no two ways about it, he'd do anything and everything – fight to the bitter end – for every member of his family.

Which brought his mind back to Bel.

As Joe started out on his bus journey, he was glad to have some time on his own. He wanted and needed some peace and quiet to think. He hadn't been surprised that Polly had asked him about Maria. She was his sister, after all, and it went without saying that she knew no boundaries as such; but he had been taken aback when Bel had also asked him about whether or not he was going to take Maria out. In fact, he had been totally flummoxed.

What should he have said? That he wanted her and not Maria. That his heart was with her and always would be?

As the bus trundled out of town and the view changed from houses to miles of farmland and fields, Joe told himself that it was time to stop his obsession with Bel. It had gone on long enough. He had a choice now: he could mope around his whole life, mooning privately for someone he simply could not have, or he could get out there and meet someone else – had already met someone else – who would make a lovely wife. Maria.

They had already courted for a year before the war. They got on well; they even made each other laugh. And there was no doubt she was a very attractive young woman. And Maria had never hidden the fact that she was more than sweet on him. Before he had gone to war she had told him that she loved him, and there had been a part of him that loved her back. At the time he had argued with himself that it wasn't the right kind of love, that he wanted the kind of love he had seen between his brother and Bel, but in the end he'd had to admit he was kidding himself, and that it was Bel he really wanted.

But Bel had only ever had eyes for Teddy. It was Teddy who Bel had chosen to love.

Now he had to finally accept that his love for Bel was not reciprocated.

He must give the love he had with Maria a chance.

He owed it to himself – and to Maria.

As the bus slowly pulled into the small terminal in the centre of Hetton-Le-Hole, Joe made a resolution: he was going to ask Maria out.

Chapter Thirty-Nine

A week later, June 1941

'*Quiet Wedding!* Oh, I'm so jealous!' Bel exclaimed. 'I *sooo* wanted to see that. I've seen the posters and it looks *fabulous!*' She ended the sentence in a put-on, haughty, upper-class accent.

Polly looked at her sister-in-law and wondered if she'd had a tipple or two, as her reaction to Joe's cinema date with Maria was a little over the top.

Joe shuffled awkwardly in the kitchen doorway, unsure whether to sit down at the table or head straight off to bed.

It had already gone ten and he had been up most of the previous night with the Auxiliary Unit in town. They had been making sure the various bunkers in the area were stocked up with canned and preserved food, should they have to go underground if an invasion were to become reality. But more than his need to catch up on his sleep was his desire to avoid any kind of cross-examination about his first date with Maria.

The film had been Maria's suggestion when he had gone to see her to ask her out. She had told him it had been released a couple of months before, and had been made despite the production studios being bombed five times; it had been this which had piqued his interest, but when he had found out that it was about a young couple on the eve of their marriage, he'd felt a little nervous.

'Was it good?' Bel continued. Her excitement showed no signs of abating. 'Was Derek Farr as dashing as he was in *Freedom Radio*? Oh . . . and was Margaret Lockwood as gorgeous as she looks in the magazines?'

Joe looked at Bel perplexed. He had no idea what *Freedom Radio* was all about – could only presume it was another movie – and he guessed the 'gorgeous' woman was the actress playing the part of the fiancée.

'Mm.' Joe scratched his head a little nervously.

'Honestly, Bel, I think you and I are going to have to go out some time. You're spending too much time cooped up in this house, up to your armpits in laundry and children. Why don't we go and see the film together later on this week?' Polly suggested.

Bel clapped her hands together as softly as possible, as Lucille was fast asleep next door; she had had a real job getting her to sleep as Joe wasn't around to tuck her in, and she was sure her daughter had become even more grizzly when she had heard them discussing Joe's date with Maria over tea.

'Yes, Polly! I'd love that!' she said, eyes wide open. Polly thought Bel looked slightly manic and resolved to make sure they did in fact make it out at the weekend.

'I do love a good wedding!' Bel added, before looking at Joe and asking, 'I'm guessing they do get married in the end?'

Joe laughed and yawned at the same time. 'You will have to go and see it yourself and find out. Anyway, I'm off to bed. See you both in the morning.'

After Joe had backed out of the kitchen and hobbled to his room, Polly whispered across to Bel, 'I wonder how it went? Do you think they're going to see each other again?' Then she immediately answered her own question.

'I don't see why not. They were both really keen on each other before Joe joined up.'

Polly looked at Bel conspiratorially. 'Interesting choice of film, don't you think? *Quiet Wedding*? Ma might finally get those grandchildren she's after.'

'God, Pol. Let's concentrate on your wedding first. Then perhaps *you* can give your ma those grandchildren,' Bel replied.

For some reason the thought of Polly getting married was far preferable to any potential nuptials between Joe and Maria.

Bel was lying wide awake in bed, and had been doing so for at least a few hours, listening to the gentle breathing of her daughter in the cot next to her bed, and keeping half an ear out in case Joe had a night terror and started shouting out.

Since the first time she had gone into his bedroom to wake him a few months ago, whenever she had heard him screaming out in his sleep from a bad nightmare, she had gone to him and gently woken him up.

After he had joined up with the Home Guard, though, his nightmares seemed to have lessened dramatically. In fact, only one time since then had Bel had to softly bring him out of his horror-laced slumber.

She was pleased he seemed to be on the mend – in all ways. He no longer needed his wound dressed, as it had now just about completely healed but, oddly enough, Bel had to admit to herself that there was a part of her that missed caring for Joe; which was absurd as she had hated it at first – had felt so much resentment towards him, had been so angry. But since she had let go of that awful, mind-altering grief, it hadn't bothered her.

And that is when the irony hit her like a slap in the face: *now that she was happy to look after Joe, he didn't need caring for. And just as she was getting used to having him around, and was actually enjoying his company, he was out and about all the time.*

Was this why she had acted like a complete loony tonight when he'd got back from the flicks?

This evening she had gone into some kind of hyperactive state. *Talk about overreacting.* But what was even harder to understand was that she was not the least bit interested in seeing the film. Everything that had come out of her mouth had been false, which was so unlike her – apart from what she had said to Polly about wanting to see her married and have children. This she couldn't wait for.

So, why did she feel so completely different about Joe getting hitched and starting a family?

Polly was her sister-in-law and Joe her brother-in-law, so logically there should be no difference.

But there was.

And she could not deny it.

As Bel continued to lie there, staring at the ceiling, the most frightening thought started to creep into her head.

Was she starting to have feelings for Joe?

Please God no.

No.

This could not be.

Could never be.

Was wrong.

And with this thought – this heart-stopping realisation – Bel's world seemed to spin off its axis for the second time that year.

Chapter Forty

Wednesday 25 June 1941

'Where's Rosie?' Gloria asked. As usual she had joined the women for lunch. They had all brought packed lunches as the weather was now behaving as it should and it was warm enough for them to sit out and have their sandwiches. Today there was a slight chill coming in from the North Sea, but it was as nothing compared to the bitter, harsh winter they had just had to endure.

'I think I saw her disappearing into the drawing office about half an hour ago and she hasn't resurfaced since then. I wonder what she's been up to in there,' Dorothy said, taking a bite of her sandwich and wrinkling her nose.

'Urgh, I think this ham's gone off! It tastes foul!' she said, prising open the two slices of buttered white bread and peering inside.

'If you can't even make a bloody sandwich, I don't think you're ever going to make anyone a good wife, Dorothy.' Gloria couldn't resist the opportunity to get a dig in. She loved working on the cranes, but she missed the women's banter.

'Don't want to!' Dorothy shot back as quick as a flash. 'Ange and I are going to be footloose and fancy free until we're old maids. No husbands. No children. We're just going to have fun. And lots of it. Aren't we, Ange?'

Angie looked at Gloria and rolled her eyes. 'Yes, Dor. That's right,' she said in a deadly serious, downtrodden manner. Gloria thought about Polly's remarks – that the pair of them were like a female Laurel and Hardy – and chuckled to herself.

'Talking of which,' Dorothy continued, as she tossed her sandwiches aside and looked into Angie's box, before nabbing one of her fresh Spam baps, 'Ange and I are going out on a double date tonight with a couple of the riveters.'

'Honestly!' Gloria said, exasperated. 'What is it with you two and riveters? I would have thought Eddie's antics would have been enough to put you both off that lot for life.'

Last year Dorothy had been distraught at finding out the man she was obsessed with (who had been the reason for her starting work at the yard in the first place) had been seeing Angie behind her back. She had found out and caused uproar in the Admiral when she had given her two-timing beau an ale shower, pouring a pint over his head. Of course, she had been upset and had felt humiliated, but some good had come out of it when she and Angie had become best buddies.

'What's this about riveters and double dates?' It was Rosie back from the main offices.

'Don't ask!' Polly said. 'It seems like the whole world is going out on dates at the moment. Dorothy and Angie. Joe and Maria . . . And,' she added cheekily, 'I think our very own boss may even be stepping out with someone?'

Everyone looked at Rosie as a slight flush started to creep across her face, causing all the women to make a right old ruckus.

'He's just a friend,' Rosie spluttered. 'Nothing more . . . Anyway, what's this about Joe? Who's this Maria?'

'I think that is called "changing the subject",' Hannah piped up.

The women started chattering over each other. Martha was asking Hannah what a 'double date' was, Dorothy was quizzing Polly about Maria, and Rosie was quietly telling Gloria that she had not heard any more news about when Jack was due back, other than that he had definitely set sail and could possibly be back in a few weeks.

'I'm not sure if that's a good thing or not,' Gloria confided. 'I think a part of me was hoping he wouldn't be back until after the baby was born. Give me more time to decide what I'm going to do.' Then she sighed. 'I can't believe I just said that! I'm missing him terribly. What a state to be in, eh?'

Rosie leaned over and squeezed Gloria's hand. 'The main thing is that you are both keeping well. How does everything feel in there?' Rosie nodded down at Gloria's huge egg-shaped belly. She knew very little about being pregnant, or having a baby, and did not pretend to know.

'All good, fingers crossed. I can feel the little nipper moving around quite a bit. Only about six weeks to go.'

'And no more visits from Vinnie?' Rosie asked with a frown.

'Not a squeak,' Gloria said, 'which suits me just fine.'

'Good, let's hope it stays that way,' Rosie said. She was so relieved that the bastard was keeping well away, but also a little puzzled. Knowing what men like Vinnie were capable of, she would have expected that he would have been back, causing more trouble.

After Gloria had turned up to work with her black eye and battered face, Rosie had been resolute that she would put a stop to this detestable man's abuse. But she had struggled to know how she was going to do it. Now it looked like something – or someone – had caused Vinnie to keep his distance. In doing so, whatever or whoever it was had taken a big, worrisome weight off her shoulders.

'Hey, Gloria!' It was Polly, who was wrapping her long chestnut-brown hair back up into her headscarf. She loved to let it loose during their breaks, but, like all the women, kept it scraped back away from her face and protected by a hat or scarf for fear of it being singed by their welds. 'Do you fancy coming to our neighbour's birthday party next Saturday? Bel's going to be there. Give you both a chance to meet. And,' she added dramatically, 'there's going to be cake there!'

Gloria's eyes lit up. 'Definitely. I'll be there. Come hell or high water!' Though her excitement at the prospect of cake was soon squashed when she spotted Helen shimmying across the yard like a catwalk queen.

'Oh no, here comes trouble, I'm off,' Gloria said, as she heaved her body up and waddled off as fast as her extended belly would allow her.

'Rosie!' Helen's voice trilled out, causing the women to quickly pack up their boxes, dust down their overalls and head over to their welding machines.

'Actually, I need to speak to you all. Everyone apart from Polly and Angela, that is. You two can tootle off.' She said the words breezily, but her eyes locked on to Polly. Both women glared at each other for a second, before Polly tore her gaze away and marched off with Angie back to their machines.

Rosie, Dorothy, Hannah and Martha stood in a semi-circle, feeling like lemons, waiting to see what Helen had in store for them.

'Sorry, girls,' she said in the most condescending manner she could get away with, 'but Hannah, your skills are needed again with Mickey in the fitting-out basin.'

'Why can't Polly or Dorothy go instead?' Rosie butted in before Helen had a chance to say anything else.

'Sorry, Rosie, but they need someone small – like your "little bird" here – to get into some awkward spots.'

Rosie forced herself to take a deep breath.

'And, I'm afraid,' Helen continued, a sneer sneaking across her face, 'Martha is needed with the riveters again. They really are short. They don't seem to be able to make up the numbers.'

Helen said all of this without once looking at Martha, who had let out a very audible huff and now stood with her sizeable arms akimbo.

'So, chop-chop, you two,' Helen said, just as the horn blared out for the start of the shift, waving them both away with a perfectly manicured hand. Rosie noticed her blood-red nails matched her lipstick perfectly.

'And now for you two,' Helen said, her voice losing its singsong lilt and dropping into a deadly serious mono-tone. 'I just want you both to know that I am well aware of what you have been doing to help Hannah . . . Rosie, I know you've been giving her the lightweight pick-up work for months now. And, Dorothy, I know you've been carrying your little pidgin-English-speaking workmate as well – taking on a good part of her workload but letting the little Czech pass it off as her own. Don't think I haven't noticed. If your little bird is not able to pull her weight, then I'm afraid she's going to be set free . . .

'And, I want you both to know that it's only down to the goodness of my heart that I haven't reported you.'

There was a deathly silence between the women for a long moment before it was broken by the sound of one of the drillers starting up nearby.

'And by the way, Dorothy.' Helen took a step forward and hissed in her face. '*I know it was you.*'

Dorothy looked at her all innocence. 'I've no idea what you're talking about.'

Helen glared at her with unguarded hatred. 'You were the squawker with the big mouth who went blabbering to that plater's wife. I knew it was one of you lot, but not which one.'

Helen took another deep breath. 'And just so you know, I won't forget. You *will* pay for what you did. If not now, then later. Mark my words.'

And with that she turned on her heel and swaggered off back across the yard.

As she did so, Dorothy stuck her tongue out at her, before turning to Rosie who was at a loss for words.

'Don't worry. She doesn't scare me,' Dorothy said. 'I'm tougher than I look. And more than anything, I'm your best and fastest welder. There's no way she could get shot of me.'

Rosie was not so sure, though. Helen's desire for retribution knew no bounds.

'Let's speak later,' she said as she spotted Hannah slopping off to the outfitting dock, her welding mask almost trailing the ground as she walked.

Rosie ran to catch up with her. 'Just hang in there,' she said when she was by Hannah's side. 'I've got a plan, which I think may work well. But you need to stick it out for another few weeks. You'll promise me you'll keep at it? For just a little while longer?'

Hannah's crestfallen face looked up at Rosie. 'I'll try my hardest,' she said.

Rosie let Hannah go on her way, but was not reassured by her promise – and she doubted whether Hannah's 'hardest' would be enough.

By the end of the day's shift, Rosie felt as mentally exhausted as she did physically.

The one thought that had kept her going all day was her weekly 'date' with Peter, who she would be with in a short while.

She had to admit to herself, though, that these were *dates*. Polly was right. She wasn't just having tea and a chat with a friend – friends didn't hold hands, or have the kind of feelings she had when they touched.

But, she argued with herself, providing it stayed the way it was, she was happy to continue as they were.

For now, anyway.

Chapter Forty-One

Saturday 5 July 1941

It had been over a week since Bel had lain wide awake in her bed in the middle of the night and asked herself if she was starting to have feelings for Joe. Her life, which had finally just started to level out, had once again suddenly been whipped up into a frenetic spin, like one of Lucille's wooden spinning tops she loved to see zigzagging across the back yard; only it had been several days now and the spinning did not show any signs of abating.

She had actually felt physically dizzy with fear.

Bel had tried telling herself that she must be having some kind of strange breakdown – a delayed reaction to the death of her husband. The thought of her being mentally unstable had bizarrely given her some comfort, for it was a far better prospect than harbouring romantic feelings towards her brother-in-law.

Whenever Joe went out on Home Guard duty, she was both relieved as well as forlorn. Relieved that she didn't have to deal with her feelings, and forlorn because she wanted to be with him. There was a part of her, a part she didn't seem able to control, that really wanted more than anything for him to stay in and simply be with her and Lucille, playing games, chatting and laughing. But she had also started to feel incredibly awkward around Joe, and she was sure he had picked up on it. She had tried to behave normally, or at least act the same way she had been with him these past few months, but she was aware her attempts at conversation were coming across as forced and stilted.

This evening she really was going to have to act her socks off as the whole household was going to a party next door at Beryl's. It was her birthday, and Agnes had decided it needed to be celebrated. Agnes had made one of her scrumptious Victoria sponges, and a big mince and onion plate pie, and Bel had made a mountain of sandwiches with a variety of fillings from a load of meat offcuts that Arthur had got from the market in town.

The house was presently buzzing with the sound of Vera Lynn's singing 'We'll Meet Again' blaring from the wireless in the kitchen, and doors were banging open and shut as they all hurried to get ready, enjoying the frivolity of getting dressed up and putting on their glad rags. Agnes was wearing her hair down for a change, and had put on her best little black dress, and was bustling to and from next door with trays of party food. The cake, now covered in little white candles, would be brought out when it was time to sing Beryl 'Happy Birthday'. Surprisingly Agnes was being helped by Pearl, who was managing to puff on a cigarette, while balancing two plates of food on each arm like a skilled silver service waitress.

'Don't you dare let any fag ash get in that food!' Agnes shouted out as they passed each other on the pavement outside.

Arthur and Joe were already next door, helping to move tables and create space for the guests. In the midst of it all, Tramp was running around, partly deranged by the lingering smell of the minced beef and the cold meats, and on alert for any more scraps that might be accidentally on purpose dropped by both Bel and Agnes.

Sensing the excitement pervading the Elliot household, Lucille was tearing around the house like a tiny whirlwind, shouting out, 'Party! Party!' And Bel was doing something she had not done since Teddy had died – she was putting on a little make-up.

'Lucille, calm down!' she shouted out to the blur of yellow she caught running past the bedroom door. Lucille was still obsessed with wearing her sunflower-yellow pinafore dress, which now only just fitted her. It was remarkable the dress had withstood yet another wash and repair, but there was no denying the time was nearing when it would either no longer fit Lucille, or it would have to be worn one last time before being chucked into the rag box. Bel dreaded the day; could well foresee her little girl's distraught reaction.

'I've got her,' Polly shouted from the kitchen, as Tramp let out a little bark as if to confirm Lucille had been brought under control. 'And, by the way, you and Ma are going to have to stop feeding this dog so much – it's getting fat!'

Bel turned back to the mirror on her dressing-room table. She applied a smudge of lipstick, and brushed a little mascara on to her already very dark eyelashes. She had pulled out an old dress she hadn't worn for so long she could not recall the last time she had put it on. It was her favourite party dress, and she was hoping its floral pattern and bright colours would hide the shameful thoughts and feelings she had been experiencing of late – and was now having to batten down on a daily basis.

'Mummy! Mummy! Go party!' Lucille came barrelling into the bedroom, along with a highly excited Tramp.

'All right, little lady.' Bel looked down at her daughter, who had already managed to get a mark on her freshly laundered dress, but who looked so happy and expectant she hadn't the heart to reprimand her.

'Mummy just needs to get her dress on and we'll be ready to go.'

Bel took off her pale pink cotton housecoat, slipped into her knee-length V-neck tea dress, and stood and looked at her reflection.

For some reason she thought she would look different, that her improper thoughts would somehow distort her looks; but they didn't. She looked the same as she always did.

'Eee, Beryl, you are a funny one!' Agnes was chuckling away with her friend, laughing at some reminiscence from the past. Nearly all the guests had arrived and the little house party was now in full swing – aided by Jimmy and Sheila's home-made wine and a bottle of port Beryl had scraped the money together to buy. People were spilling out of the front lounge and into the hallway, or stood nattering in the kitchen, nibbling on sandwiches, or relishing slices of Agnes's thick-crusted meat pie.

Beryl's three older boys were serving in the Royal Navy, and so what had been their shared bedroom had been converted back to its original use – that of a living room. Beryl, like Agnes, didn't allow smoking in the house, so those who liked a puff were standing in the back yard, which was where Pearl had been stationed most of the time, glass of port in one hand and fag in another. She had spent much of the evening chatting away to Ronald, for whom Pearl had wangled an invite at the last moment, mainly due to her putting Beryl on the spot and catching her in a good mood. Both Beryl and Agnes had observed Pearl's growing closeness to their widowed neighbour, and had speculated whether Pearl genuinely liked the man, or if she was more interested in his seemingly limitless supply of cigarettes.

Joe and Arthur were standing together, both looking a little uncomfortable but not unhappy. The two men of the household had also made an effort to look smart: Arthur was in a black three-piece suit that normally only saw the light of day for weddings or funerals, and must have been at least as old as his grandson as he'd worn it to Tommy's christening, and then again a short while later to his daughter's funeral. Joe had put on his best trousers, which were still a little loose on him, despite Agnes's best attempts to fatten him up, as well as a starched white shirt, the sleeves of which were slightly puffed up thanks to his father's shirt-sleeve holders, which had been given to him and Teddy to share when they had become young men. He had also been cajoled by Polly into wearing a navy blue tie that, Bel noticed, exactly matched the colour of his eyes.

Joe had invited Maria to the party, but she was not there as she hadn't been able to get out of her WAA duties. She had argued the case with the head driver in charge of the rota that there had not been any air raids now for well over five weeks, and all she would end up doing would be sitting on her backside the entire evening, but her words had fallen on deaf ears, and she'd had to work – party or not.

Just after seven, there was a knock on the front door, which had been left slightly ajar. It was Gloria, who had come armed with a bottle of gin that had been left untouched in her cupboard since she had found out she was expecting.

'Over here!' Polly shouted out over the heads of the other guests. She had positioned herself by the living-room doorway so that she could see Gloria as soon as she arrived, for her workmate did not know anyone at the party other than herself.

'Sorry I'm a bit late,' Gloria said, pushing the bottle of gin into Polly's hand.

'Don't worry – you haven't missed the cake!' Polly laughed. 'Come in and I'll introduce you to Beryl. You must have known – her favourite tipple is gin . . . And then I'll find Bel and the rest of the clan.'

Ten minutes later, Polly took Gloria into the kitchen to find Bel and Agnes, who were just starting to light the candles on Beryl's cake.

'Oh, Gloria! Lovely to meet you. You both!' Bel said, looking down at Gloria's sizeable bump. 'Any feelings as to whether it's a girl or a boy?'

Gloria laughed. 'If it's a girl she's going to give Martha a run for her money, that's for sure. If I get any bigger, I think I'll pop.'

Bel chuckled; she'd met Martha briefly on the night Rosie had been attacked, and had been somewhat taken aback by her outstanding physique.

Agnes smiled as she quickly blew out the burning matchstick. 'Well, as long as it's not twins!' Her jocular words were followed by an immediate look of sadness, which they had all caught pass across Agnes's face. Sometimes, for just a second, Agnes's brain played a cruel trick on her and she forgot her son was dead; believed he was still alive and would be walking through her front door any day soon.

'All right, Bel, get those pipes of yours in tune and start us off,' Agnes commanded as she forced light-heartedness back into her voice.

Bel had also been thrown momentarily by the mention of twins, but she too pushed any mournful thoughts away as she started singing, 'Happy Birthday to you . . .'

Agnes led the way, with Bel by her side, and Tramp snaking between her legs and nearly tripping her up; Polly and Gloria were at the rear. Bel's sweet, melodic voice quietened the chatter of the party, and the talk turned to song as everyone started to join in.

Beryl was standing looking a little self-conscious and more than a little tearful; her teenage daughters, Audrey and Iris, were singing by her side, daintily holding the half-full glasses of wine their mother had allowed them.

As the whole party raised their glasses and toasted Beryl a 'happy and healthy future' – as well as the safe return of her two boys – Joe couldn't drag his eyes away from Bel, who he thought looked particularly radiant this evening.

The couple of glasses of wine that Bel had hoped would help cloak her unwanted feelings had only managed to make her feel a little giddy and light-headed, and had given her a carefree, slightly flushed look.

As if sensing that she had become the focus of attention, Bel looked up and found Joe staring at her.

She held his gaze for a second before glancing down at the floor; she felt herself blush with embarrassment. When she lifted her head up again, Joe was talking to Arthur, and Beryl was blowing out the candles and closing her eyes to show she was following orders and making a wish.

'Do you want to get the plates and we'll cut the cake up?' Agnes suggested. Bel panicked that her mother-in-law had seen something in the way she had stared at Joe, and she hurried out into the kitchen to fetch the crockery, glad of an excuse to go and compose herself. When she returned, though, she was mortified to see that her brother-in-law was being introduced to Gloria.

Get a grip, Bel reprimanded herself. Of course Joe needed to meet Gloria – after all, he was going to be a part of her baby's life due to the very fact he lived here and was family.

'So, Bel's going to be looking after your little un when you go back to work.' He was leaning on his stick, which Bel knew meant his leg was starting to pain him. Gloria nodded and smiled at Bel as she handed Beryl's best dessert plates over to Agnes.

'Well, you couldn't want for anyone better,' Joe continued. 'Bel was born to be a mum. She adores children.'

'I've heard you're a natural with little Lucille too,' Gloria said. 'Polly's told us all about her niece and how she totally adores you.'

Joe laughed. 'Aye, but I don't know if I've done anything to deserve such hero-worship!'

Gloria looked at both Bel and Joe, who were standing next to each other, when all of a sudden Lucille, on hearing her name, forced her head between her mother and uncle's legs and looked up at Gloria with her striking sea-blue eyes.

'Oh, she's a bonny lass, isn't she?' Gloria said, captivated by the cherub-like face framed by a crown of corn-coloured curls.

'And the spit of her mam too!' Gloria looked at Bel, and then at Joe, and said, without thinking, 'Blimey, you can see the family resemblance, that's for sure.'

Joe smiled. He had seen his brother and, therefore, himself in Lucille. There was no denying it. And he had lost count of the number of times people had assumed his niece was his daughter. Lucille never seemed to mind the mistake made by strangers, and he could have sworn she had scowled a few times when he had corrected people.

'Here you are, Glor! I know it's what you've been waiting for!' Polly chuckled as she handed over a plate on which there was a huge slice of cake.

'She's not really come to meet you and Ma,' she said to Bel. 'This woman is driven by one thing and one thing only at the moment.'

Bel laughed and started to chat away about her many different cravings when she was expecting Lucille. Joe stood for a little while, enjoying hearing Bel chatter on, although there was a moment when he felt sad for her too.

Bel had only ever really wanted to be a mum, and when Teddy had been killed, she not only lost her husband, but also the chance of having more brothers and sisters for Lucille.

His thoughts were broken by the appearance of Pearl, who brought with her the strong smell of cigarette smoke. As usual he noticed the change it provoked in Bel – the wrinkle of her nose, followed by the look she gave her mother that told Joe she was trying hard to disguise the rising irritation her mother always seemed to cause her to feel. Knowing that Bel would ignore Pearl and pretend she hadn't noticed her for as long as possible, Joe stepped in with the introductions.

'Gloria this is Pearl, Bel's ma. Pearl, this is Gloria. She works with Polly down the yard.'

Pearl stretched out a thin bare arm and shook Gloria's free hand, which had become quite swollen of late due to her pregnancy. She had been forced to take her wedding ring off, which hadn't bothered her in the least; she was glad to have the blasted thing off her finger, but she had noticed people looking at her bump and then down at her hand and making the assumption she was a wanton, fallen woman, which, if truth be told, she was, although only she and the women welders knew that.

Pearl, ever the eagle eye, saw the ringless hand and could hardly get her words out quickly enough. 'So, the da's not here this evening?'

The softness left Gloria's eyes as she simply answered, 'No.'

Bel glowered at her mother, then ushered Gloria off to see if there was any more cake left and to meet Arthur.

'So, Joe, how's all the Home Guard malarkey going?'

Joe forced a smile. He had heard Pearl take the mickey out of the Home Guard, or what had been known as the

Local Defence Volunteers, calling them the 'Look, Duck and Vanish brigade', but that didn't bother him, nor did her cattiness surprise him.

'So, they dinnit even give yer any pay? Is that right?' she asked.

'No, Pearl, that's what's meant by *volunteering*.' Joe looked over her bottle-blonde hair to see Bel giving Gloria her own slice of birthday cake. That was Bel. She'd give her last penny to someone if she thought they needed it more than her. It was what he loved about her. When he looked back at Pearl, he struggled to put the two of them together. How could a mother and daughter be so completely different in just about every single way?

'But,' Pearl seemed intent on pursuing the subject of earnings, 'the army must have paid you something, and given you some kind of pension due to you being injured 'n all?'

'Mm,' Joe said, before spotting Lucille charging through from the hallway and tripping over the rug in quite spectacular fashion. There was a potent second's silence before Lucille's brain registered that she had hurt herself. And then came the ear-splitting siren of a long-drawn-out cry, followed by tears, sobs and snot.

Joe quickly hobbled over to the mass of yellow laid out on the floor. He bent over as best he could. On realising that her Doey was there, Lucille flung her arms out as though she was about to drown and never surface again.

'Doooeey!' she cried out, but already her elongated wail had dropped down a notch as Joe hauled her up from the floor and held her as if she was a baby chimp in his arms. Her little chest heaved as she sobbed.

'I think this little girl is what you call TOT – totally over-tired.' Bel appeared behind Joe, brushing her daughter's curls away from her angry red face.

'Bedtime,' Bel said the word in such a way it was clear there was no argument to be had.

Lucille's sobbing scaled down to a gentle snuffling.

'"Lambton Worm",' she demanded, a small bubble of salty tears and saliva forming as she opened her mouth.

Bel went to take her daughter from Joe, but the little girl clung to him like a limpet. 'No! Doey! "Lambton Worm"!'

Bel looked at Joe, who immediately answered her unasked question.

'Of course I don't mind,' he said. 'I love "The Lambton Worm"! I think I could even read it backwards if needed.' His laughter was mirrored by his little niece, now tear-free and revelling in getting her own way.

As Joe carried Lucille out of Beryl's house, with Bel following behind, Gloria and Agnes watched them leave.

'If I didn't know better I'd say they look like a lovely couple,' Gloria said, taking a bite out of her slice of birthday cake.

Agnes looked pensive; she neither agreed nor disagreed.

'I'm so sorry you've been dragged away from the party, Joe,' Bel said as they walked back over the threshold of their own home and into the quietness of the empty house. As she heard herself speak, though, she wanted to kick herself. She sounded so polite, as if she was speaking to a stranger, not someone she had known since she was a small child.

Joe looked at Bel and chortled. 'Course I don't mind. I would have thought you'd have guessed I was glad of an excuse to leave . . . You've done me a favour. I've never been a real party person. And I can't see that changing now.'

Joe thought how blind Bel was not to see how much he loved – and desired – to be alone with her, although he was pleased that was the case, as it worried him sick that his

351

passion for her would show through. So far he had some-how just about managed to keep his true feelings for her hidden – and, more importantly, in check.

He felt guilty, of course, that he still felt this way, despite starting up his courtship again with Maria. He had hoped that by being with a woman he liked and was attracted to that it would somehow dissolve the love he had for Bel.

Joe turned his attention back to Lucille, whose eyelids were already starting to droop, but kept flickering open as she struggled to keep awake.

'Unlike this little party-goer. There's going to be no stop-ping her when she gets older. I think you're going to have your work cut out.'

Bel let out a loud sigh. 'Tell me about it. She's a handful as it is.'

Joe looked at Bel, who appeared a little dishevelled. Her blonde curls kept bobbing back across her right eye, despite Bel's repeated attempts at pushing them back, and the mascara she had applied earlier had smudged a lit-tle. Joe felt the return of the passion he had hoped to have conquered by seeing Maria. But it had remained resolute. Undefeated.

'Come on then, sleepy chops, let's get you into bed,' Joe said to Lucille as he hobbled down the hallway and nudged open Bel's bedroom door with his back, before walking across to the cot and swinging his little baby mon-key into her crib. Bel followed him into the room, and he moved out of the way as Bel took off her daughter's little pinafore dress and vest.

'Put your arms in,' she said gently, as she tugged Lucille's white cotton nightie over her head, and pulled open the sleeves so that she could more easily poke her pudgy little arms through. Lucille then cosied up into her bed as Bel tucked her in.

'Snug as a bug in a rug,' Joe said, sitting down on the side of Bel's bed – the shooting pains in his leg had been unrelenting for the past hour. As soon as he stretched his leg out, the sharp stabbing ebbed away.

As he watched Bel leaning down to give her daughter a goodnight kiss, he thought he had never seen such a perfect profile. Her ivory smooth skin looked almost angelic, surrounded by a halo of naturally blonde hair.

As Bel straightened up, Lucille reached for her raggedy bunny, pulled it up to her cheek and started sucking her thumb.

'Lambton,' she managed to mumble.

Bel turned and rolled her eyes, mouthing, 'Sorry.'

Joe shook his head as if to say, *Don't be*, and Bel bent down to retrieve the tatty book from under the cot. She sat down next to Joe on the bed, like she always did when it came to reading Lucille her bedtime story, but she felt awkward, like she was with a man she didn't really know. Because of Joe's nights spent training the area's Auxiliary Units, this was the first time he had read to his niece since Bel's realisation that she had feelings for him.

Bel straightened her back and sat ramrod straight on the bed as Joe took the book from her clenched hand and opened it at the first page, which showed a cartoon-like figure of a knight in shining armour slaying a giant dragon-like worm, which had wrapped itself around a medieval castle.

Joe looked at Bel curiously, before starting, as he always did with the verse, '"Hush now, had your gobs, I'll tell you an awful story."'

Joe quietly read the story, but after a few minutes his words were interspersed by the sound of Lucille's gentle snoring.

'I think she's out for the count.' Joe turned to face Bel.

Bel had been thinking how her daughter's slumber was the complete opposite of how she herself felt, for even though it was getting late and the room was warm thanks to an uncannily balmy day, she felt wide awake. Almost alert. She had her hands clasped on her lap and had been nervously shifting about so as to make sure no part of her body was touching her brother-in-law.

Joe looked at Bel, and again felt the rise of desire – as he always did whenever he was in physical proximity to Bel. It seemed so calm and quiet here in the room. The little side lamp had enabled him to read, but the blackout curtains had darkened the room and even shut out the light from the night's full moon.

'Are you all right, Bel? You seem . . . I don't know. Different?'

Bel felt her whole body flush as she looked at Joe. Her eyes seemed to lock into his deep, soulful eyes; his enlarged black pupils made them look almost inky blue in the partial darkness. She felt her heart start hammering, and her breathing became shallow as her lips parted slightly, but no words were forthcoming.

Joe regarded Bel. Her normally pale face was flushed pink, her perfect Cupid's bow lips looked full and sanguine red. Her petite but womanly body was so close he would just have to lean forward and they would be touching. His eyes, for a moment, strayed to the V-neck of her pretty dress, which was revealing a glimpse of her full bosom, before he looked back up and into her vibrant, sparkling eyes.

And that was when he saw it.

The desire.

Her desire.

Without thinking, Joe leant towards Bel, and with the utmost gentleness he slowly kissed her lips.

Just the once. But he didn't pull away.

And neither did Bel.

Joe felt his eyes close as his mouth once again found Bel's. And this time he felt the movement of her soft lips respond and kiss him back. Equally gently. Equally softly. And equally passionately.

When they opened their eyes and their lips parted, they were both aware of each other's breathing.

Bel felt as if she was in a dream; she had become lost in that short moment of sensuous intimacy. And she had wanted to stay there for ever.

But as her eyes opened and focused on Joe, her body filled with sheer panic.

What had she done?

'Oh my God!' she said in a harsh, shocked whisper. 'That didn't happen. *It cannot happen!*'

Joe had never seen such fear in Bel's eyes before. It pulled him to his senses, and he stood up.

'Sorry,' he stuttered. 'I'm so sorry, Bel.'

And with that he immediately turned and left the room.

Chapter Forty-Two

Two weeks later, July 1941

Thanks to a temporary remission from the bomb attacks by Hitler's Luftwaffe across the whole of the country, the 'Biggest Shipbuilding Town in the World' was able to get on and do what it had been born to do – what it had been doing for the past six centuries – and that was building ships.

Despite the world war and the lack of male workers, and perhaps because of the hard work of the replacement female workforce, the town was producing a record number of ships. The town itself might still be licking its wounds and clearing away mound after mound of rubble, bricks and mortar, but its spirit was indomitable. There was an unspoken sense of pride and dignity in its part in fighting what was evil and morally wrong. And there was a growing sense of hope that light could overcome darkness, especially when news came that British forces had occupied Syria and what was being called 'a mutual assistance agreement' had been made between the United Kingdom and the Soviet Union.

Everyone in the Elliot household, like most of the townsfolk, was happily soldiering on, doing whatever they could to be a useful cog in the wheel of war.

Polly was working long and hard hours at the yard, but was content as long as she was getting her regular letters from Tommy.

Joe was battling through his painful disability to teach an eclectic mix of men and boys how best to fight the enemy on home soil – with very little weaponry or artillery.

Agnes and Bel seemed to be looking after just about every child under the age of five within a half-mile radius, as well as running what amounted to their own mini-launderette.

And Arthur was doing his best to contribute to the running of the household, having become Agnes's daily shopper.

Even Pearl had got herself a little part-time job as a barmaid in the pub down the road, the Tatham Arms, and although her motivations for getting it were a little suspect (Bel was not the only one to believe her mother's foray into work was more to do with her two favourite pastimes – booze and men – than it was about earning a wage), at least it meant she wasn't leeching from everyone else, at least not as much as before.

All seemed well. At least on the surface.

But if an outsider were to take a peek underneath the veneer of apparent wellbeing at 34 Tatham Street, they would be privy to a very different scenario.

Certainly in the case of Bel and Joe.

Since they had shared a kiss, they had both been in turmoil, although neither had spoken to anyone else about what had occurred between the two of them, nor had they uttered a word to each other about what had passed between them that night.

They had both managed to keep up very convincing appearances of outward normality. The only giveaway being that the two of them were rarely in the house at the same time.

Bel had been glad of the pandemonium created by 'Aggie's Nursery', which was now bursting at the seams thanks to the start of the school holidays. Juggling the child-care and the endless quantities of sheets and tablecloths and just about anything and everything else that could be laundered, she hadn't a minute to spare, and was happy to collapse into bed at night at around the same time she put Lucille down, which also gave her the very plausible excuse not to stay up chatting as she would normally have done with Joe.

The lack of physical let-up from work was bearable for Bel, as she had always been a hard grafter and had good stamina, despite her slender build. It was the unrelenting mental machinations which she found to be an almost unbearable burden. Her mind just never seemed to switch off.

Every night she would lie in bed and her thoughts would follow the same sequence. They would argue the case against any kind of possible relationship with her brother-in-law. And the reasons were countless:

He's Teddy's brother.

How could I do this to Teddy's memory?

God, what would Teddy think if he had seen us both that night?

What would everyone else think?

Bel desperately tried to recall the passion she had shared with her husband: his touch, their love-making, their kisses; the special times they had spent together. But it was hard, and Bel had to admit she struggled to truly recall those feelings – the reality of those moments. It had been almost two years since she had even heard his voice, never mind felt his touch, and it now seemed like another lifetime ago.

So much had happened since he had left for war. Their whole lives had changed . . . Even the physical appearance of their town had changed – Joe had commented on that a little while ago . . .

And there it was again.

Her mind weaving its way back to Joe. It was like every pathway she took ended up back at the same spot.

Joe.

There were nights when Bel cried in frustration. Tried to make herself remember Teddy. To blot out her thoughts of Joe with her remembrances of her husband. For heaven's sake, he had been her childhood love. Her sweetheart. Why couldn't she keep those memories alive? Time was causing them to disintegrate. To die.

And then Bel's chest would feel as if it was going to burst as she tried to keep her sobs silent so as not to wake Lucille, or alert the rest of the household to her disturbed emotional state.

Why did you have to die, Teddy? she kept asking.

Again and again her thoughts looped round and round. Endlessly.

And then her mind would tire, and other thoughts would push themselves through the cracks – the little openings that she did not have the energy to hold fast. And her consciousness would drift back to that night.

That kiss.

And her body would heat up and fill with a passion she had not experienced for a long time, and often she would fall asleep with the remembrance of Joe's lips on her own, kissing her gently.

'I hope Bel's all right. And she's not overdoing it,' Agnes said to Joe as he got himself ready for another night doing his Home Guard duties. 'She seems to be sleeping a lot.'

Joe struggled to respond to his mother, other than to agree and say, 'Aye, I know,' in a way which suggested that he too was puzzled.

Of course he was well aware why Bel was hitting the sack early most nights. It was the same reason Joe was keeping himself busy during the day. He had even started to give Major Black a hand with all the boring paperwork, and was now also helping out with recruitment because, just like Bel, he could not stop the constant whirring of his mind.

One moment he felt like a skylark soaring high in the sky, elated that *Bel had kissed him.*

She had loved him back.

He could still recall the smell of Bel's scent on his skin after their lips had touched and their faces had brushed – and the feel of the gentle impression of her lips on his.

The next moment, though, he would be plummeting down to earth, like a plane spinning out of control after having been shot down, and he would berate himself:

I've ruined everything.

Overstepped the mark.

The look on Bel's face had been as clear as day. A mix of shock, guilt and regret. It had clearly been a mistake on her part. One which she now obviously bitterly regretted.

Or did she?

There was the smallest sliver of ridiculous hope that Bel did have feelings for him. That it had not just been a moment of madness. He had seen the pull of attraction in her eyes, hadn't he?

Could it be that she loved him back?

But then Joe would admonish himself. This glimmer of light *had* to be extinguished, for it was an illusion. He was living in a fantasy land if he really believed that this might be the case. He had known all his life that his love for Bel would always remain unrequited.

She had loved his brother and not him.

Joe had to get on with his own life now. He had to allow himself to love someone who loved him back. And Maria did love him back. He had seen Maria just the once since the night of Beryl's party, due to their conflicting shifts; although, if Joe were honest, if he had really wanted to snatch some time with Maria, he could have made more of an effort to see her.

There was no denying he enjoyed her company and the time they spent together. And he was attracted to her and also admired her. Maria had been determined to be a part of the war effort and had joined the Women's Auxiliary Army well before the government had ruled that all single women over the age of twenty-one had to do some kind of war work.

But, during their last date, he hadn't been able to stop thinking about Bel, and he hated himself for it. Why couldn't he just allow himself to be happy with someone who was pretty much perfect for him? It was as though he had some kind of mental block which stopped him from enjoying a normal love. And his love for Bel was not normal. She was his brother's wife. He couldn't even start to imagine the kind of reaction those near to him would have, if they were to find out how much he coveted his twin's widow.

And that was what made it all the more hopeless.

Even if Bel did love him back, she would never allow herself to follow her feelings. For Teddy's sake. And for fear of what others would think, of being reviled for loving her husband's brother.

No matter which way he looked at it, Joe could only see hopelessness.

And it wasn't just Joe and Bel who had a secret they wanted to keep well hidden . . .

'Ah, how's my little Tramp? Come here, gorgeous,' Polly cajoled, giving the dog a pat.

Polly was in the kitchen on her own and was therefore allowing herself free rein to give the dog a cuddle.

Polly was finding it increasingly difficult to keep up her outward appearance of being hard and dismissive towards their new pet, as she secretly loved having the little mite around, and whenever everyone was out, she enjoyed nothing more than giving Tramp lots of love and attention.

As she bent down to stroke the dog, now rotating itself before flopping down at her feet, Polly gave the little collie-cross a slightly inquisitive look.

'Mm,' she mused out loud to the empty room as her hands gently felt Tramp's unusually firm and slightly rotund underbelly.

Chapter Forty-Three

Wednesday 23 July 1941

As DS Miller took a sip of tea, he looked across at Rosie chatting away passionately about her women welders, and felt a wave of nervousness. He had made a promise to himself. And he was determined to keep that promise.

'Honestly, I've never known a woman like her.' Rosie took a deep breath. She had had another run-in with Helen and was letting off steam.

'We women should stick together. Bloody hell, we get the short end of the stick in most things in life. As if the work isn't hard enough without women like her making it even harder still.'

DS Miller nodded his agreement, but his mind kept wandering to the long-anticipated walk home afterwards, and he had to concentrate to keep himself focused.

Rosie had been telling him how Helen had given Hannah a final official warning, and that it looked as if their little bird was going to be chucked out of the nest and left to survive on her own in a land in which she had only just sought refuge.

It was also looking more and more probable that Martha was going to be sent to work permanently with a new squad of riveters. They had a heater, a catcher, and a holder-up, now they just needed a riveter, and it looked as though Martha had been earmarked for the job.

'She'll never cope on her own. Martha's a fantastic workhorse, but she needs to be managed. It's taken us this long to cajole her out of the closed-off world she lives in most of the time. Now she actually *speaks* – and she even makes the occasional joke! That's going to disappear in a puff of smoke if she's moved to another team. Especially one full of men.'

DS Miller also knew that this would reduce Rosie's team of women welders down to just three – Polly, Dorothy and Angie. It would only be a matter of time before Helen was able to dispatch the women to other squads and then she would have succeeded in wreaking a part of her planned revenge.

He personally couldn't understand why the woman was putting so much effort into destroying Rosie's group of welders. She was never going to get what she really wanted – which was Tommy. From what Rosie had told him, the lad only had eyes for Polly, and she for him. DS Miller had thought they sounded just like he and his wife when they had been younger. Before the cancer had robbed him of her.

But now, here he was, being given a second chance of love. And again he felt the wave of trepidation.

'And Gloria? All good with her?' DS Miller asked.

'Yes, she's huge now. Just a few more weeks to go.'

'And still no sign of her husband?'

'No, thank the lord, although I did hear from one of the lads at work whose girlfriend works with him in the ropery that he was in some kind of scuffle outside his local the other week and turned up for work with quite a shiner.'

Rosie looked directly into the detective's eyes, adding, 'I couldn't help but think it was divine intervention.'

DS Miller returned the look with one Rosie could not read. He made no comment.

Rosie looked down at her watch. 'Goodness, where does the time go? I'd better get going.'

DS Miller stood up, feeling a sudden flush of nerves, and clumsily knocked the table. He did not think to ask where she was going, or what she had to rush back home for; as far as he knew, Rosie didn't do overtime. Hopefully, after tonight, he could be freer with his questions, and get to really know her.

As he held the café door open for Rosie, they both turned to quickly wave goodbye to Vera, who nodded back, as her hands were busy pouring out cups of tea.

As they stepped out on to the pavement, DS Miller took Rosie's hand and he was immediately filled with that wondrous, breathtaking sensation he had whenever he touched her. He desperately needed and wanted to hold her in his arms, to touch her face, her arms, her body. His resolve was firm. He could not keep on simply walking her home and holding her hand. He wanted more. He wanted this woman. All of her. Her mind – and her body. Their weekly meetings were now becoming torturous, as all he wanted to do was love her. Have her as his own. Or at the very least start to court her properly.

When they reached the basement flat, Rosie turned to go, but DS Miller kept hold of her hand. Rosie felt the tug on her arm and turned back to the detective. She felt her heart sink. She had known this was coming. She had sensed something a little amiss about Peter over tea; knew his mind had not been totally on their chatter. She might be a novice when it came to dating and any kind of romance, but she was experienced in the ways of men, and she had seen the flicker of yearning in her detective. The day had come that she had always known would inevitably arrive. It was time to face reality and come out of her Walt Disney world.

Peter wanted to do more than hold hands.

And she did too.

But she couldn't.

The risks were too great. The consequences could be disastrous for her life. And for the life of her sister – as well as Lily and their business.

She knew she had to sacrifice this blossoming love to ensure her own survival and that of those nearest to her.

'No, Peter,' Rosie spoke the words softly, but he saw a hardness in her that he had never observed before. 'I'm sorry, I can't.'

Rosie saw the look of devastation in her suitor's face, and a part of her wanted to feel his arms around her, to tell him how she really felt, and why this could go no further . . .

But she did not. Could not.

'I apologise if you feel I've led you on.' She stumbled through the words she knew she had to say. 'I'm so very sorry, but this can't go any further.'

DS Miller stuttered, trying to get words out, but he did not know what words he wanted to say.

'But.' He put his arm out as if he wanted to pull her back to him. 'I don't . . . I don't understand, Rosie.'

He swallowed hard. 'Why?' The question came out quietly and with great uncertainty, as if he wasn't quite sure if he was prepared or wanted to know the answer.

'I'm sorry, Peter,' Rosie said. Her own voice sounded hoarse as she struggled to keep the tears that were rising to the surface at bay.

'I don't think I can have a proper relationship with anyone . . . It's not you.'

'Why?' The detective's voice was now stronger. More confused. 'I don't understand. *Why* can't you?'

Now DS Miller did want to know, needed to know. Was desperate to know.

And Rosie also desperately wanted him to know that he was the only man she had ever wanted to be close to. But how could she tell him that without him demanding more of an explanation? He would never let her go if he knew that. If he thought there was a chance to win her round. To change her mind.

'I'm sorry, Peter. I just can't. You have to accept that. I'm so sorry. I should have said something sooner.'

And with that Rosie pulled her hand away and turned her back on her detective, disappearing down the stairs and into her little flat.

DS Miller stood there for a moment. Stunned.

Had he known this was going to happen?

Was that why he had felt so apprehensive and nervous? Had he somehow sensed it was all going to end? That his hopes of love were to be dashed away. Beaten down. Chucked out of the window.

DS Miller remained standing outside Rosie's flat, hoping she might have a change of heart and come back out and tell him that she had made a terrible mistake and that she didn't mean what she had said and that she would be his.

But she didn't.

After a while he turned and walked away.

His whole body felt numb. His mind frozen in thought.

The only warmth he felt was the lingering imprint of her hand on his as he slowly made his way back home.

Chapter Forty-Four

'Where's Kate?' Rosie demanded loudly to anyone within earshot as she marched through the front door of Lily's.

Vivian and two of the other girls who were making their way down the wide staircase stopped chatting. There was no mistaking Rosie's tone of voice. She was angry.

'I think she's with Lily upstairs,' Vivian said, wondering what had caused her normally relaxed and happy boss to appear so irritated. Even when she was upset about something, she was usually as cool as a cucumber; generally nothing much seemed to faze her. And lately she had actually seemed really happy – perhaps even a little in love. If Vivian didn't know better, she would have believed Rosie had a man in her life.

'Well, can you go and get her for me, please? And tell Lily she hasn't got a monopoly on Kate!'

Vivian forced her mouth shut. This was not the time for any backchat. She gave the other two girls she was with a puzzled look, before turning and walking back upstairs to do as she had been told. There was no way, though, that she was going to repeat what Rosie had told her to say to Lily. She had never seen Lily and Rosie exchange cross words and she didn't want to, either. She knew enough to realise it would not make for a pretty sight. Both her bosses might be as nice as pie most of the time, but all the girls were more than aware that they were both as hard as nails underneath all their finery.

When she arrived at the top room, breathing heavily as she had on a particularly tight corset this evening, Vivian conveyed Rosie's wishes in as polite a fashion as possible to Lily, whom she had found hunched over a couple of recently acquired dress patterns, Kate making amendments to them with a thick black pencil.

Vivian adored Kate. They all did. They thought she was the sweetest thing, and so incredibly shy, but it was her expertise with the needle that endeared her so much to them all – even more since clothes rationing had been introduced. They just needed to talk her through their vision for a particular kind of dress or skirt, and she would recreate it as if she had seen the picture in her head for real. She wasn't just a natural, she was a genius when it came to clothes and fashion.

The only problem was that Lily *did* hog her terribly. Vivian would have liked nothing better than to have relayed Rosie's accusations to her boss that she totally monopolised Kate, and that she had to share her out a little more, but she knew better.

'Sorry to bother you both, but Rosie has just arrived and is insisting she see Kate. How do you say it in French, Madame Lily? *Tout de suite?*'

Lily smiled. She loved it when her girls spoke even just a word of her favourite language.

Kate looked at Lily for permission to go, and Lily responded with a nod of her head. They made their way out of the room that had now been transformed into a little dressmaking studio, Vivian following her boss and Kate down the three flights of stairs. She was more than a little keen to know why Rosie was in such a hurry to see Kate.

'Did Rosie disclose the reason for this urgency?' Lily turned her head to ask.

'No,' Vivian answered, before dropping her voice, 'but she did seem a little vexed.'

When Lily got to the bottom of the stairs, she walked into the front office to find Rosie at her desk and Kate already sitting in the chair opposite, with her hands in her lap, feet close together, her back as straight as a board. Lily knew the girl's posture had been beaten into her by the nuns.

'Do you know what kind I mean?' Rosie was asking Kate. As always, Rosie was treating her old schoolfriend in the gentlest of manners, but Lily saw the look on her business partner's face and knew something had happened. Something had upset her. And when Rosie was upset, she tended to get angry.

'I think they call them "slacks",' Kate said quietly. 'That Hollywood actress Katharine Hepburn wears 'em all the time . . . they're becoming all the rage in London.'

'That's exactly what I want, Kate. What would we do without you?' Rosie was forcing herself to be jocular. She knew Kate had suffered enough awfulness to last her a lifetime. She might have felt as if she was raging inside, but there was no way she wanted Kate to pick up on any of that.

'Do you think you could make me a pair, please? Fairly quickly?' Rosie asked.

Lily stepped forward, putting her jewellery-laden hand down on the front of the desk.

'Of course she can,' she said, smiling at Kate. 'Make Rosie's new trousers first – we can pick up where we left off with the pattern alterations when you've sorted Rosie here out. Now,' she added, 'go and get yourself some supper from the kitchen. I've just made a lovely coq au vin – have as much as you like; you're still far too skinny for my liking.' She smiled at Kate, who got up and hurried out of the room, leaving Lily and Rosie alone.

'So, *trousers*?'

Lily didn't wait for an answer but gently cajoled, 'Come on, then, tell me what's happened,' as she went to pour two glasses of cognac from the crystal decanter she had just acquired, and which had been placed on top of the long, leather-embossed desktop.

Rosie slumped a little as she took her glass and looked at Lily with sadness. She knew she had to steel her heart and acknowledge that real love would never be a part of her life. It was just the way it was.

'Oh, Lily,' she sighed, 'what a weird life this is.'

'I'll drink to that,' Lily said, raising her heavy glass tumbler, and sitting down in the chair just vacated by Kate.

'Now, tell me everything,' she said, although she had a pretty good idea precisely what had caused the dark cloud of melancholy to descend upon the young woman she cared for so deeply.

She had been expecting its arrival for some time now.

Chapter Forty-Five

The next morning, across town in the Elliot household, something far less expected arrived on the doormat in the form of a Portsmouth postmarked letter addressed for the attention of Miss Pearl Hardwick.

Picking up the envelope from the doormat, Pearl was thankful no one else had seen it, thankful that for once she had been the first up as she had forgotten to prepare the fire the night before when she had come back from her shift at the pub. A couple of the regulars, who clearly had the glad eye for her, had bought her a few drinks, and that, coupled with the large brandy she kept hidden next to the beer tray, which she had slowly supped on throughout the evening, had made her more than a little tipsy; she had come back and gone straight to bed, completely forgetting to stack the fire up.

Prepping the range for the day ahead was about the only contribution Pearl made to the running of the Elliot household, and, although she hated doing it, she had learnt that it had the added bonus of endearing her to Agnes. And, whether Pearl liked it or not, Agnes was the boss and it paid to stay on her good side.

On seeing the letter, Pearl felt a wave of mixed emotions. If she had received any kind of communication from Portsmouth when she'd first came to stay with her daughter and in-laws, she would have been cock-a-hoop. But six months had passed, and now her feelings weren't quite so clear-cut.

Stuffing the envelope into her bra, Pearl hurriedly cleared out the grate and made a tiny bonfire of kindling and coal, before sparking the fire up and making herself a cup of tea.

When she heard the rest of the household start to stir, she grabbed her cigarettes and carefully carried her cuppa out to the back yard, safe in the knowledge that no one would join her if she was having a smoke.

After placing her cup and saucer down on the ground, Pearl perched herself on the wooden stool she had put out in the corner of the yard for her fag breaks. After sparking up, she pulled out her letter, slid her thumb under the back of the sealed envelope, and slowly tore it open.

Reading had never been Pearl's strong point, but luckily the words written on the white paper were both simple and to the point. It could hardly be classed as a love letter, but it was as near to one as Pearl had ever received.

The few lines of scrawled, childlike writing were, as anticipated, from Victor, her live-in lover, the man she had left in Portsmouth; the reason she had ended up back in her hometown.

Victor's almost illegible scribblings told her that he wanted her back. That this time would be different. That *he* would be different. All she needed, he wrote, was enough money for her train fare back down south – and 'a little extra' to help keep them both going for a while. He made no mention of the money needed to pay off the debts they had both accrued, and Pearl wondered how he had managed to keep their creditors at bay.

Pearl read and smoked and then smoked some more.

She had loved Victor. Probably still did. The men she had been with since she'd come back didn't count for anything. She and Victor had been a proper couple. The only downside had been that they were both as fiery as each other, especially after a few drinks. They fought like cat and dog and, more often than not, Pearl was the one to come out of it worse.

Pearl cringed inwardly when she recalled the last time she had seen Victor, how he'd chucked her and her meagre belongings out of their little end-of-terrace boarding house and on to the street after one alcohol-fuelled argument too many back in January.

'Sod off, yer stupid cow!' he had yelled from the front doorstep, so that every man and his dog could hear. 'We're finished. You're on your own now!'

Pearl had known he had meant what he'd said, and so had gathered up her few bits a nd pieces off the street, stuffed them into her beaten-up suitcase, and headed back to her hometown.

She might have been returning with her tail between her legs, but she had been damned if anyone was going to know that, which was why she had made out that she'd come back for Isabelle's sake after hearing about Teddy's death; although, gauging by her daughter's reaction, she had not believed that for one second. Her daughter wasn't stupid. She had known straight away it was an outright lie that her mother had come to comfort her in her time of need; she would never have gone to see Isabelle if she had been all right with Victor. She might have sent a little condolence card – but that would have been it.

The only reason Pearl had gone round to Agnes's was because her mate Irene had told her there was a spare room going. She knew Agnes wouldn't turn her away – knew she would never turn away anyone in need – although she hadn't been as sure that Isabelle would be so accommodating. And she had been proved right. She had seen the stubbornness in her daughter's face when she had arrived at the house that night; if it had been up to her own flesh and blood, she honestly believed she would have been turfed back out on to the street.

Pearl turned slightly as she heard the household stirring. Polly had come into the kitchen carrying Lucille, and was chatting away to the little girl, who was still half asleep.

As Pearl looked into the kitchen from her perch outside, she thought to herself that her daughter had done all right for herself. She had certainly landed on her feet marrying Teddy.

Now Pearl had her own chance of a secure future with a half-decent man, and one who wasn't going to go off and get himself killed at war. Why she wasn't singing from the treetops and waving his letter about in glee was beyond her. She really did need to give herself a kick up the back-side and, more importantly, get some money together, and get back down south. Back into her fella's arms. She certainly wasn't getting any younger and she would be damned if she was going to end up a wizened old woman all on her tod. She had been on her own most of her life, dragged herself along by her fingernails most of the time, without so much as a helping hand – so she did not intend to finish up old and alone. That much was for sure.

Chapter Forty-Six

A week later, July 1941

When Rosie woke up and realised what day of the week it was, she felt her heart sink. Normally on a Wednesday morning, as soon as she stirred from her slumber, she would be hit by an instant buzz of nervous excitement; a flutter of anticipation about meeting Peter.

But today she wouldn't be going to Vera's after work for her weekly rendezvous with the detective. Nor would she be going there ever again. Could not go.

Last week he had revealed his intentions and desire to her; his feelings had been made quite clear. He had given her no other choice than to call it a day. Now, all that she hoped for was that he would not think she had strung him along – because she hadn't, not for one moment. If anything she had tried unsuccessfully to cheat herself. She hoped he wouldn't hate her for it; hoped that he would know she cared an awful lot for him, but that it just could not go any further.

As Rosie got ready and headed out of the door for work, she started to imagine bumping into Peter, that he would tell her it was just fine and dandy for them to stay the way they were – to continue their very peculiar courtship of tea, chatter and the holding of hands.

Damn it! Stop it! Rosie cursed inwardly.
This is painful enough as it is.

As she headed down to the south dock that, as always, was swarming with workers, she told herself she should be hoping that she would *never* bump into the detective again.

So why did that prospect cause her heart to feel even heavier than it already was?

As Rosie looked up the river, trying not to seek out the Dock Police cabin on the river bend by the lock, she berated herself for inflicting this pain and mental torture upon herself. In hindsight it was as if, when she had first started meeting up with the detective, she had seen a burning building and walked straight into it – regardless of the consequences.

Why had she caused herself this upset when she had known all along there could only ever be one outcome?

Was she some kind of masochist at heart?

She must be, otherwise why had she kept on seeing him, got to know him, become closer to him? Why hadn't she just nipped this addiction in the bud from the start? Instead of feeding it? Making her want more. And now she had stopped, she was so hungry her belly ached.

As Rosie walked up to the giant iron gates of the yard, jostling shoulder to shoulder with the other workers, she forced her mind to let go of her obsessive thoughts about the detective; it was exhausting her and draining her of her energy.

She took her white clocking-on card from the out-stretched hand of the young timekeeper and forced her mind to concentrate on the here and now – for today was going to be a very busy day, in all ways.

'Morning, miss!'

It was Angie. She was always in bright and early. Rosie counted her blessings that Dorothy had convinced her to swap jobs with Gloria, as she was turning out to be a good little worker. She never complained; just got on with it. And she was always on time. Sometimes, like today, she was even in before Rosie. She had joked, saying that it was because her father, a miner at one of the local collieries, was always up at the crack of dawn, and when he was up, the whole house had to get up. Whatever the reason, though, Angie never seemed to like being at home much. If she wasn't working, she would be out with Dorothy, either on the pull in town, or going to the cinema to see the latest film. They were both united in their determination to have as much fun as possible. The pair of them were – quite simply – not going to take life seriously, not one jot.

'Miss, the bitch is coming over,' Rosie heard Angie's voice hiss over to her in a whisper.

'What was that, Angela?' Helen said in her most hoity-toity voice.

'Just telling miss I had a stitch coming on – cos I ran to work,' she said, sticking her hand on her hip and pulling her face into a grimace.

Rosie had to smile. Angie could barely read or write, but there was nothing wrong with her brain – the girl was as sharp as a pin.

'Mm,' Helen said, unconvinced, but prepared to give Rosie's new welder the benefit of the doubt; she had other things on her mind.

'Rosie, I need Martha again today with the riveters.'

There was no 'please' or 'I'm awfully sorry but . . .'

Helen was on full throttle. Her father was due back in just a few weeks. Her time was running out. There was no time for false niceties. The gloves were off.

The two women stared at each other – if they had been two dogs, their hackles would have risen.

Angie, who had been watching the women's standoff, pretended to busy herself.

'Fine,' Rosie said, before abruptly turning around and stomping over to the welding machines.

Helen glowered at Rosie's back before herself marching off.

When Martha and Hannah arrived at the welder's work area, Rosie called them over. 'Martha, you and I are going to the Admiral at lunchtime. We need to have a chat, and there's someone I'd like you to meet.'

Martha nodded solemnly.

'And, Hannah,' Rosie continued, 'come and grab a cuppa with me in the canteen. I'm parched and I want to put something to you.'

Angie's ears had pricked up. She could not wait for Dorothy to turn up. Today was going to be better than a trip to the flicks.

'I may have a solution to your problem.'

Rosie was sitting opposite Hannah in the canteen. It was relatively quiet, as the day's shift had just started. She had wanted some peace and quiet in which to chat to Hannah, instead of having to shout over the intense clattering and clanging in the yard, so had come to the cafeteria knowing it would be more or less empty.

Hannah was sitting with both her hands jammed between her knees, as if she were trying to keep them from shooting up into the air. She had a cup of black coffee in front of her. Hannah's almond-shaped dark brown eyes widened.

'Really?' She sounded the tiniest bit hopeful.

Rosie took a sip of tea and began explaining her possible 'solution'.

'A vacancy has come up for a trainee draughtsman. I remembered you saying how you used to love to draw when you were back home. And I've seen some of the sketches you've done here on bits of paper during breaks. They are very good.'

A slight blush crept across Hannah's face. 'Oh, they're just – what do you call them – doodles?'

'Well, they look like good doodles to me, Hannah. Anyway, I went to see the head draughtsman a little while ago.'

Hannah cast her mind back and recalled Angie and Dorothy chatting, wondering what Rosie had been up to when they had seen her come out of the drawing office.

'I told him about you,' Rosie continued, 'and asked him to give me a shout if anything came up. And, now it has!'

Hannah's face lit up.

'Oh, Rosie! And he's happy to have *me*? How does he know I'll be any good?'

Rosie chuckled. 'Well, I have to confess, I pinched one of your "doodles" of the ship by the quayside. He was quite impressed. He said he could not believe how exact and precise your drawing was. I think he used the word "technical". You're just what he's looking for – someone who has a natural artistic flare and also knows the ins and outs of how a ship is built.'

Rosie looked at Hannah, who was now beaming from ear to ear.

Rosie smiled, feeling good that she was at least making someone happy. 'But,' she explained, 'if you don't take to it, or you don't like it, you can leave.'

'Oh, I think I *am* going to like it. How exciting!'

'And, best of all,' Rosie added, 'there'll be no more welding.'

Hannah looked a little embarrassed. 'I'm sorry I've not been much good at that. I feel I've dragged everyone back,' she said.

'Rubbish,' Rosie reprimanded her. 'Welding is just not for you. Like Dorothy said when we were all out for a drink that day, it's time for you to ditch the Guinness and start drinking something you actually like . . . If anything, it was my fault; I should have done something about it earlier. I just became a bit obsessed with keeping my entire squad together – regardless of anything else.'

As the news started to really sink in, Hannah became more animated and seemed so much happier than she had been for months.

'I can't wait to tell the girls! No more Helen breathing down my neck. And I'll still be able to see you all – like Gloria does – at breaks and lunches.'

'Exactly, Hannah, you'll always be one of us. And I'll always be here for you, regardless of wherever you work . . . Now, shall we go and tell Helen? I'm sure she's going to be over the moon.'

Rosie's acid sarcasm made Hannah grin.

'And then we can go and meet your new boss!'

Hannah's hands sprang free from the hold they were in, and she clamped her hands together and held them to her chest, her excitement struggling to be contained.

'Oh, yes please! Thank you, Rosie. You are the best!'

As soon as the hooter sounded out for the lunch break, Martha came marching over to Rosie. She had no idea what was in store for her, but she sensed they were about to do battle, and she was happy to follow her general into the war zone.

Ten minutes later, while the women welders were all tucking into a pie and pea lunch at the canteen to celebrate Hannah's new job, Rosie and Martha were heading over to the Admiral Inn, where it had been arranged they were to meet Mr Archibald Pike, one of the yard's union representatives from the United Society of Boilermakers and Iron and Steel Shipbuilders. The odd-looking trio greeted each other with a brisk shake of hands and sat themselves round one of the small wooden tables.

The slightly plump, fleshy-faced, middle-aged Mr Pike, who was dressed in a cheap but well-pressed shiny brown suit, had already got himself a pint. He started chatting earnestly to Martha, occasionally looking across at Rosie. He then pulled out a number of official-looking forms from his battered briefcase. Between mouthfuls of frothy beer he took his time explaining various points.

Throughout their meeting, Martha wore a serious, slightly apprehensive look on her round, candid face, and either nodded in understanding, or interjected with a question when she was unsure of something.

After Mr Pike had talked for a while longer, Rosie then asked a few questions, which the man answered as concisely and as comprehensively as possible.

The two women then stood up, shook hands with Mr Pike in turn, and left him to his drink. They went back to the yard but, rather than head over to their work area, the pair walked straight across to the administration building.

'You again!' Helen sneered on seeing Rosie at her office door. As usual she completely ignored Martha.

'Have you come to tell me you're letting another one of your squad go? You won't have anyone left at this rate.' Rosie could almost see Helen's mind working overtime, wondering if she would be able to disband them sooner than anticipated if there were just the three women welders left under her charge.

'No chance, Helen. You don't think I'd make it that easy for you, do you?'

This really was brewing up to be a bare-knuckled fight.

'In case you haven't noticed, there is also someone else here in your office,' Rosie said, looking up at Martha, who seemed even larger in the confines of the small office.

Rosie took a deep breath and mentally crossed her fingers.

'Martha here has something she'd like to impart to you,' Rosie added, stepping aside a little to allow her workmate to take centre stage.

You can do it, Martha, Rosie prayed.

There was a moment's silence.

'Well, come on then, I've not got all day, you know!' Helen spat out.

Rosie's bile rose to the back of her mouth, but this was Martha's skirmish and she had to come out of it on top. Thankfully Helen's sharp words seemed to snap Martha into action.

'Here . . .' Martha said, pulling out the documentation given to her by Mr Pike, '. . . is my work contract.'

She lumbered forward, and Helen automatically took a step back, even though her desk was shielding her from the two women welders.

Helen stuck her arm out and tentatively took the papers from Martha's huge, man-sized hand.

'Page six,' Martha commanded.

Helen flicked through to the appropriate page.

'Please read,' she instructed.

Rosie could feel the euphoria rise in her.

Martha was doing it!

It took Helen a few minutes to read through the contractual jargon, but Rosie could tell by the look of pure venom spreading across her enemy's face that she had understood the basic gist of it all. When she reached the end of the page, she glared at Martha. Rosie thought it was the first time Helen had actually looked her in the eye.

'No more riveting.' Martha said simply.

'Exactly.' Rosie stepped forward. 'As I'm sure you've read Helen, Martha was contracted to work as a welder at Thompson's. If you continue to order her to work with Jimmy and his crew of riveters, you'll be in blatant breach of her contract. The only exemption to that is if her welding is below par, which we both know is never going to be the case – you've even said yourself that she's already handling twice the workload of a male welder.'

Rosie looked at Martha, who was standing expressionless, looking straight ahead of her as if she was a soldier on parade. She then turned her attention back to Helen.

'Well, that's all for today. We won't be taking up any more of your time, Helen. Good day.' And with that Rosie turned to walk out of the office, with Martha falling in behind her.

As the pair made their way out of the office and back into the afternoon sun and the fresh air, Rosie looked up at the woman who had just saved her squad of female welders.

'Well done, Martha! Well done!'

And with that Martha allowed a big, gap-toothed smile to overtake her chubby, childlike face.

Chapter Forty-Seven

As Rosie walked home, she had to force herself to be strong and not to take a diversion to Vera's café.

It was hard not to, though, but she told herself she didn't have a choice.

Today, of all days, she would have loved to have sat and chatted to Peter about what had happened with both Hannah and Martha, and she would have particularly revelled in sharing with him her glee at gaining a partial victory over Helen. Of course, she knew the civil war raging between her and Helen at the yard had not, as yet, been won or lost. She knew Helen would continue to plot and plan other forms of revenge on her welders, and, of course, on the main object of her hatred, Polly.

And she also knew that Helen would still be baying for Dorothy's blood after finding out it was her who had told Ned's wife about the lies she had spread; it worried her what punishment Helen would concoct to inflict on Dorothy, but she would just have to deal with that as and when it happened. One thing about Helen, she was no windbag – if she said she was going to do something, you could bet your boots she would; she was not one to issue empty threats. The woman was not only seriously motivated by a need for vengeance, but also by a real jealousy of the women's closeness and their friendship.

Rosie was aware that there were still battles to be fought, and that this was not the end, but at least for now, she and her welders had gained a reprieve.

As she reached her flat, Rosie's mind once again swung back to Peter. He had become a good friend, and she was going to miss that as much as anything else. It was perhaps due to their burgeoning closeness that she had managed to fool herself that, by seeing him in a purely platonic capacity, she would spare herself any heartache.

But, she had not.

They might not have made love, or even shared a kiss, but she knew the feelings she was having were those that a woman had when she was falling in love.

And she knew she had to break the fall.

The desire and love she had started to feel for this man had to end – not just in reality, but in her mind also.

This love could never be a part of her life.

Vera was pressing down on her large kitchen knife, halving one of her doorstep sandwiches with such vigour it was as if she was a butcher dissecting a particularly tough carcass. She had not been able to stop herself from glancing up every time the little bell above her door tinged, signalling the arrival of a new customer.

Every time, she felt a disappointment that the metal jangling did not herald the late arrival of the woman in the overalls with the scarred face. Vera didn't even know her name, but she felt as if she knew her. Age and experience had taught her to read a person well without ever exchanging more than a cursory hello or goodbye.

As Vera took a surreptitious look at the copper sitting on his own, she felt the tiniest bit sorry for him.

She chastised herself for becoming so sentimental in her dotage. 'Yer getting as soft as clarts in yer old age,' Vera mumbled under her breath.

The clock struck six and it was clear the woman was not going to turn up. Vera watched as DS Miller left his customary tip on the table; he had only taken a few sips of tea and had just taken a bite or two of his sandwich. She watched him weave his way around the other tables, all tightly packed into her small teashop – and as always he turned to give her a wave farewell.

He pulled the corners of his mouth up, but it wasn't enough to create a convincing smile; she caught his eye and saw the all too familiar look of heartache. A look she seemed to see too much of these days.

What a shame, Vera thought, *they seemed so smitten with each other. They positively buzzed with life when they were together.*

Why hadn't she come?

Vera told herself to stop being so pessimistic. There might be a perfectly understandable reason why she hadn't turned up. She wasn't going to give up on them. Something might just have happened and she hadn't been able to get a message to him.

Vera resolved that she was still going to save their table for them next week.

She was determined that this would not be the end of their love affair.

Chapter Forty-Eight

'Isabelle?' Pearl's face appeared around the bedroom door. She had been putting off this chat for over a week now since her letter from Victor had arrived.

'Can I come in for a moment, pet?'

Bel was sitting on her bed, reading a picture book of *Aesop's Fables*. She hadn't been able to face reading 'The Lambton Worm', and Lucille seemed happy with her mum's explanation that it was best read by Joe, and she should save it until he was able to do her bedtime story. Bel knew that Lucille would soon start to ask questions as to why Joe was no longer a part of her evening ritual, as he hadn't ventured into her room since the night of their kiss three weeks ago, but for the moment Lucille seemed content with Bel's explanation that her Doey was like the knight from 'The Lambton Worm' and he was out keeping the town safe – only that instead of protecting a castle from an awful fanged monster, he was helping guard the town against a man called Hitler.

Bel knew her daughter was too young to understand the concept of war, but she was old enough to sense the fear every time there was an air raid, and she had seen with her own inquisitive eyes the devastation and mass destruction that lay around them. Bel often wondered how this war would affect her daughter and the other children being brought up during this terrible time. She knew a lot of mothers had evacuated their children to homes out in the country, but there was no way she would do that with Lucille. The thought of her daughter being looked after by people she had not even met, never mind did not know well, was more frightening than the threat of the Luftwaffe's bombs. Bel was not going to risk anything happening to her daughter. The only people she would ever trust her child with were Agnes, Polly and, of course, Joe.

'Yes, Ma, what do you want?' Bel looked at Pearl suspiciously as she snaked her wiry body round the door and quickly sat down next to her daughter.

'Pearl! Story!' Lucille demanded.

Pearl looked at Lucille's expectant little face and at her daughter's stony face, which said, *Don't you dare say no*, and she reluctantly took the large hardback book from Bel's hand and opened it up at the first story.

'"The Young Man and the Swallow".' Pearl's gravelly voice sounded quiet and a little uncertain, which Bel put down to the fact that this was a new experience for her mother, as not once during the entirety of her own childhood had Pearl ever read Bel a bedtime story.

As Pearl made her way falteringly through the tale of the young man who spends all his money on gambling and luxurious living until he has nothing left but the coat on his back, she paused for a moment, seemingly lost in thought, before continuing to read how the man ends up selling his coat after spotting a swallow and believing spring has arrived; he then uses the money from the sale of his coat on one last bet in the hope of making his fortune. But, instead of winning, he ends up not only losing his last few pennies, but also his life when he finds the swallow frozen to death, and he too dies from the cold.

Bel had not realised the tale was so tragic, and was glad Lucille had fallen asleep and had missed the ending. Pearl also looked slightly unnerved by the tragic tale – and also unusually pensive.

'Do you want to go into the kitchen and chat, Ma?' Bel broke the sombre silence of the room. She was becoming increasingly curious as to what had impelled her mum to come to see her. It must be something she really wanted, otherwise she would not have acquiesced and read the story.

'No, no, it won't take long, pet.'

Bel interpreted this as meaning she wanted to ask her something that she didn't want anyone else overhearing.

Pearl shuffled about a little uneasily, perching on the edge of the bed but still managing to face Bel.

'Well, I was wondering . . .' She straightened her back and paused.

'Oh, for God's sake, Ma, just spit it out. What do you want?'

'Well, I was wondering,' Pearl began again, 'if . . . when Teddy was killed while he was fighting so bravely for King and country.'

Another pause.

'I was wondering if, because he was a soldier . . . and I know that the army pay their soldiers . . . whether or not they gave you any kind of widow's pension or allowance?'

Bel was stunned. It took her a few moments to find her voice. 'You are joking, aren't you, Ma?' Bel hissed at her mother vehemently, but as quietly as possible so as not to wake Lucille.

Pearl shuffled on the bed uneasily. 'Isabelle, dinnit get yer knickers in a knot. It was only a question,' she whispered back, starting to fidget around uncomfortably. 'It's only that I'm a bit short and wanted to ask you for a sub?'

Bel could feel the rage within her rise. 'What do you need money for? You've not paid a penny towards your board and lodgings since you turned up here. I know for a fact you've been keeping money back whenever you've gone out with Lucille and I've given you some spending money. And I've got a good idea you've done the same with Agnes when she's given you money to buy the shopping. No wonder she prefers Arthur to go to the market. No one might have said anything, Ma, but that's not to say it hasn't been clocked!'

Bel was now furious. 'Blimey, you've even started earning a bit at the pub. What the hell do you need more money for? More fags? More drink?'

Pearl looked at her daughter and knew she was going to have to tell her something by way of explanation. It was just a question of how much of the truth she was willing to divulge.

'I need to go back to Portsmouth for a bit and I need money for the train fare down there – as well as some money to live off . . . I know you can find some from somewhere. Agnes and you are raking it in with your little laundry business . . . and I'm sure you both get a little bit here and there for looking after all those bairns every day? And Polly . . . well, she must have a load stashed away with the amount she's on at the yard – especially with all that overtime.'

Bel shook her head in disbelief, and looked at Lucille, who was starting to stir. She kept her voice low as she leaned into her mum and spat out her anger.

'Ah, well, at least I know now why you came up here. And don't think for one minute I believed all that tosh about it being because of Teddy's death. How would *your* presence in *my* life give me any comfort whatsoever?'

Bel took another breath. 'Thought I'd come into a load of dosh did you, Ma? And that you'd be entitled to some of it being my ma 'n all? Well, you're wrong. On all counts.

'But,' Bel went on; she could hear her voice starting to shake, 'I suppose I should be glad you've actually told me that you're off again. I should be thankful for small mercies. Not like when I was a child, and you just used to up sticks and disappear without a word to anyone. So, what's it to be this time? You off for a few days? Weeks? Or is it for good this time? Me and Lucille not worth sticking around for, eh?'

Bel was so angry. Angry that the only reason her mother had turned up again in her life was for money, a roof over her head, and food in her belly.

But she was also angry with herself, for hoping that her mum might have come back to see her and Lucille. She felt like punching herself for still feeling like a child inside – hurt by her mother's seeming indifference to them both. By her complete lack of maternal love. Foolishly, she had actually started to think, to believe, that Pearl wanted to be a part of her family. To be a mother of sorts. And a grandmother – if not in name.

'You know, Ma,' Bel continued, her mind pinging about like one of those pinball machines she had seen.

'I should have known – *it was always the same with you.*' Bel's anger was now starting to break free and she was struggling to keep her voice low.

'*Money and men.* And it still is. A leopard never changes its spots . . . You got some fancy man down south you want to get back to? You've just about drained us dry here and now you want that very last drop before you bugger off again?

'Well, I have news for you, Ma, *normal* mothers are meant to *give* to their children – not take, take, take!'

Pearl looked at her daughter's hate-filled face. She was unable to see Bel's hurt or feel any kind of empathy or understanding. Her concern, as always, was for herself, and Bel's words had pushed a button inside her, releasing her own feelings of rejection. And, as was her way, Pearl's instinct was to strike back.

'Well, if I were you I'd get off my high horse,' she whispered harshly, pushing her words out from her wrinkled-up, taut mouth. 'Because you're far from perfect yourself, Isabelle.' She glared at her daughter. She knew it was wrong to say what she was about to, but she just couldn't stop herself.

'Didn't you know – *widowed* women aren't meant to be making sweet with their dead husband's brother?'

The room fell totally silent.

Bel was mortified.

Her face flamed red and her whole body felt as if it was on fire – with anger, and shame.

'How dare you make accusations like that! *How dare you?*'

Pearl looked at her daughter. 'They're not *accusations*, Isabelle,' she stressed quietly to her daughter. 'They're *facts*. Because, Isabelle, I *know*. I know *everything*,' she said, looking into her daughter's eyes, showing her that for once she wasn't hedging her bets and second-guessing – that she did, in fact, know the truth of the situation.

'I know all about your little love affair with Joe, so don't play the innocent with me. You may fool everyone else in this house with your Little Miss Perfect act, but yer don't kid yer old ma. I know exactly what you've been up to.'

'We haven't been up to anything!' Bel knew that wasn't true, but it had only been a kiss, after all. Her mother was making it sound like something really sordid.

'I saw it coming before it even happened,' Pearl said, now sounding quite pleased with herself. Boastful. 'And then I saw you both on the night of that Beryl's birthday party, when you both sneaked off early.'

Bel was feeling sick to the pit of her stomach. She had not heard anyone come into the house, but then again that whole evening seemed like a muddle to her now. She could only surmise that her mother had skulked in after them and spied on them.

'I came back to get my spare packet of fags,' Pearl told her, revelling in the fact she now clearly had the upper hand, 'and I got an eyeful of yer both kissing through the door. Yer didn't even bother to close it! Yer want to be thankful it was me that saw the two of ya smooching away like a couple of teenagers and not anyone else! God, imagine if Agnes had clapped eyes on the pair of you . . .' She paused.

'Oh, Isabelle. What a let-down. The woman welcomes you into her home as a wee bairn and this is how you repay her. One son dies, so you just help yourself to the other.'

Bel felt mortified. Her mother had spoken the words, but she had thought the same thing herself. That this was what people would think. People who had loved and cared for her. That Agnes and Polly – and even Arthur – would see her as some kind of hussy. Moving on from one brother to the next in the blink of an eye.

The shame she would feel if they found out. The embarrassment. But what would be worst of all would be seeing the disappointment on their faces.

'Anyway.' Pearl stood up and smoothed her skirt down. She knew she had successfully crushed her daughter into submission, but it irked her that the victory felt empty.

They had nothing more to say to each other. They had both said too much already. Words that could not be taken back. Or forgotten.

Pearl felt a very slight ripple of regret. Even perhaps a tinge of guilt.

'But dinnit worry, Isabelle, I'm not all bad. Yer secret's safe with me.'

As she spoke her last words, Pearl turned and quietly left the room, gently shutting the door, leaving Bel sitting as though she had been frozen in time.

Chapter Forty-Nine

Thursday 7 August 1941

'Hey, Gloria, I think you're due for a tea break.' It was Rosie's familiar voice, but her casualness sounded strained; a little false.

'Sounds like a good idea to me,' Gloria said, switching off the crane's loud engine and slowly climbing out. As she did so she put a protective arm across her bosom, which was pulling her denim overalls to their full stretch.

'Oh, I feel like I'm heaving two huge melons around with me, as well as this great big bump,' she said, carefully stepping on to the ground. She could no longer see her feet, so was feeling the ground to make sure she was on terra firma.

Rosie sat down on one of the metal chairs 'borrowed' from the drawing office and poured out a tea for Gloria and then another for herself.

'You look serious.' Gloria said, carefully sitting down next to her, 'is there anything the matter?'

Rosie looked at her friend and put her tin cup of steaming tea down. 'I'm really sorry to have to tell you this.'

Gloria felt her stomach turn over. Rosie never sounded this sombre, nor looked so grave.

'It's Jack, isn't it?' she asked. She felt her heart pound as if it was going to burst out of her chest. She could almost hear its thudding, quickening beat.

Rosie nodded and leaned over to squeeze her arm.

'Please, tell me he's not dead,' Gloria begged her.

Since the beginning of the war there had already been hundreds of the town's men – either from the Royal Navy or the Merchant Navy – declared missing or dead. Hardly a week seemed to go by without some news flash reporting that a warship, cargo vessel – sometimes even a trawler – had been torpedoed by a German U-boat, or bombed out of the water by the Luftwaffe.

'There's no news yet,' Rosie said. 'The steamship he was travelling on – the SS *Tunisia* – was bombed and sunk by Jerry a few hundred miles off the west coast of Ireland on Monday. The bosses told us today that so far they were only getting dribs and drabs of information coming through; it's sketchy to say the least.'

Gloria could feel the pinprick of tears start behind her eyes, but would not allow them to come forth.

'I'm trying my hardest to find out more,' Rosie said. 'But it's hard. Apparently the Ministry of War don't like admitting publicly that we've had a hit – bad for morale, and all that.'

Gloria tried, but found she couldn't speak. Her mind was too busy skidding around to be able to form words.

Had she lost the love of her life more or less as soon as she'd found him again?

Had her baby lost its father before they had even had the chance to meet?

Had she willed this somehow to happen when she had wished that Jack's return be delayed to give her more time to work out what she was going to do?

The guilt. It was all her fault.

Her dilemma now seemed so pathetic. So trivial. Life was what was important. Why hadn't she seen that?

Please God, let him be all right, her mind screamed out, but she seemed unable to move a muscle, never mind talk.

'You okay, Gloria?' Rosie said, moving closer to her friend, putting her arm around her shoulders and giving her a gentle hug.

'He'll be all right,' Rosie said, but even she thought that her reassurances sounded trite and empty. How did she know Jack hadn't been blown up, or drowned, or had died of hypothermia. But what else could she say? Her only thoughts now were for Gloria and her unborn child.

'You have to keep well for the baby,' Rosie said, as she felt Gloria's silent tears splash down on to her bare arm, which was wrapped around her friend. She gave Gloria another cuddle.

'Just don't give up hope,' she said. 'There's always hope.'

Chapter Fifty

Tuesday 12 August 1941

'All right everyone, I think we can now confidently say that Ma's little Tramp has definitely lived up to her name – and she is, as suspected, pregnant!' Polly announced to the entire household who were sitting squashed up around the table for dinner. Agnes had demanded they eat together because, in her words, they were all 'like passing ships in the night', and they needed to spend at least a part of an evening together.

'So,' Polly continued, 'not only will we soon be struggling to feed ourselves, as well as our new four-legged house guest here, but we're also going to have God knows how many baby Tramps to look after.'

Polly was enjoying her 'I told you nothing good would come of this' moment, which, of course, she didn't really mean. If anything, she was quite excited about the fact that the dog she secretly loved was going to have pups.

'So, Ma, you'll finally get to be a grandmother again – only to a load of tiny fur balls.' Polly chuckled, and her mother scowled back.

Joe stood to serve up the food and noticed Pearl threw Bel an odd look, which her daughter returned with one that said, *Don't you dare.*

'All right, hand your plates over,' he commanded, scooping up a big ladle of broad bean and mutton stew with dumplings.

'Age before beauty,' he joked, taking Arthur's plate. The old man was slowing down a bit these days and his hearing was getting worse.

'What's that lad?' he almost shouted.

'Us blokes have to stick together,' Joe said back. 'Let's just hope Tramp has some boy dogs to even out the numbers!'

Arthur let out a laugh before holding his nose over his plate and breathing in the mouthwatering smells of Agnes's cooking. There was never anything Agnes cooked which Arthur didn't devour with relish. Polly knew it was due to all the years there had just been him and Tommy fending for themselves. Both were great divers, but pretty poor cooks.

'And now beauty,' Joe said, taking hold of Lucille's plate and making sure she got a good chunk of meat.

'We'll have to find homes for the pups,' Agnes piped up, as Joe continued to dole out the supper. 'I may be soft, but I'm not *that* soft, and one dog is enough for this household – so if everyone could ask around.' She looked at Pearl. 'Perhaps some of your regulars might be willing to take a few off our hands?'

'Aye, I'll ask around tonight,' Pearl said, handing her plate to Joe and asking him, 'So, how's the lovely Maria? You two still courting?'

Bel felt her heart beat that little bit faster.

'Pearl. You're turning into a right nosy parker these days.' Joe forced his voice to remain light.

Everyone had fallen silent, though, eagerly awaiting Joe's answer.

Pearl cackled, 'Looks like I'm not the only *nosy parker* here.'

Joe looked at the expectant faces looking forward to his response.

'Yes,' he said, although he sounded more than a little uncertain. 'But we've not had much of a chance to date as such. Her work with the WAA is pretty full on.'

He looked over to Bel who had her eyes glued to her plate.

Realising they weren't going to eke any more information about Joe's love life out of him, the focus turned to Polly, who always had plenty to regale them with about the latest goings-on at Thompson's and what was happening with her workmates. They all knew about the problems they had been having with Hannah and Martha, and about Dorothy and Angie's shenanigans. And Agnes was always keen to hear about Rosie, whom she had nursed after she had been attacked by her uncle, and for whom she had a particular soft spot. And, of course, they were all counting down the days until the arrival of Gloria's baby.

'I can't believe how fast these past few months have gone,' Polly ruminated between mouthfuls of stew. 'She's due any day now, but she's still working – she says she'd rather be at work than sat watching the clock at home.'

Bel quietly asked if she had heard any more about Jack.

Polly's face fell and she shook her head. 'Still, we're trying to keep her positive. Hopeful. No news is better than bad news. That's what we keep telling her.'

'And from Vinnie?' Bel asked, her face hardening.

'It's all very odd. Not even a whisper. This is the longest he's stayed away from her' – she dropped her voice – 'and probably the longest he's managed to keep his hands to himself . . . Very strange, but who cares why. He's not bothering Gloria, and that's all that matters.'

Agnes, who was sitting next to her granddaughter, looked at Lucille, who seemed to be only interested in eating her dumplings, having relegated her meat to the side of the plate. Agnes knew Bel couldn't wait to have another baby in her arms; she just hoped it didn't also bring back her grief, knowing she would never have any more children with Teddy.

'Why don't we all go to the Tatham after dinner – for a special treat?' Polly suggested.

Her idea was greeted with a blast of agreement from everyone but Bel.

Polly saw the look on her sister-in-law's face, and misreading its meaning, quickly added, 'I'm sure Beryl will take Lucille for the night.'

Bel nodded, secretly hoping that for some reason Beryl would not be able to oblige, although thought it unlikely as she loved having Lucille over, as did her two daughters, who doted on her.

Bel forced a smile. 'Sounds great.'

After they all finished their supper, Agnes took Lucille next door, Pearl left for the start of her shift at the pub, and everyone else cleared and washed up before piling out of the door and sauntering the few hundred yards down to their local. When they stepped into the front bar, it was heaving.

'I think everyone's had the same idea as us tonight,' Polly shouted over her shoulder to Arthur and Agnes.

Bel was behind them, and behind her, at the rear, was Joe.

Bel felt his presence, especially as they were all having to squash through a merry throng of drinkers. One of the groups they were passing burst into raucous laughter, and a few of the men stepped back, causing Bel to topple backwards slightly.

As soon as she did so, she immediately felt Joe's hands on her shoulders steadying her. She felt his closeness and, just for the briefest of moments, his body pressed against hers.

Bel turned her head slightly to the side and, realising she wanted to say something, Joe bent his head towards her.

'Are you all right?' he asked.

Bel could feel his mouth brush the side of her face as lightly as a feather. Instinctively she felt herself starting to turn towards him.

'Joe,' she whispered the words over her shoulder.

'Yes?' Joe asked. Bel could feel his breath on her skin, sensed his body gently leaning into her own, and she felt her own body naturally responding.

Bel yearned to turn round, to hold herself against him; to feel herself enveloped in his arms, allowing herself to feel his touch.

'Ma knows,' she said, just loudly enough for Joe to hear.

Bel immediately felt his body stiffen.

'Knows what?' he asked, his hands still on her shoulders as they arrived at the bar.

Standing behind the counter, leaning on one of the beer pumps, was Pearl.

'You having trouble standing on your own two feet there, Isabelle?' she asked, looking at Joe's large, weathered hands still clasping her daughter's narrow shoulders.

Joe immediately released his grip. 'Aye, it's a bit busy here tonight. Where's the rest of the clan?' Joe asked.

'Over there, I'm gonna bring everyone's drinks across.' Pearl looked at Bel and Joe and said quietly. 'So then, what are you two sweethearts having?'

'Sorry?' Joe's face flashed anger.

'Just asking what you two are drinking?' Pearl repeated, all innocence, taking a sneaky sip of a very large brandy she had stashed away under the counter next to the slop tray.

'I'll have a pint of Vaux,' Joe said sternly. 'Bel, what are you having? Gin and tonic?'

Bel seemed to have lost the power of speech and merely nodded.

As they moved away from the bar and headed over to where Polly, Agnes and Arthur had managed to find a table, Joe once again leant his face close to Bel's.

'We have to talk, Bel.'

'I know,' she said, 'I know.'

Chapter Fifty-One

The next day everyone was up bright and early. Even Pearl. The sun had been streaming through the blackout curtains since six in the morning, enticing people to start their day that bit earlier.

Bel had got herself ready quickly, and given in to Lucille's demands to go and see her little friend called Amber, who had been named so, because she had been born with a layer of downy ginger hair which had quickly developed into a shock of apricot-coloured curls.

Bel was just about to leave the house to go into town to do some shopping and was searching around for her ration book. Pearl was out in the back yard chain-smoking and looking as if her mind was anywhere but in the here and now; Agnes was in the washhouse, possing clothes in the dolly tub as though her life depended on it; and Polly was doing a half-shift at the yard.

Arthur had made friends with another old man called Albert, who had embraced the whole Dig for Victory ethos with gusto, and Arthur had started to help his new mate out with his garden-turned-allotment near the Town Moor in Hendon. His friendship had the added benefit of providing the Elliot household with extra vegetables, although so far that had only been radishes, herbs and garden peas.

'Found it!' Bel said to herself, stuffing her little yellow paper booklet into her pocket just as Joe emerged from his room dressed in his smart Home Guard uniform.

When Bel saw Joe, she was hit by an unexpected feeling of self-consciousness. There was no denying Joe looked incredibly handsome, despite his walking stick and the slightly jaded look he had brought back with him from the front line.

'Do you mind if I walk into town with you?' Joe asked. His request sounded formal.

Bel looked at him and quietly agreed. 'No, I don't mind – like you said last night, I think we need to talk.'

Bel walked to the back door and shouted to Pearl and Agnes that she was 'off up the town', and that she would see them both later.

Agnes took a break from pummelling her washing to give her daughter-in-law a quick wave, while Pearl simply looked at both Bel and Joe, before forcing a smile through a fog of smoke. For a fleeting second Bel thought her mother looked the tiniest bit guilty, but she dismissed the thought as soon as it came into her head. That was one emotion she didn't think her ma had ever experienced in her entire life.

Within a few minutes of leaving the house, Joe and Bel were cutting up the back streets to the town centre.

'Ma saw us.' Bel just came straight out with it.

Joe looked puzzled.

'The night of Beryl's party. When we . . .' Bel let her voice trail off. 'She came back for her blasted fags and saw us. My bedroom door was open.'

Joe slowed his pace as he digested what Bel had told him. He had guessed as much from Pearl's 'sweethearts' comment in the pub.

'The thing is,' Bel said, turning to look at Joe, 'Ma's not the best person to keep a secret. She said she wouldn't say anything, but I know she won't be able to help herself.

She'll keep on dropping little hints or making snide little comments like she did last night, and Agnes and Polly will soon put two and two together.'

Joe looked at Bel and thought she looked as forlorn as she sounded.

As they reached Mowbray Road, Joe looked to make sure the road was clear. 'Come on, let's go and see the lions.'

Bel didn't say anything, but followed Joe's lead across the road, through the park entrance and towards the stone lions that had miraculously escaped the recent bombings. It was where they used to come as children, taking it in turns to sit on the back of the life-sized sculptures.

Joe didn't give two hoots if Pearl had seen them, or if she told his mother and sister – or the whole world. What mattered was this woman here beside him now.

'Bel.' He stopped by the wall on which the lion was lying, head up and alert, paws out, face turned gently to the late morning sun.

Joe understood how Bel felt. That the thought of people knowing she had been intimate with her husband's brother was so scandalous. That she had striven to lead a completely different life to that of her own mother – one of respectability – and that she would hate the thought of others thinking she was a loose woman. And a widow at that.

'Bel,' he said again, but this time he took her hand in his.

For a moment he thought Bel was going to let him hold her, let him take her in his arms – but he was wrong.

Bel wrenched her hand away from his, exploding into a furious rage. Her fists were clenched as she shouted at him.

'Don't! Don't touch me! I hate you, Joe! I hate you! I can't even bear to be near you!'

Her anger was spent more or less as soon as it had surfaced, though, and in its place came a well of tears which started to trickle down her face.

'It's all such a mess!' she lamented.

Joe looked at the woman he loved, whom he had always loved. Whom he knew better than anyone else in this world, apart from his brother. And he took her clenched fists in both his hands, making her look up at him.

'Well, I love you, Bel. And I don't care who knows it. I've always loved you. And always will. And there's nothing I can do about it.'

Joe saw the change in Bel's face, as if she had finally given up fighting, and he leant down and kissed her salty lips.

He let go of her hands and wrapped his arms around her and kissed her again and again. And she kissed him back. Tears still falling down her cheeks, but he could feel her love, her warmth, her passion.

They stayed there and kissed each other over and over again for what felt like an eternity beneath the guard of the lion.

'I want you, Bel,' Joe whispered in her ear. He took her head in his hands and kissed her heart-shaped face gently all over. 'Not just now, but for ever.'

Bel's eyes shone back at Joe, but there was a question in them. 'And Maria?' she asked hesitantly.

Bel had hated the thought of Joe being with Maria, and hated herself more for feeling jealous, especially as Maria was such a lovely person.

'I've ended it with her,' Joe said.

'But?' Bel was just about to question him about his comments over dinner last night – that the two of them were still seeing each other.

'A lie,' Joe said simply. 'I decided it wasn't fair to string Maria along. She's a lovely girl and will make someone an even lovelier wife, but it was never going to be me. I couldn't – not the way I feel about you. It wasn't fair on her . . . And,' Joe sighed, 'the reason I lied last night was that I just couldn't deal with all the questions if I'd admitted I wasn't seeing her any more.'

This time it was Bel who leaned up to Joe to kiss him.

As her kiss lingered, Joe's hands felt the outline of her back through her cotton dress, and he felt her body arch towards him, responding, showing him that she too felt the same.

When they parted he traced her face and looked down at her and deep into her large blue eyes – eyes he knew so well and that he had pictured many a night before sleep took him elsewhere.

Bel looked at Joe, her face a mixture of emotions. 'What are we going to do?' she asked.

There was so much they needed to talk about, and Joe knew he needed to reassure Bel. The war had taught him so many different lessons. Life lessons. Some good. Some bad. But the most important one was that their lives were precious. And if two people genuinely loved each other, then they must let that love live. And not bury it.

'Come on, let's take a walk in the park – what's left of it,' Joe said, looking at the cordoned-off bomb site, and putting his arm around Bel's shoulders and pulling her to him as they started ambling away from the lion's protection.

Chapter Fifty-Two

Pearl was standing outside the town's railway station on Athenaeum Street. She had put her one piece of luggage down by her side on the pavement just outside the main entrance. Even though she didn't have many belongings, she had enough to make her battered brown and green suitcase heavy for someone of her stature. She had managed to steal out of the house without anyone seeing her, which hadn't been difficult as there was only Agnes at home and she was clearly on a mission to get a record amount of laundry done before it was time to prepare the lunch.

The loud hissing and chuffing of a steam train champing at the bit to begin its journey was just sounding out, drowning out all other sounds, when a harried-looking young woman, swinging a small leather vanity case, rushed past Pearl and accidently knocked into her.

Pearl staggered a little but managed to steady herself. Victor's letter, however, fluttered free from her hand and a gentle gust of wind blew it into the side of the road.

'Watch it!' Pearl shouted to the back of the girl, now disappearing into the crowds that were crushing to get through the station barriers, eager to get down on to the platform to the waiting train.

As Pearl swung her head back, she caught sight of her letter and watched it flutter about before it landed in the gutter. She didn't move, but instead remained rooted to the spot, watching, slightly mesmerised by the sight of the single sheet of white paper as it flitted further along the gutter with the passing of each motor vehicle that trundled along the road.

Was this a sign? she wondered.

Did this mean she should stay here? Or should she just leave? Go. And not look back?

Her gaze remained fixed on the letter, and on the messy, spider-like scrawl that had been scratched on to the paper in blue ink.

What the hell was wrong with her? Why didn't she just get her backside in there, buy her ticket and get on the soddin' train?

Pearl dipped her hand into the deep pocket of her old blue trench coat and felt for her purse. In it she had enough money for the journey, but not much more. She had managed to siphon off a shilling here and there from those a little worse for wear when she was working at the Tatham.

Bel, forever the eagle eye, had been justified in accusing her of keeping back change from the chores she had done for Agnes, and from her trips out with Lucille, but it hadn't amounted to much. What she had secretly stashed away would pay for her train fare, but what was left would barely buy a bag of groceries and a packet of fags. She had hoped that Bel would give her some of her own money, or would have borrowed some from the family, but she should have guessed she wouldn't. That girl had a hard streak in her when she wanted.

Chip off the old block, Pearl thought, pleased that her daughter had at least learnt something from her.

Well, she would deal with being skint and the debts when she was down there. There would be some way round it. But, more than anything, Victor wanted her back, didn't he? They had been together for a few years, had made a home of sorts for themselves in their little rented room . . .

The squeal of the stationmaster's whistle made Pearl jump.

Why was she so jittery? Get a grip, woman! she chastised herself.

Even thinking about staying was sheer madness. She should be in there now, buying her ticket and sitting on the platform, waiting for the train that was going to take her back down south.

For pity's sake, she had only come up here because Victor had chucked her out, and now he wanted her back. She would be mad not to go. Wouldn't she?

'Train approaching platform one, the twelve o'clock service to Portsmouth, calling at . . .'

A stab of panic coursed through Pearl's body, making her heart beat faster. God, she needed a drink.

She clumsily got out her packet of Woodbines; her hand was trembling as she pulled out a cigarette and sparked it up, inhaling deeply, hoping it would give her some comfort or, better still, an answer.

If she was honest with herself, she had been in the doldrums since the night she had gone in to see Isabelle in her bedroom and asked her for a sub.

Her daughter's distraught face and angry words had grazed her conscience. She hated to admit it, but Isabelle had actually been right when she had said that she'd thought Pearl was actually starting to enjoy a normal family life. She had surprised herself, but it was true – she *did* like it. She had never had family meals around the table before, and she had made a few friends round the doors. Ronald was kind with his cigs and they enjoyed a good chinwag over a smoke. She had even quite enjoyed working in the Tatham; she had got to know some of the regulars quite well, and the perks of the job were good – the wages, the free booze, as well as the compliments and attention she received from the older blokes.

But it was her little granddaughter who always brought a smile to her face. At first she had thought the little girl would get on her nerves, like most children did – but she hadn't. She was such a lovely bairn – full of fun and cheek. In some ways Pearl saw a little of herself in the child.

'Train standing on platform one is the Portsmouth service. All aboard.'

Hearing the crackling voice of the tannoy speaker sounding out from inside the railway station, Pearl panicked. She tossed her cigarette to the side. She felt nauseous. Spotting Victor's letter, she automatically went to pick it up, but another slight gust of wind blew it out of the gutter, into the middle of the road and under a passing double-decker.

Would she end up like the man in the story she'd read to Lucille the other night, and throw her last chip into a life with Victor, only to lose everything if he chucked her out again, ending her days homeless and freezing to death?

As she moved forward, Pearl accidentally kicked her suitcase over and it fell on its side, causing the metal clasp to spring open. She stepped back and bent down to try and stuff some of her clothes that had escaped free back into the case.

Angrily, she tried to force it shut. Fighting back the tears.

'Don't turn on the waterworks!' she told herself. Words her mother had shouted at her, which she had then repeated to her own daughter.

She jammed the case shut several times, but the catch was broken; each time it rebelled and sprang open again.

'Come on!' Pearl argued with her luggage, but it was no good, the case flopped back open, allowing blouses and skirts to once again break free.

And it was then the dam behind Pearl's eyes burst forth, allowing tears to pour unhindered down her face.

But what if Isabelle wanted shot of her? Sometimes she thought her daughter looked at her as if she hated the very ground she walked on. She had even told her to her face that she thought she had been a terrible mother.

So, why not just go? Get on the damned train!

Pearl knelt on the ground next to her suitcase and put her hands to her face and cried.

And then she cried some more.

As she did so, a picture of her granddaughter's giggling little face filled her vision, and Pearl felt an unusual pull in her heart. It was a feeling she seldom had, and rarely allowed herself to feel.

After a few moments Pearl stood up and turned round.

Leaving her broken suitcase on the ground, she marched purposefully into the station.

Chapter Fifty-Three

For the next hour, Joe and Bel walked and talked. After a while they sat down on one of the park benches, felt the sun on their faces and kissed again, their fingers intertwining, Joe touching every inch of Bel's bare arm and feeling goose bumps appear. He ached for the moment when he could touch every part of her body, every inch of her skin, when they could lie together and cement their love; but he knew he would have to wait. He had waited this long. He could be patient.

Bel told Joe what her mother had said; how she had been so hurt to hear that all Pearl seemed to be after was money.

Joe recalled how Pearl had asked him at the party if he had received any compensation for his injuries, and everything started to fall into place – the real reason that Pearl had turned up was now evident.

'I hate to say it, but that woman's a bloody parasite,' Joe mused.

He felt sorry for Bel, that she had never experienced what every child should have a right to – the unconditional love of a mother. But, despite this, Bel herself had been a wonderful mum – so full of love and care. He had felt so much respect for her and how Bel had made sure she had not repeated the same mistakes with Lucille – in fact she had done quite the reverse. Lucille could not want for a better mum.

'You know, the sad thing is,' Bel said, tears filling her eyes, 'I actually started to hope Ma had changed. I mean,

I knew she wasn't going to suddenly transform into some kind of fairy godmother, but I really thought that she was starting to enjoy a normal family life with us all.'

Bel was quiet for a moment, feeling the sadness for a future that would never be. 'But she's the same old manipulative ma, only she's just managed to learn to hide it better.'

Joe sighed. Over the years, Bel had often expressed the hope that her mother would change and would eventually give her the care and nurture she had craved all her life. It was as though she refused to give up on the woman who had given birth to her, no matter what she'd done, or how cruel she'd been – and continued to be.

When Bel told him what Pearl had prophesied in regard to Agnes's and Polly's reaction to their love, he forced himself to swallow his anger.

'But, the worst thing is, she's right.' The worried expression had returned to Bel's face. 'They'll be so disappointed in me. I feel so ashamed.'

Joe put his finger on her lips and then kissed her. 'There is nothing shameful about what we feel for each other. Nothing. I never want to hear you say that again.

'I know how you must feel, and what must have been going on in your head these past few weeks, but you have to stop fretting. Teddy *wanted* me to look after you. He made me *promise* just before I was evacuated back to England,' Joe said. 'Teddy *wanted* you to be happy. For Lucille to be happy.'

Since he had come back, Joe had had plenty of time to think, plenty of restless nights lying awake, and he would often wonder if Teddy had somehow known of his love for Bel, and that in his own way his brother had been giving him permission to be with his wife by making him promise to take care of her should he die on the battlefield – and then, when Joe had been told about Teddy's last letter to Bel, a shiver had gone down his spine.

His brother's last wish to the two people he loved so dearly had been that they look after one another.

Bel looked at the intensity in Joe's open face and knew he believed what he said: Teddy had wanted her to be happy above all else – and that Joe himself had no guilt about his feelings towards her whatsoever.

Bel sighed and looked up to the light blue sky, decorated with what looked like a smattering of misshapen cotton-wool balls. She wondered if there really was a heaven – if there was some kind of life after death. If only Teddy would show her it was all right. She had loved him with every fibre of her being; couldn't bear to imagine that he would think any less of the love they had because of the feelings she now had for Joe.

Her thoughts about Teddy, however, were interrupted by the sound of a distant rumbling breaking through the peace and tranquillity of the skies above.

'Did you hear that?' Joe asked.

Bel nodded. The beginnings of panic rose up from the pit of her stomach. It didn't matter how often she heard the familiar, distant drone of an enemy aircraft, it never failed to instil in her the fear of God.

A few seconds later there followed the belated wail of the air-raid siren as it sounded out across the town.

After a peaceful three months, the town had been lured into a false sense of security.

Now the Luftwaffe had caught the home defences unawares. The town was once again under attack.

Joe and Bel looked at each other. 'Lucille!' they said in unison.

As they rushed back to Tatham Street, Bel looked up to the sky, still blazing with sunlight, but now threatening darkness, death, and destruction.

Chapter Fifty-Four

As the first bombs dropped on the north side of the river, Joe and Bel flew back through the front door of Tatham Street just in time to see Agnes charging down the hallway with two gas masks and Lucille in her arms. The poor woman looked as though she was going to collapse with sheer fright.

'Thank God you're here!'

Just then Arthur turned up outside the house, clutching a bunch of radishes.

'Come on! We've—' His voice was blotted out by the loud, punctuated sound of the ack-ack guns, frantically spilling out their bullets across the sky.

'Arthur, yer gas mask.'

'Sod the bloody mask, let's go!' Arthur turned, as Bel grabbed an ashen-faced Lucille from her mother-in-law's arms, which were still covered in soapy suds.

'Come on, Ma!' Joe ushered Agnes out through the front door and slammed it shut behind her.

As they all hurried down the road, they joined other families as they rushed towards the air-raid shelter in the basement of Tavistock House.

Bel turned to Agnes, 'Do you know where my ma is?'

'She told me she was going into town, not long after you and Joe left,' Agnes told her, seeing the look of worry on Bel's face.

'She'll be all right,' she tried to reassure her. 'She's as tough as old boots!' Agnes tried unsuccessfully to inject

418

some humour into her voice. She might dislike the woman intensely, but she hoped to God that she was safe. Heaven knew where she was, though; she had been acting strangely all morning – had seemed very subdued and not at all her usual loud, gobby self.

Bel looked round to see Joe, who had dropped behind ever so slightly and was clearly in a lot of pain. He had practically galloped back home, pushing himself forward with his stick, propelling himself the quarter of a mile or so back to their front door. She had seen the agony in his face – and the relief when they'd seen Lucille in Agnes's arms. He had never had to say the words to her but, ever since his return, she had known he would lay down his life for his brother's daughter. And, after today, she realised for her too.

Just as they neared the opening of the air-raid shelter in the basement of the grand Georgian red-brick mansion, they heard a huge explosion. Bel let out a scream. Her whole body was shaking. Joe came up behind her and grabbed Lucille from her.

'Get in. I'll pass Lucille in to you,' he ordered.

Bel climbed down the stone stairs and then turned round quickly to reach up for Lucille. Joe handed the little girl down, who had her thumb jammed into her mouth and her eyes squeezed shut. Her little legs dangled for a moment in the air, like a parachutist ready to land, as Joe carefully passed her to Bel.

Joe limped backwards and barked at his mother and Arthur to get in. They knew there was no arguing with him, and they both took it in turns to take his hand as he helped them climb, one after the other, down the first few steep steps into the darkness of their underground sanctuary.

'What about Pearl?' he asked Bel, whose face had appeared again, looking up at him through the darkness.

'Get in, Joe, she'll be fine. There's nothing you can do to help her. We don't even know where she is.'

As if on cue there was another explosion, quickly followed by another. The earth shuddered.

'Get in!' Bel shouted.

Joe climbed down the stairs and into the semi-darkness of the large stone basement. It looked as if at one time it had been some kind of wine cellar, as there were wooden shelves and wine racks but no actual bottles.

'Bloody Jerry!' An old woman's voice sounded out in the darkness, before it was illuminated by the strike of a match and the gentle glow of a gas lamp. Her deeply lined face crinkled as she spotted Lucille.

'Ah, what a bonny bairn,' she said. 'No need to be frightened, flower. We're all safe now.'

Lucille looked at the woman, who had a woollen black shawl wrapped around her shoulders and was wearing a loose blouse and a long black skirt, around which was wrapped a white apron. Bel knew it was the unofficial uniform of a fishwife, and that the woman's barrow of fish, crabs and kippers would be languishing somewhere not far from the shelter's entrance. She also knew the old woman's apron pocket would jingle with coppers were she to stand up, and that her pound notes would be safely tucked away in her garter.

Lucille seemed fascinated by the woman, who bent down and started delving around in the depths of her large carpet bag, which she had dumped next to her on the hard concrete floor. As she pulled out a huge ball of purple wool and two long knitting needles, she eyed Lucille and asked, 'Do you know how to knit, petal?'

Lucille shyly shook her head.

'Well, then shall an old fishwife show you?'

Lucille nodded her head. The old woman looked to Bel, who gave her permission by way of a tense smile.

There were only a few other people in the shelter – an older couple sat close together, holding hands, quietly chatting, and a mum and her young son, who looked around ten years old. The boy was shuffling a pack of cigarette cards, occasionally taking one out and holding it up to his mum, who was being very convincing in her show of interest.

'Where's Beryl?' Bel asked Agnes, as they all sat down on an old bench that had been pushed up against the wall. Arthur and Agnes leant back against the cold brickwork.

'In town with the girls,' Agnes said, adding in the next breath, 'Please God let Polly be all right.'

It was what they had all been thinking, but hadn't wanted to say it for the sake of causing Agnes any more worry. Bel sat down next to her and took her hand, holding it tight.

'They've got shelters in the yard. She would have been able to go straight there. She'll probably be sat with the rest of the women now, worrying about all of us.'

'It's just,' Agnes said, her voice wavering, 'the explosions sounded like they were on the north side.'

Joe was standing still, near to the entrance, in case anyone else should need to get in. He had been thinking the same thing.

'I hate that yard!' Agnes suddenly blurted out. 'Never wanted her to work there in the first place. They're like sitting ducks there, waiting for that madman to drop a bomb on them all.'

Arthur was sitting quietly next to Agnes. He wanted to try and reassure her, but didn't know what to say. If it were his daughter, he would be feeling exactly the same. Would have tried to stop her working there, just like Agnes had done. But Polly was her own woman. When she made her mind up about something, there was no stopping her. And, apart from this, if she hadn't started working there, his grandson would never have fallen in love and found his future wife.

Agnes's attention was caught by the click-clack of the fishwife's knitting and she looked over to a clearly captivated Lucille.

She then glanced across to Joe, who she noticed also looked entranced – but it had nothing to do with knitting.

As she followed his slightly misty-eyed stare, she saw that it was Bel who was the focus of his rapt attention.

She had seen the look before on Joe's face – many times. Over many years. She had always felt a little sad for Joe. She was his mother, and had been able to read every nuance of his facial expressions since he'd been a baby.

Like most mothers, she knew how to read her children, their body language, the tones of their voices – and the way they looked at others.

She had seen this look on Joe's face a few times since his return, although she knew he had been careful not to let his feelings for Bel show through, even though she also knew that couldn't have been easy – not when they all lived together and were such a close family.

But when Agnes turned her head to look at Bel, who was sitting next to her, she got a jolt of surprise – for Bel was returning her son's loving gaze. There was no denying the unspoken dialogue that was occurring between the two.

Agnes was shocked. *How come she hadn't seen it before?*

Bel was like one of her own, but she had always been harder to read. Bel had become part of the Elliot family from a young age, but she still wasn't Agnes's own blood; and although she knew her daughter-in-law well, Bel was still adept at shielding her true feelings. She had learnt to do that from a very young age – she'd been forced to with a mother like Pearl.

Joe caught his mother looking at Bel – and her startled look – and he knew in an instant that she had seen what had passed between himself and his brother's widow.

He took a deep breath and hobbled over to sit next to Bel. He took her hand and could feel her body tense. Then he looked at his mother.

'Ma, we've got something to tell you,' he said.

'No, Joe. This isn't the right time.' Bel's voice sounded quiet and nervous.

'Bel, there is never going to be a right time. And there's nothing to be ashamed of,' Joe said, looking at his mum and at Arthur, who was now watching and listening intently to what was being said. He had caught Joe taking Bel's hand in the dim light.

Agnes sat up straight and put both her hands in her lap.

'I love Bel,' Joe said, looking at his sister-in-law. 'And,' he added, 'I think Bel also loves me.'

Bel could feel herself going crimson red. She felt mortified. All her feelings of shame came rushing to the fore.

'I'm so sorry, Agnes,' she stuttered. She tried to pull her hand away from Joe's, but he held it tightly.

'I didn't mean this to happen,' she stuttered, not knowing what to say, but needing to say something. The thought of losing Agnes's love was unbearable.

'I loved Teddy so much,' she said, tears starting to well behind her eyes. Now guilt was overtaking the shame and making her feel wretched.

Arthur felt his own eyes prick. He had always thought that Bel and Joe made a lovely couple; knew without doubt that Lucille would be as pleased as punch should Joe become her stepfather, but of course he had never said anything. It was not his place.

Joe looked at Agnes for a response and her face changed and softened; she turned and took her daughter-in-law's face in her hands and said, 'I know you did, Bel. You loved my son with all your heart. I know that.'

Agnes's softly spoken words unleashed Bel's tears, which started cascading silently down her face.

'But he's gone now,' Agnes continued. The deeply felt sorrow could be heard in her voice. 'And all of our lives must go on.' Agnes wiped Bel's tears away from her face, just like she used to as a child.

'If there is a love there between you and Joe, you can't fight it. Our lives are too short and too unpredictable.'

Bel looked into her mother-in-law's eyes and knew her words were spoken from her heart.

Before she had the chance to say anything else, the all-clear siren sounded out, and Joe got up and hurried over to open up the large wooden doors to the entrance of the basement.

Lucille went bounding back to her mum, as everyone stood up, eager to leave the darkness and get back into the light.

Joe helped the old fishwife up the stairs, as well as the old couple, and then the mum and her son.

Agnes gathered her skirts up and took Lucille's hand; Arthur followed behind as they climbed the steps one by one.

As they waited for Arthur to make it to the top, Joe turned to Bel and took her quickly in his arms and kissed her. Bel kissed him back.

'I *do* love you, Joe,' she whispered in his ear.

Joe looked at Bel and felt his whole body fill with the most wondrous feeling. An incredible lightness of being.

As they both emerged out of the darkened chamber of the basement, they were temporarily blinded by the midday sunlight. Bel brushed some dust and dirt off her clothes as Joe stood and looked about him. He saw the old couple, and the mother and son, but the old fishwife was nowhere to be seen. It was as if she had just vanished into thin air, even though her wooden barrow with all her wares was still there, positioned just a few feet away from the entrance to the air-raid shelter.

'Mummy and Doey!' Lucille exclaimed aloud, positioning herself between Joe and Bel and taking hold of their hands and pulling them forward.

Bel smiled across at Joe at Lucille's undisguised joy at finally succeeding in getting what she wanted. Her beloved Doey was going to be her father. And it couldn't happen soon enough. She was beaming from ear to ear like the cat that had got the cream.

As the happy trio started to walk away, something caught the corner of Bel's eye. She automatically jerked her head to the side just as a little robin redbreast fluttered down on to the wooden handle of the fishwife's wheelbarrow. Bel stared as its little head twitched round, its black eyes blinking.

No one noticed Bel's sudden sharp intake of breath. Nor the little bird itself.

Robins had always been Teddy's favourite birds – had been for as long as Bel could remember. Whenever they were out and he spotted one, he would always point it out to Bel and tell her it was lucky and that she had to make a wish.

Bel fought back the tears as the little bird suddenly flapped its tiny wings and flew away.

This time she didn't need to make a wish, for it had already been granted.

She had been given the sign she had so desperately wanted.

Chapter Fifty-Five

Since hearing the news about Jack's ship going down, Gloria had barely slept a wink. Rosie was checking on her at least twice a day at work, and was passing on any scrap of news she heard from the powers that be. Rosie had told her that there had been fatalities, but that there had also been some survivors. Gloria had never been one to go to church, but over the past week she had been bombarding the Good Lord with a constant stream of pleas and prayers.

Gloria knew the women were concerned about her. She had tried to reassure them that she was fine and that she was just glad she was working as it helped to take her mind off her worries. But, more than anything, she knew she had to keep it together for the sake of the baby. She had started to suffer from heart palpitations and was glad she was now close to her due date.

Today was going to be her last day at work, before she finally put her feet up and waited for her and Jack's baby to enter the world. Her doctor had suggested she go into the town's Royal Hospital to give birth, especially because of her age, but Gloria had decided to have the baby at home – like she had done with her two boys. If she changed her mind, she was only a short bus journey away from the maternity ward.

When the midday klaxon sounded out, Gloria joined the rest of the women welders, and settled down with them at their spot in the partial shade by the quayside. Having unwrapped her jam sandwiches, she was using her huge, firm bump as a make-do-and-mend table.

Hannah had, as usual, also joined them. She was now two weeks into her training to become a draughtsman, or rather draughtswoman, and had taken to it like a duck to water.

Today the women were all unusually quiet – even Dorothy and Angie – and instead of chatting were simply enjoying the relative quietness, which, like clockwork, descended on the yard for exactly an hour from midday until one. The seven women were sitting in a semi-circle, looking as though they were in the stalls at the Palladium, but instead of watching a film on the big screen, they were enjoying the real-life drama of the River Wear.

The magic of the midday sun had created the illusion that the river's surface had been sprinkled with diamonds, which were now dancing on the tips of the wash, and an eclectic mix of colliers, trawlers and paddle steamers were either doing what they had been built to do, or else resting and gently bobbing about on the grey-blue waters.

The women's faces were all lifted up to the skies, enjoying both the feel of the heat of the summer sun and the cooling sea breeze. As they did so, the coast's long-billed birds dive-bombed the river, resurfacing seconds after their disappearance with what looked like a sliver of silver in their beaks.

The peace of the women's joint reverie did not last long, however.

Just a few minutes into their communal meditation, they all froze as they heard the distant murmur of what they had learnt over the past year was the approach of the Luftwaffe's deadly bombers.

For a moment the women remained stock-still – not quite believing what they were hearing.

'Oh my God! I don't believe it! Look!' Dorothy broke the silence.

As the deep mechanical murmuring became louder and louder, a huge metal Heinkel bomber appeared in the distance, bulldozing its way through the air and over the barbed-wired beaches of Roker and Seaburn. All other sounds were obliterated by the dull, relentless thumping acoustics of this airborne metal beast which was stomping its way across the skies.

The vision from above was curiously captivating, and the women welders couldn't stop themselves staring as the lone bomber released a huge bullet-shaped bomb from its underbelly.

Then another.

And another.

The muffled, thunderous explosions caused the ground to vibrate.

Seconds later a massive cloud of smoke filled the air just half a mile or so from where they stood.

'Come on, let's get to the shelter – and quick!' Rosie shouted out. The growing sound of confusion and dismay in the voices of their fellow workers started to buffet the air and could be heard alongside the thudding of hobnailed boots stamping across to the yard's shelter.

'Oh my God, I don't believe it!' Dorothy exclaimed again.

'Dor, you've already said that once!' Angie said, her voice warbling a little with nerves as she grabbed her bag and gas mask.

'No! Look!' She pointed at Gloria.

Gloria was standing, her sandwich still in her hand, a look of complete and utter shock on her face. The women's eyes all travelled down to her waist and then to the trousers of her overalls.

There was a huge wet mark.

428

It meant only one thing.

'My waters broke,' Gloria said in a shocked, quiet voice.

'Bloody hell, Glor, you don't half pick your timing!' Dorothy laughed more than a little hysterically, just as the ack-ack guns started drilling the air.

Rosie, Polly, Hannah and Martha all looked at each other with slightly desperate faces. None of them had a clue about being in labour – never mind the actual 'giving birth' part.

Never mind delivering a baby during an air raid.

'Ange, your mum's practically given birth to a whole football team,' Dorothy shouted above the chaos, 'you must have some idea what to do,' she added hopefully as she hurried over to hold Gloria up; she had gone as white as a ghost and looked as though she was about to sink into the ground.

'Yeh, but I wasn't there when she had them all, was I?' Angie shouted back, rushing over to Gloria and grabbing her other arm.

All of a sudden Gloria let out the most blood-curdling cry, which momentarily erased all other sounds.

'The baby's coming. I can feel it!' Gloria gasped. Her knees buckled and she started to go down but was buoyed up again by Angie and Dorothy.

'We need to get to the shelter!' Rosie shouted above the din of the panicked workforce, all now running for cover against the backdrop of the air-raid siren's piercing wail.

'No time!' Gloria bellowed. 'This baby's coming now whether we like it or not,' and with that she let out another deep groan that seemed to come from the very depths of her being.

Dorothy looked frantically around, her head swinging from left to right, scouring the area.

'Let's get her to the painter's shed,' Angie said, pointing over to the far side of the yard.

'Good idea,' Rosie agreed. 'At least there's some shelter there.'

The painter's shed was a huge wooden shack with a flat metal roof. Its two large doors were always kept wide open to allow the fumes to escape. Although it was unlikely to withstand a direct hit from the Luftwaffe, it would probably offer the women some protection from flying debris should a bomb explode in the yard.

'I'll take her!' Martha's voice boomed out as she stomped over, practically batting Dorothy and Angie out of the way as she grabbed her groaning workmate's arm, slung it around her neck and started hauling her the two hundred yards or so towards what was to be their makeshift delivery suite.

Rosie led the way, with Hannah fluttering alongside Martha as she dragged Gloria forward, scouring the ground, making sure the way was clear.

'Watch those leads . . . and those rivet guns,' Hannah shouted out, just in time for Gloria to look down and lift her feet over tools and machinery which had been dropped at the first sight of the enemy aircraft.

Dorothy and Angie had run ahead to the shed that was now empty, vacated by the yard's labourers and painters at the blast of the lunchtime hooter; if there had been any stragglers they would have done a runner at the sound of the impending air attack.

They both started frantically looking about at the array of abandoned pots of paints, brushes and buckets.

'Let's clear that bench over there,' Dorothy yelled, voice shaking, as she nodded over to an oblong-shaped wooden table.

Martha, now sweating profusely with the effort of practically carrying Gloria, came to a standstill at the shed's entrance.

The women all started clearing the area, while Hannah started wiping the surface of the table down with a piece of rag, trying her hardest to make it as clear and clean of dirt and debris as possible.

Guided by Martha, Gloria, now panting and emitting the odd swear word, waddled across to the wooden bench.

'Boiling water?!' Dorothy demanded.

'I'll get it . . .' Rosie ran off to where the tea boy had set up his little stove that was always in constant use, heating up water for the workers' brews.

'I'll get some clean covers.' Polly ran off in the opposite direction to the storeroom, where all the cotton rags, dust-sheets and work gear were kept.

As Gloria reached the table, she let out another gasp of pain as she was hit by another contraction. As she did so, Dorothy looked down to see Gloria was still clutching on to her jam sandwich.

'For God's sake, Glor, let go of the sandwich,' she commanded, 'I'll buy you the biggest cake I can find after this is all over . . .'

Gloria let out a cry of laughter mixed with pain as her body was hit by yet another contraction.

Dorothy cast a worried look over to Angie, 'Bloody hell, she's close.'

Just then Polly came tearing back across the yard, shouting above the ear-splitting sound of the siren, 'I've got linen – and scissors!'

As she reached the women she shook out a large dust-sheet. Hannah caught the end of it and the two women spread it out across the paint-speckled worktop as if they were two nurses making up a patient's bed.

'Martha,' Angie shouted, 'can you haul her up?'

With surprising ease, like a mother would carry a sleeping child, Martha put her thick muscular arms underneath

Gloria's legs and around the top part of her back, lifted her up and, ever so slowly and gently, placed her workmate's barrel-like body carefully on to the bench. She made it look as if she was lifting a box of feathers, not a thirteen stone pregnant woman.

Just then Rosie came back with a big metal pan; boiling hot water was slopping over the top with each hurried step.

'Sorry about this, Gloria,' Dorothy said, before turning to Polly and demanding, 'Scissors?'

Polly handed them, over and Dorothy carefully cut off her workmate's overalls.

'*Pane bože!*' Hannah said, reverting back to her mother tongue and looking as though she was going to faint there and then.

Even Rosie blanched, and Polly looked as if she was going to chuck up the little bit of lunch she had managed to eat.

The baby's head was just starting to show.

The women all stood gawping.

'For heaven's sake!' Dorothy said as she nudged her way in front of them and positioned herself at the end of the bench.

'Okay, Gloria, time to get this wee one out . . . Now *push!*'

Rosie and Angie stood on either side of Dorothy, while Hannah, Martha and Polly went to Gloria's side; as they did so Gloria, now panting heavily and creasing up with another contraction, grabbed hold of Hannah's skinny arm with one hand and Martha's very muscular arm with the other. Polly meanwhile had quickly freed her hair from her scarf and was using the square of cotton fabric to wipe sweat from Gloria's contorted face, all the while helping her to hold her head up as she strained forward.

'Your baby's coming, Glor!' Dorothy shouted.

'Noooo!' Gloria let out the longest moan, blotting out all other sounds.

As she half sat up through the sheer agony of another contraction, Gloria caught sight of the clear blue sky outside the shed. Thankfully, they hadn't heard the baneful drone of any more bombers overhead. Gloria felt her mind spinning, begging there to be no more planes, no more explosions – at least not until she pushed this baby out and got somewhere safe.

All of a sudden the image of the baby that had been found in the rubble all those months ago flashed through her mind, as did the image of Vinnie standing over her, snarling into her face.

Another agonising, searing contraction gripped her body. She felt as if she was going to pass out.

'Gloria, stay with us,' Polly commanded as she supported her workmate's head on her chest.

Gloria looked up to see Polly was also dripping sweat, and she felt straggles of her friend's long chestnut hair on her own face.

Then she felt her eyes closing. They felt so heavy. And she felt so very tired.

And it was then she saw Jack. Or at least an image of his face looking at her. Smiling.

He started to disappear from her inner vision and she forced her eyes open, desperate to see him again.

'Now, Glor!' It was Dorothy's voice. Uncannily serious. 'Do it!' she practically screamed.

The baby's head was out – its eyes clamped shut with goo.

'Push, Gloria!' Polly shouted.

'Damn it! Push!' It was Rosie's voice. Gloria had never heard her boss sound so afraid.

At that moment she felt her strength drain out of her, and she knew she had to do it. Now.

Using every last drop of energy, pulled from every part of her being, Gloria pushed.

She heard a strangled sound come out of her own mouth.

'Come on, Glor! You're nearly there.' Dorothy lifted her head up to shout out her encouragement as her hands gently eased the baby out.

'Oh my goodness!' Rosie burst into tears as she watched Dorothy gently but firmly ease the baby out. Its little feet were squashed together and its tiny blotchy pink body was curled up as if still asleep.

As Dorothy carefully lifted the baby up, her face was a picture of sheer amazement.

'Well done, Glor . . . You did it.' Dorothy voice was just a whisper, as if in reverence of the tiny being now lying in her arms. For the first time their surroundings were still and peaceful, momentarily devoid of any sound.

Standing up straight, with tears streaming down her face, Dorothy handed Gloria her baby.

'Congratulations,' she said, her voice now croaky with emotion, 'you've got a perfect little baby girl.'

Gloria's eyes glistened with tears as she took her daughter into her arms and looked at the little miracle before her.

Just then the all-clear siren started up, and Gloria's tiny baby opened her eyes and joined in with her own piercing, life-affirming wail.

The women all burst out laughing.

Hannah was sobbing her eyes out, and had her arms wrapped round Martha's thick waist. Martha's own tears were trickling down her face and landing on top of her workmate's thick thatch of black hair.

Gloria looked up at Martha and smiled. 'You were right.'

Martha grinned, as more tears dripped down her top lip and on to her chin. 'Yes,' she said, 'a girl.'

The women all looked puzzled.

'Martha told me ages ago that I was going to have a girl . . . She even knew I was pregnant before I told anyone.'

Dorothy's eyes rolled heavenward. 'Bloody Gypsy Rose Lee Martha here!'

Everyone laughed, their joy and sheer relief undisguised.

'All right everyone. We're not done yet. Who's going to cut the cord?' Dorothy swung her head around and, without waiting for a reply, took the scissors and handed them to Angie.

'Was it not enough that I learnt to weld?' she said, taking the steel cutters with trembling hands.

The women all waited with bated breath.

'Like a true professional,' Rosie said, as she watched in awe as the youngest of her squad carefully snipped the cord. 'You and Dorothy should do a sideline in midwifery.'

The women clucked their agreement as they all crowded around Gloria, who didn't seem able to tear her eyes away from her babe-in-arms.

They all stood, captivated by the sight of this wonder that they had all helped bring into the world. A world of unpredictability. A world at war.

The physical landscape where this little girl had entered the world might have been an urban field of steel and concrete, metal and machinery, but it also lay within a stone's throw of the most awe-inspiring natural scenery – a vast, seemingly endless stretch of sea that no amount of bombs could ever destroy. A place of contrast, where industry ran parallel with nature, and the swell of the river flowing out into the expanse of the North Sea somehow gave hope of the real possibility of eternity.

'I know this sounds insane, but I think I've fallen in love,' Dorothy said, touching the cheek of the little being now lying snuggled up in Gloria's arms.

There was a murmur of agreement, and more sniffles from the women.

'This is going to be the most loved baby ever!' Hannah declared.

'She's a part of our team now, whether she likes it or not,' Rosie said.

Gloria managed to drag her eyes away from her baby girl and looked up at her family of friends, who had not only probably saved her life and that of her baby, but had done so much to help her over the past few months.

She had her suspicions that one of them might have had something to do with the fact that she had not seen hide nor hair of Vinnie since he had last attacked her.

And Dorothy – the woman she had positively disliked when she had first started at the yard a year ago – had not only saved her bacon by getting Angie to swap jobs with her, but had delivered her baby as if she had done it at least a dozen times before.

'Here, give your god-daughter a little cuddle,' she said to Dorothy, as she carefully lifted her baby up towards her workmate.

For once Dorothy was speechless. As black rivulets of mascara streaked down her face, Gloria chuckled, 'That'll teach you to wear make-up at work,' her own eyes tipping happy, salty tears down her face.

Hannah grabbed Gloria's shredded overalls and quickly swaddled Dorothy's new little god-daughter in them, before placing the tiny denim-clad baby into her arms.

'Oh my goodness,' Dorothy said, her voice quavering, looking down at the little, crinkled baby now cradled in her arms. 'Do you really want me to be her godmother?'

Gloria nodded, unable to speak as the tears she was trying to stop were making her choke up.

'I'm not exactly the most saintly person you could have chosen,' Dorothy said, speaking to Gloria, but not taking her eyes off the gorgeous little baby girl snuggled up in her arms.

'That's for sure,' Gloria laughed, 'but I think you can teach her a lot – as long as you don't pass on your taste in men to her, I think you'll be perfect.'

Dorothy managed to drag her mesmerised stare off her god-daughter, and look at her friends standing around Gloria.

'Well, little one,' she said, 'time for you to meet all your aunties.' And with that she passed her god-daughter to Hannah, who murmured something to the baby in her native language, before passing the child to Martha, whose slightly protruding eyes seemed to pool with awe at the godsend in her arms.

'Beauty,' she said simply.

When Rosie took the baby, she was struck by the most incredible feeling of love. A child was something she knew she would probably never have herself, but she would be the best aunty she could, and love and protect her.

Rosie then handed Polly the baby, who cooed and told the little girl that she would soon be meeting her aunty Bel and the rest of her extended family.

Angie then gave the baby a little cuddle, and declared, 'Eee, I don't think I've ever seen anything so totally adorable ever before.' When she handed the baby back, Gloria looked at her and said, 'Thank you for doing what you did for me, Angie. For swapping jobs. I know this one,' she said, swinging her attention over to Dorothy, 'more than twisted your arm.

'And,' she added, looking around at all the women, 'before I get too sentimental – I just want to say thank you to you all. I don't know what I would have done without you.'

She started to cry, and through the tears she told them: 'I'm only going to say this the once . . . But . . . *I love you all* . . . I do.'

All the women stood, overwhelmed and smiling. All with tears pouring shamelessly down their dirt-smeared faces.

As Gloria looked at her baby through a blur of tears, Jack's smiling face came back into her mind's eye. She had been in a state of constant indecision since she had found out she was pregnant, but now she knew with certainty what she was going to do.

If, God willing, Jack wasn't now lying in a watery grave at the bottom of the Atlantic, alongside the sunken ship he had been travelling back home on, she would tell him the baby was his; that they had both created the most beautiful, perfect little girl – and that their daughter was a love child in the true sense of the word.

Gloria had no idea what would happen after that moment, but she knew in her heart that this was the right – the only – way forward. Jack had a right to know he had a child, and this little cherub now gurgling happily in her arms had a right to know who her real father was.

Who knew what would happen after that? Gloria had no idea. That, she resolved, was a worry for another day.

For now it was enough for her to know that her daughter would begin her life without any kind of lies or deceit. And Gloria would just have to deal the best way she could with the consequences of her decision to live an honest life.

'All right,' Rosie said, wiping the tears away from her face and once again taking charge of her little gang, 'let's get mother and daughter cleaned up and back home for some rest. I'm sure you must feel exhausted, Gloria?'

Gloria nodded, then immediately changed her mind. The thought of going back to her home felt unappealing. It held so many unpleasant memories for her; she didn't feel it was right that the place which had witnessed so much unhappiness over the years, so much violence, should be the first roof her little girl found herself under.

'You know,' Gloria said thoughtfully, 'my mother always told me how the first home a child should be taken into is a house of God.'

'A house of God?' Angie perked up, sounding perplexed.

'A church, you daftie!' Dorothy said.

'I've an idea!' Polly said. She was tying her hair back up into her headscarf, but still hadn't taken her eyes off the little baby, and had been thinking how excited Bel and Agnes would be to meet their new charge.

'There's a church near to us, St Ignatius. Providing it's not been bombed, we could go there and then back to mine?'

'That sounds perfect,' Gloria said.

Chapter Fifty-Six

As the women welders were making their way to the ferry landing, happily bobbing around Gloria, excitedly fussing over her baby girl, DS Miller was hurrying down the embankment to Thompson's.

His eyes were frantically inspecting the area for any bomb damage and searching all the faces coming in and out of the yard's main entrance.

When he spotted the women he stopped abruptly. And when he made out the side profile of Rosie, his whole body sagged with sheer relief.

'Thank God,' he muttered. Rosie was alive and unharmed after the town's unexpected midday air raid. That was all he needed to know.

As he watched the women from a distance, he automatically took off his trilby hat. Gloria had had her baby. And, judging by the almost ethereal aura coming from the little group of women, all was well with both mother and child.

DS Miller felt that there was a part of him that knew Gloria, as if he shared a peculiar kind of closeness to her, even though they had never met.

As he watched the women board the ferry, he saw Rosie take the tiny baby from Gloria's tired arms and cradle it in her own, carrying it carefully on to the steamer for the new-born's first trip across the Wear; a maiden journey celebrated by a fanfare of squawking seagulls circling excitedly overhead.

The rest of the women helped an exhausted-looking Gloria, who was wearing a brand new pair of overalls pilfered by Angie from the yard's storeroom, on to the boat that was now churning water ready to head back over to the south dock.

There was something about the vision of Rosie, though, as she rocked the baby gently in her arms, that deeply affected him. He didn't know if it made him feel incredibly sad, or incredibly happy.

What he did know was that he wasn't going to give up on this woman. There was something special about her, and he was not prepared to simply walk away.

What they clearly felt for one another was just too precious. He knew he couldn't let that go, or relinquish all hope of them being together.

For whatever reason, Rosie had given up on him, and he wondered if she had also given up on love. But whether or not that was true, he wasn't about to follow suit. It might take time, but he was a patient man. He could wait. There was no other woman for him.

'I don't want you to slip through my fingers – nor am I going to let you,' DS Miller said aloud.

Rosie had caused him no end of sleepless nights – from first meeting her after her uncle had been pulled from this very river, she had both intrigued him and mystified him. He felt instinctively that she cared for him, and was also attracted to him. There was most certainly a chemistry there, whether she would admit it to herself or not.

His guess was that there was something stopping her from allowing herself to be with him – and preventing her from experiencing love. But exactly what that was, he just didn't know– not yet, anyway. But he would find out. No matter how long it took him. He was determined.

He was a detective, after all.

As the ferry dragged itself across the breadth of the river, DS Miller watched as the woman he had fallen in love with disappeared from view and all he could see was a thick trail of white foaming surf.

As Polly stood leaning against the side of the ferry's iron railings, she looked at Rosie cooing down at the baby she was gentling swaying in her arms, and at the rest of her workmates, who all looked exhausted but also incredibly happy, and she realised just how much these women meant to her.

If it hadn't been for their support after Teddy had died, and their quiet understanding and words of comfort, she would have struggled to keep her head above water. Gloria might feel as if they had saved her, just as Rosie felt her women welders had rescued her from the murderous hands of her uncle, but they had all saved each other, just in different ways. Martha had come out of her shell and was no longer cut off in her own private world. Hannah had made a new home for herself and was now doing a job she liked and was good at, and which had finally given her a sense that she was being of some use to the war effort. And Dorothy had got what she had always craved – a strange kind of surrogate family; it was something she felt was also the case for Angie.

They were all true friends, who could rely on each other, and help each other out – and would always be there for each other in times of need.

As the ferry gently bobbed on the water, now a little choppy as there was a slight wind coming across from the North Sea, Polly watched Stan the boatswain go and take a peek at the baby. He made a funny face, and she could see the tiniest of hands reach up to touch his weather-beaten face.

She recalled her thoughts earlier on in the year, not long after they'd received notification of Teddy's death, and how down she had felt, and how hopeless life had seemed;

how she'd felt her brother's death had somehow signified the inability of the Allies to overcome Hitler and his evil.

She did not know whether it was because she had just witnessed new life coming into the world, but now she really had the feeling they could win this war. That they had right on their side. Light could overcome darkness. And that, more than anything, there was hope.

Death, she mused, might feel like the end, but in a strange way it also heralded a new – and often different – life.

She thought about the little baby they had just brought into the world and how it had taken its first breath at the exact same time that others, just half a mile away – fatalities in this most recent air-raid attack – had breathed their last.

Polly's mind wandered to Bel, and how the death of her husband had thrown her into a terrible state of anger and despair, but she had managed to free herself from that dungeon of deep depression, and forced herself to start living again. Albeit a different life. And one without Teddy.

She just hoped that her sister-in-law could see that not only could she *live* after Teddy had died, but that she could also *love* again.

Polly wondered how long it would take her sister-in-law to realise she had feelings for Joe. Polly had seen how Joe's love for Bel had slowly patched up her broken heart, but would Bel admit to herself the love she felt in return? And, if she did, would she allow herself to love again?

Polly hoped so.

As she looked across to Thompson's yard, sitting proudly on North Sands, she spotted the magnificent steel ship whose keel they had watched being laid at the ceremony at the start of the year.

It was now sitting, looking almost majestic, as it waited in the fitting-out quay ready to be launched and to start its new life out at sea.

Chapter Fifty-Seven

As Agnes and Arthur walked along Tatham Street, smiles spread across both their faces as they watched Bel and Joe give in to Lucille's demands and, holding on to her arms, they swung her little body off the ground amidst squeals of delight.

As they approached their front door, though, their faces dropped a little as they saw Pearl staggering around the corner from Murton Street, her blonde hair resembling a bird's nest, and her scrawny arms struggling to heave her suitcase along the pavement. Bits of her clothing were trying to break free from the sides of the case, which had been wrapped up and tied with a thin bit of rope she'd been given by one of the station porters from whom she had sought help.

Spotting her grandmother Lucille immediately let out a loud cry of, 'Pearl!'

Hearing her granddaughter's excited greeting, Pearl looked up and saw Lucille bobbing between Bel and Joe. She gave up dragging her luggage, and straightened her aching back. 'Ah, my little Lu-Lu,' she said, catching her breath. As she spoke her suitcase toppled over, causing it to break free from the confines of the loosely tied rope and release its cargo on to the pavement.

Bel and Joe let go of an impatient Lucille, tugging to be released from their grip so she could run to her grandma.

For the first time ever, Bel felt glad to see her mother. During the air raid she'd had a worried, unsettled feeling about her mum, although she wasn't quite sure why. Seeing her here now, safe and unharmed, she was hit by a wave of relief, which was followed more or less straight away by an annoyance that she still cared so much for her mother.

Bel looked at her mum's abandoned baggage. She had sensed this morning when she'd seen her ma puffing away in the back yard, looking suspiciously thoughtful, that something was up, and she realised now that her mother had clearly been intending to go back down to Portsmouth – back to whatever, or whoever, she had originally run away from – and she hadn't been going to tell Bel.

'You off somewhere?' Bel asked, looking down at the open-mouthed luggage, tongues of clothes lolling out on to the street.

'Nah,' Pearl said, looking at her daughter. Her tone had struck its usual gravelly harshness, but the way she looked at Bel was curiously soft; try as she might to disguise it, the love she felt for her daughter had managed to dodge her defences and had momentarily shone through.

'I changed my mind,' she said, picking her granddaughter up and giving her a big cuddle. 'Couldn't leave this cheeky little monkey behind,' she said, looking at Lucille, who was giggling and had started to play with the loose straggles of blonde hair on her grandma's head.

Bel looked at her mother but didn't say anything. For once she didn't feel like throwing an angry retort back at her.

She was not quite convinced her mother's words were genuine and, as always, Bel had a sneaking suspicion that although there might be a sliver of truth in her ma's purported motive for staying, she would bet there was also some other reason why she was still here and not heading back down south.

But, whatever it was, Bel knew that her mother did love her, or at least as much as Pearl's hardened heart and self-obsessive nature would allow her to love anyone, and, in return, Bel could no longer deny the love she felt for her ma.

And she realised now that, despite everything that was annoying and dislikeable about her mother, she didn't want to lose her – either as a casualty of war, or to whoever was expecting her back in Portsmouth.

Bel watched as her mother carried Lucille past her and Joe, following Agnes and Arthur into the house.

She was still looking when Pearl cast a glance back. 'Do us a favour, Isabelle,' she shouted over her shoulder, 'and bring me bag in, will ya?'

As always with Pearl, it was a demand more than a request, for she didn't wait for a reply as she stepped over the threshold of their home, still carrying a giggling Lucille on her hip.

Joe looked at Bel and shook his head. Bel grimaced in response.

Bel knew Joe was not quite as relieved about her mother's return as she herself was, but there was no malice in his demeanour, just a weary resignation that this clearly meant that Pearl was to continue to be a feature in their lives.

After bundling Pearl's clothes back into her broken suitcase, Joe hoiked it under his arm, and he and Bel both trundled into the house, where they found Agnes tearing around, checking every room and shouting out her daughter's name.

'Pol? You home?' It was half question, half plea.

But there was no reply. There was no one at home. The house was just as they had left it – empty. Polly wasn't anywhere in sight.

As Joe dumped Pearl's broken suitcase and belongings on the kitchen table, he grabbed his mother's arm.

'Ma, why don't you put us a brew on?' Joe suggested, knowing his mother had to keep busy or she would go out of her mind.

'I'm going to go to Thompson's, check she's all right . . . which she will be,' he added, trying to sound as positive as possible, but worried sick himself as it had looked and sounded as though the bombs had been dropped on the north side.

Agnes looked at her son and knew he was right; she had to keep calm, like the posters kept telling everyone to do – 'keep calm and carry on'. The only problem was she wasn't sure she would be able to carry on if anything happened to another one of her bairns.

She knew her son was right, though, and they all needed a cup of tea with perhaps a little tipple of something strong in it. She was sure she had some brandy stashed in the back of one of her cupboards.

As Agnes followed her son's orders and traipsed her way into the scullery, she stopped in her tracks – inhaled a deep glug of air – and then declared to the house:

'Oh my goodness!' She let out a chortle of disbelief. 'Everyone come and look at this!' she shouted.

Arthur, Pearl, Joe, Bel and Lucille ended up in a bottle-neck in the pantry doorway, curious to see what was causing Agnes to sound so shocked, but – judging by the tone of her voice – also a little amused.

And then they saw it.

As they peered into the small galley-like room, at the very end, cuddled up in the corner, and lying on a yellow bed made up of Lucille's favourite little pinafore dress, was Tramp – along with half a dozen tiny puppies.

'Trampie!' Lucille burst into gleeful excitement.

Bel laughed. 'Well, that's one way of finally getting her out of that raggedy dress.'

Joe put his arm around Bel and pulled her close.

Agnes was just telling Lucille she would have to wait before cuddling the puppies as they were all happily nuzzled into their mother's belly, when Polly's voice could be heard shouting down the hallway.

'Ma! I'm home!' Agnes practically fell over trying to get to the front door to greet her daughter. Tears of relief poured down her face.

'Thank God!' she cried, clasping her hands together as if she really were offering up her thanks to the heavens above.

She flung her arms round Polly, who hugged her mother back, equally relieved to find their house was still standing and, moreover, that everyone in it was alive and well.

'And I've brought someone special back to show you,' she said, turning round.

Agnes's mouth dropped open and a huge smile spread across her face, followed by another burst of tears.

'Ah, Gloria – you've had your baby!' she said, stepping forward to take the little baby from Gloria's arms.

Behind her stood the women welders: Rosie, Dorothy, Angie, Hannah and Martha. They all had identical tear streaks running down their filthy faces.

'A girl?' Agnes asked.

The women all nodded in unison.

'Oh, she's beautiful,' Agnes gasped.

Agnes looked from the women and then back down at the perfect little baby swaddled in what she thought looked like a pair of overalls.

'Name?' She was still a little breathless from the dam of tears she was trying desperately to hold back.

Gloria leant in to look at her baby daughter, touching her cheek gently and smiling, thinking how much she looked like Jack.

'*Hope,*' she said. 'Her name's Hope.'

Dear Reader,

I hope you have enjoyed *Shipyard Girls at War* – the second instalment of the Shipyard Girls series – and that you will continue to join Polly, Rosie and Gloria, and the rest of the women (and men), as they cope with the many highs and lows, as well as secrets and shocking revelations, that are thrust upon them in book three.

Hope, as I'm sure you have guessed, is the underlying theme of *Shipyard Girls at War*, just as love was in *The Shipyard Girls*.

During my research for both books, it struck me just how much love and hope were essential for those living through such a hateful war, and it occurred to me that, despite people's lives nowadays being very different to the lives of those surviving the hardships of World War II, love and hope are still just as essential today as they were then.

I hope your life is filled with both.

With love,

Nancy

x

History Notes

Very little has been written about the remarkable women who, like Polly, Rosie, Gloria, Dorothy, Angie, Martha and Hannah, worked in the shipyards during World War II.

There has never been any kind of commemoration, or indeed any praise, given to the *seven hundred* women who carried out such perilous work in such harsh conditions in the Sunderland shipyards – or, for that matter, to the women who worked in other shipyards in the North East.

These women, who not only *needed* to work but also *wanted* to be a part of the war effort, often worked seven days a week to repair and build the ships desperately needed to win the war.

Without the shipyards, the country would have been forced to surrender, as the cargo vessels being built were essential for the transportation of vital food, fuel and minerals – and, of course, troops.

It is therefore not surprising that Sunderland – then the biggest shipbuilding town in the world, which produced a *quarter* of Britain's merchant shipping at the time – was also one of the most heavily bombed towns during the war.

The women shipbuilders, many of whom had young families at home, were not only carrying out dangerous and back-breaking work, but they were also doing so under the constant threat of Hitler's Luftwaffe.

I hope the Shipyard Girls series will continue to keep the memory alive of those brave and inspirational women who played such an important role in such a crucial period of our history.